THE BARON'S APPRENTICESHIP

BETHANY HOUSE PUBLISHERS
Minneapolis, Minnesota 55438

The Novels of George MacDonald Edited for Today's Reader

Edited Title	Original Title
The two-volume story of Malcolm:	
The Fisherman's Lady	*Malcolm*
The Marquis' Secret	*The Marquis of Lossie*
Companion stories of Gibbie and his friend Donal:	
The Baronet's Song	*Sir Gibbie*
The Shepherd's Castle	*Donal Grant*
Companion stories of Hugh Sutherland and Robert Falconer:	
The Tutor's First Love	*David Elginbrod*
The Musician's Quest	*Robert Falconer*
The Maiden's Bequest	*Alec Forbes of Howglen*
Companion stories of Thomas Wingfold:	
The Curate's Awakening	*Thomas Wingfold*
The Lady's Confession	*Paul Faber*
The Baron's Apprenticeship	*There and Back*
Stories that stand alone:	
A Daughter's Devotion	*Mary Marston*
The Gentlewoman's Choice	*Weighed and Wanting*
The Highlander's Last Song	*What's Mine's Mine*
The Laird's Inheritance	*Warlock O'Glenwarlock*
The Landlady's Master	*The Elect Lady*
The Minister's Restoration	*Salted with Fire*
The Peasant Girl's Dream	*Heather and Snow*
The Poet's Homecoming	*Home Again*

MacDonald Classics Edited for Young Readers

Wee Sir Gibbie of the Highlands
Alec Forbes and His Friend Annie
At the Back of the North Wind
The Adventures of Ranald Bannerman

George MacDonald: Scotland's Beloved Storyteller by Michael Phillips
Discovering the Character of God by George MacDonald
Knowing the Heart of God by George MacDonald
A Time to Grow by George MacDonald
A Time to Harvest by George MacDonald

HAMPSHIRE BOOKS™

THE BARON'S APPRENTICESHIP

George MacDonald

The Baron's Apprenticeship
George MacDonald

Originally published as *There and Back* in 1891 by Kegan Paul Publishers, London, as a sequel to *Paul Faber, Surgeon* (now *The Lady's Confession*).

Cover by Dan Thornberg,
Bethany House Publishers staff artist.

Library of Congress Catalog Card Number
Applied for

ISBN 0-87123-655-9 (trade paper edition)
ISBN 1-55661-520-5 (Hampshire Books edition)

Hampshire Books edition published in 1994

Published by Bethany House Publishers
A Ministry of Bethany Fellowship, Inc.
11300 Hampshire Avenue South
Minneapolis, Minnesota 55438

Printed in the United States of America

Introduction

In 1891, after a lapse of twelve years since the publication of *Paul Faber, Surgeon* (*The Lady's Confession*), George MacDonald wrote the third and final book of the Thomas Wingfold trilogy, entitled *There and Back*, newly edited and retitled *The Baron's Apprenticeship* for the Bethany House series. In the story, consistent with MacDonald's own life, ten or twelve years have passed since the last Wingfold story. Thomas (now approximately forty) and Helen (thirty-seven) and their young son are no longer in Glaston but have moved; they now serve a country parish some thirty or forty miles outside London.

The people and surroundings in *The Baron's Apprenticeship* have therefore changed, but the essential themes have not, for this third book continues and concludes MacDonald's multifaceted examination of the fundamental theme concerning salvation, man's need for God, and the validity of the Christian faith in the lives of men and women.

The Curate's Awakening laid the groundwork for spiritual birth, with the "awakening" of Wingfold himself after a long struggle to come to grips with the truthfulness of Christianity as revealed in the New Testament. *The Lady's Confession* followed as the natural outgrowth of the curate's new faith—the spread of that faith into those around him. Many were touched as a result, particularly Juliet and Paul—a man and a woman with few apparent needs, but each, in fact, concealing a core of hidden sin which could be cleansed only by the forgiveness and redeeming love of Christ. Now finally in *The Baron's Apprenticeship*, the opposite dilemma of man is raised: that of moral goodness. Do those *without* ugly and obvious sin need God, too? What about the *good* man and woman? Do they stand in need of salvation as well? Is an injunction placed upon man to respond to God simply by virtue of who he is, by virtue of integrity, by virtue of being true to *the truth*?

In *The Baron's Apprenticeship*, we are introduced to Richard and Barbara, two morally virtuous young people who must each face responsibility for responding to the truth of God's existence, to the imperative of his goodness, and to the mandate of obedience to his principles. They must each ask, though their individual backgrounds and intellectual reasonings may resist the notion at first, whether or not God's existence is true, what God's character is like, and what demands are placed upon them as a result.

MacDonald here approaches the question of "salvation" from a different aspect, as he notes in the story. He presents the "thoughtful" conversion, prompted not by tearful repentance over wrongs done but instead by a dawning recognition of what *must be*: God *must* exist, he must be *good*, therefore *I must respond to him*!

As is often the case, MacDonald's characters must *reason out* the Christian faith. For MacDonald there would be no pat answers, no "humbug," as he called it. The Christian faith was a reasonable, sensible faith. God was not only the source of life's joy, contentment, meaning, and fulfillment, but his principles were *true*. And this *true-ness* pervades each of his books as the focal point for the spiritual quest within the hearts of each of his characters.

In *The Baron's Apprenticeship*, Barbara's internal quest comes first to the fore. Prompted by her own deep and unconscious reactions to the death of a pigeon, Barbara finds herself unable to accept Richard's empty statements that there is no life beyond death. A compelling, highly independent and thoughtful character—indeed, one of MacDonald's strongest fictional women—Barbara searches for "something more," bolstered by her deepening friendship with Thomas and Helen Wingfold, who are now able to act the part Polwarth played in their own lives years earlier.

And Barbara's searching and questioning ultimately prompt

Richard to reevaluate the notions he had long taken for granted. Paralleling Bascombe's interchange with Wingfold in the second chapter of *The Curate's Awakening*, the profound question which Barbara poses uncovers the shallowness and lack of *true-ness* of Richard's position. She asks: "Tell me honestly, are you *sure* there is no God? Have you gone through all the universe looking for him and failed to find him? Is there no possible chance that there may be a God?"

The glory of the world about her as well as the instincts within Barbara's heart all cry out that God must exist, and that he must be good. On her the burden of proof does not rest; everything around her and within her confirms God's presence and his goodness. To acknowledge him is but to recognize the obvious. On the other hand, upon Richard a burden of proof does rest. His denial of God, because he cannot substantiate it throughout all corners of creation, is a flawed theory; it runs contrary both to the created world and the instincts and yearnings of man's heart, based on little more than misrepresentations and a shallow spiritual upbringing.

Thus when Barbara probes into Richard's superficial denials with *Are you sure?* and *Is there no possible chance?*, he finds himself with paltry arguments on which to base an answer.

"I do not believe there is," he responds.

"But are you *sure* there is not?" presses Barbara. "Do you *know* it, so that you have a right to say it?"

Again Richard fumbles for an answer, and once more Barbara queries: "Nevertheless, are you *sure*?"

"I cannot say," he finally admits, "that I know it as I know a mathematical fact."

"Then what right do you have to say there is no God?" she asks again.

Following this interchange, Richard falls silent, then says finally, "I will think about what you say."

And because he is a man of integrity, he does think honestly about what she has said. Eventually he falls in, as had she, with the Wingfolds, who help lead him, by the example of their lives, into the fullness of God's truth.

In these three books we meet a multitude of characters along the spectrum of spiritual receptivity. In that sense, these stories can be viewed as an extended sower parable: the seed of God's truth is sown equally to all—some respond, others shut the door. In addition, MacDonald brings home the truth that the seed is not always sown in precisely the same manner. God sows the seed in a way that will most perfectly suit each individual. Some, like Paul and Juliet, respond through their deep personal sense of guilt and sin; others, like Helen and Leopold, come to know God through intense suffering and sorrow; and still others, like Wingfold, Richard, and Barbara, find themselves compelled to respond to the *truth-ness* of God's being.

Thus the three books, threaded together with the central character of Thomas Wingfold, provide a threefold picture, a parable, of God's salvation. They tell a trilogy of life-stories, and in so doing reveal God's infinite and loving means to draw the human hearts of the creation to himself.

Michael Phillips

Contents

1 Bookbinder and Son

Stretching his aching muscles and straightening from his book, John Tuke rested his glance on his son Richard. *A fine strong lad,* Tuke thought as he observed the boy at work. *And such skilled hands! Hands I never thought to hold such promise in the trade.*

But clumsiness or ugliness in infancy is sometimes promise of grace or beauty in manhood. In Richard's case, the promise was fulfilled: what had seemed repulsive to some who beheld him as an infant had given place to a certain winsomeness. He was now a handsome, well-grown youth, with dark brown hair, dark green eyes, broad shoulders, and a bit of a stoop which made his mother uneasy. But he had good health; and what was better, an even temper; and what was better still, a willing heart toward his neighbor. A certain overhanging of his brow was called a scowl by those who did not love him, but it was of minor significance—probably the trick of some ancestor.

With pride—not the possessiveness of the owner, but the liberating joy of the mentor—John Tuke watched in silence as the skillful fingers of his seventeen-year-old son moved lovingly over the volume under his care. Richard occasionally assisted his father in binding, but in general, as now, he occupied himself with his own particular devotion—the restoration of antiquity.

While learning the bookbinding trade, the young Richard had attended evening classes at King's College, where he developed a true love for the best of literature, especially from the sixteenth century. He grew to possess a peculiar regard for old books, and with the three or four shillings a week at his disposal, searched about to discover and buy volumes that, for their physical condition, would be of little worth to the bookseller. With these for his first "patients," he opened a hospital for the lodging, restorative treatment, and invigoration of decayed volumes.

Love and power combined made him look on these dilapidated, slow-wasting abodes of human thought and delight with healing compassion—indeed, with the passion of healing. The worse gnawed by the tooth of insect-time, the farther down any choice book in the steep decline of years, the more intent was Richard on having it. More and more skillful he grew, not only in rebinding, but in restoring the very tone of their constitution. Through love he moved from artisan to artist.

And in his passage into the manhood of his craft, Richard was blessed with a master who loved both him and the trade—his father John. John Tuke and his family lived on the bank of the Thames, in a poor part of a populous, busy, thriving London suburb—far from fashionable, yet not without inhabitants of refinement. Had not art and literature sent out a few shoots into it, the quarter would have kept no hold on John Tuke. He liked his trade and used his talent to the satisfaction of known customers, of whom he now had many, and his reputation had spread far beyond the immediate neighborhood. But while he worked more cheaply, quality considered, than many binders—even carefully superintending that most important yet most neglected part of the handicraft, the sewing—he never undertook cheap work.

John Tuke would never consent to *half-bind* a book, but always did a thorough job. Hence, when *carte blanche* was given to him, he would often expend upon the book a labor and value of material quite out of proportion to the importance of the book itself. Still, being a thoroughly conscientious workman who never hurried the forwarding, never cut from a margin a hairsbreadth more than necessary, and hated finger marks on the whiteness of a page, he was well known and had plenty of work. He had so much, in fact, that he often had to refuse what was offered to him. At leisure, then, he declined any job that would give him no pleasure, and as he grew older he grew more fastidious in regard to the quality of the work he would undertake.

As the boy Richard grew, his chief pleasure was to be in the shop with his father and watch him at his varying work. His knowledge of books as physical things led him the sooner to desire them as realities. Near enough for Richard to attend, and with fees within his father's means, a good dayschool presented the boy with the opportunity to discover those realities. When he was old enough for school, his father spared nothing he could spend to prepare him for his future—a future, John Tuke hoped, of greater consequence, if not greater happiness and contentment, than his own.

Richard proved to be a fair student and a voracious reader. In addition, he took such an intelligent and practical interest in the work going on at home that he began, while still a child, to experiment with paper and paste on his own. First he made manuscript books for his work at school and for the copying of favorite poems and passages from his reading. Then inside the covers of these he would make pockets for papers, and so he advanced to making small portfolios and pocket books which he would give to his friends, and sometimes—when more ambitiously successful—to a teacher. He used bits of colored paper and scraps of leather, chiefly morocco, which his father willingly gave to him, watching his progress with paternal interest and showing him various workman's techniques a little at a time. He would never come to his aid except in a real difficulty—as, for instance, when he first struggled with a piece of leather too thick for the bonds of paste and had to be shown how to pare it to the necessary flexibility and compliance.

To be able to *make* something was, Tuke believed, necessary to thorough development. He would rather have a son of his a carpenter, a watchmaker, a woodcarver, a shoemaker, a jeweller, a blacksmith, a bookbinder, than have him earn his living as a clerk in a bank. Not merely is the cultivation of such skills a better education in things human, it brings a man nearer to everything practical. Humanity unfolds itself to him the readier; its ways and thoughts and modes of being grow the clearer to both intellect and heart. The poetry of life, the inner side of nature, rises near the surface to meet the eyes of the man who *makes*. The advantage gained by the carpenter of Nazareth at his bench is the inheritance of every workman as he imitates his Maker in divine—that is, honest—work.

Perceiving the faculty of the boy, his father naturally thought it a good thing to bring him along in his trade: it would always be a possession, whatever turn things might take. And certainly the man who can gather his food off his own bench, or screw it out of his own press, must be a freer man than he who but for an inheritance would have to beg, steal, or die of hunger.

Under the watchful encouragement of his father, then, and with his great love of reading and of books, Richard delightedly entered into his apprenticeship. While still too young to wield the hammer without danger to both himself and the book in his care, the boy began to sew, and in a few weeks he was able to bring the sheets together entirely to his father's satisfaction. From the first, he set himself to do whatever work he was doing in the best way. John Tuke went on teaching him until the boy could do almost everything better than his father, until he had taught him every delicacy, every secret of the craft. Richard developed a positive genius for the work, a genius reflected, as he developed, in his powers of resurrection for working with antique volumes.

His father came to regard with wonder and admiration the redeeming faculty of his son. But in many ways Tuke was still a man of this world, and he sorely doubted if such labor would ever pay off financially. It was much easier, and therefore paid better, to reclothe than to restore! He recognized that his son was possessed of a quite original faculty for book-healing. *But alas!* he thought, *he will never be paid for the time it takes*. Nevertheless, he continued to encourage him, though mildly, in the pursuit of this neglected branch of the binding art. Through his long connections with booklovers who possessed small cherished libraries, Tuke was able to bring Richard almost as many jobs as he could handle.

But however much the youth delighted in it, he could not but find the work tiring. He often found it necessary to leave it for a walk or a solitary hour on the river. He had few companions; his parents were strangely careful about his friendships. His father held strong socialistic opinions but was, like the holders of so many higher theories, apt to forget the practice necessarily involved in his viewpoints, particularly where Richard was concerned.

As Richard developed in his love for literature, his thinking began to take the form of verse-making. His solitary walks facilitated his poetry, whether he produced anything of original value or not. Expressing oneself aids growth, which is the prime necessity of human as of all other life. Some kinds of labor are privileged to be compatible with thoughts of higher things. At the bookkeeper's desk the clerk must think of nothing but his work; he is chained to it as the galley slave to his oar. But the shoemaker may be poet or mystic, or both. The ploughman may turn a good furrow and a good verse together. And Richard could use both hands and thoughts together. It troubled his parents that they could not send him to the university, but they had determined that he must at least be a grown man, capable of looking after his own affairs, whatever the future might hold for him.

John Tuke was one of those who acknowledge some need to be kind toward his neighbor, but claim ignorance of any One who must be worshiped. And in truth, the God presented to him by his teachers was not one worthy of the least devotion. The religious system brought to bear on his youth had operated but feebly on his conscience and not at all on his emotions. By the time he was an adult he believed himself satisfied that the notion of religion—of duty toward an unseen Maker—was but an old wives' fable. The testimony of his senses, which saw and heard and felt nothing of the supposed hereafter, he accepted as stronger evidence than any amount of assertion by priests and believers. The world was around him: some things he must believe; other things no man could! One thing only was clear: every man was bound to give his neighbor fair play! He would press nothing upon Richard as to God or no God. He would not be dogmatic! He only wanted to make a man of him. And was he not so far successful? Was not Richard growing up as a diligent, honest fellow, loving books and leading a good life rather than, as a so-called "gentleman," becoming arrogant and unjust, despising the poor, and caring about nothing but himself? In the midst of such superior causes of satisfaction, it also pleased Tuke to reflect that the trade he had taught his son was a clean one, which, while it rendered him superior to any shrewd trick fortune might play him, would not make his hands unlike those of a gentleman.

His mother, however, kept wishing that Richard were better "set up," and that he looked more like his grandfather the blacksmith, whose trade she regarded as manlier than that of her husband's. Hence she had long cherished the desire that he should spend some time with her father. John, however, would not hear of it.

"He will get to working at the forge," he said, "and ruin his hands for the delicate art in which he is now so gifted."

For in certain less socialistic moods, John insisted on regarding bookbinding, in all of its branches, not as a trade, but as an art.

2 Brother and Sister

At school Richard had been friendly with a boy, gentle of nature and not much older than himself, by the name of Adam Manson. But he had suddenly disappeared from the school, and for years Richard had not seen him. One evening as he was carrying home a book, he met this fellow looking worn and sad. Adam would have avoided Richard, but he stopped him, and presently the old friendship was again struck.

Adam had had to leave school, he told Richard, because of the sudden cessation, from what cause he did not know, of a certain annuity his mother had till then enjoyed. Suddenly it became imperative that he earn his own living and contribute to her support. His sister was at work with a dressmaker, but as yet earning next to nothing. His mother was a lady, he said, and had never worked. He was himself clerking in a bank in the city with a salary of forty pounds a year. He told him where they lived, and Richard promised to call upon him the next Sunday.

Adam's mother lived in a little house of two floors. She was a handsome middle-aged woman—not so old, Richard somehow imagined, as she looked. She was stout and florid and seemed to Richard to have the *carriage* of a lady but not the speech equal to her manners. She was polite to him, but apparently not overly interested in her son's friend. Several times, however, he found her gazing at him with an expression that puzzled him. But he had a conscience too clear to be troubled by any scrutiny.

All evening Adam's face wore the same look of depression, and Richard wondered what could be the matter. He learned afterward that the mother was self-indulgent and took little care to make the money go as far as it could. Thus Adam had to toil away from morning to night at labor he hardly enjoyed, never able to have the least recreation and too tired when he came home to understand any book he attempted to read. And all the while his mother spent rather too freely the money he brought her. Richard learned also that Adam possessed no overcoat and went to the city, even in the winter, with but scanty provisions. But it was not Adam who told him this.

His sister Alice was a graceful little creature, with the same sad look her brother had, but not the same depression. She seemed more delicate and less capable of labor. Yet her hours were longer than his and her confinement even greater. Alice had to sit the whole day with her needle, while Adam was occasionally sent out to collect money. But her mistress was a kindhearted woman who was not so fashionable as to have become indifferent to the well-being of her workwomen. She even paid a crippled girl a trifle for reading aloud to them while they worked. So even if it was harder, life was not so uninteresting to Alice as to Adam, and perhaps for that reason she seemed to have more vitality.

The youths found that they still had tastes in common, although Adam had neither time nor strength to follow them. Richard spoke of some book he had been reading. Adam was politely interested, but Alice so much that Richard offered to lend it to her: it was the first time she had heard a book spoken of in such a tone of veneration.

The mother did not join in their talk, and left them soon—her daughter explained—to go to church.

"She always goes by herself," Alice added. "She sees we are too tired to go."

They sat a long time with no light but that of the fire. Adam seemed to gather courage and confessed the hopeless monotony of his life. He complained of no deprivation, only of lack of interest in his work.

"Do *you* like your work?" he asked Richard.

"Indeed I do!" Richard answered. "I would sooner handle an old book than a bunch of bank notes."

"I don't doubt it," returned Adam. "To me your workshop seems like a paradise."

"Why don't you take up the trade, then? Come to us and I will teach you. I do not think my father would object."

"I learn nothing where I am," continued Adam.

"Say you will come, and I will speak to my father."

"I wish I could! But how are we to live while I am learning?—No, I must grind away until—"

He stopped short, and gave a sigh.

"Until when, Adam?" asked his sister.

"Until death sets me free," he answered glumly.

"You wouldn't leave me behind, Adam!" exclaimed Alice, rising and putting her arm round his neck.

"I wouldn't if I could help it," he replied in a warmer tone.

"It's a cowardly thing to want to die," Richard rebuked him gently.

"I think so sometimes."

"There's your mother."

"Yes," responded Adam, without emotion.

"And how should I get on without you, Adam?" cried his sister.

"Not very well, Alice. But it wouldn't be for long. We should soon meet."

"Who told you that?" queried Richard.

"Don't you think we shall know each other afterward?" asked Adam, with an expression of weary rather than sad surprise.

"I would be a little surer of it before I talked so coolly of leaving a sister like that. I only wish I had a sister to care for."

A faint flush rose on the pale face of the girl, and just as swiftly faded.

"Then do you think that this life is only a dream?" she said, looking up at Richard with something in her great eyes that he did not understand.

"I don't know," he answered slowly. "But I would put up with a good deal before running the risk of going to sleep before my time so as to stop dreaming it."

"If Adam had enough to eat and time to read and a little amusement, he would be as brave as you are, Mr. Tuke," said Alice. "But you can't really say you believe there will be no more of anything for us after this world! I should be miserable if I thought that!"

"The best way is not to think about it at all," returned Richard. "Why should you? Look at the butterflies. They take what comes and don't grumble at their sunshine because there's only one day of it."

"But when there's no sunshine that day?" suggested Alice.

"Well, when they lie crumpled in the rain, they're none the worse that they didn't think about it beforehand! We must make the best of what we have!"

"It's not worth making the best of," cried Alice, "if there's nothing more to it than that!"

How Richard could be a lover of our best literature—much of it sacred in its influence—and talk as he did may seem incongruent. But he had come to love the literature when young, when still under the influence of the spiritual teaching, poor as it was, of his mother. But now lately, as he had approached manhood, he had begun to admire the intellectual qualities of that literature more; he had begun to fall into the fatal error of thinking truth attainable only through the forces of the brain alone.

In matters of conduct, John Tuke and his wife were well agreed; in matters of religious opinion, however, they differed greatly. Jane went to church regularly, listened without interest, and accepted without question. Had her husband attended with her, he would have listened with the interest of utter disagreement and dissent. When Jane learned that her husband no longer "believed in the

Bible," she was seized with terror lest he should die without repentance and be lost. Thereupon followed fear for herself: was not an atheist a horribly wicked man? Yet John did not seem wicked to her! She tried to think so, but couldn't. The only conclusion she could arrive at was that his unbelief must be affecting her. She begged him to say nothing against the Bible to Richard—at least before he arrived at an age old enough to decide for himself. John promised. But subtle effluences are subtle influences.

John Tuke did right, so far as he knew, and refused to believe in any kind of God; Jane did right, as far as she knew, and never imagined God cared about her. And Richard was left to discern the difference.

Tuke was a thinking man—that is, if a conversation was set in any direction that interested him, he could take a few steps forward without assistance. But he could start in no direction of himself. At a small club to which he belonged, he had come into contact with certain ideas new to him, and finding himself able to grasp them, felt at once as if they must be true. Certain other ideas, also new to him, which came self-suggested in their train, set him to imagining himself a thinker, able to generate notions beyond the grasp of people around him. He began to grow self-confident. He then took courage to deny things he had never believed, and finding that he gave offense, chose to imagine himself a martyr for the truth. He did not see that a denial involving no assertion cannot witness to any truth. Logically put, his rather flimsy position would have been: I never knew such things; I do not like the notion of them; therefore I deny them; they do not exist. But when John Tuke denied the God in his feeble notion, he denied only a God that could have no existence.

A man will be judged, however, by his truth toward what he professes to believe. And John was far truer to his perception of the duty of man to man than are ninety-nine out of a hundred so-called Christians to the doctrines they profess to believe. How many people would be immeasurably better if they would but truly believe—that is, act upon—the smallest part of what they profess to believe, even if they cast aside all the rest! But if there be a God and one has never sought him, it will be small consolation to remember that one could not get proof of his existence.

His mother continued to take the boy to church, and expose him to a teaching she could not herself either supply or supplement. It was the business of the church to teach Christianity; her part was to accept it and bring the child where he also might listen and accept. But what she accepted as Christianity is another question; and whether the acceptance of anything makes a Christian is another still.

How much of Christianity a child may or may not learn by going to church, it is impossible to say; but certainly Richard did not learn anything that drew his heart to Jesus of Nazareth, or caught him in any heavenly breeze, or even the smallest of celestial whirlwinds. He was not too advanced in years, in fact, before his growing mind began to be aware that the religion presented in his mother's church was a religion neither honorable nor elevating and was but the dullest travesty of the religion of St. Paul. Richard had, besides, read several books which, had his father been truly careful of the promise he had given his wife, he would have intentionally removed instead of unintentionally leaving about.

And in the position Richard had just taken toward his new friends, he was not a little influenced by his desire to show himself free from prevailing notions and capable of thinking for himself.

Richard told his parents where he had been, and asked if he might invite his friends for the next Sunday. They made no objection, and when Adam and Alice came, they received them kindly. Richard took Adam to the shop and showed him the job he was working on at the time, lauding what he did as giving more satisfaction than the mere binding itself.

"It would be much easier," Richard said, "to make that volume look new, but how much more delightful to send it out with a revived assertion of its ancient self!"

While the youths were having their talk, Alice was in Jane's bedroom, undergoing the probing of her hostess, the object of which the girl could not suspect. Caught by a certain look in her sweet face, Jane had set herself to learn from her what she might about her people and her background.

"Is your father alive, my dear?" she asked, her keen dark eyes riveted on Alice's face.

The girl grew red, and for a moment did not answer. Jane pursued.

"What was his trade or profession?" she inquired.

The girl said nothing, and the merciless inquisitor proceeded.

"Tell me something about him, dear. Do you remember him? Or did he die when you were a child?"

"I do not remember him," answered Alice, her voice low. "I do not know if I ever saw him."

"Did your mother never tell you what he was like?"

"She told me once he was very handsome—the handsomest man she ever saw—but cruel—so cruel!" she said. "I don't want to talk about him, please, ma'am," concluded Alice, the tears beginning to run down her cheeks.

"I'm sorry, my dear, to hurt you, but I'm not doing it from curiosity. You look so like a man I once knew, and your brother had something of the same look; I am, in fact, bound to learn what I can about you."

"What sort was the man we remind you of?" asked Alice with a feeble attempt at a smile. "Not a *very* bad man, I hope!"

"Well, not very good, if you ask me. He was what people call a gentleman."

"Was that all?"

"What do you mean?"

"Was he a nobleman?"

"Oh!—well, he was that certainly; he was a baron."

Alice gave a little cry.

"Do tell me something about him," she begged. "What do you know about him?"

"More than I choose to tell. We will forget him now," said Jane with finality.

There was in her voice a tone of displeasure, which Alice assumed to be her fault. She was consequently both troubled and perplexed. Neither asked any more questions. Jane took her guest back to the sitting room.

The moment her brother came from the workshop, Alice said

to him, "Are you ready, Adam? We had better be going."

Adam was a gentle creature and seldom opposed her. He seemed only a little surprised and asked if she was feeling ill. But Richard, who had been looking forward to a talk with Alice and wanted to show her his little library, was very disappointed and begged her to change her mind. She insisted on going, however, and he put on his hat to walk with them. But his mother called him, whispering that she would be particularly appreciative if he would go to church with her that evening. He said he did not want to go to church. But she insisted, and he yielded, though not with the best of grace.

Before another Sunday there came to Richard the invitation to spend a few weeks with his grandfather, the blacksmith. Richard was not altogether pleased, for he did not like leaving his work. And his father, he soon discovered, was less pleased than he.

"It's not just his hands," Richard heard his father saying as he passed by the door to their room.

"Then what, John? Tell me, so I will know!"

"It's being so close—too near, if you ask me! What will happen if—"

"Shush, John Tuke! Do you want the lad to hear? At least at my father's he'll be away from—"

"From what? Is what he'll be away from any better than what he'll be close to? Think, woman! If anyone knows, or sees—"

"They won't see," Jane interrupted. "What they'll see is the son of a bookbinder being made a man of by his blacksmith grandfather!"

Again, his mother prevailed. Richard agreed to go, showing deference to his mother such as few young men demonstrate. And his father, knowing the necessity of such a change, finally acquiesced.

3 Grandfather

Simon Armour was past the agility but not the strength of his youth, and he was still proud of his feats of might. Without being offensively conceited, he regarded himself superior to any baron. All he looked for from any man, whether above or below him on the social scale, was proper pay for good work and natural human respect. Several of the surrounding gentry enjoyed the free, jolly, but unpresuming carriage of the stalwart old man who could still ply a sledge hammer in each hand. He gave friendly good fellowship to the nobleman who occasionally stopped at his forge to give him some direction about the shoeing of this or that horse, and he was generally well-liked by those lower than himself as well.

He was a hard-featured, good-looking, white-haired man of sixty, with piercing eyes of deep blue and a rough voice with an undertone of music in it. There was music, indeed, all through him. In the roughest part of his history it was his habit to go to church—almost entirely for the organ. How much he understood may be a question somewhat dependent on how much there may have been to understand. But he had a few ideas in religion which were very much his own, and which, especially with regard to certain of the lessons from the Old Testament, would have considerably astonished some parsons, and considerably pleased others. He was a big, broad-shouldered man, with brawny arms, and eyes so bright that one might fancy they caught and kept for their own use the sparks that flew from his hammer. His face was red, with a great short white beard, suggesting the sun in a clean morning fog.

A rickety omnibus carried Richard from the railway station some five miles to the smithy. When the old man heard it stop, he threw down his hammer, strode hastily to the door, met his grandson with a grip that left a black mark and an ache, and picked up his case and set it inside.

"I'll be with you in a moment, lad!" he said, and with that seized a horseshoe that lay on the anvil with a long pair of pincers, thrust it into the fire, blew a great roaring blast from the bellows, plucked out the shoe—now growing white—and fell upon it as if it were a devil. Having thus cowed it a bit, he grew calm and more deliberately shaped it to an invisible idea. His grandson was delighted with the mingling of determination, intent and power, with certainty of result manifest in every blow. In two minutes he had the shoe on the end of a long hooked rod, and was hanging it beside others on a row of nails in a beam. Then he turned and said, "There, lad! That's off the anvil, and off my mind. Now for you!"

"Grandfather," remarked Richard, "I shouldn't like to have you for an enemy!"

"Why not, you rascal! Do you think I would take unfair advantage of you?"

"No. But you've got such awful arms and hands!"

"They've done a job or two in their day, lad!" he answered. "But I'm getting old now. I can't do what I once thought nothing of! Well, no man was made to last forever—no more than a horseshoe! There'd be no work for the Maker if he did!"

While they talked the blacksmith had taken off his thick leather apron, and now picked up Richard's case as if it were a handbasket, leading the way to a cottage not far from his shop. It was a humble enough place—one story with a wide attic. The front was almost covered with jasmine, rising from a little garden filled with cottage flowers. Behind was a larger garden full of cabbages and gooseberry bushes.

A girl came to the door, with a kind, blushing face and hands as red as her cheeks—a great-niece of the old smith. He passed her and led the way into a room which was half kitchen, half parlor.

"Here you are, lad—at home, I hope! Such as it is—and as much as it's mine, it's yours, and I hope you'll make it so."

He deposited the case, put on the water, and then sat down with Richard. They had tea together, with bread and butter and marmalade, and much talk about John and Jane Tuke. When the subject of bookbinding came up, Richard was surprised to discover that the blacksmith regarded it as quite an inferior and hardly a manly trade. To the blacksmith, bookbinding and tailoring were fit only for women. Not relishing his notions, Richard tried to make him see the dignity of the work.

"The difficulty is greater because of the lesser strength required," he said. "The strength itself, in certain of the operations, has to be finely scaled back and modified with extreme accuracy; while in others, all the strength a man has is necessary, especially in a shop like ours where everything is done by hand. But the fine, delicate work," he concluded, "is most tiring of all. Although I do wish I could shoe a horse as well!"

"What's to stop you?"

"Will you let me learn, Grandfather?"

"*Let* you learn! I'll learn you myself. And you'll learn soon. It's not as if you're a bumpkin to teach. The man who can do anything, can do everything!"

"Come along then, Grandfather. I want you to see that though my hands may get a blister or two, they're not the less fit for hard work because they can do delicate work. But you must have patience with me!"

"Nay, lad, I'll have great patience with you. Before many days are over, I'll wager you'll make the shoes like you was a smith yourself. But to shoe a horse as the horse ought to be shod, that comes only by God's grace."

They went back to the smithy, and there, the very day of his arrival, more to Simon's delight than he cared to show, the soft-handed bookbinder began to wield a hammer and shape the stubborn iron. So deft and persevering was he that before they left the forge that same night, he could not only bend the iron to a proper curve round the beak of the anvil, but had punched the holes in half a dozen shoes. At last he confessed himself weary; when his grandfather saw the state of his hands, blistered and swollen so that he could not even close them, he was no longer able to restrain his satisfaction.

"Come," he cried, "you're a man after all, bookbinder! In six months I should have you made into a thorough blacksmith!"

"I wouldn't undertake to make a bookbinder of you, Grandfather," returned Richard.

"Just as well, I should leave black marks all over your white pages. How much of them do you read now, as you stick them together?"

"Not a word as I stick them together. But many books are brought to me to be mended and doctored up, and from some of them I take part of my pay in reading them—scarce books, I mean, that I wouldn't otherwise find it easy to lay my hands upon."

"You would like to go to Oxford, wouldn't you, lad—and read enough to last the rest of your life?"

"You might as well think to eat enough in one year to last the rest of your life, Grandfather! Learning, like eating, must go on every day. Today's lesson won't always get you through tomorrow. But I would like to be able to lay in a stock of the tools to be got at Oxford. It would be grand to be able to pick the lock of any door I wanted to see the other side of."

"I served my time to a locksmith," returned Armour. "But we didn't hit it off, and so hit one another. When my time was up I couldn't get locksmith's work; and as I was always getting into rows, I started up for myself as a general blacksmith, in a small way, of course. But my right hand hasn't forgotten its technique in locks. I'll teach you to pick the cunningest locks in the world, whether made in Italy or China."

"The lock I was thinking of," said Richard, "was that of the tree of knowledge."

"I've heard," returned Simon with more humor than accuracy, "that that was a rather peculiar lock, kept red-hot all the time by a flaming sword."

"You don't say you believe that story, Grandfather?"

"I don't say what I believe or what I don't believe. The flaming iron I've had to do with has both kept me out of knowledge and led me into knowledge. You see, lad, when I was a boy I thought everything my mother said and my father did was old-fashioned and a bit ignorant. But when I was a man, I saw that, if I had started right off from where they set me down, I would have been further ahead. To honor your father and mother don't mean to stick by their chimney corner all your life, but to start from their front door and go forward. I went out by the back door, like the fool I was; to get into the front road, I had a long round to make before I could even get started."

"I shan't do so with my father. He doesn't read much, but he thinks, and has a good head."

"There was fathers before yours, lad. You needn't scorn your grandfather for your father."

"Scorn you, Grandfather! God forbid! Or, at least—"

"You don't see what I'm driving at, sonny. I don't mean *me*—I mean fathers of old, them that has handed down the old tales, even the old tales that you think you no longer believe and think is only old religious superstition. When an old tale comes to me from the faraway time, I don't pitch it into the road, any more than I would an old key or an old shoe—a horseshoe, I mean: the story was something once, and it may be something again! I hang the one up, and turn the other over. And if you be strong set on throwing either away, lad, you and me won't blaze together like *one* flaming sword, but will be at odds before long. Nay, old ideas is for pondering, not discarding, lad."

Richard held his peace. The old man had already somehow impressed him. Even if he had not, like his father, bid good-bye to his religious fancies, there was a power in him that was not in his father—a power like that he found in his favorite books.

"Mind what he says, and do what he tells you, and you'll get on splendidly!" his mother had said as he left home.

"Don't be afraid of him, but speak up: he'll like you the better for it," his father had counselled. "I wouldn't have married your mother if I'd been afraid of him."

Seeking to follow both counsels, Richard got on with his grandfather quite well.

4 A Lost Shoe

All things belong to every man who yields his selfishness—which is his one impoverishment—and draws near to his wealth, which is humanity—not humanity in the abstract, but the humanity of friends and neighbors and all men. John Tuke was a reasonably clever man who thought highly of his skill with his hands. His natural atmosphere was goodwill and kindliness, but he cherished the unconscious feeling that his abilities were of his own merit. He took the credit for what he was and what he could do; the idea had never arisen in his brain that he was in the world by no creative intent of his own. A man's one claim on manhood is that he can call upon God—not the God of any theology, right or wrong, but the God out of whose heart he came and in whose heart he is. This is his highest power—that which constitutes his original likeness to God. But had anyone tried to wake this idea in Tuke, he would have mocked the very sound of it. He found himself what he found himself, and was content with the find. Therefore he asked himself no questions as to whence he came. He never reflected that he might not have made himself, or that there might be a power somewhere that had called him into being that had a word to say to him on the matter. An ordinarily well-behaved man with a vague narrow regard for morals, he thought quite highly of himself. In relation to Richard he was especially pleased with himself.

With not much more thought than his father, Richard had very early noticed that for all her diligence in church-going, his mother did not seem the happier for her religion: there seemed to be a cloud on her forehead. She had inherited from her mother a heavy sense of responsibility. She had an oppressive sense of the claims of God but no personal relationship with him through which he could give his loving help to her for the duties of her life. She had no window in her soul to let in the light of heaven; all the light she had was the earthly light of duty—an invaluable and necessary thing for one properly related to God, but for her only accompanied by its own shadow of failure, giving neither joy nor hope nor strength. Her husband's sense of duty was neither so strong nor so uneasy.

She had not attempted to teach Richard more in the way of religion than the saying of certain prayers, a ceremony of questionable character. Dearly loving his mother, and saddened by her lack of good spirits, the boy had put things together—among the rest, that she was always gloomiest on Sunday—and concluded that religion was the cause of her misery. This made him welcome the merest hint of its falsehood. He had no opportunity of learning what any vital believer in the Lord of religion might have to say. His only view of Christianity was a hopelessly distorted one. Thus it is hardly any wonder that Richard grew up with the conviction that religion was worse than nothing, an evil phantom. It was not merely a hopeless task to pray to a power which didn't exist; to believe in what was not must be ruinous to the best of human nature. Therefore, the older he grew the more he began to think that the best thing he could do for his fellowman was to deliver him from this dragon called Faith. He could see the tares only; he knew nothing of the wheat—the *true* Faith—among the tares.

But the young Richard did love his kind. He gathered the chief joy of his life from a true relation to the life around him. At school he was always the champion of the oppressed; more than once for the sake of one weaker, he had gotten badly beaten. And now his protection of his kind was extended to all who, like his mother, suffered from false and outdated creeds.

His grandfather found him, as he said, a chip off the old block, and declared there was nothing the fellow could not do. By rights of inheritance, Richard's muscles grew sinewy and hard; quickly he was capable of handling a hammer and persuading iron to the full satisfaction of his teacher. In less than half the time an ordinary apprentice would have taken, Richard could hold alternate swing with the blacksmith, as, blow for blow, they pierced a block of metal to form the nave of a wheel. In ringing a wheel he soon excelled, and his grandfather's smithy being the place for all kinds of blacksmith-work, Richard quickly learned the trade. As his fortnight's holiday drew to an end, his parents wrote, saying that, as he was doing so well, they would like him to stay longer.

At the end of six weeks, Richard could shoe a sound horse as well as his grandfather. The old man had taken pains he would not have spent on an ordinary apprentice: it was worth doing, he said, and the return was great. Richard made steady progress, and gave thorough satisfaction with his work.

Late in the autumn, several houses in the neighborhood began to entertain visitors, and parties on horseback frequently passed the door of the smithy. One evening as the sun was going down, red and large—with a gorgeous attendance of clouds, for the day had been wet but cleared in the afternoon—a small mounted company came along the street. Right in front of the workshop one of the ladies discovered her mare had lost a hind shoe.

"She couldn't have pulled it off in a more convenient spot!" said a handsome young fellow as he dismounted. "I'll help you down, Bab. Old Simon will have a shoe on Miss Brown in no time!"

Richard followed his grandfather to the door. A little girl, as she seemed to him, was sliding down off the back of a huge mare. She was the daintiest little thing, as lovely as she was tiny, with clear, pale, regular features under a quantity of dark brown hair. The moment she dismounted he saw that she was not a child. And he soon discovered that it was not her beauty, but her smiling energy and vivacity that was the most captivating thing about her. Her very soul seemed to go out to meet whatever claimed her attention. As she stood by the side of the great brown creature, her head reaching but halfway up the slope of its shoulder, she laid her head against it tenderly.

A new shoe had to be forged. Simon left the task to his grandson, and stood talking to the young man. He was a handsome youth, not so tall as Richard, and with more delicate features. His face was pale and wore a rather serious, self-satisfied look. He talked to the old blacksmith, however, without the slightest assumption. There were more ladies and gentlemen, but Richard, absorbed in his work, heeded none of the company.

He was not more absorbed, however, than the girl who stood beside him: she watched every point in the making of the shoe. Heedless of the flying sparks, she gazed as if she meant to make the next one herself. Her mind seemed working in company with his hands; she seemed to be all the time doing the thing herself in her own mind. When he carried the half-forged iron to apply it for one tentative instant to the mare's hoof, the girl followed him. The mare fidgeted, but her little mistress was at her head in an instant and spoke to her, in a moment making her forget what was happening in such a far-off province of her being as a hind foot. When Richard, back at the forge, again placed the shoe in the fire, to his surprise her little gloved hand alighted beside his own on the lever of the bellows, powerfully helping him to blow. Again the shoe was on the anvil, and she again stood watching—and watched until he had shaped the shoe to his intent.

Old Simon did not move to interfere: the hoof required no special attention. Almost every horsehoof in the area was known to him.

When Richard took up the foot to prepare it for the reception of its new armor, again the mare was fidgety, and again the lady distracted her attention, comforting and soothing her while Richard trimmed the hoof a little.

"I say, my man," called the young heir, "mind what you're about there with your trimming! I don't want that mare lamed. She's much too good for apprentice hands to learn on, Simon!"

"Keep your mind easy, sir," answered the blacksmith. "That lad ain't a mere apprentice. He knows what he's about as well as I do myself!"

"He's young!"

"Perhaps younger than you think. But he knows his work."

The girl was caressing the great creature, and as Richard finished driving his second nail, the nervous animal gave her foot a jerk, and the point of the nail, through the hoof and projecting a little out the side, tore his hand so that the blood burst out in a sudden rivulet.

"Hey! that don't look much like proper shoeing!" cried the young man. "I hope to goodness that's yours and not the mare's blood."

"She's all right," answered Richard, rearranging the animal's foot.

Simon sprang forward and took the hoof from his grandson. "I'll finish, Dick!"

"It was my fault," said the sweetest voice from under the mare. "My feather must have tickled her nose."

She caught a glimpse of the bloody hand and turned momentarily white.

"I am sorry," she said. "I hope you're not badly hurt, Richard."

Nothing seemed to escape her: she had already learned his name.

"It's not worth being sorry about, miss," returned Richard with a laugh. "The mare meant no harm."

"That I'm sure she didn't—poor Miss Brown," answered the girl, patting the mare's neck. "But I wish it had been my hand instead."

"God forbid!" cried Richard. "That *would* have been terrible!"

"Hardly so great a one. My hand isn't of much use. Yours can shoe a horse!"

"Yours would have been spoiled; mine will mend and shoe just as well as before," said Richard.

It did not occur to the lady that the youth spoke better than might have been expected of a country blacksmith. She was one of the select few that meet every person on the common ground of humanity, with no thought of station or rank. She would have spoken the same way to prince or poet-laureate or blacksmith. Indeed, she treated old Betty, Sir Wilton's dairymaid, with equal respect as she showed Arthur Lestrange, Sir Wilton's heir. She was a great favorite: everybody showed her favor, for she showed everybody grace.

The old smith was finishing the shoeing and the mare, well used to him, stood perfectly quiet. Richard, a little annoyed, had withdrawn and, hardly thinking about what he was doing, had taken a rod of iron, thrust it into the fire, and begun to blow. The little lady approached him softly.

"I'm so sorry," she said.

"Please don't think of it anymore," answered Richard, "or else I will be sorry, too."

She looked up at him with a curious, interested, puzzled look, which seemed to say, *What a nice smith you are.*

The youth's manners had a certain rhythm which came of, or at least was nourished by, his love of the finer elements in literature. His breed also contributed something. Ancestors innumerable, men and women, all leave their traces in a man, and in Richard the good influences were visible and at work.

His hand kept on bleeding, and he now took a handkerchief from his pocket to bind it with. Instantly the little lady stepped forward. "It's much too black," she said, and took the handkerchief from his hand. Drawing her own from her pocket, she deftly bound up his wound with it. All of her party looked on in silence. Some of them had seen her the day before tie up the leg of a wounded dog, and had admired her for it, but this was different! She was handling a workman's hand—black and hard with labor! And it was nothing but a scratch! She was forgetting her station. But they dared say nothing; they knew her and feared what she might say in reply.

"There!" she said. "I hope your hand will be well soon. Goodbye!" She turned and followed her mare, which Simon was leading with caution through the door of the workshop, rather too low for Miss Brown.

Lestrange helped her to the saddle in silence, and before Richard realized she was gone, he heard the merriment of the party mingling with the sound of the horses' hoofs, as they went swinging down the road. The fairy had set them all laughing already!

The instant they were gone Simon showed a strange concern over the insignificant wound: he felt he had been hasty and unfair to Richard by removing him from the task in the middle of the incident. He now seemed anxious to show, without actual confession, that he knew his voice had an angry tone and that he was sorry for it. He could not have shod the mare better himself, he said. His hand had better not do anything for a day or two. Tomorrow being Saturday, they would have a holiday together.

5 The Library at Mortgrange

The next day Simon proposed that they should have a good long walk and a look at Mortgrange. "And then," he added, "we can ask about the mare and see how her new shoe fits." They had known Simon there for the last thirty years, he said, and would let them have the run of the place, for Sir Wilton and his lady were away from home. Richard had never heard of Mortgrange, but he was ready to go wherever his grandfather pleased.

They set out after breakfast to walk the four or five miles by the road that lay between them and Mortgrange. It was a fine frosty morning. Not a few yellow leaves were still hanging, and the sun was warm and bright. It was one of those days near the death of the year that make us wonder why the heart of man should revive and feel strong while Nature is falling into her dreary trance. Richard was in high spirit—for no reason but that his spirits were high. He was happy because he was happy. He had indeed begun to learn that a man must mind his duty before his happiness, and that was a great lesson to learn, but he had not yet been tried in the matter of doing his duty when unhappy. He was happy now, and that was enough. Richard took the thing that came, asked no questions, returned no thanks. He found himself here: whence he came he did not care; whither he went he did not inquire.

On their way Simon talked about the place they were going to see, and said its present owner was an elderly man, not very robust, with a wife and four children.

"That was their son that came with the little lady," he said.

"And the little lady was their daughter, I suppose," rejoined Richard, with an odd quiver somewhere near his heart.

"She's an Australian, they say," answered grandfather. "No relation."

"Is Mortgrange a grand place?" asked Richard.

"It's a fine house and a great estate," answered Simon. "More might be made of it, no doubt; and I hope one day more will be made of it."

"What do you mean by that, Grandfather?"

"I hope the son will make a better landlord than the father."

They came to a great iron gate, standing open, without any gatehouse.

"We're in luck!" said the blacksmith. "This will save us a long walk around. Somebody must have rode out and been too lazy to shut it. Perhaps we should bring the two gates together without snapping the locks. I know these locks; I put them on myself. See what a fine piece of work that gate is!"

"I could almost give up bookbinding to work on a pair of gates like those," said Richard.

"I believe you, my boy!" returned his grandfather. "Come and live with me and you shall!"

The gate admitted them to a long, winding road, with clumps of trees here and there on the borders of it. The road was apparently not much used, for it was grassy. A ploughed field was on one side and a wild heathy expanse, dotted with fir trees, on the other. Suddenly on the side of the field and gradually on the side of the heath, the ground changed to the green sward of a park.

The house of Mortgrange seemed to Richard the oldest house he had ever seen, and it moved him strangely. He said to himself that the man must be happy who owned such a house, lived in it, and did what he liked with it.

The road they had taken brought them to the back of the Hall, as the people on the estate called the house. The blacksmith went to a side door, and asked if he and his grandson might have a look at the place. The man said he would see, and, returning presently, invited them to walk in.

Knowing his grandson's passion, Simon's main thought in taking him was to bring him to the library, with its ten thousand volumes. As soon as they were in the great hall, then, he asked the servant whether they might not see the library. The man left them again, once more to make inquiry.

The grand old hall where they stood was fitter for the house of a great noble than a mere baron. But, then, the family was older than any noble family in the county, and the poor title granted to a foolish ancestor was no great feather in the cap of the Lestranges. The house itself was older than any baronetcy, for no part of it was later than the time of Elizabeth. It was of fine stone and of great size. The hall was nearly sixty feet high, with three windows on one side and a huge one at the end. Midheight along the end opposite the great window ran a gallery.

To Richard's sudden terror as he stood absorbed in the stateliness of the place, an organ in the gallery burst out playing. He looked up but could see only the tops of the pipes. The sounds rolled along the roof, reverberated from the solid walls, and crept about the corners, and the soul of the place throbbed in his ears the words of a poem centuries old, which he had read a day or two before leaving London:

> Erthe owte of erthe as wondirly wroghte,
> Erthe hase getyn one erthe a dignyte of noghte,
> Erthe appone erthe hase sett alle his thoughte,
> How that erthe appone erthe may be heghe broghte.

As he listened, his eyes settled upon a suit of armor in position, and he stood gazing upon it with fascination.

Just then the servant returned.

"Mr. Lestrange is in the library, and will see Mr. Armour," he said.

Simon and Richard followed the man through a narrow door in the thick wall, across a wide passage, and then along a narrow one. A door was thrown open, and they stepped into a solemn room. The floor of the hall was paved with great echoing slabs of stone, but now their feet sank in the deep silence of a soft carpet.

A new awe awoke in Richard. Around him, from floor to ceiling, ranged a whole army of books, mostly in fine old bindings. Their odor, however, was not altogether pleasing to Richard, whose practiced nose detected in it the faint signs of decay. The slight smell of mildewing paper, leather, paste, and glue was to Richard as the air of a poorly ventilated ward is to the nostrils of a physician. He had not seen Mr. Lestrange, half-hidden by a bookcase standing out from the wall.

"Good morning, Armour," said Lestrange. "Your young man does not seem to relish books, judging from the look on his face."

"In a grand place like this, sir," remarked Richard, "such a library as I've never seen, except, of course, at the British Museum, makes a man like myself sad to discover indications of neglect."

"What do you mean?" returned Lestrange, a bit put off.

"I beg your pardon," he said, fearing he had been rude, "but I am a bookbinder."

"Well?" rejoined Lestrange, taking him now for a sneaking tradesman on the track of a big job.

"I can tell at once the condition of an old book by the smell of it," said Richard. "The moment I came in, I knew there must be some here in a bad way—not in their clothes merely, but in their bodies as well—the paper of them. Whether a man has what they call a soul or not, a book certainly has. A gentleman I know—but he's a mystic—goes even further, and says the paper and binding is the body, the print the soul, and the meaning the spirit."

Mr. Lestrange stared. He must be a local preacher, this blacksmith, this bookbinder, or whatever he was!

"I am sorry you think the books hypocrites," he said. "They look all right." He cast his eyes over the shelves before him.

"May I look at one or two?" asked Richard.

"Do so, by all means," answered Lestrange, curious to see how far the fellow could support with proof the accuracy of his scent.

Richard moved three paces and took down a volume—one of a set, the original edition in quarto of *The Decline and Fall* bound in russia leather.

"I thought so!" he said. "Look at the joints of this Gibbon, sir. That's always the way with russia—nowadays at least! Smell that, Grandfather. The leather's stone dead! These joints, you see, are gone to powder. All russia does sooner or later. That's part of what you smell so strong in the room."

Richard replaced the book and took down one after another of the same set.

"Every one, you see, sir," he said, "going the same way! Dust to dust!"

"If they're *all* going that way," remarked Lestrange, "it would cost every stick on the estate to rebind them!"

"I wouldn't rebind any of them. An old binding is like an old picture. Just look at this French binding! It's very dingy and a good deal broken, but you never see anything like that now!"

Lestrange was not exactly stuck-up. He had feared the fellow might say anything next. But by this time the young blacksmith's admiration of the books pleased him and he became more cordial.

"Do you say *all* russia leather behaves in the same fashion?" he asked.

"Yes, now. I imagine it did not some years ago. There may be some change in the preparation of the leather. I don't know. It is a great pity! Russia is lovely to look at—and smells so good. May I take a look at some of the *old* books, sir?"

"What do you call an *old* book?"

"One not later than, say, the time of James the First. Do you have a first folio? The folio of Shakespeare of 1623? There are, of course, many much scarcer. I saw one the other day that the booksellers themselves gave eight hundred guineas for!"

"What was it?" asked Lestrange.

"It was a wonderful copy of Gower's *Confessio Amantis*—not a very interesting book, though I'm sure Shakespeare was fond of it."

"Have you read Gower then?"

"A good deal of him."

"Was it that same precious copy you read him in?"

"It was. But I hadn't time for more than about half. I will have to finish with another edition another time."

"How did you get hold of a book of such value?"

"The booksellers who bought it asked me to take it into my little book hospital. It needed a little patching."

"You say it was not very interesting?"

"Not very."

"Why did you read so much of if then?"

"When a book is hard to come by, you are the more inclined to read it when you have a chance."

All the time they talked, old Simon stood beside, pleased to note how well his grandson could hold his own with the young squire, but he said nothing.

"Where did you learn so much about our country's literature?" asked Lestrange.

"From my own reading, mostly," answered Richard. "And at King's."

"King's!" cried Lestrange.

"King's College, London, I mean," said Richard. "They have evening classes there. My father always took care that I should have time for anything I wanted to do. I go whenever I'm at home and the lecturer takes up any special subject I want to know more about."

"You'll be an author yourself someday, I suppose!"

"There's little hope or fear of that, sir! But I can't bear not to know what's in my hands. I can't be content with the outsides of the books I bind. It would be a shame to come so near light and never see it shine."

Lestrange began to feel uncomfortable. If he let this prodigy go on talking and asking questions, he would find out how little he knew about anything! But Richard was no prodigy. He was only a youth capable of interest in everything.

Further talk followed. Lestrange grew more and more interested in the phenomenon of a blacksmith that bound books and read them. He began to dream of patronage, and responsive devotion. What a thing it would be for him to undertake to pay for this youth's further education and then to have him in later years, when his own cares of property and parliament combined to curtail his leisure, available to gather information for him, to manage his tenants, to shoe his horses, to find him suitable quotations for his speeches!

"I think I'll go and have a pipe with the coachman," said the blacksmith at length.

"As you please, Armour," answered Lestrange. "I will take care of your—nephew, is he?"

"My grandson, sir—from London."

"All right! There's good stuff in the breed, Armour! I will bring him to you."

Richard went on taking book after book down and showing his host how much attention they required.

"And you could set all right for—for how much?" asked Lestrange.

"That no one could say. It would, however, cost little more than time and skill. The material would not come to much. Only, where the paper itself is in decay, I don't know about that. I have learned nothing in that department yet."

"For generations none of us have cared about books—that must be why they have gone so badly downhill—the books, I mean," he added with a laugh. "There was a bishop somewhere in the family, and I think a poet; but I doubt my father would want to lay out money on the library."

"Tell him," suggested Richard, "that it is a very valuable library—at least so it appears to me from the little I have seen of it. But it is rapidly declining in value. After another twenty years of neglect, it would not fetch half the price it might easily be brought up to now."

"I don't know that would weigh much with him. So long as he sees the shelves full and the book backs all right, he won't want anything better. He cares only about how things look."

"But the whole look of the library is growing worse—gradually, it is true, and in a measure it can't be helped—but faster than you would think, and faster than it ought to. I fear damp is getting in somewhere."

"Would you undertake to set all right if my father made you a reasonable offer?"

"I would—provided I found nothing beyond the scope of my experience."

"Well, if my father should come to see the thing as I do, I will let you know. Then would be the time for a definite understanding as to cost."

"The best way would be that I should come and work for a set time: by the progress I made and what I cost, you could judge whether to continue with the rest."

Lestrange rang the bell, and ordered the attendant to take the young man to his grandfather.

The two wandered together over the grounds, and Richard saw much to admire and wonder at, but nothing to approach the hall or the library.

On their way home Simon declared himself in favor of his working at the Mortgrange library, much to his grandson's surprise. But the idea tickled his fancy so much that Richard wondered at the oddity of his grandfather's behavior.

6 Alice

Soon after his visit to Mortgrange, the young bookbinder went home. John Tuke was shocked with the hardness and blackness of his hands. But his wife insisted their condition was no serious matter. Secretly she was proud of her boy.

Richard supposed, of course, that his father's annoyance came only from the fear that his touch would no longer be sufficiently delicate for certain parts of his work. Eager to satisfy both his father and himself that his bookmending hands had not degenerated, Richard selected the book worthiest of his labor from the ones that were awaiting his return, and set about to mend it at once—in which he was thoroughly successful.

Before doing anything else, however, he was now anxious to learn all that was known for the restoration and repair of the inside of books. In this an old bookseller friend of his father's was able to give him considerable help. He taught him how to clean letterpress and engravings from ferruginous, fungus, and other kinds of spots. He acquainted him with a process which considerably strengthened paper that had become weak in its cohesion, and when Richard had time to experiment further, he supplied him with valueless letterpress to work upon. His time was thus more than ever occupied. For many weeks he scarcely even read.

Before long, however, he thought that he must see Adam. He

went that evening to call on him, but found other people in the house who could tell him nothing about the family that had left. He would have inquired at the house in the city where Adam worked, but he did not even know the name of the firm. Once he saw him when riding on the top of an omnibus—looking feebler and paler and more depressed than ever. But when he got down he had lost sight of him, and though he ran up and down the street, he could catch no further glimpse of him.

He had considered Alice one of the nicest girls he had ever seen, but since going to the country had not thought much about her. And since seeing the fairy-like lady with the big brown mare, he had an altogether higher idea of the feminine. But Richard had not yet arrived at any readiness to fall in love, his readiness being delayed until his individuality was sufficiently developed. The man who is growing to be one with his own nature, that is, one with God who is the *naturing* nature, is coming nearer and nearer to every one of his fellow beings. This may seem a long way around to love, but it is the only road by which we can arrive at true love of any kind. He who does not walk this road will never know love as it is meant to be.

One stormy night, as Richard was returning from a house in Park Crescent to which he had delivered a valuable book he had restored, a girl came toward him, fighting against the wind with a weak umbrella, and ran into him. The collision was slight, but she looked up and begged his pardon.

"Alice!" he began.

But before he could speak again, she gave a cry and ran from him as fast as she could go. With the fierce wind and the unruliness of the umbrella, which she was vainly trying to close so that she could run better, she ran into a lamp post. Richard, close behind her, put an arm around her to catch her fall. She did not resist.

The same moment he saw a cab and hailed it. Richard lifted her into it and got in after her. But Alice came to herself, got up, and leaning out of the cab, tried to open the door. Richard caught her, drew her back, and made her sit down again.

"Richard! Richard!" she said as she yielded to his superior strength and began to cry. "Where are you taking me?"

"Wherever you like, Alice. You may tell the cabman yourself. What is the matter with you? Don't be angry with me. It isn't my fault I have not been to see you and Adam. Nobody could tell me where you moved. Give the cabman your address, Alice."

"I'm not going home," sobbed Alice.

"Where are you going, then? I will go with you. You're not fit to go anywhere alone. I'm afraid you're hurt."

"No, no! Please let me out! You must!"

"I won't. You'll fall down and be left to the police. It's horrible to think of you out in such a night. Come home with me. If you are in any trouble, my mother will help you."

"Your mother would kill me!"

"Nonsense!" he said. "What a fancy! My mother!"

"I've seen her since you went. She made me promise—"

She stopped, and Richard could get from her nothing but pleadings to be let out.

"If you don't," she said at last, growing desperate, "I will scream."

"Then let me at least take you a little nearer where you want to go," pleaded Richard.

"No, no! Set me down right here."

"Tell me where you live."

"I dare not."

"I must see my old friend Adam! And why shouldn't I see his sister? My father and mother aren't tyrants. They let me go where I please, or else they give me a good reason why I shouldn't."

"Oh, they'll do that!" returned Alice. "Let me out, Richard, please, or I shall hate you."

Even as she said it she dropped her head on his shoulder and sobbed. He tried to soothe her, but he saw that nothing would change her mind.

"Must I leave you, then, on this very spot?" he asked.

"Yes, yes! Right here!" she answered.

He stopped the cab, got out, and turned to her, but she did not accept his offered help.

"Won't you shake my hand at least?" he implored. "I didn't mean to offend you."

She answered nothing, but hurried away a step or two, then turned and lifted her arms as if to embrace him, but turned again instantly and fled away among the shadows of the flickering lamps. By the time he had paid the cabman, he saw it would be useless to follow, for she was out of sight.

The wide street was almost deserted. He turned toward home with a sense of loss and great sadness at his heart, unable even to speculate as to the cause of Alice's strange behavior. All he knew was that his mother had something to do with it. For the first time since childhood, he felt angry with his mother.

"She probably thinks I am in love with the girl," he said to himself, "and thinks she is not good enough for me! I'm not in love with her; but *any* girl I cared for I should count good enough! What can she have said to her to make her so miserable?"

He was determined to have some explanation from his mother when he arrived home. But the moment she saw where his questioning was leading she turned away, listened in silence, and then spoke with a decision that sounded as if it had anger mingled with it.

"They're not people your father and I would have you know," she said without looking at him.

"Why not, Mother?" asked Richard.

"We're not bound to explain everything to you, Richard. It ought to be enough that we *have* a good reason."

"If it is a good one, why shouldn't I know it?" he persisted. "Good things don't need to be hidden."

"That's true, they do not."

"Then why hide this one?"

"Because it is not good."

"You said it was a good reason!"

"So it is."

"Good and not good! How can that be?" said Richard, not seeing that the worst of facts may be the best of reasons.

His mother held her peace, knowing she was right, but not knowing how to answer him.

"I mean to go see them, Mother," he said.

"You'll regret it, Richard. The woman is not respectable."

"She won't bite me!"

"There's worse than biting. The Bible says the sins of the fathers are visited on the children."

"The Bible! If the Bible says what's not right, are we to do it?"

"Richard! I'll have no such word spoken again in my house!" exclaimed his mother.

"Are you going to turn me out, Mother, because I say we shouldn't do what is wrong, no matter who tells us to?"

"No, Richard. You said the Bible said what was wrong, and that's blasphemy!"

"All right then, Mother," said Richard, not wanting to argue the point, "just tell me where Adam and Alice have gone. I want to go see them."

"I don't know. I took care not to know so I wouldn't be able to tell you."

"But why?"

"Never mind why. I don't know where they are, and couldn't tell you if I would."

Richard turned angrily away, and went to his room, tired and annoyed.

In the morning his mother said to him, "Richard, I can't bear there should be any misunderstanding between you and me! The moment you are twenty-one, ask me and I will tell you everything. Believe me, I was right to stop it, for fear of what might follow."

"If you are afraid of my falling in love with a girl you don't think good enough for me, you have taken the wrong way to keep me from thinking about her."

Richard's wrong to his mother was a lack of faith in her. Where he did not understand and she would not explain, he did not give her the benefit of the doubt. He treated her just as many of us, calling ourselves Christians, treat the Father—not in words perhaps, but in feeling and actions.

At last Jane burst into tears. "You will be sorry for this one day, Richard," she said through her sobs. "Whatever I do is from love for you."

"How can it be good to me to wrong another for my sake?"

"Trust me, Richard. My own father is a blacksmith. I certainly would not look down on a dressmaker."

Richard looked at her moodily for a moment, then turned away and went to the workshop.

7 Mortgrange

In the spring a letter came from young Lestrange, through Simon Armour, asking Richard upon what terms he would undertake the work needed in the library. This time Richard was not so reluctant to leave home.

He handed the letter to his father and they held a consultation.

"There's this to consider," said the bookbinder. "If you go there for any length of time, you lose your connection here—in a measure at least—to the shop. So you couldn't charge the same, not having all the tools and advantages as working here."

"That is true. On the other hand, I should have my living expenses paid in addition."

"True, and of course that is something. We'll have to find out what the best hands in the trade get for such work."

"I'm afraid that, not knowing the finer points of the work, they will think I don't do enough, or charged them too much."

The terms they finally agreed upon appeared reasonable to Lestrange. He proposed that Richard should work for not less than a year, while Lestrange reserved the right of giving him a month's notice. These points agreed to, an agreement was drawn up and signed—much to the satisfaction of Simon Armour, whose first thought was that the work would be so easy for Richard that he would want a little exercise at the forge after hours. Richard, however, as much as he liked the anvil, was not so sure about this: there might be books to read after he had done his day's duty by their garments. He had already half laid out a plan of study for his leisure time.

It was a lovely evening when he arrived at Mortgrange from his grandfather's. He was shown to his new quarters in the mansion by the housekeeper, an elderly, worthy woman with the air of a hostess. She liked the young man. His honest, friendly carriage pleased her. He was handsome too, though not strikingly so. When he sat down to his work as lightly as a gentleman to his dinner, he gave the impression of being a painter or sculptor rather than a tradesman. His bearing suggested a desire rather than a necessity to work.

"Here is your room, young man," said Mrs. Locke.

It was a large, rather neglected chamber at the end of a long passage on the second floor.

"And I hope you will find yourself comfortable," continued the old lady in a tone that implied, *You ought to!*

"If you're wanting anything, or have anything to complain of, let me know," she added. "I thought it better not to put you in the servants' quarters!"

"Thank you, ma'am," said Richard. "This is a beautiful room for me! Do you know where I am to work?"

"I have not been informed," she answered as she left the room. "Mr. Lestrange will see to that."

Richard went to the window. Before him spread an extensive but somewhat bare park, for the trees were rather sparse. Some of them, however, were grand: many had been cut down and only the finest left. A sea of grass lay in every direction. In the distance grazed cattle and sheep and fallow deer.

The day was late in the spring; summer was close at hand. There had been rain all morning and afternoon, but the clouds were clearing away now as the sun was going down. Everything was wet, and the undried tears of the day flashed in the sunset. Nature looked like a child whose gladness had come, but who could not stop crying; so heartily had she gone in for sorrow that her mind was shaped to weeping. Most of the clouds, recently dark and sullen, were putting on garments of light as if resolved to forgive and forget, and leave no doubt of it. But the sun did not look satisfied with the day's work. Slant across the world to Richard's window came the last of his vanishing rays, blinding him as he brooded; somehow the sun seemed sad, as if atonement had come too late. In a few moments the clouds closed on the twilight, the world grew dismal, and the sadness crept into Richard; or perhaps his own hidden sadness rose up to meet the sadness of the world. He was not used to the sensation, and found himself confused by it.

In a few minutes Richard arrived at the conclusion that this momentary depression of spirits would pass as soon as he got into the library.

He went to bed and, after a dreamless night, rose to find the world overflowed with bliss. The sun was at his best, and every water drop on the grass was shining all the colors of the rainbow. Surely the gems that are dug from the earth have their prototype in the dewdrops that lie on its surface! The whole world lay before Richard as his inheritance; the sunlight gave it to him. What was it to Richard that the park, its trees, its grass, its dewdrops, its cattle, its shadows, all belonged to Sir Wilton? He never thought of the fact. He felt them his own. Was the soft, clear, fresh, damp air, with all the unreachable soul of it, not his because it was Sir Wilton's?

The highest property, Dante says, increases to each by the sharing of it with others. But the common mind does not care for such property. Did the blue, uplifted sky that spoke to the sky inside Richard belong to Sir Wilton? Sir Wilton could not claim it because he did not care for it, heard no sound of the speech it uttered. He could not prevent Richard from possessing Mortgrange in a way he himself did not and could not possess it. But neither yet were all these things Richard's in the full eternal way. Nature was a noble lady whose long visit made him glad, but she was not yet at home in his house.

The setting sun had made Richard sad; his resurrection made him glad! He dressed quickly and went to find his way out of the house. After a lengthy walk he made his way to breakfast in the servants' hall; afterward he asked one of the men to let him know when Mr. Lestrange would see him, and went to his room.

Richard had not yet become aware of any moral pressure. What is called a good conscience is often but a dull one that gives no trouble when it ought to bark loudest. Richard's was not of that sort, yet was very much at ease. He had done little that he knew to be bad and very little that he had to be ashamed of. Partly through the care of his parents he had never gotten into what is called bad company. The condition of Richard's inner being was good, rather vacant, unselfish, and yet self-contented, if not self-satisfied. He had a natural cleanliness, a natural sense of the becoming, which did much to keep him from evil. The books he chose were of the better sort. If he did not set himself with any conscious effort to rise above himself, he did do something against sinking below himself.

He got out a notebook in which he was in the habit of writing down whatever came to him, but was shortly interrupted by the entrance of a servant with the message that Mr. Lestrange was in the morning room and wished to see him.

He followed the man and found Lestrange at the breakfast table with a young woman, very ordinary looking, except for her large soft, dark eyes, and—much to his unexpected pleasure—the little lady whose mare he had shod.

He advanced halfway to the table and stood.

"Ah, there you are!" said Lestrange, glancing up. "We've got to set to work, haven't we?"

The fledgling baron, except for his too favorable opinion of himself, in which he was unlike only a very few, was not a disagreeable human and now spoke quite pleasantly.

"Yes, sir," answered Richard. "Shall I wait outside until you are through with breakfast?"

He was afraid the servant might have made a mistake by bringing him so soon.

"I sent for you," replied Lestrange curtly.

"Very well, sir. I have not yet heard whether the tools I sent on have been delivered, but there will be plenty to do in the way of preparation. May I ask if you have settled where I am to work, sir?"

"Ah, I had not thought of that."

"It seems to me, sir, that the library itself would be best, that is, if I might have a good-sized table in it, and could roll up part of the carpet. When I had to beat a book I could take it into the hallway or just outside the window. Nothing else would make any dust."

Lestrange had been wondering how to have the binder under his eye and yet not seem to be watching too closely. The family made little use of the library, and Richard's proposal seemed just the thing.

"I see no difficulty in that," he answered.

"I would need a little fire for my glue pot and polishing iron. There will be gilding and lettering too, though I hope not much—title pieces to replace, and a touch here and there to give to the tooling. No man with any reverence in him would dare more than just touch some of these delicate old gildings!"

The little lady sat eating her toast, but losing not a word that was said. Though she had said nothing, she recognized him instantly and, puzzled, was wondering what a blacksmith could do in a library.

Richard noted that her great eyes every now and then looked up at him with a renewed question, to which they seemed to find no answer. They were big blue eyes—very dark for blue. Her face was full of innocent daring, inquiry, and confidence, pale with a healthy paleness, with just an inclination to freckle. Her dark hair was so abundant and so rebellious that it had to be held firmly with gold pins. She ate daintily enough, but as if she meant to have a breakfast that should last her till lunch—when plainly the active little furnace of her life would want fresh fuel.

But it was not of her food she was thinking just now. In the man who stood there, so independent, yet so free from self-assertion, she saw a prospect of learning something. She hungered for knowledge, but, though fond of reading, was very ignorant of books. She thought like a poet, but had never read a real poem. She was full of imagination, but hardly could have told what the word meant. She had never in her life read a work of genuine imagination.

After some talk it was settled that Richard should work in the large oriel of the library. Mrs. Locke was called and the necessary orders given. Employer and workman were both anxious—the one to see, the other to make a beginning. In a few minutes Richard had located many of the books in direst need of attention—enough to keep him, turning from the one to the other as each required time in the press or to dry, thoroughly busy.

"There are a few volumes here, sir," he said midway through the morning, "that need more than I can do for them. I should like to send them to my father."

"Why to him?"

"I am best at mending. But I'm not up to my father in binding. If he could help me with those that must be bound, I would have more time with what often takes longer. You may trust him; he does not want to make a fortune."

"I will try him then," answered the cautious heir. "At least I will send him the books and see what he will charge."

"I will put the prices on them and promise that my father will charge no more," said Richard.

Lestrange was content with the arrangement, and Richard continued his work with the other volumes.

Always busy, the bookbinder soon began to be respected in the house. After his work hours were over he would read, or write when he pleased, in the library. As his labors went on, the *bookscape* began gradually to revive. Dingy and broken backs disappeared. Light and color soon began dotting the landscape of the bookshelves.

A few valuable books, much injured by time and rough usage, he had pulled apart and was soaking in certain solutions in preparation for binding them. When Lestrange came in one morning, accompanied by the curate of the parish, his eyes fell on a loose title page of a book he happened to know.

"What on earth are you doing?" he cried. "You will destroy that book! By Jove! You little know what you're about!"

"I do know what I'm about, sir. I shall do the book nothing but good," answered Richard. "It could not have lasted many more years without what I am doing."

"Leave it alone," said Lestrange. "I must ask someone else. The treatment is too dangerous."

"I'm sorry, sir, but the treatment is by no means dangerous. After a bath in this solution, the paper will hold together much stronger. The book has suffered much from damp and insects."

"No matter!" answered Lestrange, "I will not have you meddling further with that volume. Would you believe it, Hardy," he went on, turning to the curate, "to experiment on such a rare book!"

"I beg your pardon, I am not experimenting," said Richard.

"I hardly think it is such a very rare book," replied the curate. "I believe it could be replaced."

"Never!" said Lestrange. "It's inscribed personally! Didn't you look at the title page, by Jove!" he said, turning to Richard.

"I always examine the title page of a book," answered Richard. "But the signature on this one was not written by him who owned the name."

"A forgery! What do you know about it?" asked Lestrange rudely.

"Are you an expert?" inquired the curate.

"By no means," answered Richard, "but I have been a good deal with old books, and my impression is that you have got there one of the Ireland forgeries!"

"I believe it to be quite genuine!" said Lestrange.

"If you are right, there is all the more reason in what I am doing, sir."

Lestrange turned abruptly to the curate, saying, "Come along, Hardy! I can't bear to see this butchery!"

"Depend on it," returned the curate, laughing, "the surgeon knows his knife! You *know* what you're about, don't you, Mr. Tuke?"

"If I did not, sir, I wouldn't meddle with a book like this, forgery or no forgery! You should see the quantities of old worthless print I've destroyed in learning how to save such books."

"Mr. Lestrange, you may trust that man!" said the curate.

8 Barbara Wylder

Now, at the height of the social season, Sir Wilton Lestrange and Lady Ann were in London—perhaps not *enjoying themselves*, for it is doubtful whether either of them was capable of enjoying self, or anything else. Sir Wilton and Lady Ann had certainly not grown closer in love by the development of their own individualities. Where all is selfishness on both sides, other likenesses that may exist will rarely come into play. What little common ground they had once shared had long been, if not forgotten, submerged under the waters of their mutual hostility.

If Lady Ann had ever got the idea into her pinched soul that the human race is one family, it would have only strengthened her general dislike of humanity. On the whole, however, they got on rather better than might have been expected, partly in virtue of her sharp tongue and thick skin, which combination of offensive and defensive put Sir Wilton at considerable disadvantage. However sharp his retort might be, she never felt it.

Lady Ann had brought him four children: two daughters and two sons. Theodora, the elder girl, had been out for a year or two but preferred Mortgrange to London; Victoria, the younger, was under the care of Miss Malliver, a governess of uncertain age for whom Lady Ann had an uncertain liking. The elder sister was common in feature and slow in wit, but she had eyes and a heart; the younger, commonly called Vic, and not uncommonly Vixen, was clever and malicious.

Of the sons, the younger, Percy, looked to be turning out not so well. Away at school, the boy was constantly causing trouble; the authorities repeatedly threatened to send him home. He had already been dismissed from Eton. Arthur, on the other hand, was a son in whom his parents could have confidence. As Richard had already discovered, the young heir was, if not the ideal of grace and intelligence, at least not snobbish, and willing to acknowledge others' abilities.

The little lady that rode the great mare was at present their guest—as she often was, in intermittent fashion. She lived in the neighborhood, but was more at Mortgrange than at home. One consequence of this was that, as would-be-clever Miss Malliver phrased it, the house was very much B. Wyldered. Nor was that the first house the little lady had bewildered, for she was indeed an importation from a new colony rather startling to sedate old England. Her father, a younger son, had unexpectedly succeeded to the family property a few miles from Mortgrange. He was supposed to have made a fortune in New Zealand, where Barbara was born and brought up. They had been home nearly two years, and she was almost eighteen. Absurd rumors were abroad concerning their wealth, but there were no great signs of wealth about the place. Wylder Hall was kept up, and its life went on in good style, but mainly because the old servants perpetuated the customs of the house.

Her parents were not the most well-liked in the country, and had it not been for their money it is doubtful whether they would have been accepted back into English society. But everybody liked Barbara, and nobody could imagine how such a flower could have come of two such thistles. She seemed to regard everyone as of her own family. And her brain was as active as her heart. She wanted to know what people thought and felt and imagined, what everything was, how a thing was done, and how it ought to be done. She seemed to understand what the animals were thinking and what the flowers were feeling.

Barbara spent most of her life in the open air and sought the acquaintance of every living thing she saw. She was a child of the whole world. She could sit on a horse's bare back even better than with a saddle, could guide him almost as well with a halter as with a bridle, and in general control him without either. She did not remember the time she could not swim, and she ran herself against every new horse to find what he could do. She was so small that she looked fragile, but had nerves such as few men can boast, and muscles like steel. It never occurred to her not to say what she thought, believed, or felt. She was a special favorite at Mortgrange. She bewitched the man of the world, Sir Wilton, and the cold eye of his lady gleamed at the thought of her dowry. Her father hoped for someone a little higher than a mere baron for her, but he had in no way interfered.

Her father's desire was to see her so well married as to raise his own influence in the county. He was proud of her—selfishly proud. All the credit of her he considered to be his. He forgot even what share her mother might claim. But her mother, too, was proud of her—loved her indeed in a careless fashion. She had two children besides, one of whom she loved far more than Barbara and the other far less.

As for herself, Barbara would never think of love until she fell in love. It did not yet interest her, and until it did, marriage certainly never would. When she came to England it was hard to teach her the ways of the so-called civilized. Servants would sometimes be out searching for her after midnight, perhaps to find her out on the solitary heath beyond the park. She knew most of the stars, had tales and wild myths of her own, and loved the moon, the ocean, and the fields.

As to what is commonly called education, she had not had the best. Since coming to England she had had governesses, but none fit for the office. Nothing was necessary to wake Barbara's hunger and thirst; she was eager to know, and yet more eager to understand. But not one of those teachers knew enough to answer a quarter of Barbara's questions, or was even capable of perceiving that those she could not answer pointed to anything worth knowing.

She had never been taught any religion, but from her earliest recollection she had had the feeling of a Presence. For this feeling she never thought of attempting to account. Neither would she have recognized it as what I have called it. The sky over her head brought it, as did any horizon far or near. But when she went to church, none of the Presence came near her. She had no idea of ever having done wrong, no feeling that God was pleased or displeased with her, or had any occasion to be either. She did not know that the feeling of the Presence came near her in her horse, in her dog, and in the people about her. He came nearer in a thunderstorm, a moonlit night, a sweet wind—anything that woke the sense of the old freedom of her childhood. She felt the presence then, but never knew it as a Presence.

Neither did she know that there was a place where that Presence was always awaiting her—a place called in a certain old book "thy closet." She did not know that there opened the one horizon—infinitely far, yet near as her own heart. But he is there for those that seek him, not for those who do not look for him. Until they do, all he can do is to make them feel the want of him. Barbara had not begun to seek him. She did not know there was anybody to seek: she only missed him without knowing what she missed.

Barbara had no haughty pride. She spoke in the same tone to lord and humble workman. She had been the champion of the blacks in her own country, and in England looked lovingly on the gypsies in their little tents on the windy downs. Similarly, she approached the bookbinder in Sir Wilton's library not with the condescension due an inferior, but with the respect due an equal.

Hardly had Lestrange and the curate left the library when Barbara entered, noiseless as a moth. Her blue eyes—at times they seemed black, they were so dark blue—settled upon Richard the moment she entered and, resting on him, seemed to lead her up to the table where he was at work.

"What have you done to make Arthur so angry?" she asked as if they had known each other all their lives.

"What I am doing now, miss—making this book last a hundred years longer."

"But if he doesn't want you to—the book is his."

"He will be pleased enough by and by. It's only that he is afraid I will ruin it."

"Hadn't you better leave it then?"

"That would be to ruin it. I have gone too far for that."

"Why should you want to make it last so long? They are always printing books over again, and a new book is much nicer than an old one."

"So some people think. But I would always rather read an old book than a new one. And then books get so changed by printers and editors. You can never tell how faithful they have been to the author's original intent. It takes an editor who really knows and loves his subject to do a book justice. You see this little book, miss? It doesn't look like much, does it?"

"It looks miserable—and so dirty!"

"By the time I am done with it, it will be worth fifty, perhaps a hundred pounds—I don't know exactly. It is a play of Shakespeare's that was published during his lifetime."

During this conversation Richard's work had scarcely relaxed. But now that a pause came, it seemed to gather diligence.

"Why do you spend your time patching up books?" said Barbara.

"Because they are worth patching up, and because I earn my bread by patching them."

"But you seem to care most for what is inside them."

"If I didn't I should never have begun mending, I should have been content binding them."

Another pause followed.

"What a lot you know!" said Barbara.

"Very little," answered Richard.

"If you know little, then where does that leave me? I know next to nothing about books."

"Perhaps ladies don't need books. I don't know about ladies."

"I have never heard a man *or* a lady talk as you do—as if books were their friends. But books are only books, after all."

"You would not say that if once you really knew them."

"Then I wish you would teach me to know them."

"You can read, can't you, miss? And there are the books! You don't need me."

"Ah, but I can't read as you read! I can shoot and fish and run and ride and swim, and all those kinds of things. I *think* I could even shoe a horse if someone would give me a lesson or two."

"I would, with pleasure, miss."

"Oh thank you. That will be wonderful. But how is it you can do everything?"

"I can only do one or two things. I can shoe a horse, but I scarcely know anything about riding them."

"Teach me to shoe Miss Brown, and I will teach you to ride her. How is your hand?"

"Quite well, thank you."

"I would rather learn to read though—the right way, I mean."

"That would be better than shoeing Miss Brown. But I will teach you both, if you care to learn."

"Thank you, indeed! When shall we begin?"

"Whenever you like."

"Now?"

"I can't before six o'clock. I must first do what I am paid to do. What kind of reading do you like best?"

"I don't even know."

"Where do you live?" asked Richard, all the time busy with the quarto under his fingers.

"Don't you know?"

"I don't even know who you are, miss."

"I am Barbara Wylder. I live at Wylder Hall, a few miles from here. My father was the third son and never expected to have the Hall. He went to New Zealand and married my mother, and made a fortune—at least so people say: he never tells me anything. They don't care much for me. They would rather have had a boy!"

"Have you any brothers?"

"I have one," she answered. "I had two, but my mother's favorite is gone, and my father's is left, and Mama can't get over it. They were twins, but they did not love each other. How could they? My father and mother don't love each other, so each loved one of the twins and hated the other."

She mentioned the fact as if it were a thing that could not be helped. Yet the sigh which followed her words indicated trouble because of it.

Richard held his peace, rather astonished, both that a lady should talk to him in such an easy way, and that she should tell him such sad family secrets. But she seemed quite unaware of doing anything strange, and after a brief pause resumed.

"They were both fine children, but as the boys grew Mother and Father quarreled more and more about them. Each was determined and obstinate."

"Were the twins older or younger than you?" asked Richard.

"They were three years younger than I. But when I look back it seems as if I had been born into the bickering. When my father's next older brother fell ill, and there seemed a possibility of his succeeding to the property, the thing grew worse than ever; now it was which of them should be his heir. No one knew which was the elder. So from the first the boys understood that they were enemies, and acted accordingly. Each always wanted everything for himself. They were both kind to me. But there was always strife. When it came to blows, as it often did, I jumped on a horse and went away. Nobody ever missed me."

Her narrative was childlike in its insight. What could have moved her to so confide in a stranger—and a workman? In truth, she needed little moving; her nature was to trust everybody, but there were not many to whom she could talk. Miss Brown helped her with no response; to her parents she had no desire to speak; the young people she met were appalled at the least allusion to the wild ways of her past life in New Zealand, making her feel she was not one of them. Even Arthur Lestrange had more than once looked awkward at a remark she happened to make. So instead of confiding in any of them, that is, letting her heart go in search of theirs, she had taken to amusing them. In this she had succeeded so thoroughly as to be a great favorite. But it did not make her happy, did not light up the world within her.

Hence it was no great wonder that, being such as she was, she should feel drawn to Richard. Something within him made her respect him, more so than the young men of her own circle. She felt she could talk to him, confide in him. Her heart and mind were free from social prejudices. She knew that people looked down upon men who did things with their hands; but she had done many things with her hands and had often been helped by others who could do things with their hands better than she.

One of the habits which most wounded the sense of propriety in those about her was Barbara's talking about things they felt ought to be kept private. Now Barbara could keep a joyful secret, but a misery was not a nice thing to hide inside; she must get rid of it. She soon found, however, that it was no relief to talk to Arthur or his sister or the governesses. But the bookbinder was different. He was not what people called a gentleman. But he was a man who spoke out what he meant. He was such a gentlemanly workman! Of course he could not be a *gentleman* in England, but there ought to be someplace where Richard could be a gentleman just as he was, without having to be born one. She was sure he would not laugh at her behind her back, and she was not sure that Arthur or Theodora would not do that. Even more, he was ready to open for her the door into the rich chamber of his knowledge. Could it be that such a workman was a better and greater kind of man than a gentleman?

To end her story she told Richard that, since their coming to this country, her mother's favorite of the boys had died. She went nearly mad, she said, and had never been herself again. Not only had her opposition to her husband deepened into hate, but she came to hate God also. "Isn't it awful?" Barbara said, but she met no response in the honest eyes of Richard, to whom it was not such an awful thing at all.

"I have heard her say the wildest and wickedest things, whether anyone could hear her or not. There are devils going about in New Zealand. Nobody knows of that here, but it was here they got into my mother and made her defy God. Do you know what she does? She goes to church, but sits the whole time, in full view of the clergyman and everyone, and reads a novel, a yellow French one, generally."

"She disapproves of the whole thing?" said Richard.

"She used to like church well enough."

"She must do it to protest. Otherwise why would she go? Does she have a quarrel with the clergyman?"

"None that I know of."

"Then why does she go and not take part?"

"I believe she does it just to let God know she is angry with him. She thinks he has treated her cruelly and tyrannically, and she will not pretend to worship him. She wants to show him how bitterly she feels the way he has turned against her."

The absurdity of the thing struck Richard, but he didn't want to hurt the girl.

"Has the clergyman ever spoken to her about it?"

"I don't think so. I would speak to her fast enough if it were *my* church."

"He probably thinks her mind affected and doesn't want to make her worse," said Richard. "But I would think he might persuade her that, as she is not on good terms with the person who lives in the church, she ought to stay away."

Barbara looked at him doubtfully, but Richard went on.

"What sort of man is the clergyman?" he asked.

"I don't know. He seems to be always thinking about things, always asking questions and never giving the answers. Maybe he doesn't know them himself. I suppose he is a rather stupid man."

"That does not necessarily follow," said Richard with a smile, reflecting on the complexity of the questions which confronted him concerning his own trade. "Your poor mother must be very unhappy," he added.

"I suppose. I am no comfort to her. She never pays any attention to me, or she tells me to go amuse myself—she is busy. My father has his twin, and poor Mama has nobody."

At this point Barbara's friend came into the room and they went away together.

Theodora was a very different girl from Barbara. Nominally friends, neither understood the other. Theodora was the best of the family, but that did not suffice to make her interesting. She was short, stout, rather clumsy, with an honest face, entirely without guile. She did not have much sympathy, but was very kind. She never hesitated to do what she was sure was right. But she could hardly think for herself what right might be, therefore would have always been in doubt were it not for rules which governed her behavior. If all the rules she obeyed had been right, and she had seen the right in them, she would have made rapid progress; as it was, her progress was very slow. How Barbara and she managed to entertain each other was almost impossible to imagine.

Barbara left Richard almost bewitched, and considerably perplexed. He had never seen anything like her. She had indeed brought to bear upon him, without knowing it, that humbling and elevating power which ideal womankind has always had, and will eternally have upon genuine manhood. There was an airiness about her, yet a reality, a lightness, yet a force, a readiness, a life such as he could never have imagined.

Certainly, a few beauties already flowered in Barbara's garden, but a multitude of precious things waited to unfold themselves to anyone that might love her enough to give them a true welcome. Richard pictured the delight of opening the eyes of this child-woman to the many doors of treasure houses that stood in her own wall. It is the impulse of every true heart to give of its best, to infect with its own joy, and the thought of giving grandly to such a lady as Barbara might well fill the soul of a workingman with ecstasy.

Barbara had quite as much liberty as was good. Her home was a terribly dull place to her and therefore she was at Mortgrange as much as she pleased. Theodora Lestrange had taken a fancy to her, Sir Wilton was charmed with her, and Lady Ann—for her own mercenary reasons—had little to say against her. Arthur was fascinated by her grace and playfulness and tried for a while to throw his net over her, for he would fain have tamed her to come at his call. But before very long he arrived at the conclusion that nothing would tame her, at least not until she grew up a little more. She was a fine creature, he said, but hardly a woman yet. And he preferred a woman to a fairy!

But such was the report of her riches that both Sir Wilton and Lady Ann were ready to welcome her as a daughter-in-law. Sir Wilton was delighted with her gaiety and the sharp readiness of her clever tongue. As for her intellectual development, that was of so little interest to him that he never suspected Barbara of having more than a usual share of intellect to develop. She was just the wife for the future baron. But he seemed sometimes to begrudge his son the dainty little wife Barbara would make him. "The rascal will be the envy of the clubs!" he said.

9 Mrs. Wylder

Mr. Wylder was lord of the manor and chief landowner in the parish next to that in which Mortgrange lay, though his family had never been the most influential. He was not much fitted to be an English squire. He wanted to enjoy good standing with his neighbors, but lacked geniality. Proud of his family, he was arrogant and thus completely out of touch with true social interchange. Yet he remained supremely satisfied in his consequent isolation, hardly even recognized it, and never doubted himself a perfect gentleman. When he did begin to discover that the neighbors did not desire his company, he set it down to stupid prejudice against him because he had been so long absent from the country. He never did perceive the reflection of his true self mirrored in the attitudes of those around him.

Resenting the indifference of his neighbors, Mr. Wylder undertook the restoration of a certain old manor house on his property in order to fill his time. He had haunted it as a boy, chiefly for the sake of its attendant gooseberries and apples; it had since fallen into decay.

The clergyman of the parish, one Thomas Wingfold—a man who loved his fellow and would give him of the best he had, a man who was a Christian first and then a churchman—had for almost three years puzzled both heart and brain to find what could be done for these his new parishioners. He had known troubles enough as a young man in his previous parish. And after his own awakening, which came after he had occupied the pulpit for some time, he had encountered more than one individual whose outer shell took some time to penetrate. But he had learned from an unlikely dwarf in that parish that all men and women are united by a common hunger for God. Wingfold had never in two years seen so much as a glimmer of spirituality in Mr. Wylder, however, and he had seen more than a glimmer of something else in his wife. Between him and either of them their common humanity had not yet shown a spark. What he had seen of the girl he liked, but he had not seen much.

One fine frosty day in February, about twelve o'clock, Mr. Wingfold walked up the avenue of Scotch firs to call on Mrs. Wylder. He was dressed like any country gentleman in a tweed suit, carried a rather strong stick, and wore a soft felt hat, looking altogether more like a squire than a clergyman—for which most of his people liked him the better. Pious people in general seem to regard religion as a necessary accompaniment of life; to Wingfold it was life itself—with him God must be all, or he could be nothing. He was noted among the farmers for his common sense, as they called it, and among the gentry for his frankness of speech, which most of them liked. He generally walked with his eyes on the ground, but would now and then straighten his back, and gaze away to the horizon as if looking for the far-off sails of help.

He rang the doorbell of the Hall and asked if Mrs. Wylder was at home. The man hesitated, looked in the clergyman's face, and smiling oddly, answered, "Yes, sir."

"Only you don't think she will care to see me?"

"Well, you know, sir—"

"I do. Go up and announce me."

The man led the way and Mr. Wingfold followed. He opened the door of a room on the first floor, and announced him. Mr. Wingfold entered immediately that there might be no time for words with the man and a message of refusal.

Discouragement encountered him on the threshold. The lady sat by a blazing fire, with her back to a window through which the frosty sun of February was sending lovely prophecies of the summer. She was in a gorgeous dressing gown, her plentiful black hair twisted carelessly round her head. She was almost still a young woman, with a hardness of expression that belonged neither to youth nor age. She sat sideways to the door, so that without turning her head she must have seen the parson enter, but she did not move a visible hairsbreadth. She made no sign of greeting when the parson came in front of her, but a scowl dark as night settled on her low forehead and black eyebrows. Wingfold approached her with the air of a man who knew himself unwelcome but did not much mind—for he did not have to care about himself.

"Good morning, Mrs. Wylder!" he said. "What a lovely morning it is."

"Is it? I know nothing about it. The climate here is brutal."

He knew she regarded him as the objectionable agent of a more objectionable heaven.

"You would not dislike it so much if you met it out-of-doors. A walk on a day like this—"

"Who authorized you to come and offer me advice? Have I concealed from you, Mr. Wingfold, that your presence gives me no pleasure?"

"You certainly have not. You have been quite honest with me. I did not come in the hope of pleasing you—though I wish I could."

"Then perhaps you will explain why you are here!"

"There are visits that must be made, even when you are certain of giving annoyance," answered Wingfold rather cheerfully.

"That means you consider yourself justified in forcing your way into my room, before I am dressed, with the simple intention of making yourself disagreeable?"

"If I were here on my own business, you might well blame me. But what would you say to one of your men who told you he dared not go out to deliver a message you gave him for fear of the lightning?"

"I would tell him he was a coward and to go about his business."

"Well, that's what I don't want to be told by my Master, that I am a coward."

"And for fear of being told it, you dare me?"

"Well—if you want to put it like that, yes."

"I admire your courage. But I like you no more for it. You're not afraid of me and I'm not afraid of you! It's a low trade, yours."

"What is my trade?"

"To talk goody religion when there's nothing to it!"

"I'm not doing much of that sort at this moment," rejoined Wingfold with a laugh.

"You know this is not the place for it!"

"Would you mind telling me where is the place to read a French novel?"

"In church! There—what do you think of that!"

"What would you do if I were to insist on reading a chapter of the Bible here?"

"Look!" she answered, and rising, snatched a saloon pistol from the mantel and took deliberate aim at him.

Wingfold looked straight down the throat of the thick barrel and did not budge.

"I would shoot you with this," she went on. "It would kill you, for I can shoot and would hit you in the eye. I shouldn't mind being hanged for it. Nothing matters now."

She flung the heavy weapon from her, gave a great cry like an enraged animal, and began tearing at her handkerchief. The pistol fell in the middle of the room. Wingfold went and picked it up.

"I should deserve it if I did," he said quietly, as he laid the pistol on the table. "But you don't fight fair, Mrs. Wylder, for you know I can't take a pistol into the pulpit and shoot you. It is cowardly of you to take advantage like that."

"Do I read so as to annoy anyone?"

"Yes, you do. You don't dare read aloud. But you annoy as many of the congregation as can see you, and you annoy me. Why should you behave in that house as if it were your own, and yet shoot me if I behaved so in yours? Is it fair? Is it polite? Is it acting like a lady?"

"It is my pew, and I will do in it what I please. Look here, Mr. Wingfold: I don't want to lose my temper with you, but I tell you that pew is mine as much as the chair you're not ashamed to sit upon at this moment. And when he's treated me as he has, I don't see that God Almighty can complain of the manners of a woman like me!"

"Well, thinking of him as you do, I don't wonder that you are rude."

"What! You agree with me! That takes pluck!"

"I fear you mistake me."

"Of course I do. I might have known! The moment it sounds

like a parson is speaking like a man, you may be sure you mistake him!"

"You wouldn't behave to a friend of your own according to what another person thought of him, would you?"

"No, by Jove, I wouldn't!"

"Then you won't expect me to do so."

"I should think not. Of course you stick by the church!"

"The church is not my mistress, though I am her servant. God is my Master, and I tell you he is as good and fair as goodness and fairness can be."

"Ha! If he had treated you as he has treated me—then we would hear another tune! You call it good—you call it fair, to take from a poor creature he made himself the only thing she cared for?"

"And the cause of a strife that made the family in which he wanted to live a very hell on earth!"

"How dare you!" she cried, starting to her feet.

Wingfold did not move.

"Mrs. Wylder," he said, "if you dare tell God that he is a devil, I may well dare tell you that you know nothing about him, and that I do."

"Say on your honor, then, that if he had treated you as he has done me—taken from you the light of your eyes, would you count it fair? Speak like the man you are."

"I know I would."

"I don't believe you! And I won't worship him."

"Who wants you to worship him? You must be a very different person before he would care much for your worship. You *can't* worship him while you think him what you do. He is something quite different."

"Isn't that your business? Aren't you always making people say their prayers?"

"It is my business to help my brothers and sisters to know God, and to learn to worship him in spirit and truth—because he is altogether and perfectly true and loving and fair. Do you think he would have you worship such a being as you take him to be? If your son is in good company in the other world, he must be greatly troubled at the way you treat God—at your unfairness to him. But your bad example may, for anything I know, have sent him where he has not yet begun to learn anything."

"God have mercy! Is the man telling me to my face that my boy is in hell!"

"What would you have? Would you rather him be with the being you think so unjust that you hate him all the week and openly insult him on Sunday?"

"You are a hardhearted brute of a man—a devil to say such things about my boy! Oh, my God! To think that the very day he was taken ill, I struck him! Why did he let me do it? To think that he killed him on that very day, when he ought to have killed me!"

"If he had not taken him then, would you ever have been sorry you struck him?"

She burst into outcry and weeping, mingled with swearing. The soul and the demon were so entirely united in her, so entirely of one mind, that there was no room for Wingfold's prayers to get between them. He sat quiet, lifted up his heart, and waited. By and by there came a lull and the redeemable woman appeared, emerging from the smoke of the fury.

"Oh, my Harry!" she cried. "To take him from my very bosom. He will never love me again! God *shall* know what I think of it. No mother could but hate him after what he has done!"

"Apparently you don't want the boy back in your arms again."

"He's dead!" she answered, drawing herself up and drying her eyes. "I can stand a good deal, but I won't stand your toying with me! What's gone is gone! The dead feel no arms. They go to the grave and return never more!"

"But you will die, too."

"What do you mean by that? As if I didn't know I have to die one day or another. What's that to Harry and me?"

"You think we're all going to stop being and go out, like the clouds that are carried away and broken up by the wind?"

"I know nothing about it, and I don't care. Nothing's anything to me but Harry, and I shall never see my Harry again! Heaven! Bah! What's heaven without Harry?"

"Nothing, of course! But don't you ever think of seeing him again?"

"What's the use? It's all a mockery! What's the good of meeting when we won't be human beings anymore? If we're nothing but ghosts—ugh! It's all humbug! If he ever meant to give me back my Harry, why did he take him from me?"

"He gave you his brother at the same time, and you refused to love him. What if he took the one away until you should have learned to love the other?"

"I can't love Mark; I won't love him! He has his father to love him. He cares nothing for my love. I haven't got any to give him! What are you doing there—laughing in your sleeve? Did you never see a woman cry?"

"I've seen many a woman cry, but never without my heart crying with her. You come to my church and behave so badly I can hardly help crying for you. It half choked me last Sunday to see you sitting there with that horrid book in your hand, and the words of Christ in your ears."

"I didn't heed them! It wasn't a horrid book!"

"It *was* a horrid book. You left it behind you, and I took it with me. I laid it on my study table and went out again. When I came home to dinner my wife brought it to me and said, 'Oh, Tom, how can you read such books?' 'My dear,' I answered, 'I don't know what is in the book; I haven't read a word of it.' "

"And then you told her where you found it?"

"I did not."

"What did you do with it?"

"I said to her, 'If it's such a bad book, here goes!' And I threw it into the fire."

"Then I'm not going to know the end of the story! But I can send to London for another copy! How thoughtful of you, Mr. Wingfold, to destroy my property! But you didn't tell her where you found it?"

"I did not."

Mrs. Wylder was silent. She seemed a little ashamed, perhaps a little softened. Wingfold bade her good morning. She did not answer him.

Scarcely had Mr. Wingfold left the room when in came Barbara in her riding habit, with the glow of joyous motion upon her face; she had just ridden from Mortgrange.

"I've had such a ride, Mama!" she said; "straight as any crow could fly through the back fields."

"You're a madcap," said her mother. "You'll be brought home on a stretcher someday. How long were you at Mortgrange this time?"

"A week."

"Your father has his heart set on your marrying Mr. Lestrange: I can see it perfectly and I won't have it!"

"But why shouldn't I marry Mr. Lestrange?"

"Because your father has his heart set on it, I tell you! Isn't that enough? I *will not* have it—not even if it breaks your heart."

Barbara burst out in a laugh that rang like a bronze bell.

"Break my heart for Mr. Lestrange! You needn't be uneasy, Mama. I don't like Arthur Lestrange one bit and would never marry him. He's too polite. I would sooner fall in love with the bookbinder."

"The bookbinder? Who's that?"

"There's a man binding—or mending, rather—the books in the library. He's going to teach me how to shoe Miss Brown. Papa wouldn't like me to marry a blacksmith—I mean a bookbinder—would he?"

"Certainly not."

"Then would you, Mama?" said Bab demurely, with fun in her eyes.

"Tease me any more with your nonsense, and I'll set your father on you! Be off with you!"

While the two talked, another conversation, with Barbara as its subject, was going on several miles away. "Why don't you look better after your friend, Theo?" said her father when Barbara's chair was empty at dinner.

"She doesn't mind me, Papa," Theodora answered. "Do say something to her, Mama."

"'Tis not my business to reform other people's children," Lady Ann returned.

"I find her exceedingly original!" remarked the baron.

"That is her charm," responded Arthur, "but it is a dangerous one."

"Miss Wylder, with all her sweetness," said Miss Malliver, "has not an idea of social distinction. She cannot understand why she should not talk to any farmer's son or dairymaid she happens to meet. She is so familiar with them."

"Yesterday I found her talking to the bookbinder as familiarly as if he had been Arthur," said Theodora.

"She lacks self-respect," said Lady Ann. "But we must deal with her gently, and try to do her good. Her manners have in them the germ of possible distinction. I think they will come to be nearly all that could be desired in the end."

Sir Wilton knew Lady Ann's coldblooded heart, and knew that her show of tenderness toward Barbara Wylder was marred by a selfish eye cocked toward the girl's dowry. His wife's regard, though slight, of the Wylder fortunes, irritated his pharisaical pride. *She thinks to match Arthur, firstborn of her icicle brood, with that little firebrand, Barbara,* the baron mused. *But what if...* He smiled with a secret satisfaction, enjoying the imagined discomfort an unexpected turn of events might bring to his wife.

Lady Ann knew, of course, the "secret" Sir Wilton harbored—the *real* firstborn child, the son of Sir Wilton and a lowborn daughter of a common workman. The infant had not been seen since a brief year after his birth: stolen, it was assumed, by a protective nurse after the death of the mother in childbirth.

The baron had seen his son only once, in the arms of the nurse. A monster it was—indescribably ugly, with webbed fingers and toes. The little amphibian was spirited away, then, when Sir Wilton brought his new wife Lady Ann home. Both the baron and his wife were glad enough to see the child go; no real efforts to locate him and his kidnapper were made.

After a while, when Arthur and the other children came along, Sir Wilton and Lady Ann never spoke to one another about the uncertain future of the long-lost Lestrange. Perhaps he had not lived; perhaps he was far away in the obscurity of the commoners' life. Lady Ann wished him dead, but took every conceivable step to insure the security of the inheritance to her eldest.

As the hostility grew between Sir Wilton and his wife, the baron soon forgot his initial aversion to the ugliness of his phantom firstborn. He began to think—with a great deal of pleasure—how it would serve her ladyship if, after all this time, the offspring of a workman's daughter should appear, claiming his right to the Lestrange name. He lay awake at night, picturing to himself how the woman in the next room would take it—Sir Wilton and his son together! But he kept his fantasies to himself; for years he never indulged a single allusion to the idea, allowing her ladyship to refer to Arthur as the heir without the slightest hint at the uncertainty of his position.

Meanwhile, Lady Ann, dwelling on what she counted the shame of the lost child's origin, so far persuaded herself that the vanished child was baseborn that she scarcely doubted the possibility, were he to appear, of proving him illegitimate and his claim false, originated by conspiracy. Unable to learn from her husband when and where the baby was baptized, she concluded that he never had been baptized, and thus no record of his birth existed. As years went by and no whisper of his presence was heard, she grew more and more confident. She set herself to encourage Arthur's relations with the wealthy Barbara and thus to strengthen Arthur's hand in the eyes of his father.

Sir Wilton liked Barbara. He had been to school with Barbara's father, but did not favor her for that. The two men had not been friends and did not like each other any better now. But the girl amused him, and amusement was the nearest to sunshine his soul was capable of reaching. Sir Wilton was not greatly interested in the matter of his son's marriage. The well-being of his family after he was gone did not much affect him; nothing but his lower nature had ever roused him to action of any kind. How far the idea of betterment had ever shown itself to him, God only knows. Apparently he was a child of the evil one, whom nothing but the furnace could cleanse. Almost the only thing he could now imagine giving him vivid pleasure was to see his wife thoroughly annoyed. Thus, while allowing his wife the semblance of security and control, he privately reveled in his dreams of her undoing.

Now, returning to Mortgrange from London, Lady Ann found

all as she left it, with the insignificant exception of a man at the bay window of the library working to repair the books. In all other ways she had resumed the reins of the family coach.

10 The Parson's Parable

Wingfold went away wondering what could be done for the woman. What was his part, as parson of the parish, with regard to her behavior in church? Was he called upon to take public notice of her defiance to God? The Creator's discipline did not suit her, and she would let him know it! Whether it suited her necessities she did not ask or care: she knew nothing of her necessities—only of her desires. Had she had a glimmering suspicion that she was poor, angry, miserable, blind, and naked, she might have allowed God some room to show himself.

Wingfold wondered if it was his business to rebuke her behavior, or must he leave reproof as well as vengeance to the Lord. A public contention in the church was abhorrent to him, but it troubled him that some of his flock might imagine the great lady of the parish was allowed to behave herself indecorously because of her social standing.

It may seem incredible that one like Mrs. Wylder could believe in God and yet defy him. But it is one thing to believe in a god; it is quite another to believe in God! Every time we grumble at our fate, every time we are displeased, hurt, resentful at this or that which comes to us, we are of the same spirit as this half-crazed woman. One of four gates stands open to us: to deny the existence of God; to acknowledge his existence but say he is not good; to say, "I wish there was a God," and be miserable because there is none; or to say, "There is a God, and he must be perfect in goodness or he could not be," and thus give ourselves to him heart and soul.

But what was Wingfold to do about Mrs. Wylder? Was he to

allow the simple sheep of his flock to think him afraid of the squire's lady? or was he to venture an uproar in the church on a Sunday morning? He and his wife had often talked the thing over but had arrived at no conclusion. He now told her everything that had happened.

"Isn't it time to do something?" said Helen.

"Indeed, I think so—but what?" he answered.

She was silent a moment, then said, "Couldn't you preach at her?" she said with a little laugh, an odd mingling of doubt and merriment.

"I have always thought that mean," he said. "I have never done it intentionally. There was that one time," he said with a smile, "when you *thought* I was preaching to you."

"I remember—during Leopold's trouble. I didn't know whether to love you or hate you!"

He laughed. "Well, at least that turned out for the good. But it was so different."

"You're right. This case is unique. The wrong is done in the very eyes of the congregation, for the sake of its being seen. If you said something, you would not be the assailant. You would but accept, not give, the challenge. She has been pitting her position in the pew against yours in the pulpit for too long. She flaunts her novels in your face. The congregation can't help but think about her and her yellow novel instead of the things you are saying to them. For the sake of the work given you, for the sake of your influence with the people, you must do something."

"It is God she defies, not me."

"I think she defies you to speak an honest word on his behalf. She thinks you have no authority to drive from the little temple one of the cows of Bashan."

"Quite right! But you don't give me a hint what to do!"

"Am I not saying plainly that you must preach at her?"

"I just didn't expect that of you."

"A public scandal requires public attention. She has put herself before the people. She is brazen and must be treated as brazen—set in the full glare of opinion. It is all very well to make such a clamor about her boy, but she quarreled with him dreadfully. I have been told she would abuse him in language not fit to repeat, and he would scream back at her, choking with rage."

"Who told you that?"

"I would rather not say."

"Are you sure it is not mere gossip?"

"Quite sure. To be gossip a thing must go through two mouths at least, and I had it first-mouth. I tell you because I think it worth your knowing."

The next Sunday there sat the lady as usual with her novel. When the curate went into the pulpit he cast one glance at the gallery to his right, then spoke:

"My friends, I will follow the example of our Lord and speak to you today in a parable. The Lord said that some things are better said through parable because of the eyes that will not see and the ears that will not hear.

"There was once a mother left alone in the world with her little boy—the only creature in the world she cared for. She was a good mother to him, as good a mother as you can think, always kind. She never thought of herself but only her son, the apple of her eye. He was a delicate child, requiring every care she could lavish upon him, and she did lavish it. Oh, how she loved him!

"The years went by and the child grew and the mother loved him more and more. But he did not love her as she loved him. He soon began to care more for the things she gave him, but he did not learn to love the mother who gave them. Now the whole of good things is to be the messengers of love—to carry love from one heart to the other. But when they are grasped at by a greedy, ungiving hand, they never reach the heart but block up the path of love, and divide heart from heart, so that the greedy heart forgets the love of the giving heart more and more. That is the way generosity fares with the ungenerous.

"There came at last a day when she said to him, 'Dear boy, I want you to go and bring me some medicine, for I feel very poorly, and am afraid I am going to be ill.' He mounted his pony and rode away to get the medicine. Now his mother had told him to be very careful because the medicine was dangerous, and he must not open the bottle. But once he had got it he said to himself, 'It is probably something very nice and mother does not want me to have any of it!' So he opened the bottle and tasted what was in it, and it burned him terribly.

"He was furious with his mother, saying to himself that she had told him not to open the bottle just to make him do it, and he vowed he would not go back to her. He threw down the bottle and turned, and rode another way, until he found himself alone in a wild forest where there was nothing to eat and nothing to shelter him from the cold night, and the wind blew through the trees and made strange noises. He dismounted, afraid to ride in the dark, and before he knew it, his pony was gone. He became miserably frightened and wished he had not run away. But still he blamed his mother.

"The mother became very uneasy about her boy, and went out to look for him. The neighbors too, though he was not a nice boy and none of them liked him, went out to help her look for him, and they came at last to the wood with their torches and lanterns.

"The boy was lying under a tree and saw the lights and heard the voices and knew it was his mother come to find him. Then the old wickedness rose up again in his heart and he said to himself: 'Does she think she can find me so easily? Am I to come and go as she pleases?' He lay very still and crept slowly away, and thus avoided those who had come to save him. He heard one say there were wolves in the wood, but he was just the kind of boy who will not believe what is good for him. So he slipped and slipped away until at length everyone despaired of finding him, and left the wood.

"Suddenly he knew that he was alone again. He gave a great cry, but no one heard it. He stood shaking and listening. Presently his pony came rushing past him with two or three wolves behind him. He began to run, wild with fear to get out of the wood. But he could not find the way, and ran about this way and that until utter despair came upon him, and all he could do was lie still as a mouse so that the wolves could not hear him.

"As he lay he began at last to think that he was a wicked child; that his mother had done everything to make him good, and he would not be good. Now he was lost and only the wolves would find him. He sank at last into a stupor.

"He came to himself in the arms of a strange woman, who had taken him up, and was carrying him home. The name of the woman was Sorrow—a wandering woman, a kind of gypsy, always going about the world and picking up her lost things. Nobody likes her; hardly anybody is civil to her, but when she has set anybody down and is gone, often a look of affection and wonder and gratitude goes after her. Yet even with all that, very few are glad to be found by her again.

"Sorrow carried him weeping home to his mother. His mother came out and took him in her arms. Sorrow bowed and went away. The boy clung to his mother's neck and said he was sorry. In the midst of her joy his mother wept bitterly, for he had nearly broken her heart. She could not get the wolves out of her mind.

"But alas! the boy soon forgot all and was worse than ever. He grew more and more cruel to his mother, and mocked every word she said to him, so that—"

A cry came from the gallery. The congregation started in terror to their feet. The curate stopped, and turning to the right, stood gazing. In the front of the squire's pew stood Mrs. Wylder, white and speechless with rage. For a moment she stood shaking her fist at the preacher. Then in a hoarse, broken voice came the words:

"It's a lie! My boy was never cruel to me. It's a wicked lie!"

She could say no more, but stood and glared, hate in her fierce eyes, and torture in her colorless face.

"Madam, you have betrayed yourself," said Wingfold solemnly. "If your son behaved well to you, it makes it all the worse that you now behave so badly to your Father. From Sunday to Sunday you insult him with rude behavior. Till now I have held my tongue—not from fear of the rich, from no desire to spare them, but because I shrank from making the house of God a place of contention. But, madam, you have behaved shamefully, and I do my duty in rebuking you."

The whole congregation had risen to their feet staring at her. A moment longer she stood and would have brazened out the stare. But she felt the eyes of the motionless hundreds blazing away upon her, and the culprit grew naked in the presence of judging souls. Her nerve gave way; she turned her back, left the pew, and fled from the church.

Happily, Barbara was not in the church that morning.

The next Sunday the squire's pew was empty.

Wingfold felt his well-intentioned plot had failed. But though he had rough-hewed its ending, the divine hand would yet accomplish its work through it.

When the squire came to know what had taken place, he made his first call on the curate. He said nothing about his wife, but plainly wished it understood that he bore him no ill will for what he had done.

11 The Rime of the Ancient Mariner

Barbara was always glad to get away from home. While her father was paying his long-delayed visit to the curate, she was flying over hedge and ditch in a line for that gate of Mortgrange which Simon Armour and his grandson found open; Barbara had a key to it.

She went with swift, gliding step into the library. Richard was piecing the broken sections of a great old folio together, so as to prepare the book for a new cover. She carried in her hand something yet more sorely in need of mending—a pigeon with a broken wing, which she had seen lying in the park, and had dismounted to take. It kept opening and shutting its eyes, and she knew that nothing could be done for it. But the mute appeal of the dying thing had gone to her heart, and she wanted sympathy, whether for it or for herself she could hardly have distinguished.

"Ah, poor thing," said Richard. "I fear we can do nothing for it. But it will be at rest soon."

"But where?" said Barbara, to whom that moment came the question for the first time.

"Nowhere, I suppose," answered Richard.

"How can that be! Poor little thing! I won't let you go nowhere!"

Richard saw that to say more at that moment would probably be to close the door between them. Therefore he took refuge in his genuine sympathy with suffering.

"Is it not strange," he said, "that men should take pleasure in killing—especially helpless creatures like that, so full of innocent contentment? It seems to me the greatest pity to stop such a life! Did you ever notice in *The Rime of the Ancient Mariner*, the point at which the dead bird falls from the neck of the man?"

"I don't even know what you are talking about," answered Barbara. "Do tell me. It sounds like something wonderful! Is it a story?"

"Yes—a wonderful story."

He began to repeat as much of the ballad as he could, and went on, never slackening his work. The very first stanza took hold of Barbara. She sat down by Richard's table, softly laid the dying bird in her lap, and listened with round eyes and parted lips, her rapt soul at attention.

But Richard had not gone far before he hesitated.

"Have you forgotten it?" she asked.

"Not forgotten, exactly. I just became confused between the different editions; they've gotten a little mixed in my head."

"I am so sorry!" said Barbara. "It is wonderful—not like anything I have ever heard or seen or tasted before. Can't you find it in a book and read it to me?"

"I'm afraid I couldn't go find a copy just now."

"It must be somewhere here. I so want to hear the rest of the story. It wouldn't take you a minute to find it."

"I must not leave my work."

"Just one tiny minute," pleaded Barbara.

"Let me explain to you, miss. I find the only way to be *sure* I don't cheat on my time is to know of a certainty I haven't stopped for an instant to do anything for myself. Sometimes when I have stopped for a while, and then when I wanted to make up the time, I couldn't be quite sure how long it was that I owed. So that caused me to give more than I needed—which is a good enough thing to do most of the time, but which I don't want to do when I could be reading instead. When the time is my own, it is of far more value to me for the insides than to my employer for the outsides of the books. So you see, for my own sake as well as his, I cannot stop till my time is up."

"That *is* being honest!"

"I would as soon pick a pocket as undertake a job and not do it diligently."

Barbara begged no more.

"But I can talk while I work," Richard went on; "and I will try to remember."

"Please, please do."

Richard thought a little, and presently resumed the poem and went on. As he spoke, Barbara looked down at the bird in her lap.

It opened its dark eyes once more—then quivered a little, and lay still. She burst into tears.

Richard dropped his work and made a step toward her.

"Never mind," she said. "I will be all right. But I have to cry for the bird. The bird is dead, and I am glad. I will let it lie a little, and then bury it. If it be anywhere now, perhaps it will one day know me, and then it will love me. But, I can't think—that is, there must be—you don't *really* think there can be nothing after this life, do you?"

Richard was silent.

"Looking into this poor little bird's eyes has made me think as I never thought before. There *must* be more! God wouldn't—God couldn't—!"

She too fell silent, unable to complete the thoughts that were coming to her for the first time.

"But please go on with the poem," she said. "It will make me forget."

Slowly Richard resumed the narrative, with breaks here and there. Gradually Barbara's tears dried and she forgot her sorrow.

Every few stanzas Richard would stop and explain something, or answer a question Barbara had raised. Occasionally when he could not exactly remember the verses, he would extemporize in prose, to fill in the gist of the story. Barbara sat like one enchanted with a whole new world of thought and rhyme and meaning, added to in the depths of her being by the unfolding of her consciousness toward the reality of God's care for his world brought on by the death of the pigeon. Before either knew it, more than two hours had passed.

Someone had entered the room at the other end. But the sky was so cloudy and the twilight so far advanced that neither of them, Barbara absorbed in the poem and Richard in the last of his day's work, had heard anyone enter.

"Why don't you send one of the servants for a lamp?" said Lestrange.

"There is no need. I am almost done," answered Richard.

"You surely cannot see in this light!" said Arthur, who was shortsighted. "You were certainly not at your work when I came into the room."

He thought Richard had picked up the piece of leather he was parting in order to deceive him.

"Indeed I was."

"You were not. You were reading."

"I was not reading, sir. I was busy with the last of my work."

"Do not tell me you were not reading: I heard you!"

"You did hear me, sir; but you did not hear me reading," rejoined Richard, growing angry with Arthur's tone and with his unreadiness to believe him.

"You must have a wonderful memory then!" said Lestrange. "But we don't care to hear your voice in the house."

The same moment he either discovered or pretended to discover Barbara's presence.

"I beg your pardon, Miss Wylder," he said. "I did not know Mr. Tuke was amusing you."

"I suppose," returned Barbara, "that you will be ordering the nightingales not to sing in *your* apple trees next!"

"I don't understand you."

"Neither do you understand Mr. Tuke, or you would not speak to him that way."

She rose and walked to the door, but turned as she went and added: "He was repeating the loveliest poem I ever heard. I didn't know there could be such a poem!"

"It is not one I care about. But you need not take it secondhand from Tuke; I will lend it to you."

"Thank you!" said Barbara, in a tone which was not of gratitude, and left the room.

Barbara went to the door with the intention of going to the stables for Miss Brown and galloping straight home. But she thought to herself that she had no reason to leave. She was not Arthur's guest! He had been insolent to her friend who had done more for her already than Arthur was ever likely to. There was no reason she should run away from him—just the contrary! What right had he to speak so? By being a *true* workman, Mr. Tuke was a gentleman! Could Arthur Lestrange have talked like that? Could he have spoken the poetry like that? Could he shoe a horse? What if the poor man should turn out to be the real lord of the earth?

She was in danger of thinking a working man's poverty contained some essential goodness in and of itself, not realizing that, in general, the working man is just as foolish and unfit as the rich man. It is not whether a man be rich or poor that matters, but of what kind of stuff he is made.

In fact, the poor man gives the rich man his control over him by cherishing the same feelings as the rich man concerning riches, by fancying the rich man a greater man, and longing to be rich like him. A man that can *do* things is greater than any man who only *has* things.

"At any rate," concluded Barbara to herself, "I like this working man better than that gentleman."

The clock struck the hour that ended his workday. Instead of sitting down to read, Richard set out for the smithy. It was only a week since he had last seen his grandfather, but he wanted motion and desired a human face that truly belonged to him. It was rather dark when he arrived, but the old man had not yet stopped work.

The sparks were flying wild about his gray head as Richard drew near.

"Can I help you, Grandfather?" he said.

"No, no, lad; your hands are too soft by this time."

"I don't mind."

"But your strength as well as your time belongs to the man who hires you. If you weary yourself helping me, you will not do as good work for him tomorrow. Do you see sense in that?"

"Indeed, I do! You are quite right."

After an hour's talk and a cup of tea at the cottage, Richard set out on his return walk. When he had gotten only a little way into the park, a little way off on the grass a small figure glided swiftly toward him through the dusk. It was Barbara.

"I have been watching for you for so long!" she said. "They told me you had gone out and I thought you might come home this way."

"I wish I had known. I wouldn't have kept you waiting so long," said Richard.

"I want the rest of the poem," she said. "It was rude of Arthur to interrupt us as he did."

The young bookbinder was perplexed. He did not want the servants to learn they were in the park together. Yet he did not want to even hint at imprudence to her or she would be insulted. He must take care without seeming to do so. If they walked slowly they would be able to finish the poem just as they reached the house; there he could leave her and return by the lodge-gate.

"Where did we leave off?" he said.

His brief silence had seemed to Barbara but a moment spent in trying to recall.

She told him, and he continued in the same fashion as he had in the library.

The moon was now peeping, in little spots of light, through the higher foliage, casting a doubtful, ghostly shine around them. The night was warm. There was no wind except what the swift wing of a bat would now and then awake. The creature came and vanished like an undefined sense of evil at hand. But it was only Richard who thought that; nothing so ominous crossed the starry expanse of Barbara's soul. Her skirt made a soft noise as it glided past the heads of the rib-grass. Her red cloak was dark in the moonlight. She threw back the hood, and coming out of its shadow like another moon from a cloud, walked the earth with bare head. Her hands too were bare, and glimmering in the night gleam. Higher and higher rose the moon. The moon was everywhere, filling everything as they walked. Far away they saw the house, remote, scarcely reality in the dreaming night. It was much too far away to give them an anxious thought, and for long it seemed, like death, to be coming no nearer; but they were moving toward it all the time, and it was growing a more insistent fact. Thus they walked at once in the two-blended worlds of moonlight and the tale, while Richard half-chanted the music-speech of the most musical of poets, telling of the roaring wind that the mariner did not feel, of the dances of the stars, of the sighing of the sails.

When he finished, she exhaled a long, thoughtful sigh.

"Ah," she said, and looked up into the wide sky, "I should like to see the one who made all that. Think of knowing the very person who made that poor pigeon, and has got it now, and Miss Brown, and the wind. I must find him! He can't have made me and not care when I ask him to speak to me."

Richard said nothing in reply. He was not repelled by her enthusiasm, for there was nothing absurdly superstitious in it, only mildly misinformed. She could not help what she had been taught.

They went walking toward the house and were silent. The moon went on with her silentness; she never stops being silent. When they felt near the house, they fell to walking slower, but neither knew it. Barbara spoke again.

"Just imagine," she said, "if God were all the time at our backs, giving us one lovely thing after another, trying to make us look around and see who it was that was so good to us! Imagine him standing there wondering when his little one would look round and see him. If only I had him to love! Just think of all the shapes and lights and shadows and colors, and the moon and the wind and the water, all the creatures and the people—"

"And all the pain and the dying and the disease and the wrongs and the cruelty!" interposed Richard.

She was silent. After a moment or two she said, "I think I will go in now. I feel rather cold. I think there must be a fog, though I can't see it." She gave a little shiver.

He looked in her face. Was it the moon, or was it something in her thoughts that had suddenly made the sweet countenance turn gray?

"I think I want someone to say *must* to me, someone to obey," she said, after another pause. "I feel as if—"

There she stopped. Richard said nothing. Barbara went on a few steps, then turned and said, "Are you going in?"

"Not just yet," he answered. "Please remember that if I can do anything for you—"

"You are very kind. I am much obliged to you. Perhaps sometime another poem—"

"It will be hard to find another so good," returned Richard.

"Good night," she said.

"Good night," answered Richard, and walked away with loss in his heart. The poem had already ceased to please her by what he had said afterward. But he did not know that, along with the poem and the dying bird, his words had made the lovely lady more thoughtful, if less happy than before. She had begun on a road from which there was no turning back, which would open far more to Barbara's heart than had Richard's poem. But it was a road of which Richard was yet unaware.

"She has been taught to believe in a God," he said. "She is no doubt afraid he will be angry because I dared question his existence. A good God is he? How is it possible? If Nature is cruel, as she certainly is, and he made her, then he is cruel too! How could there be such a God? And if there is, it cannot be right to worship him!"

But Barbara was saying to herself, "What if he *has* shown himself to me some time—one of those nights, perhaps, when I was out till the sun rose—and I didn't know him! How frightful if there should be nobody up there at all—nobody anywhere!"

But in truth the God who knows *how not* to reveal himself must also know how *best* to reveal himself! If there be a calling child, there must be an answering father! Though her heart had, without knowing it, been calling toward him for years, now Barbara's mind began calling too; she knew she had to believe in God or die.

12 The Beginning

From an early age Richard had been accustomed to despise the form he called God which stood in the gallery of his imagination, carved at by the hands of successive generations of sculptors—some hard, some feeble, some clever, some stupid, all conventional and without prophetic imagination. Richard could see a thing to be false—that is, he could deny, but he was not yet capable of receiving what was true, because he had not yet set himself to discover truth. To oppose, to refute, to deny is not to know the truth. Whatever good may come in the destroying of the false, the best hammer of the critic will not serve to carve the celestial form of the Real; and when the iconoclast becomes the bigot of negation and declares the nonexistence of any form worthy of worship because he has destroyed so many unworthy forms, he becomes a fool. That he has never conceived a deity worth worshiping is a poor ground for saying such cannot exist.

Into the workshop of Richard's mind was now introduced by Barbara a new idea of divinity. One of the best services true man can do a neighbor is to persuade him to house his thought-children for a while that he may know what they are. From Barbara's house, almost without knowing it, Richard had taken into his a vital idea that was already working on him—the idea, namely, of a being to call God who truly was *good*, and to whom possibly man's obedience was due. The door to admit this notion was hard for him to open. The human niche, where the ideas of God must stand, was in Richard's house occupied by the most hideous falsity.

It was not pleasant to Richard to imagine anyone with rights over him; indeed, some may persist in their false ideas about God in order to avoid feeling any obligation to believe in him. For when a thoughtful man knows nothing of God's nature of devoted fatherhood, it is more than natural for him to recoil from his lesser notions of God. It is one thing to seem to know with the brain, quite another to know with the heart. But even though these new thoughts about God mingled with his visions of Barbara, through them Richard could not fail to meet something of the true idea of God. Barbara was beginning to infect him with—shall I call it the superstition of a God? It was very far from being religion yet, but the idea of a God worth believing in was coming a little nearer to him, becoming to him a little more thinkable.

He began to feel his heart drawn at times, in some strange, tender fashion previously unknown to him, to the blue of the sky, especially in the first sweetness of a summer morning. His soul would now and then seem to go out of him, in a passion of embrace, to the simplest flower. He would spread out his arms to the wind, now when it met him in its strength, now when it kissed his face. He never admitted to himself that it was one force in all the forms that drew him—that perhaps it was the very God, the All in all about him. Whether God did this, or was this, or whether it was all a result of Barbara's casting her light on the things he saw and felt, he scarcely asked. But fully he recognized the fact that nature was more alive than she had ever been to him. The thought of Barbara went on growing dear to him. And all the time a divine power of truth and beauty had laid hold upon him, and was working in him as only the powers of God can work in a man.

Instead of automatically blaming the person who does not believe in a God, we should ask first if his notion of God is a god that ought to be believed in. Perhaps the one to be blamed is he who, by inattention to the duties given him, has become less able to believe in God than he once was. Because he did not obey the true voice when it came, God may have to let him taste what it would be to have no God. A man may have been born of so many generations of unbelief that now, at this moment, he cannot believe; that now, at this moment, he has no notion of a God at all and cannot care in the least whether there be a God or not. But he can still be true to what he knows. And everything hinges upon whether he does or not. That alone can clear the moral atmosphere and make it possible for the true idea of a God to be born in him.

For some time Richard saw little of Barbara.

The heads of the house did not interfere with him. Lady Ann would now and then sail through the room like an iceberg; Sir Wilton would come in, give a glance at the shelves and grin, and walk out again with a more or less rowdy gait. Arthur was a little ashamed of having spoken to Richard as he did and had become a little more friendly. He was on the way to perceiving that, in certain insignificant things such as imagination, reading, and insight, not to mention conscience and generosity, Richard far outstripped him. And even in some of the things which had been thought a good deal of at his college, Richard was more capable than himself. In literature Arthur had already learned something from Richard, and knew it. He had indeed, without knowing it, begun to look up to him.

Richard had also discovered good in Arthur—among other things, a careful regard to his word, and to his father's tenantry, even though there yet remained, in a shallow nature like his, a good deal of condescension mingled with his behavior to his social inferiors.

The only one in the house who gave Richard trouble was the child Victoria. Gradually learning by experiment just what would annoy him, she never lost an opportunity. Richard had to endure many things from her; and what does not seem worth enduring is frequently the hardest to endure.

The behavior of the child grew worse and worse. She disturbed everything—usually the thing which Richard was most anxious to have left alone, causing him no little trouble at times to set right what she had spoiled. Her mischief was not even mingled with childish laughter; there was never any sign of frolic on her face, only the steely glitter of her sharp, black-bead eyes, full of malice. Talking to her was not of the slightest use, and it was sometimes all Richard could do to keep his hands off her to prevent her from ruining his delicate work. Sometimes she would look as blank as if she did not understand a word he said; at others she would pucker her face up into a grin of derision and contemptuous defiance.

One day when he happened to be using the polishing iron, Vixen, as her brothers aptly called her, came in and began to play with the paste. Richard turned with the iron in his hand, which he had just taken from the brasier. He was rubbing it bright and clear with a cloth; she saw this, but had not seen him take it from the fire. She grabbed at it, trying to spoil it with her pasty fingers. Just as quickly she let go of the burning steel, but did not cry, though her eyes filled with tears. Richard saw, and his heart gave way. He caught the little hand and tried to soothe her pain. She pulled it from him, crying, "You nasty man! How dare you?" and ran to the door where she turned and made a hideous face at him. That same moment Barbara walked in, saw it, and before Vixen was aware of her presence, dealt the girl such a box on the ear that she burst into a storm of wrathful weeping.

"You're a brute, Bab!" she cried. "I'll tell Mama!"

"Do, you little wretch!" returned Barbara, whose flushed face looked childlike in its indignation.

The creature left the room sobbing, and Barbara turned and was gone before Richard could thank her. He heard no more of the matter, and for some time had no further trouble with Victoria.

Barbara had the kindest of hearts, but there was nothing soft about her. She considered it a sin to spoil any animal, not to mention a child. If a sharp discipline would make a child or a dog behave better, she was not one to spare it.

13 Wingfold

Barbara had more than once heard Mr. Wingfold preach, but she had never listened, or even waked to the fact that she had not listened. She did not dislike going to church, but she liked a good many things better; and as she always did as she liked except when she saw some reason not to, she had gone to church rather seldom.

Thomas Wingfold was almost as different from Richard's idea of a clergyman, as Richard's imagined God was from any believable idea of God. The two men had never yet met, for what should bring a working man and the clergyman of the next parish together? But early one morning—he often went for a walk in the early morning—Richard saw in front of him, in the middle of a field-path, a gray-suited man seated on a stile, evidently enjoying himself an hour before sunrise. Somehow he knew he was not a working man, but he did not suspect him one of the obnoxious class which he considered the clergy. Wingfold heard Richard's step, looked round, knew him at once as an artisan of some sort, and saw in him signs of purpose and character strong for his years.

"Wonderful morning!" he said.

"Indeed it is, sir!" answered Richard.

"I love a walk in the morning better than at any other time of the day," said Wingfold.

"So do I, though I can't tell why. I've often thought about it, but I haven't yet found out what makes the morning so different."

As they chatted, Richard remarked to himself that whoever the gentleman was, he was certainly not stuck-up. They might have parted as close friends the night before instead of meeting now for the first time.

"I think," returned Wingfold, "that it must be a little like looking on the sleeping face of a loved one. As you watch such a one come awake, you see it grow into life, radiant with sunrise. In the same way, in the sunrise you can watch the thought in the twilight face of nature come awake with sunlight."

"A pretty simile," said Richard, "but I'm afraid I cannot go along with you, sir." For all the impression Barbara had made on him, he had not yet thought of the world as in any sense alive.

"Why?" asked Wingfold.

"Because I cannot allow there to be thought where no thought exists."

"Ah, you will not allow that there is personality beneath the face of nature?"

"That is what I would say, sir," answered Richard.

"You conceive the world as a sort of machine—like a clock, for instance, whose duty it is to tell the time of day?"

"Yes. Only one machine may have many uses!"

"True," said the curate; "a clock may do more for us than tell the time. It may tell how fast it is going, and it may wake solemn thought. But if you came upon a machine that constantly awoke within you—not thoughts only, but the most delicate and indescribable feelings—what would you say then?"

"Surely not that the machine was thinking!"

"Certainly not. But would you allow thought concerned in it? Would you allow that thought had preceded and occasioned its existence? Where a thing wakes thought and feeling, I say, must not thought be somewhere concerned in its origin?"

"Might not the thought and feeling come merely by associations, as in the case of the clock suggesting the flight of time?"

"I think our associations can hardly be so delicate as to have a share in bringing to us half of the thoughts and feelings that nature wakes in us. There are deeper things, hidden both in our own beings, and in the depths of the origin of nature, which are responsible. I do not want to argue; I am only suggesting that, if the world moves thought and feeling in those that observe it, then thought and feeling are somehow concerned in the world. Feeling must have put itself into the shape that awakens feeling.—Ah, there is the sun! And there are things that ought never to be talked about in their presence! To talk of some things even behind their backs will keep them away!"

Richard neither understood his last words nor knew that he did not understand them. But he did understand that it was better to watch the sunrise than to talk of it.

Up came the child of heaven, conquering in the truth, in the might of essential being. Not argument, but the presence of God silenced the words of the young doubter. The two men stood lost in the swift changes of his attendant colors. Richard refused to let any emotion influence his opinion; they must be determined only by fact and logical outline. Whatever was not to him definite could not be believed. He had no notion, however, of all he did accept without questioning.

Without a word, Richard lifted his hat to the stranger and walked on, taking with him a germ of new feeling, which would enlarge and multiply without his knowing it. When he got to the next stile and was climbing it over the fence, he looked back and saw that the man was seated once again, but now reading.

After a while, Thomas Wingfold closed his book, put it back in his pocket, rose, and began his walk home. He crossed several fields and arrived just in time to meet his wife as she came down the stairs to breakfast.

"Have you had a nice walk, Thomas?" she asked.

"Indeed I have!" he answered. "I met a young fellow who, I think, will pluck his feet out of the mud before long."

"Did you ask him for a visit?"

"No."

"Shall I write and ask him?"

"For one thing, you can't. I don't know his name, or what he is, or where he lives. But we shall meet again soon."

"Did you make an appointment with him?"

"No, but there's an undertow bringing us together. It would spoil everything if I tried to throw a net to catch him. I will not move until the tide brings him into my arms. At least that is how the thing looks to me at present. I believe enough not to make haste."

As near as he could, Wingfold recounted the conversation he had had with Richard.

"He was a fine-looking fellow," he said, "not exactly a gentleman, but almost. He looked like a man who could do things, but I could not satisfy myself as to what might be his trade. But he was more at home in the workshop of his own mind than is usual with fellows of his age. I would love to be able to put him together with our old friend Polwarth."

"It must be old Simon Armour's grandson," said Helen. "I have heard of him from several people, and your description just fits him. I know somebody that could tell you about him, but I wish I knew anybody to tell us about her—Miss Wylder."

"I like the look of that girl," said the parson warmly. "What makes you think she could tell us about my new acquaintance?"

"Only an impertinent speech of that little mischief-maker Vixen Lestrange. I forgot what she said, but it left the impression of an acquaintance between Bab, as she called her, and some working fellow the child could not stand."

"She seems to be in church, if not regularly, at least less seldom than before."

"I saw her there last Sunday. But I'm afraid she wasn't thinking much about what you were saying. I could hardly take my eyes off her, my heart was so drawn to her. There was a mingling of love and daring, almost defiance, in her look. She seemed to come awake for a moment once, but then the next looked as far off as before."

"That is good, though," said Wingfold, "because it shows there is a window in her house that may be looking in my direction: some signal may one day catch her eye! You remember how long it took us to awaken. I strongly suspect that she has a real character of her own beneath all her activity. Her mother particularly interests me! We need only to be patient, as Polwarth was with us, and see what will come."

14 Far From Home

One evening Richard went to see his grandfather and asked if he would allow him to give Miss Wylder a lesson in horseshoeing: he told him she wanted to be able to shoe Miss Brown—or any horse. Simon laughed heartily at the proposal; it was too great an absurdity to object seriously to.

"You don't know Miss Wylder, Grandfather! She'll astonish you!"

"Have you ever seen her drive a nail, boy?"

"No, but I am sure she will do it—and better than any beginner you've ever seen!"

"Well, well, lad! we'll see! we'll see! She's welcome anyhow to come and have her try. But it makes me laugh just to think of them doll hands with a great hoof in them!"

"They are little hands—she's little herself! But they aren't doll hands, Grandfather. You should have seen her box little Miss Lestrange's ear for making a face at me!"

"Well, bring her whenever you like, lad," said Simon.

It was moonlight by the time Richard drew near to Mortgrange; and near the gate, a few yards away, seated on a stone, he saw the form of a woman. At first he thought of Barbara, but almost immediately he knew there was something different about the figure off in the dark. She sat in a helpless, hopeless attitude, with her head in her hands. Slowly he approached her, and as he drew nearer he began to feel as if he had once known her. *I must have seen her in London somewhere*, he thought.

He went nearer. The form remained motionless, her head in her hands, her elbows on her knees. Something reminded him of Alice Manson.

He laid his hand on the figure, but she moved not an inch. All at once he was sure it was Alice.

"Alice!" he cried. "Good God—sitting in the cold night!"

She made no answer.

"What can I do for you?" he said.

"Nothing," she answered in a low voice that might well have been from a ghost. "Leave me," she added, as with the last entreaty of despair.

"You are in trouble, Alice!" he persisted. "Why are you so far from home? Where's Adam?"

"What right do you have to question me?" she returned, almost fiercely.

"None but that I am your brother's friend."

"Friend!" she echoed in a faint, faraway voice.

"You forget, Alice, that I did all I could to be your friend too, and you would not let me!"

She neither spoke nor moved. Her stillness seemed to say, *And I won't now.*

"Where are you going?" he asked after a hopeless pause.

"Nowhere."

"Why did you leave London?"

"Why should I tell you?"

"I think you will tell me."

"I will not."

"You know I would do anything for you!"

"I daresay!"

"You know I would."

"I don't."

"Try me."

"I will not."

Her voice grew more and more faint.

"Don't go on like that, Alice. You're not being reasonable," pleaded Richard.

"Just leave me alone!"

"I won't leave you."

"As you please. It's nothing to me."

"Alice, why do you speak to me like that? Tell me what's wrong."

Her voice was a little stronger. She raised herself and looked him in the face.

"Alice, if you won't tell me what is the matter with you, if you won't let me help you, I will sit down by you till the morning."

"What if I drop?"

"Then I will carry you away."

Her resolution to resist him seemed to break.

"I haven't had anything to eat all day."

"My poor girl. Here, put on my coat."

He was in perplexity what to do for her and stood for a moment hesitating. Alice swayed on her seat and began to fall. He caught her, and at the same moment remembered a little cottage down a lane a short way off. He picked her up in his arms and started for it.

"Richard, dear Richard!" she murmured, "where are you taking me? Where's Adam? I will let you be good to me. I can't hold out forever."

She seemed to be dreaming. He walked on without trying to answer her. His heart ached with pity for the girl.

The cottage was a very poor place, but a laborer and his family lived in it. He knocked many times. A sleepy voice answered at last, and a sleepy-eyed man half opened the door.

"What the deuce?" he grunted.

"Here's a young woman half dead with hunger and cold," said Richard. "Can you take her in?"

"Can't you take her somewhere else?"

"There is nowhere else near enough. Come, come, let us in, please. You wouldn't have her die on your doorstep!"

"I don't see the sense of bringing her here!" answered the man sleepily. "We've hardly got enough for ourselves. Wife! here's a chap says he's picked up a young woman dying of hunger—'tain't likely!"

"Let him bring the poor thing in. There ain't nowhere to put her, and there ain't nothing to give her, but she can't lie out in the cold."

"Haven't you got a drop of milk?" asked Richard.

"Milk!" echoed the woman. "It's weeks and weeks since the children's tasted of it. The wonder to me is that the cows let a poor man milk them!"

Richard set Alice on her feet, but she could hardly stand alone. The woman fetched a light, and now came to the door with a candle-end. Her husband kept prudently in her shadow.

"Poor thing! poor thing!" she said when she saw her. "Bring her in, sir. There's a chair she can sit on. I'll get her a drop of tea—that'll be better than milk. There's next to no work, and the squire, he's mad at Giles here because of some rabbit or other they says he snared—which they say was a hare, I don't know. Well, if the parson says me and my man'll be judged for sake of a hare or a rabbit, and the children starving, I'll give him a piece of my mind! But the day'll come when the rich and poor'll have a turn about. Leastways, there's something like that somewhere in the Bible.

And if it be in the Bible, it's likely to be true, for the Bible does take the part of the rich mostly."

She was a woman who liked to hear herself talk, and so she spoke as one listening to herself. Like most people, whether they talk or not, she got her ideas secondhand; but Richard was not inclined to differ with what she said about the Bible, for he knew little more, and no better about it than she. Had Parson Wingfold, who did know the Bible, heard her, he would have told her that there was not a word in it against the poor, while there were a multitude of words against the rich. The sins of the poor are not once mentioned in the Bible, the sins of the rich very often. The rich may think this hard, but Wingfold simply stated the facts and did not much care what they thought. When a man comes to judge himself and others fairly, he will understand that God is no respecter of persons, and will favor neither the rich *nor* the poor in his cause.

Richard set Alice on the one chair by the little fire; the woman was coaxing it, trying to heat the water she had put in a saucepan. Alice stared at the fire but hardly seemed to see it. The woman tried to comfort her. Richard looked around the place: the man had returned to the bed that filled one corner; a mattress in another was crowded with children; there was not even a spot where she could lie down.

"I shall be back as quickly as I can," he said, and left the cottage.

15 A Sister

He hurried back over the bare, moon-white road. He had seen Miss Wylder come that morning and hoped to reach the house, which was not very far off, before she had gone to bed. He felt she alone in that house would give him the help he needed. If she had gone back home, he would try the gardener's wife. But he needed a woman with wit as well as will. He would help himself from the larder if he could not do better—but there would be no brandy there.

Many thoughts passed swiftly through Richard's mind as he walked and ran. He could hardly imagine how Alice had come, or how it happened that she should appear at Mortgrange. But with him, as with all truly unselfish natures, thought was action. She needed aid and attention, and he would get them for her whatever the risk. Time might or might not clear the mystery of her coming. It was enough for him that the girl was now in his care. He would help without questioning, and trust to the future for explanations.

"And this is the world," he thought to himself, "that the priests would have us believe ruled by the providence of an all powerful and all good being! My heart is sore for her. I think I would give my life for her! And there *he* sits, up there in his glory, and looks down unmoved upon her suffering. I will *not* believe in any such God!"

Of course he was right in refusing to believe in such a god! But was Richard, therefore, right to believe in no God altogether? Had he really been a truthful thinker, Richard might have had a "what if" or two to propose to himself. Ought he not even now to have been capable of thinking that there might be a being with better design for his creatures than *merely* to make them happy? Here was a man judging the eternal who did not even know his name.

As he drew near the house he began to wonder what to do if Miss Wylder had gone to her room: how was he to find her? He did not know where her room was. He only knew that when she went up the stairs, she turned to the right at the top—and he knew no more.

He entered softly, went along a wide passage, and arrived at the foot of the great staircase which ascended in a half-oval, just in time to see at the top the reflection of a candle disappearing to the right. There were many chances against its being Barbara's, but with an almost despairing recklessness, he darted up and, turning, again saw the reflection of the candle from the wall of a hallway that crossed the corridor. He followed as swiftly and lightly as he could, and at the corner all but knocked down an elderly maid, whose initial fright gave way to anger the moment she saw who had run into her.

"I need to see Miss Wylder!" said Richard hurriedly.

"You have no call to be in this part of the house," returned the woman.

"I can't stop to explain," answered Richard. "Please tell me which is her room."

"Indeed I will not!"

"When she knows my business, she will be glad I came to her."

"You may find it for yourself."

"Then will you take a message to her for me?"

"I am not Miss Wylder's maid!" she replied. "Neither is it my place to wait on my fellow servants."

She turned away, tossing her head, and rounded the corner into the corridor.

Richard looked down the passage. A light was burning at the other end, with only a few doors in it. With a sudden resolve to go straight ahead, he called out: "Miss Wylder!" and again, "Miss Wylder!"

A door opened and out peeped Barbara's dainty little head. She saw Richard, gave one glance in the opposite direction, and signalled him to come to her. He did so. She was in her nightgown: it was not her candle he had followed, but its light had led him to her.

"What is it?" she said hurriedly. "Don't speak loudly; Lady Ann might hear you!"

"There is a girl in desperate trouble—" began Richard.

"Go to the library," she said. "I will come to you there. I won't be a minute."

She went in and closed her door with hardly a sound. Then for the first time Richard realized that one of the other doors might open, and the pale, cold face of the formidable lady look out. If it was her candle he had followed, she would almost have certainly heard when he called Miss Wylder. As quietly as he could, he ran gliding through passage and corridor and down the stairs. Arriving in the library, he lighted a candle, and, in case anyone should enter, pretended to be looking at books. Within five minutes Barbara was at his side.

"Now," she said, and stood silent, waiting.

He told her where and in what state he had found the girl and to what a poor place he had carried her, saying he was afraid she would die unless Miss Wylder would help him.

"We need brandy," she said. "Lady Ann has some in her room. The rest I can manage! Wait here; I will be back in three minutes."

She went, and Richard waited—without anxiety. Whatever Barbara set her hand to seemed as good as done.

She reappeared in her red cloak, with a basket beneath it.

"Open that bay window, and don't make a noise. They mustn't find it undone; we have to get in that way again."

Richard obeyed scrupulously. It was a French window, and getting out was easy.

"What if they close the shutters?" he asked.

"They don't always," she replied. "We must take our chance."

He was surprised to find her leaving the house with him and leading him to the road toward the gate.

"It's good of you to come, miss," he ventured. "Please, give me the basket."

She gave it to him, saying, "To come! What else did you expect? Did you not want me to come?"

"I never thought of your coming. I only thought you would get the right things for me."

"You don't think I would leave the poor girl to the mercy of a man who would tell her there was nobody anywhere to help her out of her troubles."

"I don't think I would have told her that."

"Perhaps. But tell me honestly," said Barbara, "for I do believe you are an honest man—tell me, are you *sure* there is no God? Have you gone through all the universe looking for him and failed to find him? Is there no possible chance that there may be a God?"

"I do not believe there is."

"But are you sure there is not? Do you know it, so that you have a right to say it, especially to a girl such as you found tonight, possibly dying?"

"I told you, I would not say such a thing to her."

"Nevertheless, are you sure?"

"I cannot say," he answered impatiently, "that I know it as I know a mathematical fact."

"Then what right do you have to say there is no God?"

Richard was silent a moment, then said, "I will think about what you say."

"Mind," said Barbara, "I don't pretend to *know* anything. But at least I *hope* there is a God, and that he is good. And I hope that the Bible is true. Have you read it all the way through, Mr. Tuke—so that you are sure about everything it says?"

"I have not," answered Richard; "but everybody knows what it says."

"Well, I don't! Nobody has taken the trouble to tell me, and I haven't read it. But I'll just tell you a little bit of my life which makes me wonder if half the things people say about God might not be wrong, things like what you say. I lived for a while in Sydney with my father and mother, and there a terrible lie was told about me, and everybody believed it, and nobody would speak to me. Somehow people are always ready to believe lies—even people who would not tell lies! As a result we had to leave Sydney, and to this day everybody there believes me a wicked, ugly girl. Now, I know I am not! I was trying to help a poor creature nobody would do anything for, and that got the lie said of me. I thought my first business was to take care of my neighbor, and I did it, and that's what came of it!"

"And you believe in a God who would let that come to you for doing good?" said Richard.

"What does God have to do with it? It was the people who were wicked to me, not God. What if there be a God who loves me? What if he cares as little what people say about me, because he knows the truth, as I care about it because I know the truth? And if such lies were told and believed about an innocent girl trying to do her duty, why may not people have told lies about God, and other people believed them?"

Richard was silent. Barbara's sore experience echoed in his heart; they had by now nearly arrived at the door of the cottage.

He knocked, received no answer, opened the door, and led Barbara in.

There was light enough from the remnant of fire to see, on a stool by its side, the woman of the house fast asleep, with her head against the wall. Her husband was snoring in bed. The children lay still on their mattress on the floor. Alice sat on the one chair, her head fallen back, and her face pale white. Beside the worn girl, Barbara looked like the incarnation of life and energy. Her cheeks were flushed from the rapid walk, and for a moment she stood radiant with the tender glow of pity as she looked down on the girl. Then with a sigh she put her arm under her head and lifted it gently. Alice's eyes opened, but they did not seem to have much life in them.

"Quick," said Barbara, "give me a little brandy in the cup."

Richard did so and Barbara put the cup to Alice's lips.

"Take a little brandy, dear; it will revive you," she said.

All Alice could see was the face of an angel bending over her. She obeyed the heavenly vision and drank what it offered. It made her cough, and their sleeping hostess jumped to her feet, but a smile and greeting from Barbara reassured her. She thanked her for her hospitality as if Alice had been her own sister, and slipping money into the woman's hand, coaxed her to make up the fire a little that she might warm some soup she had brought.

Almost at once upon tasting the soup, a little color began to return to Alice's cheek. Barbara was feeding her, and a feeble smile flickered over the thin face. To Richard, having seen but little tenderness in his mother, it was more than a gracious sight to see the love that flowed from the strong, tender girl to the delicate, starved creature to whom she was ministering.

Richard then told Barbara that, if she approved, he would take Alice to his grandfather. He was sure he would receive her graciously, and both he and Jesse would do what they could for her. But he did not know of any vehicle he could get to carry her there except for his grandfather's pony cart, and that was four miles away.

"All right!" said Barbara. "I will stay with her till you come."

"But how will you get home afterward?"

"As I came, of course. Don't trouble yourself about me; I can look after myself."

"But what if they have locked the library window?"

"Then I will do the next simplest thing. I will ring the bell and go in through the front door."

"And then they will know of your going out," said Richard, growing disturbed at the possible consequences of his hasty actions.

"That is my affair," Barbara replied. "Yours is to be off to your grandfather as quickly as you can. Don't worry about me. I shall come to no harm. Go at once and fetch the pony cart."

Richard left the cottage and set off running, not arriving at his grandfather's till the dead of night. But he had little difficulty rousing the old man. He told him all he knew about Alice and the plight he now had found her in. Simon looked grave when he heard Richard's story and learned how his daughter had attempted to keep Richard from Alice and her brother. He dressed hurriedly, harnessed the pony to the cart, and made his own preparations for going with Richard to fetch the girl. In a few minutes they were spinning along the gray road.

When they reached the hut, Barbara was standing by the door. While Richard got down and went in, she talked to Simon. Richard found Alice wide awake, staring into the fire, with a look that brought a great rush of pity into his heart, especially when he remembered how the girl had shrunk from him before. Their kind hostess had crept into bed beside her husband, and was snoring as loudly as he. Without a word he wrapped Alice in the blanket he had brought, took her again in his arms, and carried her to the cart. The sturdy old man leaned down from his perch and took her from him, placing her comfortably beside him. He put his arm around her, and with a nod to Barbara, and never a word to his grandson, drove away. Richard knew his grandfather's rugged goodness too well to mind, and was confident he would do not less but more than he promised for Alice.

He and Barbara walked slowly back to the house, neither saying much, seeming to avoid the subject of their former conversation.

When they reached a certain point, Richard drew back while Barbara went on. He saw her try the library window and fail. She then went and rang the bell. After some time the door opened, and she disappeared.

He turned away into the park, and thinking about many things, walked about until by slow gradations the sky's gray idea unfolded into the morning. He took care to let the house not only come awake but to its senses before he sought admission. When it seemed well astir, he rang the bell. The door was opened after some delay; he went straight to the library and was fairly at work by five o'clock.

16 A Conversation

Richard saw nothing of Barbara all day, or indeed any of the family except Vixen. At eight o'clock he had his breakfast, and at nine he was again in the library, so that by lunchtime he had been seven of his eight hours at work, and by half past two found himself free to go to his grandfather's.

On his way to the road through the park he met Arthur Lestrange. Richard touched his hat and would have passed, but Arthur stopped him, his face holding no friendly expression.

"Where are you going, Tuke?"

"To my grandfather's, sir," Richard answered.

"Excuse me, but your day's work is not over for some hours yet."

"If you remember, sir," he said, "our agreement mentioned no hour for beginning or ending work."

"That is true, but you undertook to give me eight hours of your day."

"Yes, sir. I was at work by five o'clock this morning and have given you more than eight hours."

"Hmm," said Arthur.

"I am quite as anxious," pursued Richard, "to fulfill my engagement as you are to have it fulfilled."

Arthur said nothing.

"Ask Thomas, who let me in this morning," resumed Richard, "whether or not I was at work in the library by five o'clock."

"Let you in!" exclaimed Arthur; "let you in before five o'clock in the morning? Then you were out all night?"

"I was."

"That cannot be permitted."

"I am surely right in believing that when my work is over, I am my own master. I had something that had to be done. My grandfather knows all about it."

"Oh yes, I remember! Old Simon Armour, the blacksmith!" returned Arthur. "But," he went on, softening a little, "you ought not to work for him while you are in my employment."

"I know that, sir; and even if I wanted to, my grandfather would not let me. While my work is yours, it is all yours."

With that he turned and left Arthur where he stood—a little relieved, though now annoyed as well that a man in his employment should not have waited to be dismissed.

Richard walked to the smithy as quickly as he could, where he found his grandfather just taking off his apron to go for a cup of tea.

"Oh, there you are!" he said. "I thought we should be catching sight of you before long!"

"How's Alice, Grandfather?"

"She's been asleep all day—the best thing for her!"

"I hope, Grandfather," said Richard, for Simon's tone troubled him a little, "that you are not angry with me. I assure you I had nothing to do with her coming here from London—that I know of. You would not have had me leave her sitting there, out in the cold all night?"

"God forbid, lad! If you thought me out of temper with you, it was a mistake. I confess the thing does bother me, but I'm not blaming *you.* You acted like a Christian."

Richard hardly relished the mode of his grandfather's praise. A man ought to do the right thing because he was a man, not because he was something else than a man! He did not yet know that a man and a Christian are precisely and entirely the same thing; that a being who is not a Christian is not a man. No one, however strong he may feel his obligations, will ever be man enough to fulfill them except he be a Christian—that is, one who, like Christ, cares first for the will of the Father.

Simon and his grandson had not yet turned the corner when Richard heard a snort he knew: there, sure enough, stood Miss Brown, hitched to the garden-paling, peaceable but impatient.

"Miss Wylder is here!" said Richard.

"Yes, lad! She has been here more than an hour. She's a fine creature."

"Yes, she's a good mare."

"I don't mean the mare. I mean the mistress!"

"Miss Wylder is a noble girl," said Richard. "But I'm afraid she got into trouble last night helping me."

"It don't sound much like it," returned the old man, as Barbara's musical laugh came from the cottage. "Alice must be doing well or she wouldn't be laughing like that."

As they entered, Barbara came gliding down the stairs in front of them, her face still radiant with the reminder of the laugh they had heard.

"Good afternoon, Mr. Armour," she said. "I didn't expect to see you so soon again, Mr. Tuke. Will you please put me up on Miss Brown?"

Richard gave his hand to Barbara, who swung up onto the mare's back.

"Good-bye," she said, and rode off.

She had ridden from Mortgrange earlier as much to get away from it as to see about Alice, for she had been irritated.

After breakfast Lady Ann had sent for her and Barbara had gone prepared for the worst.

The same maid who had been so rude to Richard had watched and seen them go out together. She locked the library window behind them, and went and told Lady Ann what she had seen.

When Barbara entered Lady Ann's dressing room, she greeted her with less than her usual frigidity.

"Good morning, my love. You were late last night!" she said.

"I thought I was rather early," answered Barbara, laughing.

"May I ask where you were?" said her ladyship, with her habitual composure.

"About a mile and a half from here, at the little cottage in Burrow Lane."

"How did you come to be there—and for so long? You were gone for hours."

Even Lady Ann could not prevent a little surprise in her tone as she said the words.

"Mr. Tuke came and told me—"

"I beg your pardon, but do I know Mr. Tuke?"

"The bookbinder in the library."

"Wouldn't your mother be astonished at your having secrets with a workingman?"

"Secrets, Lady Ann!" exclaimed Barbara. "Was I not in the process of telling you all about it? How can you accuse me of such a thing?"

"I am not accustomed to being addressed in this way, Barbara!" said Lady Ann, without either raising or quickening her voice.

"Then it is time you learned, if you are going to speak to girls as you have just spoken to me! I am not accustomed to being told that I have a secret with any man—or woman either! I have no secrets!"

"Compose yourself, my child. You need not be afraid of *me*!" said Lady Ann. "I am not your enemy."

She thought Barbara's anger came from fear, for she regarded herself as a formidable person.

"I am not afraid of you, Lady Ann," answered Barbara indignantly. "I fear no enemy."

Lady Ann found she had a new sort of creature to deal with. She had wanted to establish a protective claim on the girl—to have a secret with, and so a hold upon her. But she was discovering this was not a girl to be held quite so easily.

"Calm yourself, Miss Wylder. You will scarcely do yourself justice in English society if you give way to such temper. If you have no secrets, pray, explain the thing to me."

"Mr. Tuke told me he had found a young woman almost dead with hunger and cold by the wayside, and carried her to a cottage. I came to you, as you well remember, and asked for a little brandy. Then I went to the larder and got some soup. She would probably have been dead before the morning if we had not taken them to her."

"Why did you not tell me what you wanted the brandy for?"

"Because you would have tried to prevent me from going."

"Of course I should have had the poor creature attended to, although I confess I would have sent a more suitable person."

"I thought myself the most suitable person in the house."

"Why?"

"Because I was called upon to do it, and I had to go; and because I knew I should be kinder to her than anyone you could send."

"You may be far too kind to such people."

"You couldn't be too kind to this girl."

"It's just as I feared. She has quite taken you in. Those tramps are all the same."

"The same as other people—yes; that is, as different from each other as your ladyship and I."

Lady Ann found Barbara too much for her and changed her attack.

"But why were you so long? As you said, Burrow Lane can't be more than a mile and a half from here!"

"We could not leave her at the cottage; it was not a fit place for her. Mr. Tuke had to go to his grandfather's—four miles—and I had to stay with her till he came back. Old Simon came himself in his cart and took her away."

"Was there no woman at the cottage?"

"Yes, but worn out with work and children."

"Well, thank you for telling me, Barbara. I was certain it was some mission of mercy that led you out at such an hour. A girl in your position must be careful of what people think, you know."

"Duty to your neighbor is more important than one's reputation!" replied Barbara.

"There is nothing to be annoyed at, Barbara. I am quite pleased with what you have told me. I say only it was unwise of you not to let me know."

"It may not have been wise for my own sake, but it was for the woman's."

"There is no occasion to say more about the woman; I am quite satisfied with you, Barbara!" said Lady Ann, looking up with an icy smile.

"But I am not satisfied, Lady Ann," rejoined Barbara. "If such a thing were to happen again, I should do just the same thing. Understanding how you feel, perhaps I should not remain your guest."

After Barbara became so angry and answered Lady Ann as she did, Lady Ann took no more trouble to appease her: the foolish girl would be ashamed of herself soon and would once again accept her favor. She was not afraid of losing Barbara, for she believed her parents must be strongly in favor of an alliance with her family. She knew nothing of the personal opposition between Mr. and Mrs. Wylder; she never opposed Sir Wilton unless it was worth her while to do so, and Sir Wilton never opposed her at all—openly. It gave Lady Ann no more pleasure to go against her husband than to comply with his wishes; and she had no notion whatever of the pleasure it gave Sir Wilton to see any desire of hers frustrated.

Barbara went to the stable, saddled Miss Brown, and was away from Mortgrange before Richard, as early as he had begun, was halfway through his morning work.

She went to see Alice almost every day from that afternoon; no one could resist Barbara, and Alice's reserve, as imbedded as it was in pain, soon began to yield.

They became fast friends.

17 Alice and Barbara

It was weeks before Alice was able to leave her bed: she had been utterly exhausted.

On a lovely summer morning she woke to a sense of returning health. She lay in a neat little curtained bed, in a room with a sloping roof on both sides, covered, not with tiles or slates, but with warm thatch, thick and sound. Ivy was creeping through the chinks of the poor-fitting window frame; but through the little dormer window the sun shone freely. It was a very humble room, and Alice had been used to better furniture. But it was clean, and there was a wholesomeness and purity everywhere about her which was very welcome. For one brief moment she felt as if she had gained the haven of rest, for she lay at peace with no troubles gnawing at her soul. But suddenly a pang shot through her heart and she knew that some harassing thought was at hand. Then suddenly she remembered! She had left love and misery behind to seek help, and she had not found it! She had but lost sight of those for whom she sought the help! She could not tell how long it was since she had seen her mother and Adam: she lay covered with kindness by people she had never seen; and how they were faring, she could only guess.

Alice had little education beyond what life had given her; but life is the truest of all teachers, however little the results of her teaching may be valued by school enthusiasts. She did not know one creed from another, but she loved what she saw to be good, and knew how to send a selfish thought back to its place. She knew nothing of the Norman conquest, but she knew much of self-conquest. She wore shabby frocks, but she would not put bad work into the seams of a rich lady's dress. She had suffered much at the hands of great ladies, yet she had but to see Barbara to love her.

As she lay with her heart warming, she heard the sound of a horse's hoofs on the road. Her angel came to Alice not with flapping of great wings, but with the sounds of ringing iron shoes and snorting breath, to be followed by a girl's feet on the stairs.

"Well, how are you today?" said Barbara, sitting down on the edge of the bed.

Alice was older and taller than Barbara, but Barbara never thought about height or age: strong herself, she was instant mother to all weakness.

"Ever so much better, miss!" answered Alice.

"Now, none of that!" returned the little lady, "or I will leave the room. My name is Barbara, and we are friends—unless you don't want me calling you Alice."

Alice stretched out her thin arms to Barbara and burst into weeping.

"Will you let me tell you everything?" she cried.

"What am I here for?" returned Barbara, embracing her. "Tell me whatever you like—but nothing more."

Alice lay silent for a moment, then said, "I wish you would ask me some question. I don't know how to begin."

Without a moment's hesitation, Barbara said, "What do you do all day in London?"

"Sew, sew, sit and sew, from morning till night," answered Alice. "No sooner is one piece of cloth out of your hands till another is in them. So no matter how much you do, you never feel that you've done anything! It's a downright dreary life, miss."

"There you go again," said Barbara seriously, and Alice laughed.

"I'm so used to thinking of ladies as if they were a different creation from us, and it seems rude to call you—*Barbara*!"

"Oh, but it makes me feel so good when you do!"

"Then I *will* call you Barbara; and I will answer any question you want to put to me."

"And your mother, I imagine, is rather trying when you come home?" said Barbara, speaking from experience. "Mothers are—a good deal!"

"Well you see, miss—Barbara, my mother wasn't used to a hard life like us, and Adam—that's my brother—and I have to do our best to keep her from feeling it. But we don't succeed very well.

Neither of us gets much for our day's work. Poor Mama likes to have things nice; and now that the money she used to have is gone—I don't know how it went: she had it in some bank, and somebody speculated with it, I suppose—anyhow it's gone, and the thing can't be undone. Adam grows thinner and thinner, and it's no use. Oh, miss, I know I shall lose him!"

She wept a moment, very quietly but bitterly.

"I know he does his very best," she resumed, "but Mama doesn't see it. She thinks he should be doing more for her, and I'm sure he's dying!"

"Send him to me," said Barbara. "I'll make him well for you."

"I wish I could, miss—I mean *Barbara*!"

"Does your mother do nothing to help?"

"She doesn't know how. She hasn't learned any trade like us. She was brought up a lady. I remember her saying once she ought to have been a real lady, a lady they say *My Lady* to."

"Indeed. How was it, then, that she is not?"

"I don't know. There are things we don't dare ask Mama about. If she had been proud of them, she would have told us without asking."

"What was your father, Alice?"

The girl hesitated.

"He was a baron. But perhaps you would rather I said *miss* again."

"Don't be foolish, child!" Barbara returned.

"I suppose my mother meant that he promised to marry her, but never did. They say gentlemen think no harm of making such promises—without even meaning to keep them—I don't know—I've got no time to think about such things, only—"

"Only you have to," added Barbara. "Did he take your mother's money and spend it?"

"Oh no, not that! He was a gentleman, a baron, you know, and they don't do such things."

"Don't they!" said Barbara. "But what happened to the money? Is there any way of getting it back?"

"There's no hope of that! I'll tell you how I think it was: my father didn't want to marry my mother, for he wanted a great lady.

So he said good-bye to her and she didn't mind, for he was a selfish man, she said. So she took the money, for of course she had to raise us and couldn't do it without money—and did what they call invested it. That means, you know, that somebody took charge of it. So it's all gone, and she gets no more interest on it. And we can't always pay for the kind of things she likes. The other day she came right into the shop and said to Mrs. Harman that I could get much better wages and that she didn't give me half what my work was worth. I cried, for I couldn't help it; I was so weak and miserable, for I had hardly had any breakfast to speak of, and I just wanted my mother out of the place. But Mrs. Harman—she *is* a kind woman!—she interfered and said my mother had no right to take me away, and I must finish my month. So I sat down again and my mother was forced to go. But when she was gone, Mrs. Harman said to me, 'The best thing you can do is let your mother have her way. You just stay at home till she gets you a place that'll pay better than I do! She'll find out all the sooner that there isn't a better place to be had, for it's a slack time now. When her pride comes down a bit, you come and see whether I'm able to take you on again.' "

"Hmm!" said Barbara. "So you went home to your mother?"

"Yes—and it was just as Mrs. Harman said: there wasn't a job anyplace. I went from place to place—nearly killed myself walking about. Finally I went back to Mrs. Harman and told her. She said she couldn't have me just then but she'd keep her eye on me. I went home nearly out of my mind. Adam was growing worse and worse and I had nothing to do. At last, one night as I lay awake, I made up my mind I would go and see whether my father was as hard-hearted as people said. Perhaps he would give us enough to help us get over a week or two; and if I hadn't got work by that time, we should at least be able to bear the hunger a little longer. So the next day, without a word to Mother or Adam, I set out and came down here."

"And you didn't see Sir Wilton?"

"Who told you, miss? Did I let out the name?"

"No, you didn't. But though there are a great many barons, they don't exactly crowd a neighborhood. What did he say to you?"

"I haven't seen him yet. I went up to the house and the woman looked me all over, curious like, from head to foot, and then she said Sir Wilton wasn't at home, nor likely to be."

"What a lie!" exclaimed Barbara.

"You know him then, Barbara?"

"Yes. But never mind. I must ask all my questions first, and then it will be your turn. What did you do next?"

"I went away. But I don't know what I did. How I came to be sitting on that stone inside that gate, I can't tell. I think I must have gone searching for a place to die in. Then Richard came. I tried hard to keep him from knowing me, but I couldn't.

"You knew that Richard was there?"

"Where, miss?"

"At the baron's place—Mortgrange?"

"Lord, miss! Richard is there?"

"Yes. He's there mending their books."

"I knew nothing about him being there, or anywhere else, for I'd lost sight of him. It was mere chance he found me. I didn't know him till he spoke to me. I heard his step, but I didn't look up. When I saw who it was I tried to make him leave me. But he wouldn't. He carried me all the way to the cottage where you found me."

"Why didn't you want him to know you? What have you against him?"

"Not a thing, miss! He would be a brother to me if I would let him. It's a strange story, and I'm not quite sure if I ought to tell it."

"Are you bound in any way not to tell it?"

"No. *She* didn't tell me about it."

"You mean your mother?"

"No, I mean *his* mother."

"I am getting bewildered!" said Barbara.

"You'll be more bewildered yet when I tell you all!"

She was silent. Barbara saw she was feeling faint.

"How unkind of me to make you talk!" she cried, and ran to get her a cup of milk, which she made her drink slowly.

"I must tell you everything!" said Alice, after lying silent for a moment or two.

"You shall tomorrow," said Barbara.

"No, I must do it now, please. I must tell you about Richard!"

"Have you known him a long time?"

"My brother and he were friends at school," said Alice. "But I only came to know him about a year ago. He came to see Adam once, and then I went with Adam to see him and his family. But his mother behaved very strangely to me and asked me a great many questions. She kept looking from Adam to Richard, and then back, in the oddest way. I couldn't understand it. Then she asked me to go to her bedroom and there she told me. She was very rough to me, I thought, but tears were in her own eyes. She said she could *not* have Richard keeping company with us, for she knew what my mother was, and who my father was, and we were not respectable people, and it would never do. If she heard of Richard going to our house once again, she would have to do something we shouldn't like.

"Then she cried a lot and said she was very sorry to hurt me, for I seemed a good girl, and it wasn't my fault, but she couldn't help it. And there she stopped as if she had said too much already. I thought myself ill-used, and Adam too, for we both liked Richard, though my mother didn't think him at all our equal, or fit to be Adam's companion; for Adam was a clerk, while Richard worked with his hands. Adam said he worked with his hands too, and turned out far poorer work than Richard—stupid figures instead of beautiful books. I said I worked with my needle quite as hard as Richard with his tools; but it had no effect on my mother. Her ways of looking at things are not the same as ours, because she was born a lady."

"Never mind, Alice. Every good woman will be a lady one day—I am sure of that. It was cruel to treat you so! How can anybody belonging to Richard do such a thing? He's so gentle and good himself."

"He's the kindest of men, and I love him," said Alice earnestly. "When I told poor Adam as we went home that night that he wasn't to see any more of Richard, he couldn't help crying. I saw it, though he tried to hide it. Of course I didn't let him know I saw him cry. Men are ashamed of crying; I'm not a bit. For Richard was the only school friend who was kind to Adam. He once fought a big fellow that used to tease him.

"By the time we got home, I was so angry and told Mama all about it. But angry as I was, her anger frightened mine out of me. 'The insolent woman!' she cried. 'But I'll have my revenge of her—that you shall soon see! My children aren't good enough for her tradesman-fellow, aren't they! She said that, did she? She isn't the only one has got eyes in her head! Didn't you ever see me look at him sharp as she did at you? If ever face told tale without meaning to tell it, that's the face of the young man you call Richard! I'll take my oath who was *his* father!'

"I'm not telling you exactly what she said, miss, because when she loses her temper, poor Mama don't always speak quite like a lady. I said no more, but I thought how kindly Richard always looked at me, and my heart grew big inside to think that Adam and I had him for our very own brother. Nobody could take that away. He had notions I didn't like—for, do you know, Barbara, that he believes there's no more life after this."

She paused, frowning. "He can't have loved anybody much to be able to think that! I don't think he even believes in God at all. I'm certain you don't agree with him, miss. But I thought if he was my brother, I might be able to help change his mind about it. I thought I would be so good to him that he wouldn't want me to die forever and would then come to see things differently."

Barbara nodded, considering the possibility of such love. "Go on," she urged.

"I had no friend, not one, you see, miss—Barbara, I mean—except Adam, and he never has much to say about anything, though he's true as steel. I thought what it would be like to have a brother like Richard for a friend. Most brothers are not friends to poor girls. So I said to Mama that, now we knew all about it, there could be no reason why we shouldn't see as much of each other as we liked, seeing Richard was our brother. But she paid no heed to me."

Alice paused in her story and looked at her friend with pleading eyes. "It isn't our fault—is it, Barbara?"

"Your fault!" cried Barbara. "What do you mean?"

"People treat us as if it were."

"Never you mind. You've got a Father in heaven to see to that."

"Thank you, Barbara! You make me so happy. Well, after she had sat a while, suddenly my mother's face lit up. 'I'll not have my own children looked down on by Mrs. Bookbinder!' She said, 'He's no better than my children, and she's no better than me!'

"Barbara, I treasured every word my mother said—I was so glad all the while to think of Richard as the head of the family, even if he was, like Adam and me, not a legitimate son of Sir Wilton. I could not help thinking that I belonged to a real family, for was not the same blood in Richard and in us?

"But as much as I loved Richard and wanted him as my brother, I never wanted to interfere in his family. I remembered what his mother had said to me. He didn't know the shame of his beginnings, and so I tried to stay away from him, as his mother demanded. I met him one night in Regent Street, a terrible, stormy night, and was so flustered at seeing him, and so frightened that I might let something out that might injure him, that I treated him terribly and made him leave me alone. I had to be cruel to him, and he must have thought me awful. And now for him to appear, far away from everywhere, just in time to save me from dying of cold and hunger—isn't it wonderful?"

Barbara sat silent. It was her turn to sit thinking. Why had the strange story come to her ears? There must be something for her to do in the next chapter of it!

"Do you think Richard knows anything about this?" she asked.

"I don't think he has a suspicion he is anything but the son of the bookbinder," Alice answered.

"Should we tell him?" asked Barbara, whose characteristic honesty made her loathe to keep secrets about those she cared for.

"I don't know," answered Alice. "I have thought and thought, lying alone in the night, but never could make up my mind. I don't know if my mother was telling the truth or just seeking revenge; and there's the danger of what she might be tempted to do the moment anyone revealed her secret. Isn't it strange, Barbara, how much your love for your mother seems independent of her character?"

"I don't know; yes, I think you are right. There is my mother, who is ready to burn you to ashes before you know what she is angry about! When you trust her and go to her for help, she is ready to die for you. I love her with all my heart, but I can't say she's an exemplary woman. I don't think Mr. Wingfold—that's our clergyman—would say so either, though he professes quite an admiration for her."

At that Barbara told Alice the story of her mother's behavior in church, and how the parson had caught her.

"Nobody knows to this day," she concluded, "whether he intended to so catch her, or was only teaching his people by a parable, and she caught herself in its meshes. Caught she was, anyhow, and has never entered the church since. But she speaks very differently of the clergyman now."

"Sometimes I feel greatly tempted," resumed Alice, "to let Richard know. Whatever be the projects of other people concerning him, a man has a right to know where he came from."

"Yes," answered Barbara, "a man must have the right to know what other people know about him. I wish we knew what ground there is for inquiring into Richard's birth. But of course, Sir Wilton might not acknowledge his responsibility for any of you—"

Alice nodded gravely.

"But," Barbara concluded brightly, "I *knew* there was the air of the gentleman about that bookbinder! No ordinary workman, indeed—legitimate or not!"

The girls finally decided that, for the present, they must do nothing that might let the secret out of their keeping. They must wait and watch: when the right thing grew plain, they would do it!

18 Wingfold and Barbara

Barbara rode home with strange things in her mind. Here was a romance brought to her very door! Naturally, then, from this time onward, Barbara's thoughts rested more and more on the person and undeveloped history of the man to whom she was so greatly indebted. Richard had thrown open to Barbara regions of literature and thought previously unknown to her. On her part, she had influenced him to such an extent that he had at least become less overbearing in presenting his unbelief. The strongest bonds were thus in the process of binding them; Barbara's feeling toward Richard might very naturally develop into one of the million forms to which we give the common name of love.

As for Richard, he was already aware that his feeling toward Barbara could be nothing but love. But he understood love as few know it, giving himself fully while expecting no response and dreaming of no claim on her. Because of their different social stations, to expect any return of his devotion would have seemed to Richard an absurdity. She shone in his eyes like a lovely mysterious gem which he might wear for an hour, but which must presently, with its hundredfold shadow and shine, pass from his keeping. In truth, no man good and free could have kept her soul out of his. She was so delicate, yet so strong; so steady, yet so ready; so original, yet so infinitely responsive—what could he do but throw his doors wide to her? What could he do but love her?

And now that Barbara believed she knew more about him than he did himself; now that the road appeared to lie open between them, since he was of gentle birth—acknowledged or not—would she escape falling in love with a man whose hands of labor were mastered by a head full of understanding?

For some weeks they saw less of each other. Unconsciously, since Alice's revelation, Barbara had grown a little shy of Richard. It came mainly from her truthfulness. Without altogether defining it, Barbara regarded it as unfair to Richard, as indeed taking advantage of him, to seek his company, knowing more about him than she seemed to know. She felt even deceitful in appearing to know of him only what he chose to tell her, while in truth she suspected she knew of him what he did not know himself.

Therefore she did not now go to Mortgrange so often. Every day she went out for her gallop—alone and unattended, for she was so accustomed to the freedom of hundreds of leagues of wild country that the idea of a groom tagging along behind her was hateful.

Lady Ann and she were now on the same footing as before their misunderstanding—if indeed their whole relation was anything better than a misunderstanding. What Lady Ann knew of Barbara she misunderstood, and what she did not know of Barbara was the best of her; while what Barbara did not know of Lady Ann was the worst of her. But Barbara had told Lady Ann that she was sorry she had spoken as she had, and Lady Ann had received the statement as the expected apology.

Lady Ann's relations with Barbara were therefore not so much restored as unchanged. The elder lady neither sought nor avoided the younger, gave her always the same cold welcome and farewell, yet was as much pleased to see her as to see anybody. She regarded her as the merest of butterflies, with pretty flutter and no stay.

When Barbara went into the library, she greeted Richard as if she had just seen him the day before, asking what piece of work he was at now, and showing an interest in it as genuine as her interest in himself. If there was anything in it she did not quite understand, she made him explain it. But Richard continued to give her even more important aid in things literary, advising her what to read and what to think about as she read a certain book. He laid before her certain poems, from which he instructed her to choose those she liked best to copy out in her own hand in a manuscript book, hoping to cause them to grow in her mind until they began to assume something of the shape they had had in the author's.

To Arthur Lestrange, who had been for some time falling in love with Barbara despite the unlikeness between them, these interviews, which he never hesitated to interrupt, were hardly agreeable. He did not relish the thought that she looked to the workman rather than the employer for help in her studies. Nor was it consolation to him to be aware that he could no more give her what the workman gave her than he could teach her his bookbinding.

At Wylder Hall no questions were ever asked as to how she had spent the day. Now that her twin was gone, her mother loved her best in the world, although she never troubled her head about what she did with herself. She thought Arthur Lestrange would make a good enough husband for Bab and, having chanced upon the discovery that her husband cherished hopes of a loftier alliance, grew rather favorable to a match between them.

There was, however, a little betterment in Mrs. Wylder, and ceasing to go to church was only one of the indications of it. She had in her a foundation of genuine simplicity, and was in essence a generous soul. The source of the strange wild charm and honest strength of the daughter lay buried beneath the ruin of earthquake and tornado in the soul of the mother. The best of changes is slow in most natures; the main question is, perhaps, whether the slowness is because of feebleness, or because of the root-nature and the magnitude of what has been initiated.

Since returning to a more civilized life, Mr. Wylder had grown self-absorbed and morose. One cause of the change was that the remaining twin, his favorite, had for some time shown signs of a failing constitution. His increasing feebleness weighed heavily on his father. Barbara's heart yearned for the boy, but he was greatly attached to his nurse, and did not care for Barbara. The mother did not heed him, and the father, for very misery, could scarcely look at him: he was to him like one dead already, only not dead enough to be buried.

The bickerings between her father and mother had a great deal to do with the peculiar features of Barbara's life in New Zealand. As soon as she saw a cloud rising, she would creep away, mount one of the many horses at her disposal, and race from the house. What the object of their fighting might be, she never asked. It was plain to her that nothing was ever gained by it. Not a sentence was uttered by the one but was furiously felt as a wrong by the other. It is strange that the man who most keenly feels the wrong done him should so often be the most insensible to the wrong he does. So dominant is the unreason of the moment that the injury he inflicts appears absolute justice, and the injury he suffers absolute injustice. Yet such disputes seldom turn upon the main point at issue. War rages between kingdoms for the possession of a broken-down cottage—which, when once possessed, brings the quarrel no nearer being settled than before!

Hence it came that Barbara paid so little heed to her mother's challenge of the clergyman. Combat of that sort was too recurrent an experience of Barbara's life to find interesting. She had, indeed, sufficient respect for the forms of religion to regret that her mother should behave as she had, but she scarcely took further interest in the matter.

One day, having been in the house all afternoon, Barbara went out toward sunset to have a walk with a book. She was sauntering along a grassy public road when she almost ran into a man similarly occupied, for he was also absorbed in the book he carried. Each started back with an apology, then both burst into a modest laugh, and the curate held out his hand.

"I never saw you on your own feet before, Miss Wylder."

"Not on anybody else's, I hope!" she returned.

"Oh yes, indeed! On Miss Brown's, many a time!"

"You know Miss Brown then? She is my most intimate friend."

"I am well aware of that. Everything worth knowing in the parish, and a good deal that is not, comes to my ears."

"May I hope you count Miss Brown's affairs worth hearing about, then?"

"Of course I do! I love my animals as much as I'm sure you love Miss Brown, and I count their affairs most interesting. But indeed, I have more to be thankful for than most, for I sometimes drive a pony yet that is over forty."

"Forty years of age! That *is* interesting! I should like to see that pony!"

"You shall see her any day you will come to the parsonage. I will gladly introduce her to you, but it is getting rather late to desire her acquaintance: she does not see well and is not so good-tempered as she once was. But she will soon be better."

"How do you mean?"

"She has a process to go through, and she will come out ever so much the better."

"You're not going to have an operation performed on her—at *her* age?"

"No. She is going to have her body stripped off."

"Good gracious!" cried Barbara; then, seeing finally what he meant, she began laughing heartily.

"So then," she said, "you believe animals have souls?"

"I do. Although I can't prove it," answered Wingfold. "I can't actually prove anything."

"Then why do you believe it?" asked Barbara.

"Belief and proof have little or nothing to do with each other. I believe many things I cannot prove. I believe in God, but I could never begin to prove his existence to one who wanted to argue the point."

"But," persisted Barbara, with Richard in her mind, "how are you to be sure of what you can't prove?"

"When you love a thing, you already believe enough to put it to the proof of trial rather than the proof of brains. Shall I search heaven and earth for proof that my wife is a good and lovely woman? The signs of it are everywhere; the proofs of it nowhere."

They walked along for a while, side by side, in silence. Which had changed direction to walk with the other, neither knew. Barbara was beginning already to feel that safety which almost everybody sooner or later came to feel in Wingfold's company. In the closest talk about the deepest things, he never lay in wait for a victory, but took his companion, as one of his own people, into the end after which he was striving.

"Do you think it very bad of a man not to believe in a God?"

"That depends on the sort of God he imagines that he either does or does not believe in. Most people have totally wrong conceptions of God. A thousand times would I rather see a man not believe in God at all than believe in an evil god that could cause suffering and misery as if he were a devil. But if a man had the same notion of God that I have—a God who is even now doing his best to take all men and women and beasts out of the misery in which they find themselves—and did not at least desire that there might be such a God, then I confess I would have difficulty in understanding how he could be good. When one looks at the gods that have been offered through the years who are not worth believing in, it might be an act of virtue not to believe in them."

"One thing more, Mr. Wingfold—and you must not think I am arguing against you or against God, I just want to understand—might not a man think the idea of a God such as you believe in too good to be true?"

"Why should he be able to think anything too good to be true? Badness itself can have no life in it. If a thing be bad, it cannot possibly be true. But if the man really thought as you suggest, I would ask him, 'If such a being did exist, would you be content never to find him, but to go on forever saying, *He can't be. He can't be! He's so good he can't be!* Supposing one day you find him, will you say to him: *If you had not been so good, if you had been just a little bad, then I would have believed in you*'?"

"But if the man could not believe there was any such being, what could be done for him to give him the heart to look for him?"

"God knows—God *does* know. It all depends on whether such a man had been doing what he knew he ought to do, living as he knew he ought to live, or whether he had by wrong-doing injured his deepest faculty of understanding."

"And if the man was one who sought to do right, who tried to help his neighbor—yet still denied the God that most people seem to believe in? What would you say then?"

"I would say, 'Have patience. If there be a good God, he cannot be altogether dissatisfied with such a man. I do not know when any man or woman has arrived at the point of development where he is capable of really believing in God: the innocent child who has never heard of Jesus may be capable, and a gray-haired intelligent man of science incapable. If he be such a person as you have described, I believe that, no matter how uninteresting he may say the question of a God is to him, the God of patience is taking care of him, and the time must come when something will make him want to know whether there be a God, and whether he can get near to him.' I would say, 'He is in God's school; don't be too troubled about him, as if God might overlook and forget him. He will see to all that concerns him. He has made him, and he loves him, and he is doing and will do his very best for him.' "

"Oh, I am so glad to hear you speak like that!" cried Barbara. "I didn't know clergymen were like that. I'm sure they don't talk like that in the pulpit!"

"Well, you know a man can't just chat with his people in the pulpit in the same way he can when he has one friend alone to himself. There are hundreds there, and they are all very different.

There are multitudes who could not understand a word of what we have been saying to each other."

Their talk the rest of the way was lighter and more general; and to her great joy Barbara discovered that the clergyman loved books the same way the bookbinder loved them. But she did not mention Richard.

The parson took leave of her at a convenient exit from the park, rejoicing that, in his dull parish, where so few seemed to care whether they were going back to be monkeys or on to be men, he had yet found two such interesting young people as Richard and Barbara.

Wingfold had come upon Richard again at his grandfather's, talked a little more with him, and found him not so far from the kingdom of heaven but that he cared to deny a false god; and he had just discovered in Barbara, who so seldom went to church and who came of such strange parents, one in whom the love of God was not merely innate, but keenly alive. The heart of the one recoiled from a god that was not; the heart of the other was drawn to a God of whom she knew little: were not the two upon converging tracks? What to most clergymen would have seemed the depth of a winter of unbelief seemed to Wingfold a springtime full of the sounds of rising sap.

"What man," he said to himself, "knowing the compassion that some men have for their fellowmen, can doubt that, loving the children, they must one day love the Father! Who more welcome to the heart of the eternal Father than the man who loves his brother, whom also the unchanging Father loves!"

Wingfold scarcely thought about the church, and never mistook it for the kingdom of God. He was a servant of the church universal, of all that believed or ever would believe in the Lord Christ, therefore of all men, of the whole universe—and first, of every man, woman, and child in his own parish. But though he was the servant of the boundless church, no church was his master. He had no master but the Lord of life. Therefore the so-called prosperity of the church did not interest him. He knew that the Master works from within outward, and believed no danger possible to the church, except from within.

The will of God was all Wingfold cared about, and if the church was not content with that, the church was nothing to him, and might do with him as it would. He gave himself altogether to the Lord, and therefore to his people. He believed in Jesus Christ as the everyday life of the world, whose presence is just as needed in bank or shop or House of Lords, as at what so many of the clergy call the altar. When the Lord is known as the heart of every joy, as well as the refuge from every sorrow, then the altar will be known for what it is—an ecclesiastical antique. The Father permitted but never ordained sacrifice; in tenderness to his children he ordered the ways of their unbelieving belief. So thought and said Wingfold, and if he did not say so in the pulpit, it was not for fear of his fellows regarding him as a heretic but because so few of his people would understand. He would spend no strength in trying to shore up the church; he sent his lifeblood through its veins, and his appeal to the Living One, for whose judgment he waited.

The world would not perish if what is called the church did go to pieces; a truer church, for there might well be a truer, would arise out of her ruins. But let no one seek to destroy; let him that builds only take heed that he build with gold, silver, and precious stones, not with wood, hay, and stubble! If the church were so built, who could harm it? If it were not in part so built, it would be as little worth pulling down as letting stand. There is in it a far deeper and better vitality than its blatant supporters will be able to ruin by their advocacy, or the enviers of its valueless social position by their assaults upon that position.

Wingfold never thought of associating the anxiety of the heiress with the unbelief of the bookbinder. He laughed with delight when some time later he learned their relation to each other.

The next Sunday Barbara was at church, and never afterward willingly missed going. She sought the friendship of Mrs. Wingfold, and found at last a woman she could heartily look up to. She found in her also a clergyman's wife who understood her husband and fell thoroughly in love with his way of teaching people. Like Thomas, Helen never sought to make one in the parish a churchman, but tried to make everyone she influenced a scholar of Christ, a child of his Father in heaven.

19 The Shoeing of Miss Brown

Miss Brown was in need of at least one pair of new shoes, and her mistress had been waiting for an opportunity for a lesson in shoeing her. Therefore, two days later, on a lovely autumn evening, Barbara rode Miss Brown across the fields, avoiding the hard road even more carefully than usual.

The red-faced, white-whiskered, jolly old Simon stood at the smithy door to receive her: he had been watching for her, and had heard the gentle trot over the few yards of road that brought her in sight. With a merry greeting he helped her down from the great mare. She would have shaken hands with him, but he would not: it would make her glove as black as his apron, he said. Barbara immediately pulled off her glove and gave him her dainty little hand, which the blacksmith took at once, being too much of a gentleman not to know where respect gives way to rudeness. He clasped the lovely loan with the sturdy reverence of his true old heart, saying her hand should pay for her footing in the trade.

"Lord, miss, ain't I proud to make a smith of you!" he said. "Only you must do nothing but shoe! I can't let you spoil your hands! And here comes Dick for his part."

Richard came up, brought Miss Brown in, and put her in her place. The smith knew exactly what sort and size of shoes she wanted, and had them already so far finished that but a touch or so was necessary to make them an absolute fit. Barbara tucked up her skirt, and secured it with her belt. But this was not enough for Simon. He had a little leather apron ready for her, and nothing would satisfy him but that she protected herself entirely from the dirt. Until this was done, he would not allow her to touch hammer or nail.

Richard did not offer to put on the first shoe; he believed she had watched the operation so often that she must know perfectly what to do. And he was not disappointed. She proceeded like an adept smith. Happily, Miss Brown was very good. She was neither hungry nor thirsty, and had had just enough exercise to make her willing to stand and breathe for a while. Richard hardly found himself astonished, after all her careful observation, at Barbara's coolness as she tucked the great hoof under her arm, or even at the accurate aim which brought the right sort of blow down on the head of nail after nail. But he was astonished at the strength of her little hand, the hardness of her muscles, and the knowing skill with which she twisted off the ends of the nails: the quick turn necessary.

Very quickly the mare was shod without accident, and Richard felt no anxiety as he lifted the little lady to her back; she cantered away as if she had been presented with fresh feathery wings instead of new iron shoes.

He was a little disappointed, however, for he had hoped to walk part of the way back alongside Miss Brown. In truth, Barbara had expected that he would, but a sudden shyness came upon her and made her start up at speed the moment she was in the saddle. Simon and Richard stood looking after her.

But then with a sharp scramble she turned. She came back at a quick trot and was back beside the two men in a moment. Barbara had come to herself and thought that it was a pity to get no more pleasure or profit out of the afternoon than just a horse-shoeing!

"She's all right!" she cried.

She thanked the old man once more in such a pretty fashion that he felt lord of the world. Then Richard and she moved away together in the direction of Mortgrange, and left Simon praying God to give them to each other before he died.

They had not gone far when Richard stopped.

"Oh, miss," he said. "I must go back. Neither of us went to see Alice."

She regarded him without response or word or look for a moment.

"Alice is gone," said Barbara quietly at length.

He stood and stared. Barbara saw him turn white and understood he mistook her meaning.

"She went home to her mother yesterday," she added.

Richard gave a great sigh of relief.

"I thought you meant she was dead," he said, "and I had not been so good to her as I might have been!"

"Richard," said Barbara—it was the first time she had called him by his name since their first meeting—"did anybody in the world ever do all he might to make his friends happy?"

"No, miss. Probably not. There must always be more that might have been done. But can you tell me why Alice went away without letting me know?"

"She had a good reason," answered Barbara.

"I can't imagine what it could be," he returned. "I hadn't come to see her for several days, but she couldn't be too offended by that. Did her mother send her money?"

"Not that I know of."

"Perhaps my grandfather lent her some. I wonder why she dislikes me so much!"

Barbara could not tell him that Alice was afraid to bid him good-bye lest, in her weakness, she should throw her arms around him and begin kissing him! Then she would have to tell him he was her brother; she therefore had to go without a word.

"She is far from disliking you," said Barbara.

"Why then didn't she tell me so that I might have given her money for her journey?"

"There was no need of that," returned Barbara. "She is my sister now, and a sovereign or two is nothing between us."

"Oh, thank you! But I am afraid it will be long before she is able to work again. It would be of no use to tell my mother, for somehow she seems to have taken a great dislike to poor Alice. I am positive she does not deserve it. My mother is the best woman I know, but she is very stiff when she takes to disliking someone. Have you got her address? Adam would take money from me, I think, but I don't know where he is."

"I will see she has everything she needs," answered Barbara.

"Bless your lovely heart, miss. But I fear nothing much will reach them as long as their mother is alive. She takes everything for herself. There's Adam, cold and thin and miserable, without even an overcoat in the bitterest weather! And Alice working so hard and so thin! And Mrs. Manson well dressed and eating the best money can buy. Such women as she have no right to be mothers!"

"Shall I tell you what our clergyman said to me the other day?" returned Barbara.

"Yes, I don't mind what you say, because the God you would have me believe in is like yourself. And if such a God could be, I'm sure he would set everything right again as soon as he could."

"Mr. Wingfold said that it was not fair, when a man had made something for a purpose, to say it was not good before we knew what his purpose with it was. 'I don't even like my wife to look at my poems before they're finished,' he said. 'But God can't hide away his work till it is finished, as I do my verses, and we ought to take care what we say about it. God wants to do something better with people than people think.' "

"Is he a poet?" asked Richard. "But when I think how he looked at the sunrise—he must be. That man doesn't talk a bit like a clergyman; he talks just like any man. I couldn't help liking him and wishing I might meet him again. But I think I could put a question or two to him yet that would puzzle him."

"I don't know," returned Barbara; "but one thing I am sure of, that, if you did puzzle him, he would say he was puzzled and must have time to think it over."

"That is honest. But do you think, miss, that you could get Adam's address from Alice? His office is not where it used to be."

"I am sure I could."

"You see, the time is coming when I shall have to go back to London."

There was a tone and slight tremble in his words. It was to this, not to the words themselves, which Barbara made reply.

"Will anyone dare say we shall not meet again?"

"The sort of God you believe in, miss, would probably not say it," he answered; "but the sort of God my mother believes in would."

"I know nothing about other people's gods. Indeed," she added, "I know very little about my own; but I want to know more, and Mr. Wingfold is teaching me."

"Take care he doesn't talk you into anything. Only I doubt he would try to do that."

"He will persuade me of nothing that doesn't seem to me true—be certain of that, Richard. And if it please God to part us, I will pray to him to let us meet again. You have been very good to me."

Richard was not elated by her words. He only thought, *How kind of her!*

20 Vixen

The next day, before noon, Richard was busy as usual in the library. Doors and windows were shut against draughts, for he was working with gold-leaf on the tooling of an ancient binding. A door opened, and in came the goblin of the house. Perceiving what Richard was about, she came bounding in, and making a willful wind with her pinafore, blew away the leaf he was dividing and knocked a book of gold-leaf to the floor. The book-mender rose, took her in a firm grasp, and proceeded to expel her. She threw herself on the floor, and began to scream. Richard picked her up, laid her down in the hall, and closed and locked the door by which she had entered. Vixen lay where he had deposited her, and went on screaming. By and by her screaming ceased and a few minutes later the handle of the door was tried. Richard took no notice. Then came a knock. Richard called out, "Who's there?" but no answer came except a repetition of the knock, to which he paid no attention. The knock was repeated twice more, but Richard went on with his work. Suddenly another door, which he had not thought of locking, burst open and in sailed Miss Malliver, the governess, tall and slight, with the dignity she put on for her inferiors, to whom she was as insolent as she was cringing to those above her.

"Man!" she exclaimed, the moment her wrath would allow her to speak, "what do you mean by your insolence?"

"If you allude to my putting the child out of the room," answered Richard, "I mean that she is rude, and that I will not be annoyed with her."

"You shall be turned out of the house."

"In the meantime," rejoined Richard, who had a natural repugnance to Miss Malliver and was now thoroughly angry, "I will turn you out of the room too, and for the same reason."

"I dare you!" cried Miss Malliver.

Richard quietly laid aside the tool he was using, and approached her deliberately. Not believing he would presume to touch her, the woman kept her ground defiantly until his hands were on the point of seizing her. Then she uttered a shriek and fled. Richard closed the door behind her, locked it also, and returned to his work.

But he was not to be left in peace. Another hand came to the door, and a voice demanding entrance followed the foiled attempt to open it. He recognized the voice as Lady Ann's and rose to admit her. But her ladyship stood motionless on the doormat, erect and cool. Anger itself could not warm her; the fact that she was angry was plain only from the steely sparkle in her gray eyes.

"You forget yourself! You must leave the house!" she said.

"I have done nothing, My Lady, except what it was necessary to do. I did not hurt the child in the least."

"That is not the point. You must leave the house."

"I should at once obey you, My Lady," rejoined Richard, "but I am not at liberty to do so. Sir Wilton has the command of my time till the month of May. I am bound to be at his orders, whether I choose or not, except he tell me to go."

Lady Ann stood speechless and stared at him with her icicle-eyes. Richard turned away to his work. Lady Ann entered and shut the door behind her. Suddenly her behavior had turned very peculiar, for in his anger, Richard had flashed on her a look which she knew but could not identify, and which somehow frightened her. She could not rest until she could shape and identify the reminiscence! But Lady Ann could not isolate the look, and so went on talking to him, keeping to the point, trying again to raise the same expression passing swiftly across his face.

"Mr. —, —I don't know your name," she resumed, "—no respectable house could harbor such behavior. I grant Sir Wilton is partly to blame, for he ought not to have allowed the library to be turned into a workshop. That, however, makes no difference. This kind of thing cannot continue!"

Richard went on with his work and made no reply. Lady Ann looked in vain for a revival of the expression that had struck her.

"You must not imagine yourself of importance in the house," she resumed, "simply because a friend of the family happens to be interested in the kind of thing you do—very neatly, I admit, but—"

She stopped short. At this allusion to Barbara, Richard's rage boiled up with a swelling heave. Lady Ann turned pale—pale even for her—murmured something inaudible, put her hand to her forehead, and left the room.

Richard's anger fell. He thought at first that he had frightened her. "Oh, well," he said to himself, "perhaps they will leave me alone now." He closed the door she had left open behind her, unlocked the other, and fell once more to his work.

For the time the disturbance was over. When Miss Malliver and Vixen, lingering near, saw Lady Ann walk past, holding her hand to her forehead, they also turned pale with fear: the man must be terrible indeed to have silenced their lady in her own house, and had his own way with her! Vixen dared not go near him again for a long time.

But Lady's Ann's perturbation did not last. She said to herself that she was a fool to imagine such an absurdity. She remembered to have heard, though at the time it had held no interest for her, that the bookbinder had relatives in the neighborhood. Such a likeness might meet her at any turn: the kind of thing was a constant occurrence about estates of this sort. It improved the breed of the lower orders, and was no business of hers. A child had certainly been lost, with a claim to the succession; but was she therefore to be appalled at every resemblance to her husband that happened to turn up? As to that particular child, she would *not* believe that he was alive! He could not be!

Lady Ann had lived so long in dread lest the missing heir appear to claim his own that but a simple look of anger on the young bookbinder's face became for her the Lestrange look; it troubled her and set in action so important a train of thought. It might be a false conjecture but for the present, unnecessary as she was determined to think it, she yet resolved to do all that was left her to do: she would watch. And while she watched, she would take care that the young man was subjected to no annoyance. She did not want his angry face to suggest to anyone else, as it already had herself, the question of his origin.

Thus Richard heard nothing more of his threatened expulsion from Mortgrange.

21 Barbara's Duty

That same afternoon Barbara appeared before the front windows of the house, perched upon her huge yet gracious Miss Brown. Usually Arthur was on the lookout for her, but today he was more upset than usual with her for keeping back the encouragement he imagined he deserved; therefore he was paying no attention today.

He was confident that he loved Barbara. He did not know or suspect that two weeks of the London social season would make him nearly forget her. He was not a bad sort of fellow, had no evil vices, was not a snob or a cad. His worse fault was pride in himself because of his family—pride in everything he had been born to. He was not jealous of Barbara's pleasure in Richard's company. The slightest probe of such a feeling toward a man so infinitely beneath him would have been degrading. To compare himself to the bookbinder for the briefest moment would have been to insult all the Lestranges that ever lived. Tuke had no *raison d'être* but work for the library that would one day be Arthur's, and by its excellence add to the honor of Mortgrange. He forgot that Richard had opened his eyes to its merit, and imagined himself the discoverer of its value: did he not pay the man for his work? And is not what a man pays for his own? The workman in the library knew as much about the insides as about the outsides of the books, Arthur conceded, but that fact accorded the bookbinder no dignity in his eyes, though it did make him a bit more friendly to him.

Little Vixen ran out to Barbara and made herself less unpleasant than usual: she was preparing, by what blandishment she was mistress of, to put forward a complaint against the man in the library. She accompanied Barbara to the stable and as they walked back together gave her such an account of what had taken place that Barbara, distrusting the child, nevertheless felt a little anxious. She knew Richard's spirit, knew that he would never show her ladyship any falseness, and was afraid lest he should have to leave the house as a result of what had occurred. She must see Lady Ann and give her the opportunity to say whatever she might on the matter.

Barbara was under no pledge of secrecy to Alice or anyone; she was free to do what might seem for the best—that is, Richard's good.

"I am sorry to find you feeling poorly, Lady Ann," she said when she entered the lady's room. Vixen had told her that the horrid man had made her mama quite ill; and Barbara found her with her room darkened, and a cup of green tea on a Japanese table beside the couch.

"It is only one of my headaches, child," returned Lady Ann.

"From what Victoria tells me, something serious must have happened to annoy you."

"Nothing at all worth mentioning. He is an odd person, that workman of yours!"

"He is peculiar," granted Barbara, "but I am certain he would not willingly make anyone angry."

"Children will be troublesome," said her ladyship.

"Particularly Victoria," returned Barbara. "Mr. Tuke cannot bear to have his work put in jeopardy."

"Very excusable in him."

Barbara was surprised at her consideration and thought she must somehow be pleased with Richard.

"It would astonish you to hear him talk sometimes," she said. "There is something remarkable about the young man. He must have a history somewhere!"

Barbara had been wondering whether it was altogether fair to Sir Wilton and his family to conceal the identity of the baron's son. The question of Richard's legitimacy held no significance for one such as Barbara, but next to Richard himself, weren't they the ones most concerned in it? Had they no right to some preparation for the changes the disclosure would bring to their lives? For all these reasons she had determined that very morning, should the opportunity present itself, to give Lady Ann a hint of the truth about the bookbinder.

In addition, Barbara was one of those to whom concealment is a positive pain. She had a natural hatred, most healthy and most Christian, to all secrets as such. She constantly wanted to say all that was in her, and when she could not, she felt grieved.

"He may have had good blood in him on one side," suggested Lady Ann. "He was rude to me, but I daresay it was the child's fault. He seems intelligent."

"He is more than intelligent. I suspect he could be a genius if given the chance."

"I should have thought him a tradesman all over."

"But his intelligence might make a gentleman of him."

"No. It might make him grow to look like one, that's all."

"Isn't that the same? Isn't it all in the look?"

"By no means. A man must be born a gentleman or he is nothing," said Lady Ann.

She spoke condescendingly, as to an ignorant person from the colonies, where they could not be expected to understand such things.

"But if his parents were gentlefolk?" suggested Barbara.

"Birth predetermines style," said Lady Ann, "though education and society do their share as well. But bad blood does occasionally get in."

"I wish I knew what makes a gentleman!" sighed Barbara. "I

have been trying to understand the thing all my life. Tell me, Lady Ann—to be a gentleman, must a man be a good man?"

"I'm sorry to say," she answered, "it is not necessary in the least."

"Then a gentleman may do bad things and still be a gentleman?"

"Yes—that is, *some* bad things."

"Do you mean—not *many* bad things?"

"No, I mean certain kinds of bad things."

"Such as cheating at cards?"

"No. If he were found doing that, he would be expelled from any club in London."

"May he tell lies then?"

"Certainly not! It is a very ungentlemanly thing to tell lies."

"Then if a man tells a lie, he is not a gentleman?"

"I do not say that; I say that to tell lies is ungentlemanly."

"Does that mean that he may tell *some* lies, and yet be a gentleman?"

Lady Ann was afraid to go on. She saw that to go on answering this colonial girl with her troublesome freedom of thought and question might land her in a bog of contradictions.

"How many lies may a gentleman tell in a day?" pursued Barbara with characteristic directness.

"Not any," answered Lady Ann.

"Does the same rule hold for ladies?"

"Y–e–s—I should say so," replied her ladyship with hesitation, for she suspected being slowly driven into some snare. She knew she was not particularly careful to speak the truth if a lie would suit her purpose better.

As they talked, the feeling came upon Barbara and grew that she was herself not acting like a lady in going so much to Lady Ann's house, and being received by her as a guest, when all the time she knew something her hostess did not know, something it was important for her to know, something she had a right and a claim to know. It was unfair to leave them unwarned.

"I want to talk to you about something, Lady Ann," she said.

"You can't but know that a son of Sir Wilton's was stolen when he was a baby and never found."

It was the first time for many years that Lady Ann had heard the thing alluded to. Her heart seemed to make a somersault, but not a visible muscle moved. What *could* the girl be hinting at? Were there reports about?

"Everyone knows that!" she answered. "It is but too true. It happened after my marriage. I was in the house at the time. What of it, child? There can be little hope of his turning up now—after twenty years."

"I believe he has turned up. I believe I know him."

"It may be so," she answered quietly, "but it hardly interests me. A child was born in this house and stolen out of it; but his mother was a low woman; she was not the wife of Sir Wilton."

"He was not a legitimate child, then," Barbara rejoined. "But, still—" Her strong sense of justice was beginning to arouse the temper that Lady Ann had seen once before.

"I am sorry I had to mention the thing," interrupted Lady Ann, "for I can see it is upsetting to you. There may be many such children fathered by Sir Wilton's lack of wisdom. But it matters little to the future of Mortgrange, I daresay. Of course I know where the particular report you allude to comes from. *Any* man, bookbinder or blacksmith, may put in a claim. And he will probably find many to back him."

"You imagine Mr. Tuke told me he was Sir Wilton's son, Lady Ann? You are mistaken. He does not know himself that he is even supposed to be."

"Then who told you? Is it likely his friends have gotten him into the house with him knowing nothing of their designs?"

"How do you know it was he I meant, Lady Ann?"

"You told me so yourself."

"No. That I did not! I *know* I didn't, Lady Ann. What made you fix your thoughts on him?"

Lady Ann saw she had committed herself.

"If you did not tell me," she rejoined, "your peculiar behavior to the man must have led me to the conclusion!"

"I have never concealed my interest in Mr. Tuke, but—"

"You certainly have not!" interrupted her ladyship, who suffered both in temper and loss of prudence from annoyance at her own blunder.

"Please, hear me out, Lady Ann. What I want to say is that my friendship for Mr. Tuke began long before I learned the fact concerning of which we have been speaking."

"Friendship! Ah, well—scarcely decorous! But as to what you call *fact*, I would counsel a little caution. I repeat that, if the man be the son of my husband, which may be difficult to prove, it is of no consequence to anyone: Sir Wilton was never married to his mother. I am sorry he should have been born out of wedlock; at the same time I cannot be sorry that he will never come between my Arthur and the succession. The baron's inheritance and title are reserved for the legitimate heir."

Here Lady Ann saw a change on Barbara's face. Entirely concerned until now with Richard's loss by not being acknowledged, it now occurred to her for the first time what she herself would gain if indeed he were rejected because of his illegitimacy: no one could think she had approached him as a friend, or more, because he was going to be a rich man! She might behave to him as she pleased—though of course people would talk of her going below her station, but who cared for that? There could be no suspicion of low motive on her part. And with this realization a slow smile spread across her face. Barbara was free to approach Richard without people thinking she did so because of his position.

It did not take Lady Ann long to interpret the glow on Barbara's face to her own satisfaction. Undoubtedly, the girl had heard the report and believed that the bookbinder had some claim to the estate; that uncertainty had kept Barbara back from encouraging Arthur, pursuing instead her unpleasant intimacy with this Tuke. The sudden change on her countenance indicated her relief in finding that Arthur, and not Tuke, was to be the heir! How could she but prefer her Arthur to a man smelling of leather and glue, a man without the manners or education of a gentleman! He might know a few things that gentlemen did not care to know, but even those he got only out of books! He could not do one of the many things her Arthur did. He could neither ride nor shoot nor dress nor dance.

He was tall, but he was clumsy. No doubt he was handsome in a vulgar sort of way, but when angry he was ugly enough!

The girl remained silent.

"You will oblige me, my dear Barbara," she said, "by not alluding to this rumor. It might raise doubt and could do serious harm."

"There are others who already know it, and believe it," answered Barbara.

"Who are they?"

"I do not feel at liberty to tell their names. I thought you had a right to know what was said, but I have no right to mention where I heard it."

Lady Ann grew thoughtful again and became convinced that Richard had indeed told her and that Barbara had not spoken the truth. It is so easy for those who lie to imagine that another is lying! And is it impossible for such a one as Lady Ann to imagine that Barbara would not lie when she had a strong reason for doing so. She believed also that Richard had gotten into the house in order to learn things that might serve in the establishing of a claim as the firstborn son—despite the question of legitimacy.

"It will be much better if you keep silent concerning the report," she said. "I do not want the question stirred up. If the young man—or any young man, I mean—should claim the heirship, we must meet the issue as it ought to be met; till then, promise me you will be silent."

She needed time to think, for she feared in some way to compromise herself. And in any case, the longer the crisis could be postponed, the better her prospects!

"I will not promise anything," answered Barbara. "I dread making promises."

"Why?" asked Lady Ann, raising her eyebrows.

"Because promises have to be kept, and that is sometimes very difficult, and because sometimes you find you shouldn't have made them."

"But if you ought to make the promise," suggested Lady Ann.

"Then you must make it. But where there is no *ought*, I think it wrong to bind yourself. What right have you, when you don't know what may be wanted of you, to tie your own hands and feet?"

"Does friendship demand nothing? You are our guest!"

"One's friends may have conflicting interests!" said Barbara.

Lady Ann was becoming more and more convinced that Richard was at the root of the affair, and she hated him. What if he *was* the heir and it could be proved? The thought was sickening. With the greatest effort she kept up her facade of indifference before Barbara. How was she to assure herself concerning the fellow? How could she discover what he knew, and how much he could prove? She could not even think with that little savage sitting there, staring out of her wide eyes!

"My sweet Barbara," she said, "I am so much obliged to you for letting me know. I will not ask any promise from you. Only you must not unnecessarily bring trouble upon us. If the thing were talked about, some unprincipled lawyer would be sure to take it up and raise a hubbub, and thousands of ignorant honest folk would be duped of their money to enrich the rascal. I heard a distinguished judge once say in a similar case that even if the claimant *were* the real heir, he had no right to the property, having so long neglected the duties of it as to make it impossible to be certain of his identity. Such people are never of any service to the country. It is a wrong to all classes when a man without education succeeds to property. For one thing, he will always side with the tenants against the land. And what service can any such man render his country in Parliament? Without suitable training there can be no genuine right."

To all this Barbara had been paying little heed. She was revolving in her mind whether she ought to tell Richard what she had just heard. But she could come to no conclusion.

She rode all the way home thinking about it. If Richard could never claim an inheritance, it would be unfair to trouble him. But he might have a just claim; what then? She must seek counsel! But from whom? Not of her mother! And just as certainly not of her father! She had no grounds for trusting the judgment of either.

Having gotten rid of Miss Brown, she walked to the parsonage.

But she did not there find such a readiness to give advice as she had expected after she had told Wingfold her story.

"The issue is not my business," he said.

"Not!" returned the impetuous Barbara. "I thought you were interested in the young man! You told me the other day that he had seen you again and had a long talk with you."

"Yes, we had a nice talk. And of course I am interested in him, as I am in everyone. Tell me then, Miss Wylder: are you interested in the young man because he might have a claim to Sir Wilton's fortunes?"

"Certainly not!" answered Barbara with indignation.

"Then why should I be?" pursued the parson. "What is it to me? I am not a county magistrate. His person interests me, not his station or his title."

"I cannot understand you, Mr. Wingfold!" protested Barbara. "You say you are there for the people, yet you will not move to see right done!"

"I would move a long way to see that Mr. Tuke cared to do right: that is my business. It is not much to me, and nothing of my business, whether Mr. Tuke be rich or poor, a baron or a bookbinder; it is everything to me whether Mr. Tuke will be an honest fellow or not."

"But if he should prove to have a right to the property?"

"Then he ought to have the property. But it is not my business to discover or enforce the right. My business is to help the young man make little of the matter, whether he find himself the heir, or a much injured man through his deceived mother. Tell me whose servant I am."

"You are the servant of Jesus Christ."

"—Who said the servant must be as his master. Do you remember what he said when a man came asking to see justice done between him and his brother? He said, 'Man, who made me a judge and divider over you? Take heed and beware of covetousness.' My responsibility is to do as Jesus did, and to follow what he said—nothing more. It may be *your* business to see about it; I don't know; I rather doubt it. My advice would be to keep quiet a while longer, and see what will come. There appears no reason for hurry. The universe does not hang on the question of Richard's rights. Will it be much to you whether your friend go into the other world as the late heir, or the late owner of Mortgrange, or as the late son of John

Tuke, the bookbinder? Will the dead be moved one way or the other? In other words, is there any eternal difference between the two?"

22 The Parson's Counsel

It was a good thing for both Richard and Barbara that Barbara was now under other influences than Richard's. The more she saw of Mr. and Mrs. Wingfold, the more she felt she had come into a region of reality and life. Both of them understood that she was a rare girl and spoke as freely in front of her as if she had been a sister of their own age. And Barbara likewise spoke with total freedom to them, both of her past and her family, as well as her great desire to help Richard believe in God.

It was not her desire to see him "converted"; indeed, the word would have had little meaning to Barbara. Certain attempts at what is called conversion are but manifestations of greed for power over others; swellings of the ambition to propagate one's own creed and proselytize victoriously; hungerings to see self reflected in another convinced. In such efforts lie dangers as vulgar as the minds that make them, and love the excitement of them. But genuine love is far beyond such groveling delights.

Barbara was one who, so far as human eyes could see, had never required what is commonly termed conversion. She had but to go on, recognize, and do. She turned to the light by a holy will as well as holy instinct. She needed much instruction, and might yet have fierce battles to fight, but to change direction for such as Barbara must be to turn them the wrong way; for the whole energy of her being was in the direction of what was right. She needed but to be told a good thing—not *told that a thing was good*—and at once she received it—that is, obeyed it, the only way of receiving a truth. She responded immediately upon every reception of light, every expansion of true knowledge. She was essentially *of* the truth; therefore when she came into relation with such a soul as Wingfold, a soul so much more developed than herself, her life was fed from his and began to grow faster. For he taught her to know the eternal Man who bore witness to her Father, and Barbara became his child, the inheritor of the universe. Fortunately, her life had not been loaded to the ground with the degrading doctrines of a wrathful God whose so-called justice is perversely satisfied with the blood of the innocent for the punishment of the guilty. From the whole swarm of that brood of meager, incomplete teachings she was protected—by pure lack of what is generally regarded as a *religious education.* Such teaching is the mother of more tears in humble souls, and more presumption in the proud and selfish, than perhaps any other influence out of whose darkness God brings light. Neither ascetic nor mystic nor doctrinist of any sort, caring nothing for church or chapel or observance of any kind for its own sake, Barbara believed in God, and was coming to believe in Jesus Christ. And glad she was as she had never been before that there was such a person as Jesus Christ!

Wingfold never sought to influence her in any way concerning her workman-friend; he only sought to strengthen her in the truth.

One day when they were all three sitting together in the twilight, he said to his pupil:

"Now, Miss Wylder, don't try to convince the young man of anything by argument. If you succeeded, it would do no good. Opinion is all that can result from argument, and opinion concerning God—even right opinion—is of little value when it comes to *knowing* God. The god Richard denies is a being that could never exist. Talk to Richard, not of opinion, but of the God you love—the beautiful, the strong, the true, the patient, the forgiving, the loving. Let him feel God through your enthusiasm for him. You can't prove to him that there is a God. A god who could be proved would not be worth proving. Make his thoughts dwell on a God worth having. Wake the notion of God such as will draw him to wish there were such a God. Many religious people will tell you God is different from what I say. 'God is just!' said a carping theologian to me the other day. 'Yes,' I answered, 'and he cannot be pleased that you should call that justice which is injustice, and attribute it to him!' There are many who must die in ignorance of their heavenly Father's character, because they will not of their own selves judge what is right.

"Set in Richard's eye a God worth believing in, a God like the Son of God, and he will go out and look to see if such a God may be found. He will call upon him, and the God who is will hear and answer him. God is God to us not that we may prove that *he is*, but *that we may know him*; and when we know him, then we are with him, at home, at the heart of the universe, the heirs of all things.

"All this is foolishness, I know, to the dull soul that cares only for things that can be proved. 'You cannot prove to me that you have a father,' says the blind sage, reasoning with the little child. 'Why should I prove it?' answers the child. 'I am sitting on his knee! If I could prove it, that would not make you see him; that would not make you happy like me! You do not care about my father, or you would not stand there disputing; you would feel about until you found him.' If a thing be true in itself, it is not capable of proof; and that man is in the higher condition who is able to believe it as it is. If there is a higher power than intellect, something that goes deeper, causing and even including our intellect, if there be a creative power of which our intellect is but a faint reflex, then the child of that power, the one who acknowledges and loves and obeys that power, will be the one to understand it.

"Men accept a thousand things without proof every day, and a thousand things may be perfectly true and have no proof. But if a man cannot be sure of a thing, does that automatically mean it is false? Neither can any man prove God's existence to be false. There is no proof of the intellect available in either direction. The very chance that a good thing *may* be true is a huge reason for an honest and continuous and unending search. But the final question is always this: Have you acted, or rather, are you acting according to the conscience which is the one guide to truth?"

"But," said Barbara, "perhaps the man would say that we see such suffering in the world, that the being who made it cannot possibly be both strong and good, otherwise he would not allow it. Richard has said that very thing to me."

"He might be both strong and good, yet have some reason for allowing it, or even causing it, which those who suffer will themselves one day see. For the infliction of suffering can be to greater purpose, though many cannot see that. A year ago my little boy displeased me horribly by something he did. People say, 'Children will be children.' But I see little consolation in that. They're made to be good children, just as men are made to be good men. Without telling you what he did, all I will say is that he did a mean thing. I told him I must whip him; that I could not bear doing it, but that I would rather even kill him and be hanged for it than that he should be a damned, mean, contemptible little rascal. I imagine that sounds awful, but—"

"Not in the least," said Barbara. "I like a man to curse what is bad and go down on his knees to what is good."

"Well, what do you think the little fellow said?—'I will be good, Papa!' he cried. 'Please don't be hanged for my naughtiness! Whip me and make me good!' "

"And then you couldn't do it?"

"I cried," said Wingfold, almost crying again as he said it. "I couldn't help it. The child took out his little pocket-handkerchief and dried my eyes, and then prepared himself for the spanking. And I whipped him as I never had before, and hope in God shall never have to do again. When it was over and I sat holding him, both of us with tears in our eyes, he said, 'I will try never to make you cry again, Papa.' And ever since then I have been thinking about the suffering in the world. I don't like pain a whit better than any other person, and I don't bear it nearly as well as Helen. But it doesn't bother me in the least—in brain and heart, I mean—that God sends it.

"After whipping my son, I knew that the tears the Lord wept over Jerusalem were not only wept by him, but by the Father as well. Whoever says that God cannot suffer does not understand. God *can* weep, and weeps more painful tears than ours; for he is God and we are his little ones. The suffering we see around us hurts God more than it hurts us, or even more than it hurts the man or woman upon whom it falls. But he hates things that most men think nothing of, and will send any suffering upon them rather than have them continue indifferent to them. Men say, 'We don't care about being good!' but God says, 'I know my own obligations, and you shall not be bad as long as there are any resources left in the Godhead.' I know that most mothers in my congregation would call me a cruel father after hearing what I just have told you. They would rather have me weak, and love my child less. They would rather their own child should be foul in the soul than be made clean through suffering. But I also know that they do not see how ugly is evil. Tell the tale your own way to your workman-friend, and may God help him to understand it!"

"I am glad you spanked the darling," said Barbara. "I shall love him more than ever."

"You should see how he loves his father!" said Helen.

Barbara rose to go.

"You'll be on your watch," said Wingfold, "for any chance of me serving your mother?"

"I will," replied Barbara.

The next morning she got on Miss Brown and rode to the forge, where Simon always made her welcome. She knew that Richard was to be there. They left Miss Brown in the smithy and went for a walk together; Barbara was careful to follow the parson's advice. Their talk was mostly about her life in New Zealand. Now that she knew God more, and believed more in him, she was able to communicate long-vague feelings about her own history with more definite shape. She understood herself better, and was better able to make Richard understand her. And in Richard, by degrees, through the sympathy of affection, was growing the notion of a God it would not be hard to believe in. But he had not yet come to long that he should exist, or to desire him. His hour was not yet come.

Naturally his manners were growing more refined from his relations with the gracious, brave, sympathetic, unconventional girl, so strong yet so gentle, so capable in indignation, so full of love. He was gradually developing the pure humanity that lay beneath the rough artisan. He was, in a word, becoming what in the kingdom of heaven every man must be—a gentleman, and more than a gentleman.

All this time Barbara was pulled in two ways: for Richard's

sake she would have him heir to Mortgrange; for her own she would be rid of the shadow of having sought the baron in the bookbinder. But more and more the confidence of Lady Ann gained force with her—that Richard was not the heir. At first she had greatly doubted her, but now she said to herself: "She could hardly be mistaken, and she *cannot* have lied." In consequence she grew yet more free, more at home with Richard. She listened to all he had to tell her. Thus they learned from each other, subtly and subconsciously—she from him intellectually, he from her spiritually.

They strolled together in the field behind the smithy, within sight of the cottage, for an hour or so; then hearing from the smithy the impatient stamping of Miss Brown, and fearing she might give the old man trouble, they hastened back. Richard brought out the mare. Barbara sprang on a big stone by the door, and mounted without his help. She went straight for Wylder Hall.

As they had walked up and down the field, Arthur Lestrange had passed on foot some distance away; he saw them, and went home in a quiet, though heated, anger.

23 Lady Ann

It would have been difficult for Arthur himself to say whether rage or contempt was stronger in his heart when he saw the lady he thought he loved walking in a field, back and forth, in close talk with the bookbinder. She had never walked like that with *him*! She clearly preferred the bookbinder's society to his—and made no secret of it!

What did Barbara mean by it? Scorn alone kept Arthur from hating Richard. As for Barbara, he attributed her disregard of propriety, and the very possibility of her being interested in such a person, to the mode of life in the half-savage country where she had been born and reared. The worst of his torment was that Richard was a good-looking fellow. And yet he was a mere working-man—what *could* be her intent?

The girl was uncontrollable. She would pay attention to nothing he might say. How could such a bewitching creature so lack refinement? If her face showed itself in London, she would be the belle of the season. If he did not secure her, some poor duke would pounce on her!

What was he to do? He would only bring scorn on himself by appearing jealous of the tradesman. The idea of her being in love with the fellow was preposterous! The notion was an insult! He *must* put a stop to it! He must send the man away. It would be a pity for the library. It was beginning to look beautiful, and would soon have been the most distinguished in the county. But there were other bookbinders! And what did the library matter! But she would be sure to suspect why the fellow was sent packing and might take offense. She might never enter the house again. Therefore, he must leave the thing alone—for the present! But he would be on his guard!

While the son was thus desiring riddance of the man he had brought into the house, the mother was pondering the same thing. Should the man remain in the house or leave it? That was the question with her also. And if they asked him to leave, what would be the pretext? She was growing more and more uncomfortable with the possibilities.

The thing was, of course, a conspiracy to supplant the true heir! If Sir Wilton had kept to his own rank and made a suitable match, none of this misery would have come upon them. Lady Ann's god was the head of the English aristocracy, and a baseborn illegitimate could not, in the nature of things divinely ordained, have the same rights as her son. An age-long process of degeneration had been going on in her race, and she was the result; she was well-born and well bred for feeling nothing except herself. How fearful that through the generations the body may go on perfecting while the heart goes on degenerating! Lady Ann was indeed born capable of less than most; but had she attempted to do the little she could, she would not have been where she was: she would have been toiling up the hill of truth, with her success to be measured, like the widow's mite, by what she had not.

All her thoughts were now occupied with the *rights* of her son and, through him, of the family. Sir Wilton had been for some time ailing, and when he went, they would be at the mercy of any other heir than Arthur, just as miserably whether he were the true heir or an imposter. Lady Ann cared nothing for the right. The law of the land was to be respected, no doubt, but your own family—most of all when land was concerned—was worthier still!

The best thing would be to rid the place of the bookbinder—but how? She would rather remain ignorant whether he was legitimate or not, whether, in fact, he was her husband's son. She could not consult Sir Wilton. Arthur and he got on quite as well as could be expected of father and son—their differences never came to much. But, on the other hand, Sir Wilton had a demoniacal pleasure in frustrating anyone he didn't like. Therefore it would be far better that he should have no hint, especially from her, of what was in the air.

Thinking over her talk with Barbara, she could not be certain that Richard believed the report himself, or that he had incited Barbara to take his part. In any case it was better to get rid of him. It was dangerous to have him in the house. He might be spending his night trumping up evidence! At any moment he might appeal to Sir Wilton as his father. But even worse, he would be unable to prove anything right off, and if her husband would but act like a man, they might impede the attempt beyond the possibility of its success.

She was all but confident the child was not already baptized when stolen from Mortgrange. That fact must have its weight with Providence! God would never favor the succession of such a one to the title and the estate—he would never take the part of one who had not been baptized! She would dispute his identity to the last, and assert him as an imposter. Her duty to society demanded that she should not give in!

Suddenly she remembered the description her husband had given her of the ugliness of the infant; this man was decidedly handsome! Then she remembered that Sir Wilton had told her of a membrane between certain of his fingers—horrible creature! She must examine the imposter!

Arthur was very moody at dinner; his mother feared some echo of the same report as caused her anxiety had reached him, and took the first opportunity of questioning him. But neither of Lady Ann's sons had learned to have such faith in their mother as to tell her their troubles. Arthur would confess nothing. She, in turn, was far too prudent to disclose what was in her mind: there was no telling what he might do in the folly of his youth.

The same afternoon Richard was mending the torn title of a copy of *Fox's Book of Martyrs.* Vixen had forgotten her former fright and her evil courage had returned. Opening the door of the library so softly that Richard heard nothing, she stole up behind him and gave his elbow a great push just as, with the sharpest of penknives, he was paring the edge of a piece of old paper, to patch the title. The penknife slid along the bit of glass he was paring upon and cut his other hand. The blood spouted, and some of it fell upon the title page. Richard was angry: it was an irremediable catastrophe, for the paper was too weak to bear any washing. He grabbed the child, intending again to carry her from the room and lock the door. Then first Vixen saw what she had done and was seized with horror—not because she had hurt the bookbinder, but because she could not stand the sight of blood. She gave one wavering scream and dropped to the floor.

Richard thought she was pretending a faint, but when he picked her up he saw that she was unconscious. He laid her on a couch, rang the bell, and asked the man who answered it to take the child to her governess. The man saw blood on the child's dress, and when he reached the schoolroom with her, informed the governess that she had had an accident in the library. Miss Malliver, with one of her accomplished shrieks, dispatched him to tell Lady Ann. In a few moments Vixen came to and told a confused story of how the man had frightened her. Miss Malliver, who would hardly have been sorry had Vixen's throat been cut, rose in wrath and would have swooped down the stairs upon Richard.

"Leave him to me, Malliver," said Lady Ann, and went down

the stairs. She entered the library and saw Richard's hand tied up in his handkerchief.

"What have you done to yourself, Mr. Tuke?" she said, making a motion to the wounded hand.

"Nothing of any consequence, My Lady," he answered, rising and standing before her. "I was using a very sharp knife and it slipped into my hand. I hope Miss Victoria is better."

"There is nothing much the matter with her," answered her ladyship. "The sight of blood always makes her faint."

"Would you mind showing me the wound?" she continued. "I am something of a surgeon."

To her disappointment he persisted that it was nothing. Lady Ann was foiled. Why should the man be so unwilling to show his hands?

"Your work must be very interesting," she said.

"I am fond of it, My Lady," he answered, wondering at her friendliness but ready to meet any kindness. "If I had a fortune left me I would find it hard to drop it. There is nothing like work—and books—for enjoying life."

"I daresay you are right. But go on with your work. I have heard so much about it from Miss Wylder that I should like to see you at it."

"I am sorry, My Lady, but I shall be fit for next to nothing for a day or two because of this hand. I dare not attempt going on with what I am now doing."

"Is it very painful? You ought to have it seen to. I will send for Mr. Hurst."

He assured her that it was the quality of his work he was thinking of, not his hand, and added that, if Mr. Lestrange had no objection, he would take a short holiday.

"Then you would like to go home!" said her ladyship, thinking that it would be easy then to write and tell him not to come back—if only Arthur could be persuaded to do it.

"I would like to go to my grandfather's for a few days," answered Richard.

This was by no means what Lady Ann desired, but she did not see how to oppose it.

"Well, perhaps you had better go," she said.

"If you please, My Lady," rejoined Richard, "I must see Mr. Lestrange first. I cannot go without his permission."

"I will speak to my son about it," answered Lady Ann and went away, feeling that Richard would make a dangerous enemy. She did not hate him; she only regarded him as an adverse force to be encountered. In the meantime, the only thing clear was that he had better be removed from the neighborhood! Sir Wilton had hardly seen the young man. If there was anything about him capable of rousing old memories, it was best it should not have the chance! Sir Wilton was not fond of books, and it could be no great pleasure to him to have the library set to rights. As it was, he was annoyed at being kept out of it, for he liked to smoke his cigar there, and shuddered at the presence of a workingman except in the open air. She was certain he would not feel aggrieved if the project were abandoned halfway through. The only person she feared might oppose Tuke's departure was Arthur.

24 Dismissal

She went to find her son, told him what had happened to the young man, and proposed to him that he should go to his grandfather's for a few days. *Send him where he and Barbara would be constantly meeting!* thought Arthur. *I cannot have him go there! I would rather give up the library altogether!* There should be no more bookbinding at Mortgrange, Arthur decided. He would send Richard the books in London; he should have the work all the same, but not at Mortgrange!

"I am rather tired of him," he answered his mother. "We have had quite enough of him; the work seems to be taking too long, and this is a good opportunity for getting rid of him. I am rather sorry, for it was good for the books, but I can just as well send them to

London and have them done there. The man has been making himself disagreeable, it seems, and I do not want to quarrel with him. It is far the best thing simply to let him go. I liked him at first; perhaps I showed it more than was good for the fellow, so that he began to presume upon it."

This was far better than Lady Ann had expected. Arthur went at once to Richard, and told him they found it inconvenient to have the library used as a workshop any longer, and must make a change.

Richard was glad to hear it, thinking they meant to give him another room, and said he could work just as well anywhere else: he just needed a dry room with a fireplace. Arthur told him he had arranged for what would be more agreeable to both parties—namely, that he should do the work at home. It would cost more, but he was prepared for that. He might go as soon as he pleased, and they would arrange by letter how the books should be sent—so many at a time.

Richard suspected something more behind his dismissal than the affair with Miss Vixen, but he was too proud to ask for an explanation. Mr. Lestrange was completely within his rights, but he felt aggrieved nevertheless and was sorry to have to leave the library. He would probably never again have the chance of restoring such a fine library—working among such books had been a rare delight! He could always make a living, but this had been a pleasure!

And he would be sorry not to see more of Mr. Wingfold, a man unlike any clergyman he had ever seen. Richard had indeed known nothing of any other clergyman out of the pulpit; and most are less human, therefore less divine, in the pulpit than out of it.

But his far worse sorrow was leaving Miss Wylder. The thought brought a keen pain to his heart. That she was miles above him was no reason why he should not love her. His low position, in fact, and the absence of any thought in the direction of marriage left but the wider room for the love infinite. In a man capable of loving in such fashion, there is no limit to the growth of love. Richard thought his soul was full, but a live soul can never be full; it is always growing larger and always being filled.

Almost like one stunned, he went about his preparations for departure.

"You will go by the first train in the morning," said Arthur, happening to meet him in the stable yard, where Richard had gone to see if Miss Brown was in her usual stall. "I have told Robert to take you and your tools to the station in the spring cart."

"Thank you," returned Richard. "I shall not require the cart. I will leave the house tonight and shall send for my things tomorrow morning. I have them almost ready now."

"You cannot go to London tonight!"

"I am aware of that, sir. I will not be going to London for a few days."

"Then where are you going? I wish to know."

"That is my business, sir."

Arthur felt a shadow cross him—almost like fear: he had but driven Richard to his grandfather's and perhaps made an enemy of him besides. And he could not shake the thought that what he had done to Richard was not quite the thing for a gentleman to do. His trouble was not that he had wronged Richard, but that he had wronged himself, had not acted like his ideal of himself. He did not think of what was right, but of what befitted a gentleman. Such a man is in danger of doing many things unbefitting a gentleman, for the measure of a gentleman is not a man's ideal of himself.

His uneasiness grew as day after day went by and Barbara did not appear at Mortgrange. He was not aware that Richard saw no more of her than himself. For Richard waited there a week, but no Barbara came to the smithy. He could not endure the thought of going away without seeing her once more. He must at least once thank her for what she had done for him. And he must let her know why he had left Mortgrange.

Then he thought of the clergyman. He would go and say good-bye, and possibly from him he might hear something of her.

Wingfold caught sight of him approaching the house and opened the door to him. Taking him to his study, he asked him to sit down.

"I came," said Richard, "to thank you for your kindness to me and to ask about Miss Wylder. Not having seen her for a long time,

I was afraid she might be ill. I am going away."

There was a tremor in Richard's voice he was unaware of.

"I am sorry to say you are not likely to see Miss Wylder," he answered. "Her mother is ill."

"I hardly thought to see her, sir. Is her mother very ill?"

"Yes, very ill," answered Wingfold.

"With anything infectious?"

"No. Her complaint is just exhaustion—mental and nervous: a breakdown, if you will. She is too weak to think, and can't even feed herself. I am afraid her daughter will be worn out waiting on her before long. She devotes herself to her mother with a great spirit and energy. She never seems tired, but it is hardly any wonder she should be in good spirits: it is the first time in her life, she says, that she has been allowed to be of any use to her mother. And the woman is suffering no pain, and that makes a great difference. But more than anything, her mother has grown tender to her, and so grateful. And her father has grown kinder to her mother—a thing previously unknown. But what is this you tell me about going away? The library cannot be finished!"

"No, sir," answered Richard; "the library is left in mid-ocean of decay. I don't know why they have dismissed me. The only thing clear is that they want to be rid of me. What I have done I can't imagine. There is a little girl of the family—"

Richard told how Vixen had behaved to him from the first and what had happened as a result.

"But," he concluded, "I do not think it can be that. I should like to know what it is."

"Then wait," said Wingfold. "If we only wait long enough, every reason will come out. You know I believe we are meant to go on living forever; and I believe the business of eternity is to bring grand hidden things out into the light.—But I am deeply sorry you're going."

"I don't see why you should be, sir," answered Richard sincerely, his look and tone conveying nothing of the rudeness which seemed to be in his words.

"Because I like you, and feel sure we should understand each other if only we had time," replied the parson. "It's a wonderful thing to come upon one who knows what you mean. It's just like heaven. I hope you don't think I'm talking shop; I can't help it."

"I should never say you talked shop. I don't think you would say I was talking shop if I went on about the beauties of a Grolier binding. You would know I was not talking from love of profit, but love of beauty."

"Thank you. You are a fair man, and that is even more than an honest man. I don't speak from love of religion. I don't know that I do love religion."

"I don't understand you now."

"I'm very fond of a well-bound book; I should like all my new books bound in levant morocco. But I don't *care* overly much about it. I could do well enough without any binding at all."

"Of course you could, and so could I! Or any man that cared for the books themselves."

"Exactly! In the same way I don't care about religion much, but I could not live without my Father in heaven. I don't believe anybody can live without him."

"I see," said Richard.

He thought he saw, but he did not see, and could not help smiling in his heart as he said to himself, *I have lived a good many years without him!*

Wingfold saw the shadow of the smile and blamed himself for having spoken too soon.

"When do you go?" he asked.

"I think I shall go tomorrow. I am at my grandfather's now."

"If I can be of use to you, let me know."

"I will, sir; and I thank you heartily. There's nothing a man is so grateful for as friendliness."

"The obligation is mutual," said Wingfold.

25 The Wylders

A new experience had come to Mrs. Wylder. Her passion over the death of her son, her prolonged contention with her husband, her protest against him whom she called the Almighty, and the public consequences of the same, had all combined and resulted in a sudden sinking of the vital forces of her life. She who had once been a burning fiery furnace was now like a heap of cooling ashes on a hearth. She had never before known what it was to feel unfit. Power and strength had so constantly seemed part of her very self that she had never thought of them. But now suddenly they were drained away from her.

Her Bab was now the mother's one delight. Whereas her love for her lost twin had been mostly partisanship, defense, and opposition, her love for Barbara was tenderness and no pride. Finding the castle of her self, which she had regarded as impregnable, now crumbling under the shot of the enemy, she found herself defenseless, and thus discovered refuge in her little maid, the daughter she had for so long ignored. The loss of all that the world counts *first things* is a thousandfold repaid in the waking to higher need. It proves the presence of the divine in the lower good, that its loss is so potent. A man may send his gaze over the clear heaven and suspect no God. But when the stifling cloud comes down, folds itself about him, shuts from him the expanse of the universe, he begins to long for a hand, a sign, some shadow of presence.

Mrs. Wylder was not that far yet, but she had sought refuge in love; and what is the love of child, or mother, or dog, but the love of God shining through another being? The one important result of her illness, finding refuge in the love of her daughter, brought her to love Barbara. The next point in her eternal growth would be to love the God who made the child she loved, and whose love shone upon her through the child. By nature Mrs. Wylder was a strong woman whom passion made weak, hardening her will into selfish determination, then pulling it into helpless obstinacy. Where the temple of God has no windows, earthquakes must sometimes come to tear off the roof that sunlight may enter. Her earthquake had come, and Barbara's mother lay broken so that the spirit of her daughter might enter the soul of her mother—and with it the Spirit of him who, in the heart of her daughter, made her who she was.

Her illness had lasted a month, when one day her husband, at Barbara's request, came to see her. She feebly put out her hand, and for a moment the divine child in the man opened its heavenly eyes. He took the offered hand kindly, faltering a gentle-sounding commonplace or two, and left her happier, with a strange little bird fluttering in his own heart.

Mrs. Wylder began to recover, but the recovery was a long one. As soon as she thought her well enough, Barbara told her that Mr. Wingfold had been to ask about her almost every day and asked whether she would not like to see him. Her mother was in a quiet condition, noncombative, involving no real betterment, only a weakening of the will to fight. But such a condition gives opportunity for the good and loving to be felt.

The sufferer resembles a child that has not yet been severely tempted. With recovery come stronger claims by the powers of God. But these claims will be resisted by old habits, resuming their force as physical and mental health returns—and then comes the tug of war. For no one can be saved without the will being supreme in the matter, without choosing to resist the wrong and do the right. Wingfold never built much on bed-repentance. But he welcomed the fresh opportunity for a beginning. He knew that pain and sickness do clean some dirt from the windows looking toward the infinite, and that the unknown world from which we came does sometimes look in, waking the unconscious memories that lie in every child born into the world. God is the God of patience, and waits and waits for the child who keeps him waiting and will not open the door.

Wingfold went to see Mrs. Wylder, but took care to press nothing upon her. He let her give him the lead. She spoke of her weakness, and the parson drew out her moan. She praised her Barbara, and the parson praised her again in words that opened the mother's eyes to new beauties in her daughter. She mentioned her weariness, and the parson spoke of the fields and soft wind and the yellow shine of the buttercups in the grass. Her heart was gently drawn to the man whose eyes were so keen, whose voice was so mellow and strong, and whose words were so lovely and sweet, saying the things that were in her own heart but would not come out.

One day he proposed to read something, and she consented. I will not say what he read. But he was successful in interesting Mrs. Wylder, which was no wonder, for she had a strong brain as well as a big heart. More than half her faults came of an indignant sense of wrong. She had passionately loved her husband once, but he had soon ceased even the pretense of returning her affection.

After a fierce struggle against the lessons life would have her taught, a struggle that continued into her fortieth year, she was now at length a pupil in another school, where her bed was the schoolroom, the book of Quiet her first study. Her two attendants were a clergyman and her own daughter, and her one teacher God himself; in that schoolroom the world began to open to her a little. Wingfold had no equal in being able to make another think without seeming to aim at that specifically. He called out the thoughts lurking in men's souls, and set them to dealing with those thoughts, not with him. Many were slow to discover that he was a divine musician, playing upon the holy strings of their hearts. They thought the tunes came alive in their own air—as indeed they did, only another hand woke them. To work thus, he had to lay bare his own feelings; where it was brotherly to show feeling, he counted it unchristian to hide it.

Barbara was happy all day long. She had learned from Wingfold that the bookbinder was gone, but was at the time too busy to question him about the reasons. Till her mother was well, it was enough to know that Richard had wanted to see her, doubtless to tell her all about it. She often thought of him, what he had done for her, and what she had tried to do for him; she was certain he would one day believe in God. She did not suspect any quarrel with the people at Mortgrange. She thought perhaps the secret concerning him had come out and he did not choose to remain in a house where he was known but not acknowledged. As soon as she was able she would go and hear of him from his grandfather. There was no hurry. She would certainly see him again before long. And he would be sure to write. It did not occur to her that a man in his position would hardly venture to contact her again without some renewed approach on her part. Thus, for a long time she was not uneasy.

How is it that a child begins to be good? Upon what fulcrum rests the knife-edge of change? As indistinguishable is the moment in which the turn takes place, equally perplexing to keenest investigation is the part of the being in which the renovation begins. Who shall analyze repentance? You cannot see it coming! Before you know it, there it is, and the man is no more what he was. His life is all at once upon other lines. The wind has blown! We saw not where it came from or where it went, but the new birth is there. It began in the spiritually infinitesimal, where all beginnings are. Then it grew, till one day the outer shell was cracked.

Meanwhile, the change was begun in Mrs. Wylder. But the tug of war was still to come.

Lady Ann had not once been to see her since first calling when she arrived. Naturally, she did not take to her. In the eyes of Lady Ann, Mrs. Wylder was a vulgar, arrogant, proud, fierce woman; she felt in every way her superior. Mrs. Wylder was not particularly annoyed that Lady Ann did not call a second time. She did not care enough to mind; neither she nor her daughter felt the least deference to Lady Ann's exalted position.

But now that danger, not to say ruin, appeared to loom on the horizon, Lady Ann must, for the sake of her son, wronged by his father's indiscretion, leave nothing to chance! Arthur had come to Wylder Hall repeatedly in the last month, but Barbara had not seen him. Therefore, she would go herself and pay some court to the young heiress. She was anxious to learn whether the girl's absence from Mortgrange was merely because of her mother's condition, or because she was angry with Arthur.

Barbara received her heartily and they talked a little, Lady Ann imagining herself very pleasing: she rarely condescended to make herself agreeable, and thus measured her success by her exertion. She found Barbara in such good spirits that she pronounced her heartless not to have visited them for so long. She begged her to leave her mother for an hour or two now and then and ride over to Mortgrange. Incessant care for the ill would injure her own health, Lady Ann said, and health was essential to beauty. Barbara protested mildly, saying that she was the only person fit to nurse her mother. When her ladyship, for once oblivious of her manners, grew importunate, Barbara flatly refused.

"You must pardon me, Lady Ann," she said. "I cannot and will not leave my mother."

Then the notion occurred to Lady Ann that it might be wise in the future to make a little more of the mother to whom the girl seemed so devoted. But meeting Mr. Wylder in the avenue as she left, and stopping her carriage to speak to him, she changed her mind and resolved to curry favor with the husband instead of the wife. Up to now she had scarcely seen Mr. Wylder, and knew about him only by unfavorable hearsay; but she was charmed with him now, and drew from him a promise to go and dine at Mortgrange.

Bab went singing back to her mother, never passing a servant, male or female, without a kind word. If asked what made her so happy, she would have answered that she had nothing to make her unhappy; and there was more philosophy in the answer than may at first appear. For certainly the normal condition of humanity is happiness; simply the absence of anything to make us unhappy should be enough to make us happy.

Mr. Wylder went and dined with Sir Wilton and Lady Ann. The latter did her best to please him and was successful. It had always been an annoyance to Mr. Wylder that his wife was not a lady. In the bush he did not feel it, but now he saw the many ways she was inferior. It consoled him to hear Lady Ann praise his daughter, her beauty, her manners, her wit—praise her for everything. She hinted that it would be of the greatest benefit to Barbara to have the next season in London. The girl had met nobody and might, in her innocence, being such an eager and warmhearted creature, with her powers of discrimination but little cultivated, make unsuitable friendships that would lead to entanglement. On the other hand, well chaperoned, she might well become one of the first ladies in the county. She took care to let Barbara's father know—or think he knew—that, although her son would be only a baron, he would be rich, for the estates were in excellent condition and free of encumbrance; there was, she hinted, a fine chance of enlarging the property, neighboring land being on the market at a low price.

Mr. Wylder had indeed hoped for a higher match, but Lady Ann, being an earl's daughter, had influence with him. The remaining twin was so delicate that it was very doubtful he would live long enough to succeed to Wylder Hall. If he did not, and land could be bought to connect the two properties of Mortgrange and Wylder, the estate would be far the finest in the county; when, as Lady Ann implied, means might be used to draw down the favor of Providence in the form of a patent of nobility.

To Lady Ann, London was the center of courtship. Arthur, she said to herself, would show himself to better advantage there than in the country. The place where she had been nearest to falling in love herself was a ballroom: the heat had apparently half-thawed her.

Mr. Wylder thought Lady Ann was right, and the best thing for Barbara would be to go to London; Lady Ann would accompany her, and she would doubtless be the belle of the season. Her chance would be none the worse of making a better match than Arthur Lestrange. Who could tell whom she might meet?

Oddly enough, no similar reflection occurred to Lady Ann; far more eligible men than her son might well be drawn to such a bit of sunshine as Barbara. But what in Barbara was most attractive, Lady Ann was least capable of appreciating.

26 London

Richard got out of his third-class carriage into the first of the London fogs of the autumn. He took his case in one hand and his bag of tools in the other, and went out of the great dim station to look for an omnibus. How dull the streets were! Into the far dark, the splendor of Barbara had vanished. Various memories of her—a look, a smile, a dress, a laugh, a certain button half-torn from her riding habit, the feeling of her foot in his hand as he lifted her to Miss Brown's back—would enter his heart unbidden. The way she drove the nails into her mare's hoof; the way she put her hand on his shoulder as she slid from the saddle; the commanding love with which she spoke to the great animal, and the way Miss Brown received it; the sweet coaxing respect she showed his blacksmith grandfather—a thousand attendant shadows glided in procession through his mind and heart. He forgot the bus and went tramping through the streets with his bags—he had sent home his heavier things earlier—thinking of Barbara. She came into his world as a star ascends above the horizon of the world, raising him as she rose. She was a power within him. He could not believe in God, but neither could he think belief in such a God as she believed in degrading.

Everything, he said to himself, *depends on the kind of God one believes in.* He wondered how many ideas of God there might be, for everyone who believed in him must have a different idea. *Some of them must be nearer right than others,* he thought; but he had not the slightest perception that he was beginning to entertain the notion of a real God. For he saw that the ideas of the best men and women must be similar and must point to some object rather than an empty center. He had not yet come to consider the fact that the *very best* of men said he knew God, that God was like himself only greater, that whoever would do what he told him should know God and know that he spoke the truth about him, that he had come from him to tell the world that he was truth and love. Richard had started on a path leading toward those conclusions, yet all was at this point vaguest speculation.

He was far from perceiving that no man is a believer, no matter what else he may do, except he give his will, his life to the Master. No man is a believer who does not obey him. Thousands talk about him for every one who believes in him in this sense. Thousands will do what the priests and scribes, their parsons and pastors, say for every one who searches to find what he says and to obey it—

who takes his orders from the Lord himself, and not from other men. A man must come to the Master, listen to his word, and do what he says. Then he will come to know God, and know that he knows him.

Richard did not once ask himself, *Does she love me?* He said, *She cares for me; she is good to me. I wish I believed as she does that I might hope to meet her again in the house of God.*

It was Saturday night, and he had to go through a weekly market—a hurrying, pushing, loitering, jostling crowd, gathered thick about the butchers' and fishmongers' shops, the greengrocers' barrows, and the trays upon wheels with things laid out for sale. Suddenly a face flashed upon him and disappeared. He was not sure that it was Alice's, but it suggested Alice so strongly that he turned and tried to overtake it. Slowed down by his luggage, however, which caught upon the hundreds of legs, he soon saw the attempt was hopeless. Then painfully he remembered that he did not have her address and had no way to communicate with her. He still longed to know why she had left him without a word, and what her avoidance of him meant. Even more, he desired to help her.

But Barbara was her friend. Barbara knew her address! He would ask her to send it to him! It would be a reason to write her! His heart gave a bound. Who could tell, maybe she might please to send him the fan-wind of a letter now and then, keeping the door, just a chink of it, open between them. He walked the rest of the way with a gladder heart; he was no longer without a future—there was something to do, something to wait for! Days are dreary unto death which wrap no hope in their misty folds.

His father and mother received him with more warmth than he had ever known them to show. They were in good spirits about him, for they had all the time been receiving news of him and Barbara, with not a word of Alice, from old Simon. Jane's heart swelled with the ambition that her boy should as a workingman gain the love of a well-born girl.

Mrs. Tuke loved the boy she had always considered her son, but she was constantly haunted with a vague uneasiness—about what, Richard could never persuade her to disclose. This undefined uneasiness, however, was sufficiently powerful to repress the show of her love, and to make her go to church regularly. Her pleasure in going was not great, but she was nonetheless troubled that Richard did not care about going. She sojourned still in the land of bullocks and goats—she went to church with the idea that she was doing something for God in going. Until we know God, we seek to obey him by doing things he neither commands nor cares about; while the things for which he sent his Son, we regard of little or no importance.

Mrs. Tuke noted that whenever Richard was quiet, a shadow settled on his face and he looked lost and sad; it occurred to her that of course he must miss his Barbara. In the evening he asked his mother if she would not like him to go to church with her, feeling that in church he would be nearer Barbara, for he knew that now she went often. But alas, while he sat there he felt himself drifting farther and farther from her. The foolish statements of the preacher made him regret he had gone. They awoke all his old feelings of repulsion. There was no ring of reality, no spark of divine fire, no common sense. The clergyman was not a hypocrite in any sense. He was in some measure even a devout man. But there was no glow, no enthusiasm in the man—neither could there be, with the notions he held. His God suggested a police magistrate more than a loving Father. Richard would gladly have left the place and wandered about outside until the service was over; only for the sake of his mother did he sit out the misery.

He had written his letter to Barbara; a long time of waiting followed, but no waiting brought any answer. Lady Ann had dropped a hint, and Mr. Wylder had picked it up—a hint subtle, but forcible enough to make him keep an outlook on the letters that came for his daughter. When Richard's arrived, it did not look to him that of a gentleman. Where his own family was concerned Mr. Wylder was not the most delicate of men: he opened the letter and found in it what he called a rigmarole of poetry and theology. "Confound the fellow!" he said to himself. Lady Ann did well to warn him. There should be no more of this! The scatterbrain girl took after her mother!

He never said a word about the letter. He feared the little girl he pretended to protect and did not want to rouse her against him.

So Richard's letter went into the fire and Bab never read the petition of her poor friend.

The next morning Richard went to the shop and took up the first job that fell to his hand. He told his father of Lestrange's proposal about the library, and Tuke counseled to accept it.

Richard made no objection. He would gladly keep the door open to any place where Barbara's shadow might fall. But when they wrote to arrange the thing, no notice was taken of the letter, and a gulf seemed to yawn between the houses.

Thus began a dreary time for Richard. Now, for the first time, he began to know what unhappiness was. But as dead as his work seemed, he could not remain indoors a moment after it was done. Whatever the weather, out he went, heedless of cold or wind or rain. His mother grew worried about him, attributed his unrest to despair, and feared she might have to tell him the secret source of her uneasiness. But she longed to avoid breaking up the happiness of seeing him about the house. And he would most certainly leave, once he was apprised of the truth. It would be so much easier to go on as they were doing. A day would come when she would have to part with him, but that day was not yet. She dreaded uncaging her secret, dreaded the changes it would work.

Her husband left the matter entirely to her. It was her business, he said, from the first; he would let it be hers to the last.

Richard soon began to recover both from the separation and from his disappointment about the letter. But nothing shook his faith in Barbara; he was sure that whatever might be the cause of her silence, it came from no fault in her.

And soon he found that he now looked upon the world with eyes from which a veil had been withdrawn. Barbara gone, Mother Earth came close to comfort her child. He had learned much since he had gone to the country. He had gone nearer to nature, and now that Barbara was gone, the memories of nature came nearer to him: he remembered her and was glad. Soon he began to find that, both with regard to nature and those whom we love, absence is, for very nearness, often better than the presence itself. Nature had always been to him an abstraction; now it gradually began to dawn upon him that the things about him wore meanings. Thoughts clothed in beautiful forms were everywhere about him, over his head, under his feet, in his heart; and as often as anything brought him pleasure, either through memory or in present vision, it brought Barbara, too.

As his thoughts progressed along these paths, the personhood of God stole gradually upon him, not from anything he had heard at church, but chiefly as a result of his association with Wingfold and Barbara, with nature now working on him in their absence. If God were a person, an individual, and if he loved individual humanity in return—ah, he would be a God to be believed in! Barbara believed that such a God lived all about and in us! Mr. Wingfold said he was too great to prove, too near to see, but the greater and nearer, the more fit to be loved!

The God Barbara believed in was like Jesus Christ, not at all like the God his mother believed in. Jesus was someone who could be loved. He was gentle and cared for individuals. And he said he loved the Father! And how could such a one as he be the Son of any but an equally kind, equally gentle, equally loving Father? Yet Richard's eyes saw such disharmony in the world around him. Nature herself could be mild one moment, cruel the next. And how could he reconcile the seemingly indiscriminate suffering which existed everywhere? How could, he asked again, as he had been asking for years, a good and loving and kind God have created a world where so much was wrong?

The thought, halfway to an answer, did not come to Richard then: What if we are not yet able to understand nature's secret, therefore not able to see it although it lies open to us? What if the difficulty lies in us? What if nature is doing her best to reveal? What if God is working to make us know—if we would but let him—as fast as he can?

One idea will not be pictured, cannot be made present to the mind by any effort of the imagination—one idea requires the purest faith: a man's own ignorance and incapacity. When a man knows, then first he gets a glimpse of his ignorance as it vanishes. Ignorance cannot be the object of knowledge. We must *believe* ourselves ignorant. And for that we must be humble of heart. For God is infinite, and we are his little ones, and his truth is eternally better than the best shape in which we see it.

Jesus is perfect, but our idea of him cannot be perfect. Only obedient faith in him and in his Father is changeless truth in us. Even that has to grow, but its growth is not change. We glimpse a greater life than we can feel; but no man will arrive at the peace of it by struggling with the roots of his nature to understand them, for those roots go down and out, out and down infinitely into the infinite. By acting upon what he sees and knows, hearkening to every whisper, obeying every hint of the good, following whatever seems light, man will at length arrive. Thus obedient, instead of burying himself in the darkness about its roots, he climbs to the treetop of his being; there, looking out on the eternal world, he understands at least enough to give him rest.

In his climbing, the man will somewhere in his upward progress of obedience awake to know that the same Spirit is in him that is in the things he beholds. God is in the world, the atmosphere, the element, the substance, the essence of his life. In him he lives and moves and has his being. Now he lives indeed; for his Origin is his, and this rounds his being to eternity. God himself is his, as nothing else *could* be his.

But Richard was yet far from raising his head above the cloudy region of moods into the blue air of the unchangeable. As the days went by and brought him no word from Barbara, the darkness began to gather around him. The sad consolations of nature by degrees left him; they became all sadness and no consolation. The winter of his soul crept steadily upon him, laden with frost and death. He went back to his stern denial of God, thinking he had no need of a God because he had no hope in any. He lost his love of reading. The books which came to him now he no longer ministered to with his mind and heart, but only with his hands. He hated the very look of poetry. Where, in such a world as he now lived in, could live a worthy God? Richard made his own weather, and it was bad enough. Fortunately, no law compels a man to keep up the weather or the world he has made. Never will any man devise or develop mood or world fit to dwell in. He must inhabit a world that inhabits him, a world that envelops and informs every thought and imagination of his heart.

In Richard's world, the one true, the one divine thing was its misery, for his misery was his need of God.

27 A Drunken Disclosure

One day, in the midst of his suffering, the realization suddenly flashed into Richard's mind what a selfish fellow he was: his own troubles had made him forget Alice and Adam! He must find them!

He knew the street where the firm employing Adam used to have its offices. He went to the old address and found that one of the men there chanced to know where the firm had moved. The next day he told his father he would like to have a day off. He walked into the city, and found the place easily enough, but no Adam. He had not been there for a week, they said. No one seemed to know where he lived, but Richard went on inquiring until at length he found a cabman who lived in the same street. He set out for it at once.

It was a long walk; the neighborhood where at last he found the house was a very poor one, and the house one of the dingiest of all. The door stood open. He walked in and up to the second floor, where he knocked at the first door on the landing. A feeble sound, hardly a voice, answered, and Richard opened the door. There sat Adam, muffled in an old rug, sitting in front of a wretched fire. He held out a pallid hand and greeted him with a sunless smile, but did not speak.

"My poor dear fellow!" said Richard; "what is the matter with you? Why didn't you let me know?"

Tears came to Adam's eyes and he struggled to answer, but his voice was gone. He seemed horribly ill—perhaps dying. He took a piece of paper from his pocket, and a scribbled conversation followed.

"What is the matter with you?"

"Only a bad cold."

"Where is Alice?"

"At the shop. She will be back at eight o'clock."

"Where is your mother?"

"I don't know; she is out."

"Is there anything I can do for you?"

"What does it matter? I do not know anything. It will soon be over."

And this is the fate of one who believes in God! thought Richard. "Would you take a few shillings?" he said to Adam. "It is all I happen to have on me. Then I will come and see you again soon."

Adam shook his head and wrote, "Money is of no use—not the least."

"Isn't there anything that might do you good?"

"I can't get out to get anything."

"Your mother would get it for you!"

He shook his head.

"What about Alice?"

Adam gave a great sigh and said nothing. Richard laid the shillings on the chimney piece, and proceeded to make up the fire before he went. He could see no sort of coal scuttle, no fuel of any kind. With a heavy heart he left him and went down into the street, wondering what he could do.

As he drew near the public house that chiefly poisoned the neighborhood, its door opened and out came a woman in black, wiping her mouth under her veil with a dirty pocket handkerchief. Her red face was swollen with the signs of much alcohol; she walked erect, and went perfectly straight, but looked as if she would begin to stagger were she to relax in the least. As she passed Richard he recognized her: it was Mrs. Manson. He stopped to speak to her, but saw immediately that she was far from sober.

She started at the sight of him and gave a snort of anger.

"What are you doing here!" she cried. "What do you want—coming here to insult your betters! You, Tuke the younger! You, the son of the bookbinder! You're no more John Tuke's son than I am. You're the son of that rascal, my husband! Go to him; don't come to me! You're nothing but a baseborn wretch. Oh yes, run to your mother. Tell her what I say! Tell her she was lucky to get hold of her tradesman! I was never so lucky!"

Something about the woman's disclosure rang to Richard as if it might possibly be true. As the woman staggered away, Richard gave a stagger, too. He sat down on a doorstep to recover himself, but long after he had resumed his walk he went like one half stunned. He had often felt that his father did not particularly care for him. Then there was his mother's strangeness. His mother! His mother made him an outcast! The thought was sickening!

Perhaps the woman lied! But no; something questionable in the background of his life had been unrecognizably showing from the first of his memory! All was clear now! His mother's cruel breach with Alice and her determination that there should be no interaction between the two families—it was all explained. He *must* know the truth. He would ask his mother—but how *could* he ask her? How could any son go to his mother with such a question? He dared not! Why should he add to his own misery by making his mother more miserable! Such a question from her son would go through her heart like the claws of death. Had she not had trouble enough? Could he not spare her knowing that he knew?

But even this horror held its germ of comfort: he had his brother Adam and his sister Alice to care for. He now had the right to compel them to accept his aid.

He thought and thought, and saw that in order to help them he must make a change in his business relations with his father: he must have command of his earnings. To ask for money would arouse questions, and he could not let his mother know that he went to see them. He must have money about which no questions would be asked. That terrible mother of theirs! It was good to know that his mother was not like *her*!

The first thing, then, was to ask his father to take him on as a journeyman and give him journeyman's wages. He knew his work was worth more, but that would be enough. Out of his wages he would pay his share of the housekeeping, and do as he pleased with the rest. Buying no more books, he would have a nice little weekly sum for Alice and Adam. But how was the money to reach them in the form of food? That greedy, drunken mother swallowed everything! To her, the sole satisfaction in life was to eat and drink, if not what she pleased, at least what she liked. He would not have his hard-earned money go to make her drunk and comfortable.

Now he understood why Barbara had not written. She had known him as the son of honest tradespeople and had no pride to make her dislike him. But she must have learned from Alice that he was illegitimate, and had decided to drop him. It was not altogether fair of Barbara—for he was certainly not at fault himself. But he fought hard in his mind to keep from blaming her. It would kill him to think less of her. In all the world, Barbara was most like the God she believed in. He could not stand losing the memory of her. Let him at least keep that!

With his heart like a stone in his bosom, he reached the house, a home to him no more, and he managed to act even a little better than he had for several weeks. He was doing the best he could without God; surely the Father was pleased to see the effort of his child. To suffer in patience was a step toward himself. No doubt self was a strong ingredient in the process—not the best self, which is able to forget itself, but at least the better self that chooses what good it knows.

The same night he laid his request for fixed wages before his father, who agreed to it at once. His wife agreed, with a pang, to what he counted a reasonable sum for Richard's board. But she would not hear of his paying for his lodging; that was more than the mother heart could bear. But the trouble remained on his mind, for a long week must go by before he could touch any wages.

Every night, the moment his head was on the pillow, the strain of his stoicism gave way. Then first he felt alone, utterly alone, loneliness that penetrated his soul and settled there. The strong stoic, the righteous unbeliever, burst into tears. They were the gift of the God he did not know—or rather, the God he knew but a little without knowing that he knew him—and they somewhat cooled his burning heart. But the fog of fresh despair steamed up from the rain, and its clouds closed down upon him. What was left him to live for? All was gray! The world lay in clearest, barest, coldest light, its hopeless deceit and its misery all revealed! At least there was no mockery now! The world was not pretending to be happy! What a devilish thing was life—a mask with no face behind it, a form with no soul! A bubble blown out of lies with the breath of a liar!

All of a sudden he was crying, as if with a loud voice from the bottom of his heart, though not so much as a sound rose in his throat. *Oh, thou who made me, if you are anywhere, if there be such a one as I cry to, unmake me again! Be merciful for once and kill me. Let me cease to exist! Let me die!*

But immediately rose up a surge of shame for his selfishness, praying for his release, while he abandoned his fellows to their misery!

"No!" he cried aloud, "I will not pray for that! I will not put myself above my fellows! O God! if you have any pity—pity your creatures! If you are anywhere, speak to me and let me hear. If you are God, if you live and care that I suffer, and would help me if you could, then I will live, and bear what I face, and wait. Only let me know you are, and that you are good and not cruel. If I only had a friend who would stand by me and talk to me a little, and help me! I have no one, no one, God, to speak to! If you will not hear me, then there is nothing! God, I pray thee, exist! You know my desolation!"

A silence came down upon his soul. Before it passed he was asleep and knew no more till the morning waked him—to sorrow indeed, but from a dream of hope. With but a few keys, yet with great variety, life struck every interval between keen sorrow, lethargic gloom, and grayest hope; and Richard's days passed and passed.

The moment he received his wages from his father at the end of the week, Richard set out for Everilda Street, Clerkenwell, a little anxious at the thought of encountering the dreadful mother but hoping she would be out of the way.

When he reached the place he found no one at home. He hung about, keeping a sharp watch on each end of the street; before long Adam appeared, stooping like an aged man, and moving slowly.

His face brightened when he saw his friend, but a fit of coughing immediately followed.

"When did you have your dinner?" asked Richard.

"I had something in the middle of the day," he answered feebly; "and when Alice comes she will perhaps bring something with her. But we don't care much about eating," he added with an unreal laugh.

"It's no wonder you don't get rid of your cold!" returned Richard. "Come along and have something to eat."

"I can't leave Alice to come home and not find me," objected Adam.

"We can bring something back for her," suggested Richard.

He seemed to yield, but his every motion was full of indecision. Richard took his arm and led him to a nearby coffee shop, where, the sight of food waking a little hunger, the poor fellow did pretty well for one who looked so ill. As he ate he revived and began to talk a little.

"It's very good of you, Richard," he said. "I suppose you know all about it."

"I don't. What is it? Anything new?"

"No, nothing! It's all so miserable!"

"It's not miserable," answered Richard, able to comfort another with words which could not comfort himself, "so long as we are brothers!"

Tears came to Adam's eyes. Illegitimate half brothers, both were stuck on the bottom of society despite the gentle blood that flowed through their veins.

"You *do* know!" he said. "That is good, though it be only in misfortune! I am sorry for you. But though I am a wretched creature, you are a strong man, Richard. I shall never be worth calling your brother!"

"You can do one great thing for me."

"What is that?"

"Live and grow well."

"I wish I could; but that is just what I can't do. I am on my way home."

"I would gladly go with you."

"Why?"

Richard offered no answer, and silence followed.

Adam got up. "Alice will be home soon," he said. "She will think I have become too sick to get home and will be worried about me."

"Let's go, then!" said Richard.

When they reached the street they saw Alice on the doorstep waiting anxiously for her brother. The moment she caught sight of them she ran away along the street. Richard would have followed her, but Adam held him.

"Never mind her tonight. She doesn't know that you know. I will tell her, and when you come again, you will find her different. Come again as soon as you can—at least, I mean, as soon as you like."

"I will come tomorrow," answered Richard. "Do you want me to go now?"

"It would be better for Alice."

"But where shall I find you tomorrow?"

They arranged their meeting and parted.

The next day they found a better place for their meal. Richard thought it better not to go all the way home with Adam, but learned from him where Alice worked and what hour she left. The following night, therefore, he went to wait for her not far from the shop.

At last she came along, looking very thin and pale, but she brightened when she saw him and joined him without the least hesitation.

"How do you think Adam is?" he asked.

"I've not seen him so well for a long time," she answered. "But that is not saying much," she added with a sigh.

They walked along together. With a taste of happiness even once a week, Alice would have been a merry girl. She was so content to be with Richard that she paid no attention to where he was taking her. But when she found him going into a coffee shop, she drew back.

"No, Richard," she said. "I can't let you feed me and Adam, too. Indeed I can't!"

"Nonsense," returned Richard. "I want some supper, and you must keep me company."

"It's all right for Adam, but not for me," she insisted. "He's ill. But I'm a strong girl—"

"Look here!" said Richard. "Aren't you my sister—and don't I know you haven't had enough to eat?"

"Who told you that?"

"No one. Any fool could see it with half an eye!"

"Adam has been telling tales!"

"He has said nothing. I earn so much a week now, and after paying for everything, I have money left to spend as I please. If you refuse me as your brother, say so, and I will leave you alone."

She stood motionless and made him no answer.

"Look here!" he said; "there is the money for our supper. If you will not go with me and eat it, I will throw it into the street."

With her ingrained respect for the preciousness of money, Alice did not believe him.

"Oh, no, Richard, you would never do that!" she said.

Almost the same instant the coins rang faintly in the middle of the street, and a cab passed over them. Alice gave a cry almost of bodily pain and started to run after them and pick them up. Richard held her tight.

"It's your supper, Richard!" she almost shrieked, struggling to get away after the money.

"Yes," he answered, "and yours goes after it unless you come in and share it with me."

As he spoke he showed her his other hand with shillings in it.

She turned and entered the shop. Richard ordered a good meal.

Alice stopped in the middle of her supper, laid down her knife and fork, and burst out crying.

"What *is* the matter?" asked Richard in alarm.

"I can't bear to think of that money! I must go and look for it!" sobbed Alice.

Richard laughed, for the first time in days.

"Alice," he said, "the money was well spent: I got my own way with it!"

As she ate and drank, a little color rose in her face, and on Richard fell a shadow of the joy of his Creator, beholding his work, and seeing it good.

28 A Door Opened in Heaven

Some men hunt their fellows to prey upon them; Richard hunted and caught his brother and sister that they might feed upon the labor of his hands. To Adam and Alice, their newfound brother, strong and loving, was an angel from heaven. Richard found no similar comfort in them, but through no fault of his own. To see them improve in looks and in strength did, of course, comfort him, but they had few thoughts to share with him—had little coin for spiritual commerce. Even their religion had little shape or color. What there was of it was genuine, but it was much too weak to pass over to help of another. Divine aid of a different sort, however, was waiting for him. Richard had followed the most basic of God's principles: he had *done* what was given him to do; he had helped those given him to help. He was thus on the upward path toward further revelation, soon to find his deepest heart's cry answered by the one his lips had long denied.

A gentleman who employed Richard happened one day, in conversation with him, to take up the subject of music. Despite Richard's ignorance on the subject, the man's remarks found sufficient way into his mind to make him realize what little experience he had had in this regard. As the conversation continued, Richard became still more interested, resulting in his attending a concert at the St. James's Hall the next Monday night. In the crowd waiting more than an hour at the door of the orchestra to secure a seat for a shilling, not one knew so little of music as he. But the first throbbing flash of the violins cleft his soul as lightning cleaves a dark cloud, and set his body shivering as with its thunder—and lo, a door was opened in heaven! After that he went every Monday night to the same concert room. It became his church, the mount of his ascension, the place where his spirit soared. All that was best and simplest in him awakened as he listened. What fact did the music prove? None, whatever. Would not the logic of science have persuaded him that the sea of mood and mystic response to the music was but an illusion? But if it was only illusion, how could such illusion be possible? How could it contain such bliss? What he felt, he knew that he felt. The feeling was *in him*, but waked by some power *beyond him*. The voice of the power was a voice all sweetness and persuading, a voice of creation, calling up a world of splendor and delight.

One night, after many such nights, he sat entranced, listening to the song of a violin, alone and perfect, soaring and sailing—and Barbara in his heart was listening with him. He had given up hope of seeing her again in this world, but not all hope of seeing her again somewhere; and her image had not grown less dear. The song, like a heavenly lark, folded its wings while yet high in the air, and ceased. All was over and the world was still. But the face of Barbara kept shining from the depths of Richard's soul, as if she stood behind him, and her face looked up reflected from its ethereal ocean.

All at once he was aware that his bodily eyes were resting on the bodily face of Barbara, as if his strong imagining of her had made her be. His heart gave a great bound, then stood still, as if for eternity. But the blood surged back to his brain, and he knew that together they had been listening to the same enchanting spell of the violin. He had felt, without knowing it, the power of her presence. He gazed and gazed, filled with the joy of seeing her again. She was so far off that he could gaze at will, and thus distance was a blessing. As he gazed he became aware that she saw him, and that she was aware of his eyes on her. There was no change on her face, no sign of recognition, but he knew that she saw and knew. In his modesty he neither perceived nor imagined more. His heart received no thrill from the pleasure that throbbed in the heart of the lovely lady at sight of the poor sorrowful workman; neither did she in her modesty perceive on what a throne of gems she sat in his heart. She saw that his cheek was pale and thin, that his eyes were larger and brighter; she little thought how the fierce sun of agony had ripened his soul since they parted.

For the rest of the concert the music sank to a soft delight. But now it took second place; the delight in seeing dulled his delight in hearing. All became one in his consciousness. Barbara was the music and the music was Barbara. He saw her with his ears; he heard her with his eyes. But as the last sonata sank to its death, suddenly the face and the tones parted company and he knew that his eyes and her face must part next. Her face was already far away. She had left him; she was looking for her fan, preparing to go.

He was not far from the door. He hurried softly out, ran into the open air as into a great cool river, went round the house, and took his stand at one of the doors. There he waited like one watching the flow of a river of gravel for the shine of a diamond. But the flow diminished to threads and drops, and the diamond never shone.

He walked home, nevertheless, as if he had seen the end of sorrow: how much had been given him that night! Such an hour! He could endure the world, even worse than it was, with an experience like that but once in ten years! He had been so miserable and was now content. He was even strong to be miserable again!

Before the next Monday he had learned all the exits of the Hall, and the relations of the hallways to its doors. But he fared no better, for whether again he mistook the door or not, he did not see Barbara come out. But he had been with her throughout the whole concert, and he now had reason to hope she might be present often. The following Monday, nevertheless, she was not in the Hall: had she been, he said to himself, his eyes would have found her.

Two weeks passed, and Richard had not again seen Barbara. He began to think she must have gone home. A gentleman was with her the first night, whom he took for her father; the second, Arthur Lestrange was by her side: neither of them had he seen since.

She might have come to London to prepare for her marriage with Mr. Lestrange! The thought came to Richard suddenly, immediately followed by despair. *She must of course be married someday!* He had always taken that for granted, but now, for the first time, the thought came near enough to burn. In vain he tried to persuade himself that Barbara would not listen to such a suitor as Arthur. But the more he thought of the idea, the more likely it grew in his mind that she might indeed marry Lestrange. Mortgrange and Wylder Hall were conveniently near, and he had heard his grandfather speculate that Barbara must one day inherit the latter. The thought was a growing torment. His heart sank into a new well of misery, from which the rope of his thinking could draw up nothing but suicide. Richard cast that idea from him. It was cowardly to hide one's head in the sand of death! So long as he was able to stand, why should he lie down? If a morrow was on the way, why not see what the morrow would bring?

Once more the loud complaint against life awoke and raged. What an evil, what a wrong was life! Again and again he cried out against God for the misery he had caused. Even if he had not caused it, could he not prevent it? And if he could prevent it, then why did he allow it?

It is surely a notable argument against the existence of God, that they who believe in him believe in him so wretchedly! So many carry themselves to him like peevish children. Richard half-believed in God, only to complain of him altogether. Would it not be better to deny him altogether than to murmur and rebel against him?

But perhaps it is better to complain, if one complains to God himself. Does he not then draw nigh to God with what truth is in him? And will he not then fare as Job, to whom God drew nigh in return, and set his heart at rest?

Finally, Richard began to wonder whether even an all-mighty and all-good God could have contrived such a world that nobody in it would ever complain of anything. What if he had plans too large for the vision of men to take in, and they would not trust him for what they could not see? Why should not a man at least wait and see what God was going to do with him, perhaps for him, before he accused or denied him? At worst, he would be no worse for the waiting!

His thinking was stopped by a sudden flood of self-contempt. What did it matter whether *he* was happy or not if all was well with her? A man was free to sacrifice his happiness. He would do that for her sake! For her sake he would still seek her God; perhaps he might find him. What if there was a way so much higher than ours as to include all the seeming right and seeming wrong in one radiance of righteousness? The idea was hardly conceivable! But he would try to hold by it. What we rightfully conceive bad must be bad to God as well as to us; but may there not be things so far above us that we cannot take them in, that seem bad because they are so far above us in goodness that we see them only partially and untruly?

He would try to trust! He would say, "If you are my Father, be my Father, and comfort your child! Perhaps things are not as you would have them, and you are doing what can be done to set them right. Give me time to trust you. Explain the things I am unable to understand."

Thus he thought as he walked home late one Monday night. He was walking westward, with his eyes on the ground, along the broad pavement on the house side of Piccadilly. Lost half in misery, half in thought, he was stopped by a little crowd about an awning that stretched across the footway. The same instant rose a murmur of admiration, and down the steps from the door came tripping the same Barbara to whose mold his being seemed to have shaped itself. He stood silent as death, but something made her cast a look on him, and she saw the large eyes of his suffering fixed on her. She gave a short, musical cry, and turning, darted through the crowd, leaving her escort at the foot of the steps.

"Richard!" she cried, and catching hold of his hand, laid her other hand on his shoulder—then suddenly became aware of the gazing faces, not all pleasant to look upon, that came crowding closer about them.

She pulled him toward a carriage standing at the curbstone.

"Jump in," she whispered. Then turning to the gentleman, who in a bewildered way thought she had caught a prodigal brother in the crowd, "Good-night, Mr. Cleveland," she said. "Thank you."

One moment Richard hesitated; but he saw that neither place nor time allowed anything but obedience, and when she turned again, he was already seated.

"Home!" she said to the coachman as she got in, for she had no attendant.

"I must talk fast," she began, "and so must you; we have not far to go together. Why did you not write to me?"

"I did write."

"Did you?" exclaimed Barbara.

"I did indeed."

"Then what could you think of me for not answering?"

"I thought nothing you would not like me to think. I was sure there was an explanation."

"Of course. You knew that! But how ill you look!"

"It is from not seeing you anymore at the concerts," answered Richard.

"Tell me your address, and I will write to you. But do not write to me. When shall you be at the Hall again?"

"Next Monday. I am there every Monday."

"I shall be there, and will take your answer from your hand as I come out by the Regent Street door."

She pulled the coachman's string.

"Now you must go," she said. "Thank God I have seen you. Tell me when you write if you know anything of Alice."

She gave him her hand. He got out, closed the door, took off his hat, and stood for minutes in the cold clear night, hardly sure whether he had indeed been side by side with Barbara or in a heavenly trance.

29 Doors Opened on Earth

He turned and walked home, but with a different heart. The world was folded in winter and night, but in his heart the sun was shining! Did Barbara know about him? Had Alice told the terrible secret? If she knew, and did not withdraw her friendship, he could bear anything! He would be happy now, would try to keep happy as long as he could, and try to be happy when he could not. She was with him all the way home. Every step was a delight.

He slept a happy sleep and in the morning was better than for many days—so much better that his mother, who had been watching with uneasiness and wondering whether she ought not to say something and bring matters to their inevitable crisis, began to feel at rest about him. She had not a suspicion of what troubled him the most.

Richard now knew who was his father, but he did not understand about his mother; from this half-knowledge rose the thickest of the cloud yet overshadowing him. He had been proud that he came of such good people as his father and mother, but it was not the notion of shame to himself that greatly troubled him; it was the new feeling about his mother. He did not blame her and never felt unready to stand up for her. What troubled him was that she must always feel shame before him. He could not bear to think of it. If only she would say something to him, that he might tell her she was his own precious mother, whatever had befallen her!

Already good had come of Mrs. Manson's attack: Richard felt far more goodness from his mother, and loved her better now that he believed himself her shame.

As soon as the next day's work was over, Richard sat down to write to Barbara. But he had no sooner taken the pen in his fingers than became doubtful about what to say. He could not open his heart about any of the things troubling him most! Putting aside the recurrent dread of her own marriage, how could he mention his mother's wrong and his own shame? How was he, such a common fellow, to draw near to her loveliness with such a tale! It would be a wrong to his own class to discuss such things, and would but prove him unfit for the company of his social superiors. It would but prove that one of his nurture could not be regarded as a gentleman. And more than any of that, how could he speak of his mother's hidden pain when she could not even tell him!

He could write to her of Alice! She had asked him to do so. Richard thought it strange that she should ask about Alice. But Alice had not told him that she was unable to keep the money sent by Barbara from falling into the hands of her mother and going to drink. Unwilling to expose her mother, and not wanting Barbara to spend her money in such a way, Alice had contrived to have her checks returned, as if they had changed addresses and their new address was unknown. Therefore, Barbara had heard as little from Alice as she had from Richard.

Richard wrote what he thought would set her at ease about them, but scarcely had he finished when he remembered, with a pang of self-reproach, that the time of his usual meeting with Alice was past, and that Adam, too, was in danger of going to bed hungry. He set out at once for Clerkenwell—on foot, despite the hurry he was in, for he was saving every penny to get new clothes for Adam.

He sped as quickly as he could go, anxious to get to the house before the mother came in. He stopped on the way to buy some slices of ham and some rolls, then ran on again. It was a frosty night, but by the time he reached Everilda Street he was far from cold. He was rewarded by finding his brother and sister at home, alone, and not too hungry.

He had just had time to empty his pockets and receive a kiss from Alice when they heard the uncertain step of their mother coming up the stairs, stopping now and then, and again resuming the ascent. Richard rose and attempted to leave through one of their two doors just as she was entering the other. But she changed her mind at the last moment, entered the other door, and caught him in the very act of making his exit.

She flew at him, seized him by the hair, and began to hit at him and abuse him. "True son of your father!" she screamed drunkenly. "Everything on the sly, and never look an honest woman in the face!"

Richard never said a word, but let her tug and revile him until no strength remained in her, when she let him go and dropped into a chair.

The three went halfway down the stairs together.

"Don't mind her," said Alice with a great sob. "I hope she didn't hurt you much."

"Not a bit!" answered Richard.

"Poor mother!" sighed Adam. "She's not in her right mind. We're in constant terror that she's going to drop down dead!"

"She's not a very good mother to you," said Richard.

"No, but that has nothing to do with loving her," answered Alice; "and to think of her dying like that and going straight to the bad place. Oh, Richard, what *shall* I do? It drives me crazy to think of it!"

The door above them opened and the fierce voice of the mother fell upon them. But it was broken by a fit of hiccupping, and she went in again, slamming the door behind her.

That night Richard could not rest; he had caught a cold and was feverish. When he did sleep, he kept starting awake from troubled dreams. In the morning he felt better, and rose and began his work, shivering occasionally. All week he was unwell, but thought the attack nothing but an ordinary cold. When Sunday came he stayed in bed, hoping to get rid of it. The next day he was worse, but he insisted on getting up. He must not seem to be ill, for he was determined, if he could stand, to go to the concert. It was all he could do to stick to his work, with weariness and shortness of breath and sleepiness. But he held on till the evening, when he slipped from the house, and with the help of an omnibus, made his way to the Hall.

It was dire work waiting till the door to the orchestra seats was opened. The air was cold, his lungs heavily oppressed, and his weakness almost overpowering. But paradise was within that closed door, and he was passing through the pains of death to enter into bliss! When at length it seemed to yield to his prayers, he almost fell in the rush, but managed to find a seat.

The moment the music began he forgot every discomfort. With the first chord of the violins, as if ushered in by the angels themselves, Barbara came flitting down the center of the side space toward her usual seat. Now he felt entirely well. All was peace and hope and bliss. Even Arthur Lestrange beside Barbara could not blast his joy. He saw him occasionally offer some small attention; he saw her carelessly accept or refuse it. Barbara gazed at him anxiously, he thought. But he did not know he looked sick; he had forgotten himself.

When the concert was over, he hastened from his seat. The moment he reached the open air the cold wind seized him, but he conquered in the struggle and reached the human torrent exiting into

Regent Street. Against it he made his way gradually until he stood near the inner door of the Hall. In a minute or two he saw her come, slowly with the crowd, her hand on Arthur's arm, her eyes anxiously searching for Richard. The moment she found him, her course took a drift toward him, and her face grew white as his, for she saw plainly that he was ill. They edged nearer and nearer; their hands met through the crowd; their letters were exchanged, and without a word they parted. As Barbara reached the door, she turned one moment to look for him, and he saw a depth of angelic care in her eyes. Arthur turned and saw him too, but Richard was so changed he did not recognize him, and thought the suffering look of a stranger had roused the sympathy of his companion.

How he got home Richard could not have told. Before he reached the house he was too ill to know anything except that he had something precious in his possession. He managed to get to bed—and did not leave it for weeks. A severe attack of pneumonia prostrated him, and he knew nothing of his condition or surroundings. He had not even opened his letter. He remembered occasionally that he had a precious something somewhere, but could not recall what it was.

When he came to himself after many days, he awoke with a wonderful delight of possession, though whether the object possessed was a thing, a thought, a feeling, or a person he could not distinguish.

"Where is it?" he said, hardly knowing that he spoke till he heard his own voice.

"Under your pillow," answered his mother.

He turned his eyes and saw her face as he had never seen it before—pale and full of love and anxious joy. There was a gentleness and depth in the expression that was new to him. The divine motherhood had come nearer the surface in her boy's illness.

Partly from her anxiety about what she had done and what she had yet to do, the show of her love had, as the boy grew up, gradually retired; her love burned more and shone less. If Jane Tuke had been able to let her love appear in a form that suited its strength, the teaching of his father would have had little power over Richard; certainly he would have been otherwise impressed by the faith of his mother. He would have been prejudiced in favor of the God she believed in, and would have sought hard to account for the ways attributed to him.

Nonetheless, only through much denial and much suffering would he have arrived at anything worth calling faith. And the danger would have been great of his drifting into an indifference that does not care that God should be righteous, ready to call anything just which so-called spiritual leaders declare God does—without concern whether it be right or wrong, or whether he really does it or not. He would have supposed the Bible said things about God which it does not say, things which, if it did say them, ought to be enough to make any honest man reject the notion of its authority as an indivisible whole.

Had Richard embraced his mother's faith, he would have had to encounter all the wrong notions of God, dropped on the highway of the universe by the nations that went before in the march of humanity. He would have found it much harder to work out his salvation, to force his freedom from the false forms imposed upon truth by interpreters of little faith.

"What did you say, Mother dear?" he returned, all astray, seeming to have once known several things, but now knowing nothing at all.

"It is under your pillow, Richard," she said again, very tenderly.

"What is it, Mother? Something seems strange. I don't know what to ask you. Tell me what it means."

"You have been ill, my boy."

"Have I been out of my mind?"

"You have been wandering with the fever, nothing more."

"I have been thinking so many things, and they all seemed real! And you have been nursing me all the time!"

"Who should have been nursing you, Richard? Do you think I would let anyone else nurse my own child? Didn't I nurse the—"

She stopped abruptly; she had been on the point of saying, "—the mother who bore you?" Her love for her dead sister was one with her love for the living child. But Richard seemed to take no notice. He lay silent for a time thinking—or rather, trying to think, for he felt like one vainly trying to get the focus of a three-dimensional picture. His mind kept going away from him. He knew himself able to think, yet he could not think. It was a revelation to him of the absolute helplessness of our being.

"Shall I get it for you, dear?" asked his mother.

The morning after the concert he had taken Barbara's letter from under his pillow and would not let it out of his hand. Fearing he could tear it to pieces, his mother tried to remove it several times, but the moment she touched it, he would resist her. When in his restless turning he dropped it, he showed himself so miserable that she could do nothing but put it in his hand again, and he would then lie perfectly quiet for a while. At length, dreaming of Barbara he forgot his letter, and his mother again put it under his pillow. With the Lord, we shall forget even the Gospel of John.

She took out the crumpled, frayed envelope and gave it to him. The moment he touched it, everything came back to him.

"Now I remember, Mother!" he cried. "Thank you. I will try to be better to you. I am sorry I ever upset you!"

"You never upset me, Richard," said the mother heart. "Or if you ever did, I've forgotten it. And now that God has given you back to us, we must see whether we can't do something better for you!"

Richard was so weary that he did not care to ask what she meant, and in a moment was asleep, with the letter in his hand.

When at length he was able to read it, it caused him great pleasure, and some dismay. Her father was determined she should marry Mr. Lestrange, but her mother was against it. There was as much dissension at home as ever. She believed Lady Ann had talked her father into it, for he had not always favored the idea. There was now greater reason why both Lady Ann and her father should desire it, for there was every likelihood of her being left sole heir to the property; her brother could not, the doctors said, live many months. She was sure her mother was trying to do right, and she herself did all she could to please her father, but nothing less than her consent to his plans for what he called her settlement in life would satisfy him—and that she could not give.

She hoped Richard was not forgetting their talks in the old days. If it were not for those memories, she could not now bear life.

She was almost never alone and in constant danger of interruption, so that he must not wonder if her letter broke off abruptly. She was leading, or rather being led, a busy life of nothing at all—a life not worth living. Her father, set on, no doubt, by Lady Ann, had brought her to London, while her mother was still not well enough to accompany them, so that she had had to go where and do what Lady Ann pleased. But her mother had come at last, had stood by her, as she said: she would have no Lady Ann interfering with her girl! She had herself married a man she had not learned to respect, and she was determined her daughter should make her own choice—or stay unmarried if she pleased. She was not going to hold her child down for them to bury in money! With this the letter broke off.

Barbara's openness about her parents was in perfect harmony with her simplicity and straightforwardness. She was proud of her mother, and the way she put things therefore told all to Richard.

He had a bad night, with delirious dreams, and for some days made little progress. His anxiety to get well, that he might see Barbara, and also that he might again see Alice and Adam about whom he was much afraid, slowed his recovery.

Thinking about Mrs. Manson's drinking herself to death, and the harm she was doing to her son and daughter as well, he began to wonder whether God's hand could be even in such a pitiful situation as that. How wise must be a God who, to work out his intent, would take all the conduct, good and bad, all the efforts of his children, and out of them all bring the right thing! If he knew such a God, one to trust in absolutely, he would be able to go to sleep without one throb of anxiety about anyone he loved. The perfect love would not fail because one of his children was sick!

One of the benefits of illness is that, either from general weakness or from the brain's being cast into a state of rest, habits are broken for a time; and more simple, childlike, and natural modes of thought and feeling come into action, whereby right has a better chance. Some sicknesses may well open windows into the unseen. A man's self-stereotyped thinking is unfavorable to revelation; his mind works too strongly in its familiar channels. But illness, in weakening these habits and breaking down these channels, strengthens more primary and original modes of vision. More open to the influences of the divine question are those who are not frozen in their own dullness, cased in their own habits, bound by their own pride to foregone conclusions, or shut up in the completeness of human error, theorizing beyond their knowledge and power.

Having thus in a measure given himself up, Richard began to grow toward the light. What a joy to think that a man may, while still unsure about God, yet be coming close to him! How else should we be saved at all? For God alone is our salvation; to know him is salvation. He is in us all the time, otherwise we could never move to seek him. Only in faith can we be saved: there is no good but him, and not to be one with that good by obedience is to be unsaved; but the poorest *desire* to draw near to him *is* an approach to him. Very unsure of him we may be; how should we be sure of what we do not yet know? But the unsureness does not nullify the approach. A man may not be sure that the sun is risen, may not be sure that the sun will ever rise, yet he has the good of what light there is. Richard was fed from the heart of God without knowing that he was partaking of the Spirit of God. He had been partaking of the creation of God all his life. The world had been feeding him with its beauty and essential truth, with the sweetness of its air, and the vastness of its sky of freedom. But now he had begun, in the words of St. Peter, to be a partaker of the divine nature.

It was a long time before he was strong again. His mother took him to the seaside, where in a warm, secluded bay on the south coast he was wrapped closer in the garments of the creating and reviving God. He was again a child, and drew nearer to the heart of his mother than he had ever drawn before. Believing he knew her sad secret, he set himself to meet her every wish. He spoke so gently to her that she felt she had never until now had him her very child. Richard had started on a voyage of self-discovery. When a man finds he is not what he thought, that he has been talking greatly but only imagining he belonged to the world of greatness, he is on the way to discovering that he is not up to his duty in the smallest matters. When, for very despair, he finds life impossible, then he begins to know that he needs more than himself; that there is none good but God. Richard was beginning to feel in his deepest nature—where alone it can be felt—his need of God.

All betterment must be radical, for a man can know nothing of the roots of his being. His existence is God's; his betterment must be God's, too—God's through honest exercise of that which is highest in man—his own will, God's best handiwork. By actively willing the will of God, and doing what of it lies within his power, the man takes the share offered him in his own making, in his own becoming. In willing actively and operatively to become what he was made to be, he becomes creative—so far as a man may. In this way also he becomes like his Father in heaven.

Richard grew in graciousness and in favor with God and his mother. Often she wondered whether the time had not come for revealing her secret, but now one thing, now another deterred her. One time she feared Richard's agitation in his present state of health; another, she thought it unfair to the husband who had behaved with such generosity to give him no part in the revelation.

Once, to comfort him when he seemed depressed, she ventured to say, "Would you like to go to the university, Richard? To Oxford? Or Cambridge?"

"What makes you ask that, Mother?" He looked up with a smile.

"Perhaps it could be managed," she answered, leaving him to suppose his father might send him.

"You think I shall never be able to work again? Look at that!" he returned, extending an arm on which the muscle had begun again to put in an appearance.

"It is not for strength," she answered. "For that you could do well enough. But the dust! It's so irritating to the lungs! And stooping all day long!"

"Never mind, Mother. I'm quite up to it, dust and all—or at least shall soon be. We mustn't be anxious about others any more than about ourselves. Doesn't the God you believe in tell you so?"

"Don't you believe in him then, Richard?" asked his mother with a trace of sadness.

"I think I do—a little—in a sort of way—believe in God—at least I am beginning to. But I hope to believe in him ten thousand times more!"

His mother sighed. She made him no reply, and presently reverted to their former topic.

"I think it might be managed—someday!" she said. "You could go on with your trade afterward if you liked. Why shouldn't a collegeman be a tradesman? Why shouldn't a tradesman know as much as a gentleman?"

"Why, indeed, Mother! If I thought it wouldn't be too much for you and Father, there are not many things I should like better than going to Oxford. You are good to me like God himself!"

"Richard!" His mother was shocked. She thought she served God by going to church, not by being like him in every word and look of love she gave her boy.

The mere idea of going to the university, and thus taking a step nearer to Barbara, began immediately to better his health. It gave him many a happy thought, many a cottage and castle in the air, with more of a foundation than he knew. But his mother did not revert to the subject again, and one day suddenly the thought came to Richard that perhaps she meant to apply to Sir Wilton for the means of sending him. Castle and cottage fell in silent ruin. His soul recoiled from the idea—as much for his mother's sake as his own. Having married his reputed father, she must have no more relation—especially for his sake—with Sir Wilton! So at least thought Richard. He was sorry he had said he should like to go to Oxford. If his mother alluded to the thing again, he would tell her he had changed his mind and would not interrupt the exercise of his profession as surgeon to old books.

30 The Cave in the Fire

The spring advanced; the days grew a little warmer, and at length—partly from economic considerations—Richard and his mother determined to go home. When they reached London, they found a great difference in the weather. Fog and drizzle, frost and fog, were everywhere. At once Richard was worse, but nevertheless he felt compelled to get what news he could of Adam Manson. He dreaded hearing he was no more in this world. The cold wintry weather, and the return to poor and sparse nourishment caused by Richard's illness must have been hard on him. So the first morning he felt it possible, he took his way to the city. There he learned that the company had dispensed with Adam's services because his attendance had become so irregular.

Sad at heart, Richard set out for Clerkenwell. He was hardly able for the journey—but what if Adam were dying! He would brave the mother for the sake of the son. He got into an omnibus which took him a good part of the way, and walked the rest. When at length he looked up at the dreary house, he saw the blinds of the windows drawn. Depressed, moody, and fearful, he went up the stairs to the darkened floor.

When he knocked at the front room, that in which Alice slept with her mother, Alice opened it, looking more small and forlorn than he had yet seen her, with hollower cheeks and larger eyes, and a smile to make an angel weep.

"Richard!" she cried with a voice in which the very gladness sounded like pain. A pink flush rose in her poor wasted cheeks, and she lay still in his arms as if she had gone to live there.

In his pity he could not speak one word.

"How ill you look!" she murmured. "I knew you must be ill; I thought you might be dead! Oh, God *is* good to leave you to come back to us!" Then she burst into tears. "How wicked of me," she sobbed, "to feel anything like gladness with my mother lying there, and me not able to do anything for her! We shall never see her again!"

"Don't say that, Alice! Never say *never* about anything except it be bad. But how's Adam?"

"He'll never get up again!" she answered, with a touch of bitterness. "If he had been left to me, we should have got along somehow. I could have taken care of him, and worked for him. But he's past hope now."

O God! cried Richard in his heart, where an agony of will wrestled with doubt, *if you are God, hear me, and take pity on her, and on us all!* "May I go and see him?" he asked Alice.

"Surely, Richard. But shouldn't I let him know first? The surprise might be too much for him."

Their talk had waked him, however, and he knew his brother's voice. "Richard! Richard!" he cried, so loud that it startled Alice: he had not spoken above a whisper for days. Richard opened his door and went in. But when he saw Adam he could scarcely recognize him, he was so wasted. His eyes stood out like balls from his sunken cheeks, and the smile with which he greeted him was all teeth, like the helpless smile of a skull. Overcome with tenderness, Richard stooped and kissed his forehead, then stood speechless, holding the thin leaf of a hand. Adam tried to speak, but his cough came on, and his brother begged him to be silent.

"I will go into the next room with Alice," he said, "and come to you again. I shall see you often now, I hope. I've been sick or I would have been here fifty times."

In the next room lay the unmoving form of the mother. A certain something of human grace had returned to her countenance. Richard did not like looking at her; he felt that not loving her, he had no right to let his eyes rest on her. But she had been sinned against like his own mother; he must not fail her with what sympathy was due her.

"Don't think hard of her," said Alice, as if she knew what he was thinking. "She didn't have the strength of some people. I don't believe she could help it. She had been accustomed to having everything she wanted."

"I pity her with all my heart," answered Richard.

She threw her arms around his neck and clung to him as if she would never again let him go.

"But what am I to do?" she said, releasing him. "If I stay at home to nurse Adam, we must both die of hunger. If I go away, there is nobody to do anything for him!"

"I wish I could stay with him!" returned Richard. "But I've been ill so long that I have no money, and I don't know when I shall have any. I have just one shilling in my possession. Here—take it, dear."

"I can't take your last shilling, Richard!"

"Don't worry about me," he said. "I shall have everything I need. It makes me ashamed to think of it. You must just get on for a while as best you can while I think what to do. Only there's the funeral expense to think of."

Alice gave a cry choked by a sob.

"There is no help!" she said in a voice of despair. "The parish is all that is left us!"

"It doesn't matter much," said Richard. "For myself, I don't care what becomes of me after I'm gone. She won't care how her body gets put under the earth. Go to the parish and put your mind at ease about her. Tell Adam I hope to see him again soon; I must not stay now. I won't forget you, Alice—not for an hour. Ask someone in the building here to look in on him while you are away. I shall do something for him soon. Good night, dear!"

With a heavy heart Richard went. It was all he could do to get home before dark, walking all the way. His mother was greatly distressed to see him so exhausted; but he managed not to tell her what he had been about. He had some tea and went to bed, remaining there all the next day. And while he was in bed, it came to him clear and plain what he must do. It was certain that for a long time he could do nothing for Adam and Alice out of his own pocket. Even if he got to work immediately, he could not take his wages as before, seeing his parents had spent most of their savings upon his sickness and recovery.

But there was one who *ought* to help them! Especially in such a time of great need they had a right to the help of their own father! He would go to his father and their father. As the words rose in his mind, he wondered where he had heard something like them before.

The next day he asked his father and mother to let him spend a week or two with his grandfather.

Two days later, well wrapped to keep out the cold, he took his place in a slow train, and at the station was heartily welcomed by his grandfather. It was not long before he was settled in the room occupied by Alice. He felt like a usurper, leaving her in her misery to settle in the heart of the comfort that once had been hers. He had to tell himself that it was foolish, for he was there for her sake.

He took his grandfather at once into his confidence, begging him not to let his mother know; and Simon, who had in former days experienced something of the hardness of his true-hearted daughter, entered into the thing with a brooding kind of smile. He saw no reason why Richard should not make the attempt, but shook his head at the prospect of success. No doubt the baron thought he had done all that could be required of him. He would have preferred that Richard rest a day before encountering him, but when he heard in what condition he had left Alice and her brother, he said no more. The next morning he had his pony and cart ready to drive him to Mortgrange.

With feelings unlike any he had ever before experienced, Richard drew near to the familiar place and looked again upon the familiar sights. The house that he had entered so often as a workman he now entered as a son. What manner of son was he, and how would he be received should he take it upon himself to disclose his identity? But he had resolved to say nothing. He was there for another purpose.

Richard's heart beat fast as he passed through the gate and walked up to the front door. After a moment's bewilderment, the servant who answered his ring recognized him and expressed concern that he looked so ill. When he asked to see Sir Wilton, the man, thinking he came to resume the work so suddenly abandoned, said he was in the library having his morning cigar.

"Then I'll just step in," said Richard, and the footman gave way as to a member of the household.

Sir Wilton, now an elderly and broken man, sat in his chair. Richard, partly from the state of his health, even with all the courage he could gather, quailed a little before the expected encounter. But he remained outwardly quiet and seemingly cool. The sun was not shining into the room and it was rather dark. Sir Wilton sat with his back to the one large bay window, and Richard received its light on his face as he entered. He stood an instant, hesitating. The baron did not speak, but sat looking straight at him, staring indeed as at something portentous. At the moment when the door opened to admit him, Sir Wilton was thinking of the monstrous baby stolen from him, and wondering if the creature were still alive and as hideous as twenty years before.

Sir Wilton had been annoyed with his wife that morning, and it was always a bitter thing to him not to be able to hurt her in return. But because of her cold imperturbability, revenge was impossible no matter what he might say. Therefore, as often as he sat in silent irritation with her, the thought of his lost child never failed to present itself. What a power over her ladyship would he not possess if only he knew where the heir to Mortgrange was! He was infernally ugly, but the uglier the better! If he could only find him, he swore he would have a merry time with his lady's pride! After so many years the poor lad might, ugly as he was, turn out to be presentable; if so, by heaven, that smooth-faced gentleman Arthur would have to shift for himself!

Suddenly Richard appeared, and before his father had time to settle what it could all mean, the apparition spoke.

"I am very sorry to intrude upon you, Sir Wilton," he said, "but—"

Here he paused.

"But you've got something to tell me—eh?" suggested Sir Wilton. He was on the point of adding, *If it be where you got those eyes, I may have to ask you to sit down!* but he checked himself, and said only, "You'd better make haste, then; for the devil is at the door in the shape of my cursed gout!"

"I came to tell you, Sir Wilton," replied Richard, plunging at once into the middle of things, which was indeed the best way with Sir Wilton, "about a son of yours—"

"What!" cried Sir Wilton, putting his hands on the arms of his chair and leaning forward as if on the point of rising to his feet. "Where is he? What do you know about him?"

"He is lying at the point of death—dying of hunger, I may say."

"Rubbish!" cried the baron, contemptuously. "You want to get money out of me! But you shan't! Not a shilling, not a penny!"

"I do want to get money from you, sir," said Richard. "I kept the poor fellow alive—kept him in dinners at least, him and his sister, till I fell ill and couldn't work."

At the word *sister* the baron grew calmer. It was nothing about the lost heir! The other sort did not matter; they were no use against the enemy!

Richard paused. The baron stared.

"I haven't a penny to call my own or I should not have come to you," resumed Richard.

"I thought so! That's your orthodox style! But you've come to the wrong man!" returned Sir Wilton. "I never did give anything to beggars."

He did not in the least doubt what he heard, but he scarcely knew what he answered—wondering where he had seen the fellow. But the stolen infant was ugly; there was not the remotest suggestion that this handsome fellow might be the same.

"You are the last man, Sir Wilton, from whom I would ask anything for myself," said Richard.

"Why so?"

Richard hesitated. To let him suspect the same claim in himself would be fatal to his plans.

"I swear to you, Sir Wilton," he said, "by all that men count sacred, I come only to tell you that Adam and Alice Manson, your son and daughter, are in dire need. Your son may be dead; he looked like it three days ago, and he had no one to attend to him; his sister had to leave him to earn their next day's food. Their mother was a corpse lying in the other of their two poor rooms."

"Oh, she's gone, is she? That changes the case. What became of all the money I gave her? It was more than her body was worth; soul she never had!"

"She lost the money somehow, and her son and daughter starved themselves to keep her in plenty, so that by the time she died, they were all but dead themselves."

"A pair of fools."

"A good son and daughter, sir!"

"You are attached to the young woman, eh?" asked the baron, looking hard at him.

"Very much, but hardly more than to her brother," answered Richard. "God knows if I had the strength I would work myself to the bone for them and not ask you for a penny!"

"I provided for their mother! Why didn't they look after the money? *I'm* not accountable for *them*!"

"Aren't you accountable for giving the poor things a mother like that, sir?"

"By Jove, you have me there! She *was* a bad lot—a most infernal liar! Young fellow, I don't know who you are, but I like your pluck! There aren't many I'd let stand talking to me like that! I'll give you something for the poor creatures—that is, mind you, if you've told me the truth about their mother! You're sure she's dead? They'll not have a penny if she's alive!"

"I saw her dead with my own eyes, sir."

"You're sure she wasn't shamming."

"She couldn't have shammed anything so peaceful."

The baron laughed.

"Believe me, sir," said Richard, "she's dead—and by this time buried by the parish."

"God bless my soul! Well, it's none of my fault!"

"She ate and drank her own children!" said Richard with a groan, for his own strength was failing. He sank into a chair.

"I will give you a check," said Sir Wilton, rising and going to a writing table in the window. "I will give you twenty pounds for them in the meantime—and then we'll see—we'll see—that is," he added, turning to Richard, "if you swear by God that you have told me nothing but the truth!"

"I swear," said Richard solemnly, "by all my hopes in God the Savior of men, that I have not knowingly said a single word that is untrue or incorrect."

"That's enough. I'll give you the check."

He turned again to the table, sat down, searched for his keys, unlocked and pulled out a drawer, took from it a checkbook, and settled himself to write with deliberation, thinking all the time.

"Have the goodness to come and fetch your money," he said tartly when he was finished.

"With pleasure!" answered Richard, and went up to the table.

Sir Wilton turned on his seat, and looked him in the face, full in the eyes. Richard steadily encountered his gaze.

"What is your name?" said Sir Wilton at length. "I must make the check payable to you."

"Richard Tuke, sir," answered Richard.

"What are you?"

"A bookbinder. I was here all the summer, sir, repairing your library."

"Oh! bless my soul! Yes, that's what it was! I thought I had seen you somewhere! Why didn't you tell me so at first?"

"It had nothing to do with my coming now, and I did not imagine it of any interest to you, sir."

"It would have saved me the trouble of trying to remember where I had seen you!"

Then suddenly a light flashed across his face.

By heaven, he muttered, *I understand it now! They saw it—that look on his face! By Jove! But now; she never saw* her! *She must have heard something about him, then!*—"They didn't treat you well, I believe," he said aloud. "Turned you away at a moment's notice! I hope they took that into consideration when they paid you?"

"I made no complaint, sir. I never asked why I was dismissed."

"But they made it up to you—didn't they?"

"To take money for ill-usage is to submit to it, it seems to me, and I don't submit to ill-usage, sir."

"By Jove, there are not many would call money ill-usage! Well, it wasn't right, them sending you away without notice, with the job not half completed, and I'll have nothing to do with it!—Here," he went on, wheeling round to the table and drawing his checkbook toward him, "I will give you another check for yourself."

"I beg your pardon, sir," said Richard, "but I can take nothing for myself. Don't you see, sir? As soon as I was gone, you would think I had come for my own sake."

"I won't, I promise you. I think you a very honest fellow."

"Then, sir, please continue to think me so, and don't offer me money."

"Lest you should be tempted to take it!"

"No, lest I should annoy you by what I do with it."

"Tut, tut! I don't care what you do with it! You can't annoy me!"

He wrote a second check, blotted it, then finished the other, and held both out to Richard.

"I can't give you so much as the other poor beggars; you haven't the same claim upon me!" he said.

Richard took the checks, looked at them, put the larger in his pocket, walked to the fire, and placed the other in the hottest cave of it.

"By Jove!" cried the baron, and again stared at him: he had seen another do precisely the same thing—with the same action, to the very turn of her hand, and with the same choice of the central gulf of fire!

Richard turned to Sir Wilton, and would have thanked him again on behalf of Adam and Alice, but something welled up in his throat, and with a grateful look and a bend of the head, he made for the door, speechless.

"I say, I say, my lad!" cried Sir Wilton, and Richard stopped.

"There's something in this," the baron went on, "more than I understand! I would give a big check to know what is in your mind! What does it all mean?"

Richard looked at him, but said nothing; he was fascinated by the old man's gaze.

"Suppose now," said Sir Wilton, "I were to tell you I would do whatever you asked me, so far as it was in my power—what would you say?"

"I would ask you for nothing," answered Richard.

"I make the promise: I say solemnly that I will give you whatever you ask of me—provided I can do it honestly," said the baron. Then the thought came to him, *What an infernal fool I am to talk so! But I must know what it all means! I shall find out some way!*

"I can ask you for nothing whatever, sir; but I thank you from my heart for my poor friends, your children. Believe me, I am grateful."

With a lingering look at his father, he left the room.

31 Duck-Fists

The godless old man was strangely moved. He rose, but instead of ringing the bell, hobbled after Richard to the door. As he opened it, he heard the hall door close. He went to it, but by the time he reached it, the bookbinder had turned the corner of the house to the spot where his grandfather was waiting for him.

He found him in his cart, expectant, his pony eating the grass at the edge of the road. Before the old man got his head pulled up, Richard was in the cart beside him.

"Drive on, Grandfather," he panted in triumph. "I've got it!"

"Got what, lad?" returned the old man, with a flash in his eyes.

"What I wanted. Money. Twenty pounds."

"Bah! Twenty pounds!" returned Simon with contempt.

"But of course," he went on, "twenty pounds will be a large sum to them, and give them time to look about and see what can be done. And now I'll tell you what, lad: if the young man is fit to be moved when you go back, you just bring him here — to the cottage, I mean—and it won't cost him a penny. I've a bit of a nest egg, and who knows but the place may suit him as it did his sister. You look into it when you get home."

"I will indeed, Grandfather! You're a good man."

Richard felt in his soul that, little reason as he had to be proud of his descent, he had at least one noble grandfather.

"Middling," returned the old man, laughing. "I'm not so good as my Maker meant me to be, and I'm not so bad as the devil would have me. But if I was the power above, I wouldn't leave things as they are. I'd have them a bit straightened out before I died."

"That is just what God is always doing, Mr. Wingfold would say."

"I know the man. Since you went, he's been once or twice to the smithy to ask about you. He's one of the right sort, I can tell that. He's a man, he is—most of them don't walk and talk and look like men! If more of the clergy was like Mr. Wingfold, why, the devil wouldn't have a chance."

They were spinning along the road, halfway home, when they became aware of a quick, sharp trot behind them. Neither looked around, but the next moment the horseman came alongside the cart and slackened his pace.

"Sir Wilton wants to see Mr. Tuke," he said. "He made a mistake in the check he gave him."

An arrow of fear shot through Richard's heart. What did it mean? Was the precious thing going to be taken from him? Was his hope to be destroyed? He took the check from his pocket and examined it: he could see nothing amiss with it. The next moment, however, he noticed that it was payable at a branch bank in the town of Barset, near Mortgrange. He concluded that the baron had, with more care than he would have expected of him, thought that this would cause trouble, so had sent his man to bring him back that he might replace the check with one payable in London. His heart warmed toward his father.

"I see," he said. "I'm sorry to cause you the trouble, Grandfather."

Simon turned the pony without a word, and they went trotting briskly back to Mortgrange. Richard explained what he thought was the matter with the check.

"I'm glad to find him so considerate!" said the old man. "It's a bad cheese that don't improve with age! Only men ain't cheeses!"

The moment he saw that Richard was indeed gone, the baron swore to himself that the fellow was his own son. He was his mother all over—anything but ugly, and far fitter to represent the family than the smooth-faced ape Lady Ann had presented him with! Then a doubt came into his mind: the boy's mother, lowborn as she was, had a sister somewhere; a son of hers might have stolen a likeness to the lady.

Alas for his grip on Lady Ann! The pincers melted in his grasp, and she was gone! It *was* a pity! If he had been a better man, he would have taken better care of the child, ugly as he was, and would have had him now to plague Lady Ann! But there was something odd about the child—something more than mere ugliness—

something his nurse had shown him in that very room! By Jove! what was it? It had something to do with ducks or geese or swans or pelicans! He had mentioned the thing to his wife, he knew; she was sure to have remembered it! But he was not going to ask her! Very likely she had known the fellow by it, and therefore had sent him out of the house! Yes! yes! by Jove! He had webs between his fingers and toes! He might have got rid of them, no doubt, but he must see this fellow's hands!

All this passed swiftly through Sir Wilton's mind. He rang the library bell furiously, and sent a groom after the bookbinder.

They drove in at the gate but stopped a little way from the house. Richard ran to the front door, found it open, and went straight to the library. There sat the baron.

"I thought to myself," said Sir Wilton the moment he entered, "that I had given you a check on the branch at Barset, when it would probably suit you better to have one headquartered in London."

"It was very kind of you to think of that, sir," answered Richard.

"Kind! I don't know about that. I'm not often accused of that weakness!" returned Sir Wilton, rising with a grin in which there was more of humor than ill nature.

He went to the table in the window, sat down, unlocked a drawer, took out a checkbook, and began to write a check.

"What did you say was your name?" he asked. "These checks are all made to order, and I should prefer your drawing the money."

Richard gave him again the name he had always been known by.

"Tuke! Beast of a name!" said the baron. "How do you spell it?"

Richard's face flushed, but he would not willingly show anger to one who had granted the prayer of his sorest need. He spelled the name to him as calmly as he could. But the baron had a keen ear.

"Oh, you needn't be crusty!" he said. "I meant no harm. One has fancies about names, you know. What did they call your mother before she was married?"

Richard hesitated. He did not want Sir Wilton to know who he was. He felt that if the relation between them was known, he would be forced to behave to his father in a way he would not like. Yet he must speak the truth!

"Her name was Armour, sir," he said.

"Hey!" cried the baron with a start. Yet he had all but expected it.

"Yes, sir, Jane Armour. My grandfather is Simon Armour, the blacksmith."

"Indeed." The baron's murmur was barely audible. "Jane," he muttered to himself. "What motive could there be for misinforming the boy about the Christian name of his mother?"

Richard stood perplexed. Sir Wilton had responded oddly to his mother's maiden name. He had said Mrs. Manson was a liar: might not her assertion of a relation between them be as groundless as it was spiteful? The baron had at once acknowledged the Mansons, but showed no recognition on hearing *his* mother's name. There might be nothing whatever in Mrs. Manson's story; he might, after all, be the son of John as well as of Jane Tuke!

"Here, put your name on the back there," said the baron, having blotted the check. "I have made it payable to your order, and without your name it is worth nothing."

"It will be safer to endorse it at the bank, sir," returned Richard.

"I see you know what you're about!" grinned Sir Wilton, thinking, *the rascal will be too much for me!* "But," he continued, "I see, too, that you don't know how to sign your own name! I had better alter it to *bearer*, with my initials! Curse it all! your paltry check has given me more trouble than if it had been for ten thousand! Sit down there, will you, and write your name on that sheet of paper."

Richard knew the story of Talleyrand—how, giving his autograph to a lady, he wrote it at the top left-hand corner of the sheet, so that she could not write above or in front of it an order for money or a promise of marriage or anything else which would bind him. Yielding to an absurd impulse, Richard did the same. The baron burst into loud laughter, which, however, ceased abruptly.

"What comical duck-fists you've got!" he cried.

"My feet are more that way than my hands," replied Richard. "Only *some* of my fingers have got the web between them. My mother made me promise to put up with the monstrosity till I came of age. She seems to think some luck lay in it."

"Your mother!" murmured the baron, and kept eyeing him. "By Jove," he said aloud, "your mother! Who *is* your mother?"

"Tuke, sir, my mother's name is Jane Tuke!"

"Born Armour?"

"Yes, sir."

By heaven! said the baron to himself, *I see it all now—the nurse—perhaps she was a cousin to Rebina—perhaps . . . Simon, the old villain, would know all about it!*

He sat silent for a moment.

"Hmm! Now tell me, you young rascal," he said, "why didn't you put in a claim for yourself instead of those confounded Mansons?"

"Why should I, sir? I didn't want anything. I have all I desire—except a little more strength to work, and that is coming."

The baron kept gazing at him with the strangest look on his wicked, handsome old face.

"There is something you *should* have asked me for!" he said at length, in a gentler tone.

"What is that, sir?"

"Your rights. You have a claim upon me before anyone else in the whole world! I like you, too," he went on in yet gentler tone, with a touch of mockery in it. Apparently he still hesitated to commit himself. "I must do something for you!"

The son could contain himself no longer.

"I would ask nothing, I would take nothing," he said, as calmly as he could, though his voice trembled and his heart throbbed with the beginnings of love, "from the man who had wronged my mother!"

"What do you mean, you rascal?" the baron burst out. "I never wronged your mother! Who said I wronged your mother, you scoundrel? I'll take my oath *she* never did! Answer me directly who told you so!"

His voice had risen to a roar of anger.

His son could do the dead no wrong by speaking the truth.

"Mrs. Manson told me—" he began, but was not allowed to finish the sentence.

"Like the liar she always was!" growled the baron. "The beast ought to have died on the gallows, not in her bed! Ah, she was the one to plot, the snake! In this whole curse of a world, *she* was the meanest devil I ever came across, and I've known more than a few!"

"I know nothing about her, sir, except as the mother of Adam, my school friend. She seemed to hate me! She said I belonged to you and had no right to be better off than her children."

"How did she know you?"

"I don't know, sir."

"You are like your mother, but that snake never could have set eyes on her! Give me that check! Her beasts won't have a farthing! Let them rot alive with their dead mother!"

He held out his hand: the second check lay on the table, and Richard had the former still in his possession. He did not move, nor did Sir Wilton urge his demand.

"Did I not tell you?" he resumed. "Did I not say she was a liar? I never did your mother a wrong—nor you, either, though I did swear at you a bit, you were so infernally ugly. But I don't blame you. You couldn't help it! Lord, what a display the woman made of your fingers and toes, as if the webs were something to be proud of, and made up for the face! Can you swim?"

"Fairly well, sir," answered Richard, carelessly.

"Your mother swam like a Naiad, was it—or Nereid? I forget—confound it!"

"I don't know the difference in their swimming."

"Nor any other difference, I daresay."

"I know the former was a nymph of a river, the other of the sea."

"Oh! you know Greek, then?"

"I wish I did, sir; I was not in school long enough. I had to learn a trade and be independent."

"By Jove, I wish I knew a trade and was independent! But you shall learn Greek, my boy! There will be some good teaching in *you*! I never learned anything! But how the deuce do you know about Naiads and Nereids and all that bosh if you don't know Greek?"

"I know my Keats, sir, though I had to plough through him with my dictionary."

"Good heavens!" said the baron, who knew as little of Keats as his young Vixen. "I wish I had been content to take you with all your ugliness, and bring you up myself, instead of marrying Lot's widow!"

Richard thought to himself that he preferred the upbringing he had, but he said nothing. Indeed, he could make nothing of the whole business. How was it that, if Sir Wilton had done his mother no wrong, his mother was the wife of John Tuke? He was bewildered.

"You wouldn't like to learn Greek, then?" asked his father.

"Yes, sir. Indeed I would!"

"Why don't you say so, then? I never saw such a block! You *shall* learn Greek! Why do you stand there looking like a dead oyster?"

"I beg your pardon, sir! May I have the other check?"

"Check?"

"The check there for my brother and sister," answered Richard, pointing to it where the baron had laid it, on the other side of him.

"Brother and sister?"

"The Mansons, sir," persisted Richard.

"Oh, give them the check and be hanged to them! But remember, they're no brother and sister of yours, and must never be alluded to as such, or as persons you have any knowledge of. When you've given them that"— he pointed to the check which still lay beside him— "you drop their acquaintance."

"That I cannot do, sir."

"There's a good beginning now! But I might have expected it! You tell me to my face you won't do what I order you?"

"I can't, sir; it wouldn't be right."

"Fiddlesticks!—Wouldn't be right! What's that to you? It's my business. You've got to do what I tell you."

"I must go by my conscience, sir."

"Oh, hang your conscience! Will you promise or will you not? You're to have nothing to say to those young persons."

"I will not promise."

"Not if I promise to look after them?"

"No, sir."

His father was silent for a moment, regarding him—not all in anger.

"Well, you're a good-plucked one, I allow! But you're the greatest fool, the dullest young half-wit, notwithstanding. You won't suit me though you are web-footed! Why, hang it, boy! don't you understand yet that I'm your father?"

"Mrs. Manson told me so, sir."

"Oh, rot Mrs. Manson! She lied; she told you I wronged your mother!"

"And did you not, sir? My mother had but one husband, and he is—"

"You fool! You are my son; whatever I may choose to give you is my own to give as I see fit."

Richard's heart gave a bound as if it would leap to heaven. Even acknowledged as a son, he had no hope of the land; nor did he care for the books; illegitimate, he could never be worthy of Barbara. But he could meet the needs of Adam and Alice! The voice of his father went on.

"You know now, you idiot," it said, "why you can have nothing more to do with that cursed litter of Mansons!"

Richard's heart rose to meet the heartlessness of his father.

"They are my brother and sister, sir!" he said.

"And what does it matter to you if they are! That's my business, not yours! You had nothing to do with it! You didn't make the Mansons!"

"No, sir. But God made us all, and says we're to love our brothers."

"Now, don't you get pious on me! It won't pay here! Mind you, nobody heard me acknowledge you! By the mighty heavens, I will deny knowing anything about you! You'll have to prove to the court of chancery that you're my son. By Jove, you'll find it stiff! Who'll advance you the money for such a suit? You can't do it without money! Nobody cares whether it be Sir Richard or Sir Arthur! The property's not entailed. But don't imagine I should mind telling a lie to keep the two together. I'm not a nice man; I don't mind lying!

I'm a bad man—that I know better than you or anyone else, and you'll find it uncomfortable to differ and deal with me both at once."

"I will not deny my own flesh and blood," said Richard.

"Then I will deny mine, and you may go rot with them!"

"Then I am no worse off. I will work for them and myself," said Richard.

Sir Wilton glared at him. Richard made a stride to the table. The baron grabbed up the check. Richard darted forward to seize it. Was his truth to his friends to be the death of them? He *would* have the money! It was his! The baron had told him to take it!

What might have followed I dare not think. Richard angrily approached his father, then he remembered that he had not given him back the former check, and Barset was quite within reach of his grandfather's pony. He turned and made for the door. Sir Wilton read his thought.

"Give me that check!" he cried, hobbling to the bell.

Richard darted out; the man, far off down the hallway, came to answer the bell. He hastened to meet him.

"Jacob," he said, "Sir Wilton rang for you. Just run down with me to the gate, and give the woman there a message for me."

He hurried to the door, and the man, doubting nothing, followed him.

"Tell her," said Richard as they went, "if she should see Mr. Wingfold pass, to ask him to call at old Armour's smithy. She does not seem to remember me! Good day! I'm in a hurry!"

He leaped into the pony cart, while Jacob began the long walk down the drive to the gate from the house, unaware that the baron was frantically awaiting his arrival in hopes of detaining Richard.

"Barset!" he cried, and the same moment they were off at full speed, for Simon saw that something was up.

"Let's see what this blessed pony can do! Every instant is precious!"

Never asking the cause of his haste, old Simon did his best, and never had the pony gone with a better will. He seemed to know speed was needed.

No hoofs came clamping on the road behind them. They reached the town in safety, and Richard cashed his check—all the more easily that Simon, a well-known man in Barset, was seen waiting for him in his wagon outside. The eager, anxious look on Richard's face, and the way he clutched at the notes, might otherwise have waked suspicion. As it was, he only aroused curiosity.

The man whom Richard had decoyed appeared at length, some time later, before his master, whose repeated ringing had brought the butler first. When Sir Wilton, after much swearing on his, and bewilderment on the servant's part, made out the trick played on him, his wrath began to evaporate in amusement: he had been outwitted and outmaneuvered—by his own son! Even in the face of such an early outbreak of hostilities, he could not help being proud of him. He burst into a half-cynical laugh, and dismissed the man to hopeless speculation on the meaning of the affair.

Simon encouraged Richard to send the banknotes by the mail and stay with him a week or two. But Richard insisted on taking them himself; no other way seemed safe. And he could not possibly rest until he had seen his mother and told her all. He said nothing to his grandfather of his recognition by Sir Wilton and what followed: he was afraid the old man might take the thing in his own hands and go to Sir Wilton himself.

Questioning his grandfather, he learned that Barbara was at home, but that he had seen her only once. She had one day appeared suddenly at the smithy door, with Miss Brown all in a foam. She asked about Richard, wheeled her mare round, and was off homeward, straight as an arrow.

They were near a station at Barset, and a train was almost due. Simon drove him there straight from the bank, and before the blacksmith was home, Richard was halfway to London.

Short as was his visit, he had gotten from it not merely all he had hoped for, but almost all he needed. His weakness had left him; he had twenty pounds for his brother and sister. And was he not also a little step nearer to Barbara? True, with the very revelation he had been disowned; he was no closer to legitimacy, but he had lived without his father till now, and could very well go on to live without such a father! As long as he did what was right, right was on his side! As long as he gave others their rights, he could waive his own! A fellow was not bound, he said, to insist on his rights.

Borne swiftly back to London, his heart was full of gladness with which to console the heavy hearts of Adam and Alice. Twenty pounds was a huge sum to take them—as much as Alice could earn in six months or a year! He could himself earn such an amount in a little while—possibly in two or three months if he applied himself, but how long would it take him to *save* this much? Now here it was, whole and free, powerfully ready to be turned at once into food and warmth and hope!

32 Baron and Blacksmith

The more Sir Wilton's anger subsided, the more his heart turned to Richard, and the more he regretted that he had begun by quarreling with him. Sir Wilton loved his ease, and was not a quarrelsome man. He could dislike intensely, he could hate heartily, but he seldom quarreled; and if he could have foreseen how his son would take the demand he made upon him, he would not at the outset have risked it. He liked Richard's looks and carriage. He liked also his spirit and determination, though he wished his first experience of them different. Very little refining would make him a man fit to show to the world and be proud of as his son. His satisfaction with Richard on these grounds was augmented by an additional, peculiar, secret pleasure in the discovery of him—the youth was a lump of dynamite under his wife's lounge, of which no one knew but himself, which he could at any instant explode. It was sweet to know what he *could* do, to be aware, and alone aware, of the fool's paradise in which his lady and her brood lived! But already, through his own hot-headed precipitation, his precious secret was in peril! Perhaps *he* had been the fool after all, rather than that rascal of a son of his, with his blasted principles!

The fact that he had let Richard slip away gave him considerable uneasiness. His thought was, at the ripest moment of Lady

Ann's frosty indifference, to make her palace of ice fly into pieces about her with his revelation. What a delight it would be to watch her perturbation! And now he had opened his hand and let his bird fly!

Sir Wilton did not know Richard's prudence. Like the fool every man of the world is, he judged from Richard's greatness of heart, and his refusal to forsake his friends, that he was a careless, happy-go-lucky sort of fellow, who would bluster and protest. As to the march he had stolen on him in order to escape to Barset to cash the check, he did not resent that. When pressed by no selfish necessity, he did not care all that much about money. In fact, his son's promptitude greatly pleased him.

The fellow shall go to college, he thought; *and I won't give my lady even a hint of it all before I have made of him the finest gentleman and the best scholar in the county! He shall be both! I will teach him billiards myself!*

"By Jove!" Sir Wilton laughed aloud, "it is more of a pleasure than I have a right to expect at my years! To think of an old sinner like me being blessed with such a victory over his worst enemy! It is more than I could deserve if I lived to the age of Mephistopheles—or Methuselah—or whatever his name was! I shouldn't like to live so long, there's so little worth remembering! I wish forgetting things wiped them out! Hang it, it may be all over Barset by this time, that Sir Wilton's lost son has turned up!"

He rang the bell, and ordered his carriage.

"I must see the old fellow, the rascal's grandfather!" he kept on to himself. "I haven't exchanged a word with him for years! And now that I think of it, poor Armour was a very decent sort of fellow! If he had but once hinted what he was, every soul in the parish would have known it. I *must* find out whether he's in on my secret! I can't *prove* it yet, but perhaps he can!"

Simon Armour was not altogether astonished to see the Lestrange carriage stop at the smithy; he thought Sir Wilton had come about the check. He went out, and stood in hairy arms and leather apron at the carriage door.

"Well, Armour, how are you?" said the baron.

"Well and hearty, sir, I thank you," answered Simon.

"I want a word with you," said Sir Wilton.

"Shall I tell the coachman to drive around to the cottage, sir?"

"No. I'll get out and walk there with you."

Simon opened the carriage door and the baron got out.

"That grandson of yours—" he began the moment they were in Simon's little parlor.

Simon started. *The old bloke knows!* he said to himself.

"—has been too much for me!" continued Sir Wilton. "He got a check out of me whether I wanted to give it to him or not!"

"And got the money for it, sir!" answered the smith. "He seemed to think the money better than the check!"

"I don't blame him, by Jove! There's decision in the fellow! They say his father's a bookbinder in London!"

"Yes, sir."

"You know better! I don't want humbug, Armour! I'm not fond of it! Tell me straight!"

"You told me people said his father was a bookbinder, and I said, 'Yes, sir.' "

"You know as well as I do it's all a lie! The boy is mine. He belongs neither to bookbinder nor blacksmith!"

"You'll allow me a small share in him, I hope! I've done more for him than you, sir."

"That's not my fault!"

"Perhaps not. But I've done more for him than you ever will, sir."

"How do you think that?"

"I've made him as good a shoesmith as ever drove nail! I don't say he's up to his grandfather at the anvil yet, but—"

"An accomplishment no doubt, but not exactly necessary to a gentleman!"

"It's better than dicing or card-playing!" said the blacksmith.

"You're right there! I hope he's learned neither. I want to teach him those things myself. He's not a bad-looking fellow!"

"There's not a better lad in England, sir. If you had brought him up as he is, you might have been proud of your work."

"*He* seems proud of somebody's work! Prouder of himself than his prospects, by Jove!" said Sir Wilton, feeling his way. "You should have taught him not to quarrel with his bread and butter!"

"I never saw any reason to teach him that. He never quarreled with anything at my table, sir. A man who has earned his own bread and butter ever since he left school is not likely to quarrel with it."

"You don't say *he* has done so?"

"I do—and I can prove it! Did you tell him, sir, that you were his father?"

"Of course I did! And before I said another word, there we were quarreling—just as it was with me and my father."

"He never told me!" said Simon, half to himself, and ready to feel hurt.

"He didn't tell you?"

"No, sir."

"Where is he?"

"Gone to London with your money."

"Now, Simon Armour—" began the baron with assertiveness in his tone.

"Now, Sir Wilton Lestrange!" interrupted Simon. "Please remember you are in my house!"

"Tut, tut! All I want to say is that you will spoil everything if you encourage the rascal to keep low company."

"You mean?"

"Those Mansons."

"Are your children low company, sir?"

"Yes. I am sorry, but I must admit it. Their mother was low company."

"The children are not the mother," said Simon. "I know the girl and she is anything but low company. She lay ill in my house here for six weeks or more. Ask Miss Wylder. If you want to be on good terms with your son, don't say a word against your daughter or her brother."

"I like that! On good terms with my son! Ha, ha!"

"Remember, sir, he is independent of his father."

"Independent! A beggarly bookbinder!"

"Excuse me, sir, but an honest trade is the only independence. You are dependent on your money and your land. Where would you be without them? And you made neither. We, my grandson and I, have means of our own," said the blacksmith, and held out his two brawny hands. "The thing that is beggarly," he resumed, "is to take all and give nothing. If your ancestors got the land by any good they did, you did not get it by any good you did; and having got it, what have you done in return?"

"By Jove! I didn't know you were such a radical!" returned the baron, laughing.

"Men like you, sir, make what you call radicals. If the landlords had used what was given to them to good ends, there would be no radicals—or not many—in the country! But when you call it yours and do nothing for it, I am radical enough to think no wrong would be done if you were deprived of it!"

"What! are you taking to the preaching stump at your age?"

"No, sir. I have a trade I like better, and have no call to involve myself in your affairs, however ill you may have used your land. But there are those that think they have a right to take the land from landlords like you, and I would no more leave my work to prevent them than I would to help them."

"Well, well! I didn't come to talk politics: I came to ask a favor of you."

"What I can do for you, sir, I shall be glad to do."

"It is merely this—that you will for the present say nothing about my son having turned up."

"I could have laid my hand on him any moment these past twenty years; and I can tell you where to find the parish book with his baptism in it. That I've not spoken proves I can hold my tongue; but I will give no pledge. When the time comes, I will speak."

"Are you aware I could have you severely punished for concealing his whereabouts?"

"Do your best! I'll take my chance. But I would advise you not to allow the issue to come into court. Words might be spoken that would hurt. I *know* nothing myself, but there is one that could and would speak. Better let sleeping dogs lie."

"Oh, hang it! I don't want to wake them! Most old stories are best forgotten. But what do you think: will the boy—what's his name?"

"My father's, sir—Richard."

"Will Richard, then, as you have taken upon yourself to call him—"

"His mother gave him the name."

"What I want to know is, will he go and spread the thing, or leave it to me to tell when I please?"

"Did you tell him to hold his tongue?"

"No. He didn't give me time."

"That's a pity! He would have done whatever you asked him."

"Would he?"

"He would—so long as it was a right thing."

"And who would be the judge of that?"

"Why the man who had to do it or not do it, of course! But if he didn't tell me, he's not likely to go blazing it abroad!"

"You said he would go to his mother first: his mother is nowhere."

"So some might say. But not I!"

"Never mind that. Who is it he calls his mother?"

"The woman that brought him up—and a good mother she's been to him!"

"But who is she? You haven't told me who she is!" cried the baron, beginning to grow impatient, and impatience and anger were never far apart with him.

"No, I haven't told you; and I don't mean to tell you till I see fit."

"And when, pray, will that be?"

"When I have your promise in writing that you will give her no trouble about what is past and gone."

"I will give you that promise—always provided she can prove that what was past and gone is come again. I shall insist upon that!"

"Most properly, sir! You shall not have to wait for it.—And now, if you will take me to the post office," responded the blacksmith, "and I will send a telegram to Richard, warning him to hold his tongue."

"Good! Come!"

They walked to the carriage, and Simon, displacing the footman, got up beside the coachman. He was careful, however, to be set down before they got within sight of the post office.

The message he sent was:

I know all, and will write. Say nothing but to your mother.

When Richard reached London he went straight to Clerkenwell. There he found Adam, in bed and unattended, but covered up warm. The room was tidy but very dreary. When Richard related to Adam his success with Sir Wilton, he thanked him with such a shining face that Richard saw in it the birth of saving hope.

"And now, Adam," he said, "you must get better as fast as you can. The first minute you are able to be moved, we'll ship you off to my grandfather's where Alice was."

"Away from Alice?"

"Yes. But you must remember there will be more for her to eat, and more money to get things comfortable with by the time you come back. Besides, you will grow well faster, and then perhaps we shall find some better work for you than that hideous clerking and money-counting."

The joy on Adam's face was nearly all the reward Richard needed for what he had done and sacrificed for the sake of his brother. He made a fire, set on the kettle, and went to buy some things, that he might have a nice supper ready for Alice when she came home. Next he found two clean towels and covered the little table, forgetting all his troubles in the gladness of being able to minister to others.

When Alice came in she heard Adam cough and hurried up the stairs, but before she reached the top of the second landing she heard such a merry laugh that she was filled with wonder and gladness. What could have made Adam laugh like that? She opened the door and there sat the only joy of their life, their brother Richard, looking much like himself again. What a healer, what a strength-giver is joy! She sprang forward and burst out weeping.

"Come and have supper," he said. "I've been out to buy it, and haven't much time to help you eat it. My father and mother don't know where I am. But we shall eat, and I shall tell you what I have been about."

With a happy heart Richard made his way home, for he left happy hearts behind him.

His elation was short-lived. When he opened the door to greet his parents, his mother was not in the least surprised to see him and she looked strangely troubled.

"What does this telegram mean?" she asked, holding it out toward him.

"I don't know, Mother," he replied. "Won't you give me a kiss first?"

She threw her arms about him.

"You won't stop saying *Mother* to me, will you?" she pleaded, fighting with her emotion.

"It will be a bad day for me when I do!" he answered. "My mother you are and shall be. Whatever do you mean?"

She showed him the curious telegram, and he realized that Sir Wilton and his grandfather had been in touch. Perhaps things might be worked out between him and his father after all.

"You've got your real father now, Richard!" said his mother.

But she saw an expression on his face that made her add, "You must respect your father, Richard, now that you know him for your father."

"Respect him!" Richard shot back. "After what he did to you? How can you apply the word 'respect' to him, Mother? He wronged you, and left me to be called 'bastard.' I care not for myself, but for your sake, I cannot respect him."

"But you must," his mother responded, tears welling up as she looked tenderly upon her boy. "He has done no wrong to your mother, beyond withholding a love of which he was incapable."

Richard, stunned speechless, stared at her.

"You are not illegitimate, my son," she whispered. "You are Sir Wilton's heir. And I am not your mother."

33 The Bookbinder's Heritage

It would be but stirring a muddy pool to inquire what forces compelled Sir Wilton Lestrange to marry a lowborn woman. His motives were mainly low ones, as demonstrated by their intermittent character and final cessation. The marriage to a social inferior brought about great surprise, and just as much annoyance, among the families of the county—many of their own grandmothers failing to remind themselves that they had been no better known to the small world than Lady Lestrange.

The union caused yet more surprise, though less annoyance, among the men of Sir Wilton's clubs: they set him down as a greater idiot than anyone had previously imagined him. Had he not been dragged to the altar by a woman whose manners and breeding were hardly on the level of a villa in St. John's Wood? Did anyone know whence she sprang, or even her name before Sir Wilton replaced it with his own?

Even Sir Wilton himself displayed no pride in his lady. His mother, a lady less dignified than eccentric, out of pure curiosity asked him to enlighten her concerning her origin, and received for answer from the high-minded baron, "Madam, the woman is my wife!" After that the prudent dowager asked no more questions. Sir Wilton, in fact, soon came to begrudge his wife the fact that he had married her and so generously bestowed upon her his name. The marriage was the fruit of but a momentary passion. Springing up suddenly, just as suddenly it died away, dropping from a loveless attraction to coldness, then to positive hatred.

And what of the woman, the other half of this union without heart? Although she was, after a fashion, in love with him, it was still not in her favor that Robina Armour, after experiencing his first advances, should have at last consented to marry Sir Wilton Lestrange. For what she was really in love with was the gentleman of her own imagining whom she saw in the baron; while the baron, on his part, was what he called *in love* with what he called *the woman.* As he was overcome by her beauty, so was she by his rank. Yet despite this misplacement of grounds for marriage, the blacksmith's daughter was in many respects a woman of good sense, with much real refinement, and a genuine regard for right. Sir Wilton had never loved her with what was best in him. Had his better nature been awake, it would have justified the bond and been strengthened by it.

Lady Lestrange's father was a good blacksmith, occasionally drunk in his youth, but persistently sober now in his middle-age. He had accounted it the prime duty of existence to take care of oneself, and communicated much of this belief to his younger daughter. After marrying Sir Wilton, however, Death knocked at her door with the cry of her first child, and she went with him when the child was but an hour old.

Not one of her husband's family was in the house when she died. Sir Wilton himself was in London, as he had been for the last six months, preferring the city and his club to Mortgrange and his wife. When a telegram informed him that she was in danger, he did go home; but when he arrived she had been an hour gone, and he congratulated himself that he had taken the second train.

There had been between them no approach to any depth of union. When what Sir Wilton called love had evaporated, he returned to his mire with a resentful feeling that the handsome woman—his superior in everything genuinely human, if not in rank—had bewitched him to his undoing. The truth was, she had ceased to charm him. The fault was not in her; it lay in the dulled eye of the swiftly deteriorating man, which grew less and less capable of seeing things as they were and transmitted falser and falser impressions of them. The light that was in him was darkness.

He was decent enough, however, not to parade his relief about. He retired to the library, lit a cigar, and sat down to wish the unpleasant fuss of the funeral over, and the house rid of the disagreeable presence. Had the woman died of some disease which he himself might one day have to face, her death might, as he sat there, have chanced to raise for an instant the watery ghost of an emotion. But as it was, he had no sympathetic interest in her death any more than in herself. Relaxing back in the easiest of chairs, he revolved in his mind the turns of last night's play at the theater, until it occurred to him that he might soon by a second marriage make amends in the eyes of his neighbors for their disapproval of his first. So pleasant was the thought that he fell asleep brooding upon it.

Some time passed, and suddenly he awoke, looked, rubbed his eyes, stared, rubbed them again, and stared. A woman stood in front of him; had he seen her before? No, surely he had never seen her anywhere! What an odd, inquiring, searching expression was looking at him out of her two hideous black eyes! And what was that in her arms—something wrapped in a blanket?

The message in the telegram recurred to him: a child! The bundle must be the child! Confound the creature! What did it want?

"Go away," he said. "This is not the nursery!"

"I thought you might like to look at the baby, sir!" the woman replied.

Sir Wilton stared at the blanket.

"It might comfort you, I thought," she went on, with a look he felt to be strange. Her eyes were hard and dry, red with recent tears, glowing with suppressed fire.

Sir Wilton was courteous to most women, but respected none. It was odd, therefore, that he should now feel embarrassed. The machinery of his self-content had somehow gotten out of gear; anyhow, no answer came. He had not the smallest wish to see the child, but was unwilling, perhaps, to appear brutal. In the meantime, the woman was parting and turning back the folds of the blanket with gentle, moth-like touch, until from behind it dawned a tiny human face for the baptism of its father's first gaze.

The woman held out the child to Sir Wilton, as if expecting him to take it. He jumped to his feet, sending the chair a yard behind him as he did, stuck his hands in his pockets, and with a look of disgust, cried, "Take the creature away!"

But he could not lift his eyes from the face nestled in the blanket. It seemed to fascinate him. The woman's eyes flared, but she did not speak.

"Uglier than sin!" he half hissed, half growled. "I suppose the animal is mine, but you needn't bring it so close to me. Take it away—and keep it away. I will send for it when I want it—which won't be in a hurry!"

"He is as God made him," remarked the nurse, quietly in spite of her growing wrath.

"Or the devil!" suggested his father.

The woman looked like a tigress. She opened her mouth, but then closed it again.

"I may say what I like of my own," said the father. "Tell me the goblin is not mine and I will be respectful as you please. Prove it, and I will give you a hundred pounds. He's ugly! He's hideous! Deny it if you can!"

The woman held her peace. Even to herself she could not call the child particularly pleasant to look at. She gazed on him for a moment with pitiful, protective eyes, then covered his face as if he were dead. But she did not move.

"Why don't you go?" said the baron.

Instead of replying, she began to remove the coverings at the other end of the bundle and presently disclosed the baby's feet. The baron gazed, wondering. She took one of the little feet in her hand and spread out the five pink baby toes. Between every pair of toes stretched a thin, delicate membrane. She laid the foot down and took up the other, which showed the same peculiarity. The child was web-footed, as distinctly as any properly constituted duckling! Then she lifted the tiny hands and showed, between the middle and third finger of each, the same sort of membrane rising halfway to the points of them.

"I see!" said the baron with a laugh that had no merriment in it. "The creature is a monster! Well, if you think I am to blame, I can only protest that you are mistaken. I am not web-footed! The duckness must come from the other side."

"I hope you will remember, Sir Wilton!"

"Remember? What do you mean? Take the monster away."

The woman rearranged the coverings of the little legs.

"Won't you look at your lady before they put her in her coffin?" she said.

"What good would that do her? She's past caring! No, I won't!

Why should I? Such sights are not pleasant."

"The coffin's a lonely chamber, Sir Wilton. Lonely to lie all day and all night in."

"She's past feeling loneliness, I daresay!"

"You are heartless, Sir Wilton!"

"Mind your own business. If I choose to be heartless, I have my reasons. Take the child away."

Still she did not move. The baby, young as he was, had thrown the blanket from his face, and the father's eyes were fixed upon it. While he gazed the nurse would not stir. He seemed fascinated by its ugliness.

"My God!" he said—for he had a habit of crying out as if he had a God—"The little brute hates me! Take it away, woman, before I strangle it!"

With a glance whose mingled anger and scorn the father did not see, the nurse turned and went.

He kept staring after her till the door shut, then fell back into his chair, exclaiming once more, "My God!" What or whom he meant by the word, it would be difficult to say.

"How could the woman have presented the world such a travesty? It's like nothing human! It's an affront to the family! They say your sins will find you out! It was a sin to marry the woman! What a fool I was! But she bewitched me. Curse the little monster! I won't be able to breathe till I am out of the house. Where was the doctor? He ought to have seen it! Hang it all, I'll go abroad!"

Ugly as the child was, to many an eye the first thing evident in him would have been his strong likeness to his father.

As tenderly as if he had been the loveliest of God's children, the woman bore her charge up the staircase and through corridors and passages to the remote nursery, where, in a cradle whose gay furniture contrasted sadly with the countenance of the child and the fierceness of her own eyes, she gently laid him down. Long after he was asleep she continued to bend over him, hardly able to restrain herself from clasping him again in her arms.

A dramatic fitness was evident even in the selection of this bold and outspoken nurse who was now the baby's only protector. She was the child's aunt.

Jane Tuke had been married four or five years, but had no children. Lady Lestrange's elder sister, she had arrived to be with her sister at the birth of her child. So great was Lady Lestrange's disappointment in her husband that she regarded the coming of his child almost with indifference. Jane, on the other hand, had an absolute passion for children. She had married a quarter for faith, a quarter for love, and a whole half for hope of being a mother. As displeasing as this infant was, to have him as her own son would have made the world a paradise to Jane. Her heart burned with divine indignation at the wrongs already heaped upon her nephew. The more the baby was rejected, the more hers he became! He belonged to her, for she was the only one who loved him. No vision or riches ever produced such a longing as this woman's longing after the child of her sister.

The body that bore the child was laid in the earth. His mother had helplessly forsaken the infant, but the God in another woman had taken him up: there was a soul to love him, two arms to carry him, a strong heart to shelter him.

Sir Wilton returned to London, and there enjoyed himself—not much, but at least comfortable in the knowledge that no woman sat at Mortgrange with a right to complain that he lived a life of pleasure without her. He moved in society, beginning to assume the staidness, if not dullness, of a man whose first youth has departed; but he was only less frolicsome, not more human. He was settling down to what he had made himself; no virtue could claim a share in the diminished rampancy of his vices.

With the first unacknowledged signs of approaching age, the idea of a quieter life, with a woman whose possession would make him envied, grew mildly attractive. A brilliant marriage could, in addition, avenge him in the minds of those who had despised his first choice. With judicial family-eye, therefore, he began to survey the eligible women of his acquaintance. To his disadvantage, an heir already lay crying in the nurse's arms, for any woman who might willingly be mother to the inheritor of such a property as his would certainly not find the notion attractive that her firstborn would be her husband's *second* son. But who could tell—possibly he would be lucky and the heir that fate had palmed upon him might be doomed to go the way of so many infants!

He spread the report that the boy was sickly, and the notion that he was not likely to live prevailed about Mortgrange. However it was originated, this rumor was nourished by the fact that he was seen so seldom. In reality, there was not a healthier child in all England than Richard Lestrange.

Sir Wilton's relations took as little interest in the heir as they did Sir Wilton himself, and few of them ever found reason to visit Mortgrange. The aunt-mother, therefore, had her own way with him. She was not liked in the house, the servants said she cared only for the little toad of a baron, and they would do nothing for her comfort. They had a shadow of respect for her, however: if she encouraged no familiarity, she did not meddle and was independent of their aid. Even the milking of the cow which had been set apart for the child, she did herself. She sought no influence in the house, and was both little loved and little heeded.

Sir Wilton had not again seen his heir, now almost a year old, when the rumor reached Mortgrange that the baron was about to be married.

Naturally, the news disquieted Jane. She hoped, however, that the stepmother might care as little for the child as the father did, and that he would therefore—for some years, at least—be left to her care. The loving woman lived in fear that they might be parted; more terrible was the thought that her baby might become a man like his father.

34 Stepmother

The rumor of Sir Wilton's marriage was, as rumor seldom is, correct. Before the year was out, Lady Ann Hargrove, sister to the Earl of Torpavy—an old family with a drop or two of very bad blood in it—became Lady Ann Lestrange. Whether love had part in the affair was questionable, considering the baron's history. His lady understood her husband's character pretty well. She might have preferred a husband different from Sir Wilton, but she was twenty-nine, and her brother was poor despite his title. If she waited much longer, she might never marry at all.

When they arrived at Mortgrange the man wore a look of careless all-rightness, tinged with an expression of indifferent triumph; he had what he wanted. What his lady might think of her side of the bargain he neither thought nor cared. The woman, whatever her reflections, would never reveal them to a soul. Her pale, handsome face was never false to herself, never betrayed what she was thinking, never broke the shallow surface of its frozen dignity. No trace, no shadow of disappointment clouded the countenance of Lady Ann that sultry summer afternoon as she drove up the treeless avenue. She had been trained to fashionable perfection, even though the vague animal in her nature was just visible: in the curve of her thin lips as they prepared to smile, one could discern the veiled snarl and bite. Her eyes were gray, her eyebrows dark, her complexion a clear fair, her nose perfect, except for a sharp pinch at the end of the bone; her nostrils were thin but motionless; her chin was defective, and her throat as slender as her horrible waist.

After his lady had had a cup of tea, Sir Wilton proposed taking her over the house, which was old and worthy of inspection. In their progress they came to a door at the end of a long passage. Sir Wilton did not know what the room was used for or he would have passed it by. But since its windows offered a fine view of the park, he opened the door and Lady Ann entered. Sudden displeasure shortened her step; she found herself bearing down on a woman too occupied with the child on her knee even to look up at their entrance. A moment later she did look up to see the dreaded stepmother looking straight down on her baby. Their eyes encountered. Jane met an icy stare, Lady Ann a gaze of defiance. Not a word did the lady utter, but to Jane her eyes and her very breath seemed to say with scorn, *Is that the heir?* Sir Wilton did not venture a single look: he was ashamed of his son, and already a little afraid of his wife. As she turned toward the window, however, he stole a glance at his offspring: the creature was not quite so ugly as before—not quite so repulsive as he had pictured him. But, good heavens! He was on the lap of that same woman whose fierceness had upset him almost as much as his child's ugliness! He walked to the window after his wife. She gazed for a moment, turned with indifference, and left the room. Her husband followed; a glance of fear, enmity, and defiance went after them.

The contrast between the two women could hardly have been more striking. Jane's countenance was coarse, but its rugged outline was almost grand. Her hair grew low down on her forehead, and she had deep-set eyes. Her complexion was rough, her nose large and thick. Her mouth was large also, the curve of her lip sweet, occasionally humorous. Her chin was strong, and the composite of her face might be called masculine; but when she silently regarded her child, it grew beautiful with the radiant tenderness of protection.

Her visitors left the door open behind them; Jane rose and shut it, sat down again, and gazed at the infant. Perhaps he vaguely understood the sorrow and dread on her face, for he started to cry. Jane clasped him to her bosom: she felt certain she would not long be permitted to stay and care for him! In the lady's silence, her jealous love heard the voice of doom pronounced against her darling. What precise doom she dared not ask herself. That she should be his guardian no more was unthinkable, an idea for which there should be no place in her soul! Unfathomable as the love between man and woman is the love of woman to child.

She spent a restless night, certain the decree of banishment was soon to go out against her. She must go, yet her heart cried out that he was her own. In the same lap his mother had also lain, carried by day, and at night folded in the same arms—Jane herself but six years old. Never had there been a difference between the two sisters until Robina began to listen to Sir Wilton, whom Jane could not endure. When she responded to her sister's cry for help, she made her promise that no one should know who she was, she should simply be taken for and treated as a hired nurse. Why Jane stipulated this, it was hard to say, but so careful were they both that no one at Mortgrange suspected the nurse as having the same blood as the ugly heir left in her charge. No one dreamed that the child's aunt had forsaken her own husband to nurse him. She, in turn, had promised her sister never to leave him, and this pledge only strengthened the bond of her passion. The only question was *how* to be faithful to her pledge and *what* to do when she was relieved of her duties. Seeing those thin, close-pressed lips in her mind's eye, Jane knew she could not count on remaining where she was beyond a few more days.

Jane Tuke was not only a woman capable of making up her mind, but a woman of resource, with the advantage of foresight. Often she had thought about the very possibility she was now facing. That same night, after her darling was asleep, she sat at work with needle and scissors far into the morning, making alterations on an old print dress. For several nights thereafter she was similarly occupied, though not a scrap or sign of the labor was visible in the morning.

The anticipated crisis came within two weeks. Lady Ann did not show herself a second time in the nursery but, sending for Jane, informed her that an experienced nurse was on her way from London to take charge of the child, and her services would not be required after the next morning.

"For of course," concluded the lady, "I could not expect a woman of your years to undertake a nurse's place!"

"Please, your ladyship, I will do so gladly," said Jane, eager at least to postpone the necessity which was being forced upon her.

"I intend you to go—*at once*," replied Lady Ann. "That is, the moment Mrs. Sweeny arrives. The housekeeper will take care that you have your month's full wages in lieu of advance warning."

"Very well, My Lady! Please, your ladyship, when may I come and see the child?"

"Not at all. There is no necessity."

"Never at all?"

"Decidedly not."

"Then may I at least ask why you are sending me away so suddenly?"

"I told you that I want a properly qualified nurse to take your place. My wish is to have the child more immediately under my own eye than would be agreeable if you kept your place. I hope I speak plainly!"

"Quite, My Lady."

"And let me, for your own sake, recommend that you behave more respectfully when you find another place."

Jane went in silence, seeming to accept the inevitable, too proud to wipe away the tear whose rising she could not prevent—a tear not for herself, nor for the child, but for the dead mother whose place was usurped by such a woman. She walked slowly back to the nursery where her charge was asleep, closed the door, sat down by the cot, and sat for a while without moving.

Then her countenance began to change, and slowly went on changing, until at last, as through a mist of troubled emotion, out upon the strong, rugged face broke the glow of resolve. A maid more friendly than the rest brought her some tea, but Jane said nothing of what had occurred. When the child awoke, she fed him and played with him a long time, until he was thoroughly tired. Then she undressed him, laid him down, and set about preparing his evening meal. No one could have perceived in her any difference, but a subdued excitement shone in her glowing eyes. When the supper was ready, she went to her box, took from it a small bottle, and poured a few dark-colored drops into the food.

"God forgive me! It's but this once!" she murmured.

The child seemed not quite to relish his supper, but did not refuse it, and was presently asleep in her arms. She laid him down, took a book, and began to read.

35 Flight

She read until every sound in the house had died, every sound from attic to cellar. In the silence she rose, laid down her book, softly opened the door, and stepped even more softly into the narrow passage. She listened for a moment or two, then stole on tiptoe to the main corridor and listened again. She walked to the head of the great stairway and there stood and listened. Then she crept down to the drawing room, saw there was no light in the library, billiard room, or smoking room, and with stealthy feet returned to the nursery. There she closed the door she had left open and took the child. He lay in her arms like one dead. She removed everything he wore and dressed him in the garments she had been making for the last two weeks out of clothes of her own. When she was done he looked like any laborer's child, and nothing in his face contradicted the appearance of his attire. She regarded the result for a moment with a triumph of satisfaction, laid him down, and proceeded to put away the clothes he had worn.

Over the top of the door was a small cupboard in the wall. She had never looked into it until the day before, when she opened it and found it empty. She placed a table under it and a chair on the table, climbed up, laid in it everything she had taken off the child, locked the door of it, put the key in her pocket, and got down. Then she took the cloak and hood he had till then always worn out-of-doors, laid them down beside the wardrobe, and lifting the end of it with a strength worthy of a blacksmith's daughter, pushed them with her foot into the hollow between the bottom of the wardrobe and the floor of the room. This done, she looked at the clock on the mantel shelf, saw it was one o'clock, and sat down to recover her breath.

The next moment she was on her knees sobbing. By and by she rose, wiped the hot tears from her eyes, and went carefully about the room, gathering up small items and putting them into her box. Having locked it, she stuffed a number of small pieces of paper into the lock, using a crochet needle to get them well into the works of it. Lastly, she put on a dress she had never worn at Mortgrange and picked up the child, who was still in a dead sleep. She wrapped him in an old shawl, and stole with him from the room.

Like those of a thief, her eyes looked this way and that as she crept to a narrow stair that led to the kitchen. She knew every turn and every opening in this part of the house, and for weeks had been occupied in her imagination with the daring idea she was now carrying out.

She reached the door that was most likely to offer her a safe exit, unlocked it quietly, and stood in a little paved yard from which another door in an ivy-covered wall opened into the kitchen garden. The moon shone large and clear, but the shadow of the house gave her cover. It was the month of August, warm and still. For the first time in her life she wished for darkness. Along the wall she stole, clinging to it for safety. Another door led into the shrubbery surrounding the cottage of the head gardener, from which a back road led to a gate to the highway. Along the road's honest, unshadowed spaces she must then walk miles and miles before she could even begin to hope herself safe.

She stood at length in the broad moonlight, gazing down the white, far-reaching road. Her heartbeat stifled her; she dared not look down at the child. The moon itself even looked suspicious! For an instant she wished herself back in the nursery. But she knew that she would only have to do it all over again: it *had* to be done! She could never leave the child of her sister to be in the way, with those who hated him, where his helpless life would be in danger! She could not!

But while she was thinking, she did not stand still. Softly, with great strides, she stalked along the road. She knew the country; she was not many miles from her father's forge, and at moments she almost seemed to hear the ring of his hammer through the still night.

She kept to the road for three or four miles, then turned aside on a great moor stretching far to the south. Daybreak was coming fast, and she must find some cottage or natural shelter so that the light would not betray her. When the sun had made his round and yielded his place to the friendly night once again, she would start afresh. In her bundle she had enough for the baby; she herself could hold out many hours without food. A few more miles from Mortgrange and no one would know her! They could never, from any possible description, be suspected by the garments they wore! She had hidden their usual attire; Sir Wilton might take for granted they had gone away in it.

She did not slacken her pace till she had walked five miles more. Then she stood a moment, gazing about her. The great heath was all around, solitary as the heaven out of which the solitary moon was watching them. Even then she would not stop to rest except for the briefest breathing space. On and on she went for another five miles, as near as she could judge, until the moorland was behind her. Then at length she sat down upon a stone, and a timid flutter of safety stirred in her bosom, followed by a gush of love victorious.

Her treasure! Not once on the long way had she looked at him. Now she folded back the shawl and gazed on the sleeping countenance. Who but she could have a right to the child? Surely not a coldhearted, cruel stepmother who would give him to a hired woman! She jumped to her feet, and hurried on. The boy was no light weight, and she had other things to carry besides; but before seven o'clock she had cleared some sixteen miles, in a line away from Mortgrange as straight as she could keep.

She neared a village whose name she knew, but she dared not show herself lest some inquiry might later reach it and lead to the discovery of the route she had taken. Therefore she turned aside into an old quarry to spend the day. The child was now awake, but still drowsy. She gave him a little food, and ate the crust she had saved from her tea the night before. During the long hours she slept off and on a good deal, and when evening came she was quite fit to resume her tramp. To her joy it became cloudy, giving her courage to enter a little shop she saw on the outskirts of the village and buy some milk and bread. From this point she kept to the road. If she had the opportunity she might now take help from a cart or wagon. She was not without some money, but was afraid of the train. So she wandered, weary, but with great purpose, toward London, and the populous suburb where her husband awaited her.

It was the middle of the day before they were missed. Their absence caused no commotion for a time; the servants said the nurse must have taken the child for his usual walk. But the nurse from London arrived; after renewed search and inquiry, nothing was heard of them, and their disappearance could no longer be kept from Lady Ann. She sent a servant to inform her husband.

Sir Wilton asked a question or two of her messenger, said the thing must be seen to, finished his cigar, threw the stump in the fire, and went to his wife. They at once began to discuss, not steps to be taken for the recovery of the child, but the woman's motive for stealing him. The lady insisted it was revenge for having been turned away. She would no doubt, she said, put an end to his life as soon as she reached a suitable place: she had seen murder in her eyes! The father's opinion was that there was no such danger. Though he did not mention it, he remembered the peculiarity of the woman's behavior when he first saw her.

"There is no limit," he said, "to the unnatural fancies of women; some are disgustingly fond of children, even of other women's children." Plain as the infant was, Sir Wilton did not doubt she had taken a fancy to him and therefore could not bear to part with him. True, the element of revenge could have some small share in the deed. As far as he was concerned, he concluded, she was welcome to the child!

Lady Ann gave no answer. She was not easily shocked, and it would have caused her no particular consternation simply to regard the disappearance as final. But something must at least *appear* to be done! If they just let the matter drop, unpleasant things might be said, and uncertainty was always full of annoyance!

"You must be careful, Sir Wilton," she remarked. "Nobody thinks you believe the child your own."

Sir Wilton laughed.

"I never had a doubt on the subject. I wish I had; he's not to my credit. If we never hear of him again, all the better for the next!"

"True!" rejoined Lady Ann. "But what if, after we have forgotten all about him, he were to turn up again?"

"That would be unpleasant—and is indeed a reason why we should look for him. Better to find him than live in doubt! Besides, the world would be cruel enough to hint that you had made away with him; it's what ought to have been done when he first appeared. I give you my word, Ann, he was a positive monster, actually web-footed—like any frog!"

"You must let the police know," said the lady.

"That the child is web-footed? No, I don't think so," said Sir Wilton.

He got up, went out, and ordered a groom to ride hard to the village and tell the police what had happened. Within the hour a constable appeared, come to inquire when the fugitives were seen last and what they wore—the answer to which question set the police looking for persons very different in appearance from Jane and her nursling. Nothing was heard of them, and the inquiry, never prosecuted with any vigor, was by degrees dropped entirely.

John Tuke was in bed asleep when suddenly he opened his eyes and saw beside him the wife he had not seen for twelve months, with the stolen child in her arms. When he heard how the stepmother had treated her, and how the baby was likely to fare, he was filled with indignation. He thoroughly appreciated and approved of his wife's decision and energy, but he saw that the deed exposed them to frightful consequences if it were discovered.—And discovered it must be, eventually. But when he understood the precautions she had taken, and thought about how often the police fail, he had better hopes of escape. Even amid the risk, it never occurred to John Tuke to return the child to the scene of his wife's crime. They would accept both child and consequences as they might come.

When Jane had left for Mortgrange they had agreed that her husband should say she was gone to her father's. Since nobody where they lived knew who or where her father was, nobody had any possible clue as to where she had been. For some time after her return she did not show herself, leaving it to her husband to say she had come back with her baby. Then she began to appear with the child, and so managed her references to her absence that no one dreamed of his not being her own, or imagined that she had left her husband for any other reason than to be tended during and after her own childbirth at her old home. After a few years, even the fact of his not having been born in that house was forgotten, and Richard grew up as the son of John Tuke, the bookbinder, with not a single doubt as to his parentage.

36 Uncle-Father, Aunt-Mother

"Thus," Jane Tuke concluded, "you became son of our hearts, though not our bodies."

Richard had listened thoughtfully to his mother's tale, unaware, to any great extent, of what her revelation meant to him. Most immediately, it meant that she was free of shame and accusation. She was not an ignoble woman—and how his heart rejoiced in the truth!

"Much of what Sir Wilton—my father—said to me now makes sense," Richard mused. "He said he had caused my mother no disgrace, but I could not understand how I could reconcile his assurance with what Mrs. Manson said."

"Mrs. Manson is—was—a vile and despicable woman!" Jane Tuke spat out. "She was ill-used by Sir Wilton and left with two illegitimate children to raise, so she struck out at you with her poison."

"Alice and Adam are my brother and sister—" Richard began to protest, but his mother cut him off.

"Those two again!" she sputtered. "I told you—"

"I know, Mother," he answered. "You wanted to protect me from loving my sister as I should not have loved her. But there was never any danger of that. She was always a sister to me—"

"Sister!"

"Sister indeed!" he returned. "And now—"

"Now," she finished for him, "you can take your proper place at Mortgrange. I would never have taken you away at all if that woman hadn't sent me away for no reason but to have a nurse of her own choosing and control over you. How could I leave my sister's child in the power of such a woman? Day and night, Richard, I was haunted with the sight of her cold face hanging over you. I was certain the devil might have his way with her when he chose: there was no love in her to prevent him. In my dreams I saw her giving you poison, or with a penknife in her hand and her eyes shining like ice. I could not bear it! I knew I was committing a crime in the eyes of the law, but I felt a stronger law compelling me, and I said to myself, 'I will be hanged for my child, rather than that my child should be murdered! I will *not* leave him with that woman!' So I took you, Richard!"

"Thank you a thousand times, Mother! I am sure it was the right and best thing for me! How much I owe to you and my uncle! I must call you *mother* still, but I am afraid I shall have to call my father *uncle*."

"It won't hurt him, Richard; he has been a good uncle to you, but I don't think he would have taught you the things he did if you had been his very own child."

"He has done me no harm, Mother—nothing but good," said Richard. "And so you are my mother's sister?"

"Yes, and a good mother she would have been to you! You must not think of her as a grim old woman like me! She was but twenty-six when you were born and she died. She was the most beautiful woman I ever saw, Richard!—Never another woman's hand has touched your body but hers and mine."

He took her hand and kissed it. Jane Tuke had never had her hand kissed before, and would have drawn it away. The lady within was ashamed of her rough hands, not knowing they had won her her ladyhood, for there are no ladies but true women. What lovely ladies will walk into the next world out of the rough cocoon of their hard-wrought bodies—not because they have been working women, but because they have been true women. Among working women as among countesses, there are last that shall be first, and first that shall be last. No doubt the next world will resume the patterns of this one more directly than most people think—only it will be much better for some, and much worse for others, as the Lord has taught us in the parable of the rich man and the beggar.

"No, Richard," resumed his aunt, "your father was not a good man, but he may be better now, and perhaps you will help him to be better still."

"It's doubtful I may get such a chance," returned Richard. "We've had a pretty fair quarrel already!"

"He can't take your birthright from you!" she cried.

"That may be—but what *is* my birthright? He told me the land was not entailed; he can leave it to anyone he likes. But I'm not going to do what he would have me do—that is, if it be wrong," he added, not willing to reopen the discussion of the Mansons at the moment. "To be a sneak would be a fine beginning! If that's to be a gentleman, I will be no gentleman!"

"Right you are, my son!" said Tuke, who that moment came in.

"Oh, Uncle!" cried Richard, jumping to his feet.

"*Uncle!* Ho! ho! What's up now?"

"Nothing's up, but all's out, Father," answered Richard. "You knew, and now I know. How shall I ever thank you for what you have done for me, and been to me, and given me!"

"Precious little, my boy! I wish it had been a great deal more."

"Shall I tell you what you have done for me? You made a man of me first, by giving me a trade and making me independent. Then again, by that trade you taught me to love the very shape of a book. Baron or no baron—"

"What do you mean?"

"My father threatens to disown me."

"He can't take your rank from you. We'll have you Sir Richard anyhow! And I'd let them see that a true baron—"

"—is just a true man, Uncle!" interposed Richard; "and that you've helped to make me. Being independent and helping others, not being a baron, will make a gentleman of me. That's how it goes in the true world, anyhow."

"The *true* world! Where's that?" rejoined Tuke.

"And that reminds me of another precious thing you've given me," Richard went on. "You've taught me to think for myself."

"Think for yourself indeed, and talk of any world but the world we've got?"

"If you hadn't taught me to think for myself," returned Richard, "I should have thought just as you did. But I've been thinking for myself a great deal, and I now believe that, if there be nothing more after we die, then life is so ridiculous that even the dumb, deaf, blind, heartless God you seem to believe in could not have been guilty of making it!"

"Ho! ho! That's the good my teaching has done you? Well, we'll have it out by and by! In the meantime, tell us how it all came about—how you came to know, I mean. You're a good sort, whatever you believe or don't believe, and I wish you were really ours!"

"In reality I am yours!" protested Richard, but his mother broke in:

"Would you dare, John," she cried, "to wish him ours to his loss?"

"No, no, Jane! You know me! It was but a touch of what you call the old Adam—and I the old John! We've got to take care of each other! We're all agreed about that!"

"Come and let's have our tea!" said the mother, "and Richard shall tell us how it worked round that the old gentleman knew him. I remember him when he was young enough to be no bad match for your mother—in terms of looks, I mean. There wasn't a more beautiful woman than my sister Robina in all England, I'm bold to say—not that it takes much boldness to say the truth!"

"It takes nearly as much as I have right now," returned Richard, realizing that he now had to tell what had made him go to his father.

He had only begun when a black cloud rose on his mother's face and she nearly jumped from her seat.

"I told you, Richard, you were to have nothing to do with those creatures!" she cried.

"Mother," he answered, "was it God or the devil that told me I must be neighbor to my own brother and sister? Hasn't my father done them wrong enough that you should side with him and want me to carry on the wrong? I heard the same voice that made you want to run away with me. You were ready to be hanged for me; I was ready to lose my father for them. He, too, said I must be done with them, and I told him I wouldn't. That was why I got you to put me on journeyman's wages, Uncle. They were starving, and I had nothing to give them. What am I in the world for, if not to set right, as far as I may, what my father has set wrong? You see, I *have* learned something from you, Uncle!"

"I don't see what," returned Tuke.

He had been listening with a grave face, for he had his pride, and did not relish his nephew's being hand-in-glove with his base-born brother and sister.

"If a man's ideas of doing good don't apply to those closest to him," resumed Richard, "where on earth is it to begin? Must you turn your backs on those nearby and go to Russia or China for somebody to minister to? If Sir Wilton Lestrange were to come into this room this minute, you would offer him a chair. But his children you would order out of the house!"

"I wouldn't do that," said Mrs. Tuke.

"Mother, you *did* turn them out of the house—I beg your pardon, but you know it was the same thing. You visited the sins of the father on the children."

"Bravo!" cried his uncle. "I thought you couldn't mean it!"

"Mean what, Father?"

"That rot about God you said a while ago."

"Father, I have changed. It would take the life out of me now to believe there was no God. I was wrong not to believe in him. But the God I have come to hope in is a different person from the God my mother's clergy have taught her to believe in, and a different God than you think you don't believe in."

"Different? How so?"

"Different because of Jesus Christ. Do you know him, Father?"

"I know the person you mean, my boy."

"Well I now know what *kind* of person he is, and he said God was just like him. And I will believe in a God that is like him, if I can find him, with all my heart and soul—and so would you, Father, if you knew him. You will say, perhaps, that he isn't anywhere *to* know, but as someone pointed out to me, you haven't a right to say that until you've been everywhere to look."

He had spoken eagerly, and some may think he ought to have held his tongue. But neither father nor mother took offense. The mother, unspeakably relieved by what had taken place, was even ready to allow that her favorite preacher might "perhaps dwell too much upon the terrors of the law."

37 A Meeting

The next day's mail brought a letter from Simon Armour, saying in his own peculiar way that it was time the thing was properly understood between all the parties involved; but that they must honor the baron's wishes and disclose nothing yet: he believed Sir Wilton had his reasons. They must, therefore, as soon as possible, make it perfectly clear to him that there was no break in the chain of their proof of Richard's identity. He proposed, therefore, that his daughter and Richard should come for a visit.

The suggestion seemed good to all concerned. Though she knew what she had done was criminal, Jane Tuke did not shrink from facing Sir Wilton side by side with the nephew she had carried to him twenty-one years earlier. To her surprise she found that she almost enjoyed the idea.

Richard cashed the money order the old man had sent them, and they set out for his cottage.

The same day Simon went to Mortgrange and saw the baron, who agreed at once to go to the cottage to meet his sister-in-law.

The moment he entered the little parlor where they waited to receive him, he made Mrs. Tuke a polite bow and held out his hand.

"You are the sister of my late wife, I am told," he said.

Jane made a dignified curtsey, her resentment, even after a lapse of twenty years, rising once again at the sight of the man who had behaved so badly to her sister.

"You carried off the child?" asked the baron.

"Yes, sir."

"I am glad I did not know where to look for him. You did me the greatest possible favor. What these twenty years would have been like, with him in the house, I dare not think."

"I did it for the child's sake," said Jane.

"I am perfectly aware it was not for mine," returned Sir Wilton. "Ha, ha! you looked as if you had come to stab me that day you brought the little object to the library and presented his fingers and toes to me as if, by Jove, I was the devil and had made them so on purpose! I tell you, Richard, if that's your name, you rascal, you have as little idea what a preposterously ugly creature you were, as I had that you would ever grow to be—well, half fit to look at! But it doesn't follow you're the least fit to be owned to. You're a tradesman, every inch of you! You don't look like a gentleman in the least, though your aunt looks as if she would eat me for saying it.

"Now listen to me, all of you. It's no use your saying I've acknowledged him. If I choose to say I know nothing about him, then as I told the rascal himself the other day, you'll have to prove your case, and that will take money! If you prove it, you still will get nothing but the title, and much good that will do you! So you had better make up all your minds to do as I tell you—that is, not to say one word about the affair, but just hold your tongues. I'm not going to have people say my son shows the tradesman in him. He will be all the gentleman I can make him!

"So you're off to the university directly, young man," Sir Wilton said, "and I don't want to hear of or from you until you've taken your degree! You shall have two hundred pounds a year and pay your own fees—not a penny more! You're not to attempt to communicate with me. If there's anything I ought to know, let your grandfather come to me. Only, mind, I make no promises! If I should leave everything to the other lot, you will have no right to complain. With the education I give you, the independence your uncle has given you, and the good sense you have, you're well provided for. You can be a doctor or a parson, you know. The Reverend Sir Richard Lestrange! It doesn't sound too bad.

"Only mind this," the baron concluded, "if once you say who you are as long as you're at the university, or before I give you leave, I will be done with you. I won't have any plan of mine interfered with for your vanity. Don't any of you say who he is. It will be better for him. If it be but hinted at who he is, he'll be courted and flattered. And remember, he mustn't go beyond his allowance."

This expression of the baron's desires, if not quite satisfactory to everyone concerned, was altogether delightful to Richard.

"May I say one word, sir?" he asked.

"Yes."

"I've not read a page of Latin since I left school and never knew any Greek."

"Ah, I forgot your predicament! You shall have a tutor to prepare you! But you shall go to Oxford with him. I will not have you loafing about here. You may remain with your grandfather till I find one, but you're not to come near Mortgrange."

"I may go to London with my mother, may I not?" asked Richard.

"I see nothing against that. It will be even better."

"If you please, Sir Wilton," said Mrs. Tuke, "I left evidence at Mortgrange of what I should have to say."

"What sort of evidence?"

"Things that belonged to the child and myself."

"Where?"

"Hid in the nursery."

"My lady had everything moved, and the room freshly papered after you left. I remember that distinctly."

"Did she say nothing about finding anything?"

"Nothing. Of course, she wouldn't!"

"I left a box of my own, with—"

"You'll never see it again."

"The things the child always wore when he went out were under the wardrobe."

"Say nothing about them. I am perfectly satisfied, and believe every word you say. I believe Richard there the child of your sister Robina and myself; and it shall not be my fault if he doesn't have his rights. At the same time I promise nothing, and will manage things as I see best."

"At your pleasure," answered Mrs. Tuke.

"Would you mind, sir, if I went to see Mr. Wingfold before I go?" asked Richard.

"Who's he?"

"The clergyman of the next parish, sir."

"I don't know him—don't want to know him. What have you got to do with *him*?"

"He was kind to me when I was here before."

"I don't want you to have much to do with the clergy."

"You said I might go into the church."

"That's quite another thing. You would have the thing in your own hands then."

Richard was silent. There was no point to argue.

The moment Sir Wilton was gone, Simon turned to his grandson.

"As to seeing Mr. Wingfold, or Miss Wylder either, do just as you please, as long as you don't let out his secret."

"No, Grandfather. If I had not asked him, perhaps I might. But to ask him, and then not do what he told me would be sneaking."

"You're right, my boy. Hold on that way and you'll never be ashamed."

For the meantime Richard went to London with his mother and went on helping his uncle, going often to see his brother and sister. When Adam was able for the journey, both Richard and Alice went with him; they were met at the station by Simon. After Adam was comfortably settled, his brother and sister went back to London together. Alice took a single room and began her work once more, but with new courage and hope; Richard returned to bookbinding until his father had found a tutor for him.

With the help of the head of the university to which Sir Wilton had resolved to send his son, a tutor was at length found—happily for Richard, one of the right sort. They went to Oxford together, and set to work at once. It would be difficult to say which of the two reaped the more pleasure from the relationship, or which, in the duplex process of teaching and learning, gained the most. For the tutor had in Richard a pupil of practiced brain yet fresh, a live soul ready, for its own need and nourishment, to use every truth it came near. Sunlight and air came through his open windows. Finding Richard knew ten times as much of English literature as himself, in this department his tutor became the pupil's pupil; and listening to his occasional utterance of a religious difficulty, new regions of thought opened in him, to the deepening and verifying of his nature.

Richard gained little distinction at his examinations. He did well enough, but was too eager after real knowledge to care about appearing to know more than he actually did.

He made friends, but not many close friends. He sorely missed ministration to Adam and Alice. But it continued to grow upon Richard that, if there be a God, it is the one business of a man to find him, and that, if he would find him, he must obey the voice of his conscience.

As to the outward show of the man, Richard's carriage gradually improved. Interaction with young men of "society" influenced his manners, while all the time he was gathering the confidence of experience. His rowing and the daily run to and from the boats, along with other exercises prescribed by his tutor, strengthened his shoulders and lungs. He was fast growing more than presentable.

Old Simon was doing his best for Adam. He would hear nothing of his going back to London, or attempting anything in the way of work beyond a little in the garden. He was indeed unfit for anything more.

The blacksmith himself was making progress—the best parts of him were growing fast. Age was turning the strength into channels and mill-streams, which before, wild-foaming, had flooded the meadows.

38 Wylder Hall

Barbara's brother, her father's twin, was fast following her mother's to that world each of us must learn about for himself. As the poor fellow grew weaker, his tutor became less able to console him, but the love of his sister had always leaned toward him, ready at the least opening of the door of his heart to do for him what she could. One day on the lawn he tripped and fell. The strong little Barbara took him in her arms and carried him to his room. When two drops of water touch, the mere contact is not of long duration;

so the hearts of the sister and the dying brother rushed into each other. After this they were seldom apart. A new life had waked in the very heart of death and grew and spread through the being of the boy. His eye became brighter, not with fever only, but with love and contentment and hope; for Barbara made him feel that nothing could part them; that they had been born into the world for the hour when they should find one another.

He would come creeping up to her as she worked or read and sit on a stool at her feet, asking for nothing, wishing for nothing, content to be near her. But Barbara's book or work was soon laid aside. He was bigger than she, but the muscles of the little maiden were like springs of steel, informed with the tenderest, strongest heart in all the county, and presently he would find himself lifted to her lap, his head on her shoulder, the sweetest voice in all the world whispering lovely secrets in his willing ear, her face bent over him with the stoop of heaven over the patient, weary earth. In her arms his poor wasting body forgot its restlessness; the fever that irritated every nerve, burning away the dust of the world, seemed to pause and let him grow a little cool.

One day the mother peeped in and saw them seated thus. Motherhood, strong in her, though poisoned by her strife with her husband, moved and woke at the sight of her natural place occupied by her daughter.

"Let me take him, poor fellow!" she said.

Barbara rose with him in her arms. The mother sat down and Barbara laid him in her lap. Grown through her recent illness both weaker and tenderer, she began silently weeping. He looked up and a tear dropped on his face.

"Don't cry, Mama. I will be good!" he said.

He was much too old for the baby speech that came from his mouth, but as he grew weaker, he had grown younger in his helplessness. She clasped him to her, and from that moment she and Barbara shared him between them.

While in London, Barbara went to all the parties to which she was expected to go, and enjoyed them—after her own fashion. She loved people, and loved their company up to a point. But often the crowd and the glitter would vanish from around her, and she would be once more on the back of Miss Brown, racing across some grassy field, chasing the setting sun. Then with a sigh would Barbara return to herself, the center of many regards.

Arthur Lestrange found himself no nearer to her than before—farther off in reality, for in London he was but one among many that sought her. But her behavior to him was the same in a crowded room in London as in the garden at Mortgrange. She spoke to him kindly when he addressed her, and behaved so that the lying hint spread about by Lady Ann, that they had been for some time engaged, was easily believed.

Her father had several times said to her that it was time she should marry, but had never gotten nearer anything definite; her eyes would flash and her mouth close tight—reminding him that her mother had been more than enough for him, and he had better not throw his daughter into the opposition as well. He saw clearly enough that he would never be able to prevail against her liking; but it would be an infernal pity, he thought, if she would not have Lestrange; for the properties would marry splendidly, and then who could tell what better title might not be granted in time!

Lady Ann would not let her hope go. She grew daily more fearful of the cloud that hung in the future: out of it might at any moment step the child of her enemy, the low-born woman who had dared to be Lady Lestrange before her! For her Arthur not to succeed him would be a morsel to sweeten her husband's death for him, to spite the woman he had married! At one crisis in their history he had placed a will in her hands that left everything to her son; but he might have made ten wills after that one for all she knew! She knew she had done nothing to please him; she had, in fact, never spent a thought on making life good for the man she had married. She wished she might try to make herself agreeable to him. But it was too late! Sir Wilton would instantly imagine a rumor of the lost heir and be on the alert. If only he hadn't yet made a later will! He must die someday—why not in time to make his death of use?

The same week in which Sir Wilton had given that will into his lady's keeping, he executed a second, in which he made the virtue of the former depend on the nonappearance of the lost heir. Of this will he said nothing to his wife. Even from the grave he would hold a shadowy yet potent rod over her and her family! Lady Ann, however, suspected something of the sort, and spent every secret moment searching for some such hidden torpedo. But there was one thing which Sir Wilton protected better than his honor—his bunch of keys.

After the return of the Lestranges and the Wylders to their country homes, having prevailed on Mrs. Wylder to pay her a visit, Lady Ann connived to gain her cooperation in the alliance of the houses. She opened upon her with the same artillery she had employed against her husband. Mrs. Wylder sat for some time quietly listening but looking so much like her daughter that Lady Ann saw the mother's and not the father's was the alliance to seek. Thereupon she pulled out the best gun in her battery, as she thought, and began to hint her fear that Miss Wylder had taken a fancy to a person unworthy of her.

"Girls who have not been much in society," she said, "are not unfrequently the sport of strange infatuations! I myself knew an earl's daughter who married a baker! I do not, of course, imagine *your* daughter guilty of the slightest impropriety—"

Scarcely had the word left her lips, when a fury stood before her—eyes flashing and mouth set.

"How dare you hint that my Bab has not behaved with prudence!" cried Mrs. Wylder like a thundercloud.

Lady Ann was not of a breed familiar with fear, but for the first time in her life, except in the presence of her mother, a more formidable person than herself, she did feel a little afraid.

"I did not mean to offend you," she said, growing a little paler, but at the same time more rigid.

"What sort of mother do you take me for? Offended, indeed! Would you take it kindly, I should like to know, if I had the audacity to say such a thing of one of your girls?"

"I spoke as to a mother who knew what girls are like!"

"You don't know what my Bab is like!" cried Mrs. Wylder in a tone of imprecation.

Lady Ann was offended, and seriously: how could she ally herself with such a woman? But she was silent. For once in her life she did not know the proper thing to say.

Mrs. Wylder rose, turned away, and with a backward glance of blazing wrath, left the room and the house.

"Home, and be quick about it!" she said to the footman as he closed the door of the carriage, and she disappeared in a whirlwind.

From the library Sir Wilton saw her stormy exit and departure. "By Jove!" he said to himself, "a hundred to one my lady was insolent to her! Said something cool about her madcap girl, probably! *She's* the right sort, by Jove, that little Bab! If only my Richard now, leathery fellow, would glue onto her! I'll put him up to it, I will! Arthur and she indeed! As if a plate of porridge like Arthur would draw a fireflash like Bab! I'd give my soul to have such a girl!"

It did not occur to him that his soul for Barbara would scarcely be fair barter.

The instant she reached home, Mrs. Wylder sent for her daughter, and demanded, fury still blazing in her eyes, what she had been doing to give that beast of a Lady Ann a right to talk.

"Tell me first how she talked, Mama," returned Barbara, used to her mother's ways and not annoyed at being addressed so. "I can't have been doing anything very bad, for she's been doing what she can to get me and keep me."

"She has? And you never told me!"

"I didn't think it worth telling you. She's been setting Papa on to me, too."

"Oh, I see! And you wouldn't set him and me on each other! Well, I'll have no buying and selling of my goods behind my back! If you speak one more civil word to that young Lestrange, you shall hear from me!"

"I will not speak an uncivil word to him, Mama; he has never given me occasion to. But it wouldn't break my heart never to see him again either. If you like I won't go near the place. Theodora's the only one I care about—and she's as dull as she is good."

"What did the kangaroo mean by saying you were sweet on somebody not worthy of you?"

"I know what she meant, Mother; but the man is worthy of a far better woman than me—and I hope he'll get her someday."

Thereupon little Bab burst into tears, dreading that her good wish for Richard should be granted otherwise than she meant it. She did hope to be a better woman before it was too late.

"Come, come, child! None of that! I don't like it. I don't want to cry on top of my rage. What is the man? Who is he? What does the woman know about him?"

At once Barbara began and told her mother the whole story of Richard and herself. The mother listened. Old days and the memory of a lover, not high in the social scale, whom she had to give up to marry Mr. Wylder, came back upon her, and her heart went with her daughter's before she knew what it was about. Her daughter's love and her own seemed to mingle in one dusky shine, as if the daughter had inherited the mother's experience. The heart of the mother would not have her child, like herself, gather only weed-flowers of sorrow among the roses in the garden of love. She had learned this much, that the things the world prizes are of little benefit to the heart of a woman. But when Barbara told her that this same Richard, the bookbinder, was the natural but illegitimate son of Sir Wilton, she started to her feet, crying:

"Then the natural bookbinder shall have her, and my lady's legitimate fool may go to the dogs! You shall have *my* money, Bab, anyhow."

"But Mama dear," said Barbara, "what will Papa say?"

"Poof!" returned her mother. "I've known him too long to care what he says!"

"I don't want to offend him," returned Barbara.

"Don't mention him again, child, or I'll turn him loose on your bookbinder. Am I to put my own daughter through the same torture I had to suffer by marrying him! God forbid! When you're happy with your husband, perhaps you'll think of me sometimes and say, 'My mother did it! She wasn't a good woman, but she loved her Bab!' "

A passionate embrace followed. Barbara left the room with a happy heart, and went—not to brood on her love, but to her brother's room, where she had heard his feeble voice calling her. Upon him her gladness overflowed.

39 Miss Brown

That same evening Barbara rode to the smithy in hopes of hearing some news of Richard from his grandfather. The old man was busy at the anvil when he heard Miss Brown's hoofs on the road. He dropped his hammer, flung the tongs on the forge, and, leaving the iron to cool on the anvil, went to meet her.

"How are you, Grandfather?" said Barbara, with unconscious use of the word.

Simon was well pleased to be called grandfather, but too well bred to show his pleasure.

"As well as hard work can help me to be. How are you yourself, my pretty little lady?" returned Simon.

"As well as nothing to do—except nursing poor Mark—will let me be," she answered. "Please, can you tell me anything about Richard yet?"

"Can you keep a secret?" rejoined Simon. "I'm not sure I'm being altogether within the law, but if I didn't think you fit, I shouldn't say a word."

"Don't tell me if it is anything I shouldn't know."

"Well, I'll tell you at my own risk, for you're the right sort to trust. I'll bind you with no promises, only don't tell anyone of it without letting me know first. It's just this—Richard's gone to the university!"

Bab slid from Miss Brown's back, flung her arms, with the bridle on one of them, round the blacksmith's neck, and kissed the old man for the good news.

"Miss! Miss! Your clean face!" cried the blacksmith.

"Oh, Richard! Richard! You *will* be happy now!" she said. "But will he ever shoe Miss Brown again, Grandfather?"

"Many's the time, I trust," answered Simon. "He'll be proud to do it. If not, he never was worth a smile from your sweet mouth."

"He'll be a great man someday!" she laughed, with a little quiver of the mouth.

"He's a good man now," answered the smith. "As long as a son of mine can look every man in the face, I don't care whether it be great or small he is."

"But wouldn't it be better still if he could look God in the face?"

"You're right there, my pretty dove!" replied the old man; "only a body can't say everything out in one breath. But you're right, you *are* right!" he went on. "I remember well the time when I thought I had nothing to be ashamed of; but the time came when I was ashamed of many things, and I'd done nothing worse in the meantime either! When a man first gets a peep inside himself, he sees things he didn't look to see—and they stagger him a bit! Now mind, I haven't told you what university he's gone to. But I will let him know that I've told you that much, because he couldn't tell you himself, being he's bound to hold his tongue."

Barbara went home happy: his grandfather recognized the bond between them! As to Richard, she had no fear of his forgetting her.

With more energy still she went about her duties; and they seemed to grow as she did them. As the end of Mark's sickness approached, he became more and more dependent on her. He loved his father deeply, but his father never stayed more than a moment or two in the sickroom. Mark at length went away to find his twin; and his mother and Barbara wept.

One morning, the week after Mark's death, Mr. Wylder asked Barbara to go with him to his study—where, indeed, about as much study went on as in a squirrel's nest. It was right and natural while she was a girl with a brother that she should be allowed a great deal of freedom, he told her. But now, circumstances being changed, such freedom could no longer be given her: she was now sole heiress, and must behave as an heir, namely, by consulting the interests of the family. In those interests, he continued, he intended to strengthen as much as possible his influence in the county. It was also time that, for her own sake, she should marry; and better husband or fitter son-in-law than Mr. Lestrange could not be desired. He was well-behaved and good-looking, and when Mortgrange joined with Wylder, they would have far the finest estate in the county!

"I am sorry to go against you, Papa," said Barbara, "but I cannot marry Mr. Lestrange."

"Stuff and nonsense! Why not?"

"Because I do not love him."

"Fiddlesticks! I did not love your mother when I married her! You don't dislike him, I know! Now don't tell me you do, for I won't believe you!"

"He is always kind to me, and I am sorry he should want what is not mine to give him."

"Not yours to give him! What do you mean by that! It may not be yours, but it is mine! Have you not learned yet that when I make up my mind on an issue, it is done?"

Where husband and wife are not one, it is impossible for the daughter to be one with both, or perhaps with either; the constant and foolish bickering to which Barbara had been a witness throughout her childhood had tended to poison rather than nourish respect. Though the idea of parent must be venerated, a parent is not God. Child must leave father and mother and all for God—that is, for what is right, which is his very will—only the child must be sure it is for God, and not for self. If the parent has been the parent of good thoughts and right judgments in the child, those good thoughts and right judgments will be on the parent's side; if he had been the parent of evil thoughts and false judgments, they may be for him or against him, but in the end they will work for division. Any general decay of filial affection must originate with the parents.

"I am not a child, I am a woman," said Barbara. "And I owe it to him who made me a woman to take care of myself."

"Mind what you say. I have rights, and will enforce them."

"Over my person?" returned Barbara, her eyes sending out a flash that reminded him of her mother, and made him angrier than ever.

"If you do not consent here and now," he said sternly, "to marry Mr. Lestrange—that is, if, after your mother's insolence to Lady Ann—"

"My mother's insolence to Lady Ann!" exclaimed Barbara, drawing herself, in her indignation, to the height of her small person.

"—if, as I say," her father went on, "he should now condescend to ask you—I swear—"

"You had better not swear, Papa!"

"I swear you shall not have a foot of my land."

"Oh, is that all? There you are in your right, and I have nothing to say."

"You insolent hussy! You won't like it when you find it done!"

"It will be the same as if Mark had lived."

"It's that cursed money of your mother's that makes you impudent!"

"If you left me penniless, Papa, it would make no difference. A woman that can shoe her own horse—"

"Shoe her own horse!" cried her father.

"Yes, Papa! You couldn't! And I *made* two of her shoes the last time! Wouldn't any woman that can do that, wouldn't she—to save herself from shame and disgust—wouldn't she take a place as a housemaid or shop girl rather than marry the man she didn't love?"

Mr. Wylder saw he had gone too far.

"You know more than is good!" he said. "But don't you mistake: your mother's money is settled on you, but your father is your trustee! Take care how far you push him!"

"Not to love is not to marry—not if the man was a prince!" persisted Barbara.

She went to her mother's room, but said nothing of what had passed.

The next morning she ran to saddle Miss Brown. To her astonishment her friend was not in her box, nor in any stall in the stable; neither was anyone around to ask what had become of her. For the first time in her life, everybody had gotten out of Barbara's way. In the harness room, however, she came upon one of the stableboys. He was in tears. When he saw her, he turned to run, looking as if he had had a piece of Miss Brown for breakfast, but she stopped him.

"Where is Miss Brown?" she said.

"Don't know, miss."

"Who knows then?"

"Perhaps Master, miss."

"What are you crying for?"

"Don't know, miss."

"That's not true. Boys don't cry without knowing why!"

"Well, miss, I ain't *sure* what I'm crying for."

"Speak out, man! Don't be foolish."

"Master give me a terrible cut, miss."

"Did you deserve it?"

"Don't know, miss."

"You don't seem to know anything this morning!"

"No, miss."

"What did your master give you the cut for?"

"'Cause I was crying."

Here he burst into a restrained howl.

"What were you crying for?"

"Because Miss Brown was gone."

"And you cried without knowing where she was gone?" said Barbara, turning almost sick with apprehension.

"Yes, miss," affirmed the miserable boy.

"Is she dead?"

"No, miss, she ain't dead; she's sold!"

The words were not yet out of his mouth when he turned and bolted.

"That's my gentleman-papa!" said Barbara to herself. Had she been any girl but Barbara, she would have cried like the boy. But not once from that moment did she allude to Miss Brown in the hearing of father or servant.

One day her mother asked her why she never rode anymore, and she told her. The wrath of her mother was like a tigress. She sprang to her feet and bounded to the door. But when she reached it, Barbara was between her and the handle.

"Mother! Mother dear!" she pleaded.

The mother took her by the shoulders, thinking she would fling her across the room. But she was not so strong as she had been, and found the little one hard as nails: she could not move her an inch.

"Get out of my way!" she cried. "I will kill him."

"Mama, listen! It happened a month ago! I said nothing—for love's sake!"

"Love! Dare you tell me you love that wretch of a father of yours! I will kill *you* if you say you love him!"

Barbara threw her arms round her mother's neck, and said: "Listen, Mama: I do love him a little bit; but it wasn't for love of him I held my tongue."

"Bah! Your bookbinder fellow! What does he have to do with it?"

"Nothing at all. It wasn't for him, either. It was for God's sake I held my peace. If *all* his children quarreled like you and Daddy, what a house he would have! It was for God's sake I said nothing; and you know, Mama, you've made it up with God, and you mustn't go and be naughty again!"

The mother stood almost silent and still. She turned to her chair, sat down, and again was still. A minute later, her forehead flushed like a flame, turned white, then flushed and paled again several times. Then she gave a great sigh, and the conflict was over. She smiled, and from that moment she also never said a word about Miss Brown.

But in the silence of her thoughts, Barbara suffered for what might be the fate of Miss Brown. In her mind's eye she kept seeing her turn her head with sharp curved neck in her stall, or shoot it over the door of her box, looking and longing for her mistress, and wondering why she did not come to pat her, or feed her, or saddle her for the joyous gallop across grass and green hedge; and the heart of her mistress was sore for her. But at length one day in church, they read the Psalm in which came the words, "Thou, Lord, shalt save both man and beast!" and they went to her soul. After more reflection she saw that the reasonable thing was to let God look after his own; Miss Brown was his, and he would care for her.

The mother was sending all over the country to find who had Miss Brown; she had not inquired long before she learned that she was in the stables at Mortgrange. There she knew she would be well treated, and therefore told Barbara the result of her inquiries.

40 The Baron's Will

Barbara now went more often to Mr. and Mrs. Wingfold. By this time, through Simon Armour, they knew something about Richard, but none of them felt at liberty to talk about him.

Barbara now had a better guide in her reading than Richard. What in Barbara Richard had begun well, Wingfold was carrying on better. With his help she was now studying a variety of subjects. Wingfold had himself passed through all Richard's phases, and through some that were only now beginning to show in him. Therefore he was well prepared to help her—both intellectually and spiritually.

"Why do I never see you on Miss Brown?" Wingfold asked Barbara one day.

"For a reason I think I ought not to tell you."

"Then don't tell me," returned the parson.

But by a mixture of induction and intuition, he saw into the situation perhaps more than Barbara realized, and did what he could to make up for it, by taking her every now and then on a long walk or drive with his wife and their little boy. He gave her strong, hopeful things to read. Heart and brain, Wingfold was full of both humor and pathos. In their walks and drives, many a serious subject would give occasion to the former, and many a merry one to the latter. Sometimes he would take a nursery rhyme for his theme, and expound upon it so that at one instant Barbara would burst into the gayest laughter, and the next have to restrain her tears. Rarely would Wingfold enter a sickroom, especially in a poor cottage, with a long face and a sermon in his soul. Almost always he walked lightly in, with a cheerful look and some kind of odd story on his tongue, well pleased when he could make the sufferer laugh—better pleased sometimes when he had made him sorry. He did not find those that laughed the readiest the hardest to make sorry. He moved his people by infecting their hearts with the feeling in his own.

Having now for many years cared only for the will of God, he was full of joy. For the will of the Father is the root of all his children's gladness, of all their laughter and merriment. The child that loves the will of the Father is at the heart of things; his will is with the motion of the eternal wheels; the eyes of all those wheels are opened upon him, and he knows whence he came. Happy and fearless and hopeful, he knows himself the child of him from whom he came, and his peace and joy break out in light. He rises and shines. No other bliss than the will of the Father, creative and energetic, exists on earth or in heaven.

Arthur Lestrange was sharply troubled when he found he was to see no more of Barbara. He went again and again to Wylder Hall, but neither mother nor daughter would receive him. When he learned that Miss Brown was for sale, he bought her for love of her mistress. All the explanation he could get from Lady Ann was that the young woman's mother was impossible—she was more than half savage.

Time's wheels thereafter moved slowly at Mortgrange. Sir Wilton missed his firstborn. Whatever annoyed him in his wife or any of her children fed his desire for Richard. Arthur did not please him. He had in no way distinguished himself—and some men are annoyed when their sons prove only a little better than themselves.

The only comfort in the house occupied the soul of Lady Ann: she had heard nothing of the bookbinder! She had grown so complacent that when Danger was not flattening his nose against the windowpane, she was at peace. A lawyer of her own had the will in his keeping, and she had come upon no trace of another.

But Sir Wilton had become dissatisfied with his agent and had sent for his lawyer from London to look into his factor's accounts and make a thorough investigation. In addition, he made one further use of him of which his wife heard nothing: he had him draw up another will, in which he left everything to Richard, only son of his first wife Robina Armour. With every precaution for secrecy, the will was signed and witnessed; when the lawyer would have taken it with him, the baron refused to give it up. He laid it aside for a week, then had the horses hitched to his carriage, and drove to find Mr. Wingfold, of whom he had heard from Richard. When he saw him, Sir Wilton, man of the world, was impressed by the simplicity of the clergyman without a touch of the clerical, without any look of what he called *sanctity*.

The baron asked for a private interview, and told the parson he wanted to place in his keeping a certain paper, with the understanding that he would not open it for a year after his death, and would then act upon the directions contained in it.

"Provided always," Wingfold stipulated, "that they require of me nothing unfit, impossible, or wrong."

"I pledge myself that they require nothing unworthy of the cloth," said Sir Wilton.

"The cloth be hanged," said Wingfold. "Do they require anything unworthy of a man—or, if you think the word means more—of a gentleman?"

"They do not," answered the baron.

"Then you must write another paper, stating that you have asked me to undertake this, but that you have given me no hint of the contents of the accompanying document. This second you must enclose with the first, sealing the envelope with your own seal."

Sir Wilton at once consented, and immediately did as Wingfold desired.

"I've checkmated my lady at last!" he chuckled as he drove home. "She would have me the villain to disinherit my firstborn for her miserable brood! She shall find my other will, and think she's safe! Then the thunderbolt! My lady's money won't be much for that litter of hers!"

He always spoke as if Lady Ann's children were none of his. Her ladyship had, in fact, taught him to do so, for she always said, "*My* children!"

That night he slept with an easier mind. He had kept putting the deed off, regarding it as his abdication; now that it was done he felt more comfortable.

Wingfold suspected in the paper some provision for Richard, but could imagine no reason for letting it lie unopened until a year should have passed from the baron's death. Troubling himself nothing, however, about what was not his business, he put the paper carefully aside—but where he would see it now and then, lest it should pass from his mind. With Sir Wilton's permission he told his wife what he had undertaken, so that she might carry it out if he were prevented from doing so.

Time went on, and communication diminished between Mr. Wylder and his family. He had returned to certain old habits and was spending money rather fast in London.

In the fourth year Richard wrote to his father, through his grandfather, informing him he had his B.A. degree and was awaiting further orders. The baron was heartily pleased with the style of his letter, and in the privacy of his own room gave way to his delight at the thought of his wife's approaching consternation. At the same time, however, he was not a little uneasy. The eyes of his wife had become almost a terror to him. Their gray ice, which had not grown clearer as she grew older, made him shiver. Why should the stronger so often be afraid of the weaker? Perhaps the conscience happens to side with the weaker; or perhaps the weaker is able to make the stronger feel worse than uncomfortable. The baron dared not present his son to his wife except in the presence of at least one stranger.

He wrote to Richard, appointing a day for his appearance at Mortgrange.

41 The Heir

The morning was lovely as Richard, his heart full of hope and intense joy, stopped at the station nearest to Mortgrange and set out to walk there in the afternoon sun. June folded him in her loveliness of warmth and color. Often he had walked the same road, a contented tradesman; a gentleman now, with a baron for his father, he knew that he would always love the tradesman-uncle more than the baron-father. He was grateful to his father for his reception of him, and for his education; but he could not be proud of him as he was of his mother and his aunt and uncle and grandfather.

His only anxiety was that his father might again lay upon him the command to cease communication with his brother and sister. He lifted his heart up to God, and vowed that not for anything the earth could give would he obey. The socialism he had learned from his uncle had undergone a baptism to something infinitely higher. He prayed God to keep him clean of heart and able to hold by his duty. He promised God that he would not forsake his own, would not break the ties of blood for any law, custom, prejudice, or pride of man. The vow made his heart strong and light.

Every father, thought Richard, *who loved his children, ought to make them independent of himself, that neither clog, nor net, nor hindrance of any kind might hamper the true working of their consciences: then would the service they rendered their parents be precious indeed! Then, indeed, would love be lord, and neither self, nor fear of man, nor fear of fate be a law in their life!* He himself was independent: he could bind books and be content. How much harder it would be for a poor, tradeless man like Arthur to make such a resolve! His father had trained him to do nothing; therefore his dependence upon him was total.

He had not sent word to his grandfather that he was coming, and had told his father that he would walk from the station—which suited Sir Wilton, for he felt nervous, and was anxious there should be no stir. So Richard came to Mortgrange as quietly as a star to its place in the twilight.

When he reached the gate and walked in as he had of old, he was challenged by the woman who kept it. Of all the servants, she and Lady Ann's maid had alone treated him with rudeness; now she was not polite even though she did not recognize him. Neither was he recognized by the man who opened the door. Many changes had passed upon him, for he was now twenty-five, and fully a man.

Sir Wilton was in the library waiting for him. A gentleman was with him, but he kept in the background, seemingly absorbed in the titles of a row of books.

There you are, you rascal! his father was on the point of saying as Richard came into the light of the one large window; instead, he gazed at him for an instant in silence. Before him was one of the handsomest fellows his eyes had ever rested upon—broad-shouldered, tall, and straight, with a thoughtful yet keen face, every feature fine and solid, and dark brown hair with night and firelight in it, and a touch of the sun here and there at moments. The situation might have been embarrassing to a more experienced man than Richard, but he stood quite at ease, neither hands nor feet giving him any of the trouble so often caused by those outlying provinces. He stood like a soldier waiting the word of his officer.

"By Jove!" said his father; and there was another pause.

The baron was growing prouder of his son by the moment. He had never had a feeling like it before. He saw his mother in him.

She's looking at me straight out of his eyes! he said to himself.

"Aren't you going to sit down?" he said to him at last, forgetting that he had neither shaken hands with him nor spoken a word of welcome.

Richard moved a chair a little nearer and sat down, wondering what would come next.

"Well, what are you going to do?" asked his father.

"I must first know your wish, sir," he answered.

"Church won't do?"

"No, sir."

"Glad to hear it! You're much too good for the church! No offense, Mr. Wingfold! The same applies to yourself."

"So my uncle on the stock-exchange used to say!" answered Wingfold, laughing as he turned to the baron. "He thought me good enough, I suppose, to be a priest of mammon."

"I'm glad you're not offended. What do you think of that son of mine?"

"I have long thought well of him."

At the first sound of his voice, Richard had risen, and now approached him, his hand outstretched.

"Mr. Wingfold!" he said joyfully.

"I remember now!" returned Sir Wilton. "It was from him I heard of you, and that was what made me seek your acquaintance. He promises to turn out fairly, don't you think? Shoulders good; head well set."

"He looks like a powerful man!" said Wingfold. "We shall be happy for a visit, Mr. Lestrange, as soon as you care to come to us."

"That will be tomorrow, I hope, sir," answered Richard, faltering a bit at the use of the unfamiliar name.

"Stop, stop!" cried Sir Wilton. "Enough with your plans; we know nothing for certain yet! By the way, if your stepmother doesn't make you particularly welcome, you needn't be surprised, my boy!"

"Certainly not. I could hardly expect her to be pleased, sir."

"Not pleased! Not pleased at what? Now, don't you presume and take things for granted! How do you know she will have anything to be displeased about? I never promised you anything! I never told you what I intended! Did I ever?"

"No, sir. You have already done far more than ever you promised. You have given me all any man has a right to from his father. I am ready to go to London at once and make my own living."

"How?"

"I don't know yet. But I would have the freedom of a choice—thanks to you and my uncle."

"In the meantime, you must be introduced to your stepmother."

"Then—excuse me, Sir Wilton—" interposed the parson, "do you wish me to regard my old friend Richard as your son and heir?"

"As my son, yes. As my heir—that will depend—"

"On his behavior, I presume!" Wingfold ventured.

"Nothing of the sort!" replied the baron testily. "Would you have me doubt whether he will carry himself like a gentleman? The thing depends on my pleasure. There are others besides him."

He rose to ring the bell.

"Now, Richard," said his father as Richard rose, "don't play the part of a servant. Nothing shows want of breeding more than for a man to serve himself in his own house. Wait for things to come to you!"

"I will try to remember, sir," answered Richard.

"Do. We shall get on all the better."

At the words the baron was seized, as by the claw of a crab, with a sharp twinge of his gout. He caught at the back of a chair, hobbled with its help to the table, and so to his seat. Richard restrained himself and stood rigid. The baron turned a half-humorous, half-reproachful look on him.

"That's right!" he said. "Never help where you're not asked. I wish my father had taught me as I am teaching you! Ever had the gout, Mr. Wingfold?"

"Never, Sir Wilton."

"Then you ought every Sunday to say, 'Thank God that I have no gout.'"

"But if we thanked God for all the ills we don't have, there would be no time to thank him for any of the blessings we do have!"

"What blessings?"

"So many, I don't know where to begin to answer you."

"Ah, yes! You're a clergyman! I forgot. It's your business to thank God. For my part, being a layman, I don't know anything in particular I've got to thank him for."

"If I thought a layman had less to thank God for than a clergyman, I should begin to doubt whether either had anything to thank him for. Why, Sir Wilton, I find everything a blessing! I thank God I am a poor man. I thank him for every good book I fall in with. I thank him when a child smiles at me. I thank him when the sun rises or the wind blows on me. Every day I am so happy, or at least so peaceful, or at the worst so hopeful, that my very consciousness is a thanksgiving."

"Do you thank him for your wife, Mr. Wingfold?"

"Every day of my life."

The baron stared at him a moment, then turned to his son.

"Richard," he said, "you had better make up your mind to go into the church! You hear Mr. Wingfold! I shouldn't like it myself; I would have to be at my prayers all day!"

"Ah, Sir Wilton, it doesn't take time to thank God! It only takes eternity."

Sir Wilton stared. He did not understand.

"Ring the bell, will you?" he said. "The fellow seems to have gone to sleep."

Richard obeyed, and not a word was spoken until the man appeared.

"Wilkins," said his master, "go to my lady and say I beg the favor of her presence in the library for a moment."

The man went.

"No aversion to cats, I hope!" he added, turning to Richard.

"None, sir," answered Richard gravely.

"That's good! Then you won't be taken aback!"

In a few minutes Lady Ann sailed into the room, the servant closing the door so deftly behind her that it seemed without moving to have given passage to a spirit.

The two younger men rose.

"Mr. Wingfold you know, My Lady!" said her husband.

"I have not had the pleasure," answered Lady Ann, with a slight motion of her head, like the hard bud at the top of a long stalk.

"Ah, I thought you did! The Reverend Mr. Wingfold, Lady Ann! My wife, Mr. Wingfold! The other gentleman, Lady Ann—"

He paused. Lady Ann turned her eyes slowly on Richard. Wingfold saw a slight, barely perceptible start, and settling of the jaws.

"The other gentleman," resumed the baron, "you do not know, but you will soon be the best of friends."

"I beg your pardon, Sir Wilton, I do know him! I hope," she went on, turning to Richard, "you will keep steadily to your work. The sooner the books are finished the better!"

Richard smiled, but what he was on the point of saying, his father prevented.

"You mistake, My Lady!" said the baron. "The gentleman is my son, and will one day be Sir Richard."

"Oh!" returned her ladyship, without a shadow of change in her impassivity; Wingfold, however, detected the slightest movement of squint in the eye nearest him. She held out her hand.

"This is an unexpected—"

For once in her life her lips were truer than her heart; they did not say *pleasure.*

Richard took her hand respectfully, sad for the woman whose winter had no fuel, and who looked as if she would be sad to all eternity. Lady Ann stared him directly in the eye.

"My favorite prayer book has come to pieces at last: perhaps you would bind it for me?"

"I would be delighted to," answered Richard.

"Thank you," she said, bowed to Wingfold, and left the room.

Sir Wilton sat like an offended turkey cock, staring after her. *By Jove!* he seemed to say to himself.

"There! that's over!" he cried, coming to himself. "Ring the bell, Richard, and let's have lunch. Richard, *no* gentleman could have behaved better! I am proud of you! It's blood that does it!" he murmured to himself.

As if he had himself compounded both his own blood and his son's in the stillroom of creation, he took all the credit of Richard's *savoir faire*. He did not know that the same thing made Wingfold happy and Richard a gentleman. Richard had a higher breeding than was known to Sir Wilton. At the court of courts, whence the manners of some other courts would be swept as dust from the floors, the baron would hardly gain admittance!

Lady Ann went up the stairs slowly and perpendicularly, a dull pain at her heart. The cause was not so much that her son was the second son, as that the son of a blacksmith's daughter was—she took care to say *at first sight*—a finer *gentleman* than her Arthur. Rank and position, she vaguely reflected, must not look for justice from the jealous heavens! They always sided with the poor! Just look at the Psalms—the rich and noble were hardly dealt with!

The baron was merry over luncheon. The servants wondered at first, but before the soup was removed they wondered no more; the young man at the table, in whom not one of them had recognized the bookbinder, was the lost heir to Mortgrange! He was worth finding, they agreed—one who could hold his own! The house would be merrier now—thank heaven! They liked Mr. Arthur well enough, but here was his master!

The meal was over, and the baron always slept after lunch.

"You'll stay to dinner, won't you, Mr. Wingfold?" he said, rising.

"Richard, ring the bell. Better send for Mrs. Locke at once and arrange with her where you will sleep."

"Then may I choose my own room, sir?" asked Richard.

"Of course—but better not too near my lady's," answered his father with a grim smile as he hobbled from the room.

"Mrs. Locke," said Richard, when the housekeeper came, "I want to see the room that used to be the nursery—in the older time, I mean."

"Yes, sir," answered Mrs. Locke pleasantly, and led him up two flights of stairs and along corridor and passage to the room Richard had occupied before. He glanced around it and said, "This shall be my room. Will you kindly get it ready for me?"

She hesitated. It had not been repapered, as Sir Wilton had thought, and had said to Mrs. Tuke! To Mrs. Locke it seemed uninhabitable by a gentleman.

"I will send for the painter and paper-hanger at once," she replied, "but it will take more than a week to get ready."

"Please, leave it as it is," he answered. "You can have the floor swept, of course," he added with a smile, seeing her look of dismay. "I will sleep here tonight, and we can settle afterward what is to be done to it. There used to be a portrait," he went on, "over the chimney-piece, the portrait of a lady—not well painted, I imagine, but I liked it: what has become of it?"

Then first it began to dawn on Mrs. Locke that the young man who mended the books and the heir to Mortgrange were the same person.

"It fell down one day, and has not been put up again," she answered.

"Do you know where it is?"

"I will find it, sir."

"Do, if you please. Whose portrait is it?"

"The last Lady Lestrange's, sir." *But bless my stupid old head! It's his own mother's picture he's asking for!* "You'll pardon me, sir! The thing's more bewildering than you'd think! I'll go and get it at once."

"Thank you. I will wait till you bring it."

"There ain't anywhere for you to sit, sir!" lamented the old lady.

"If I'd only known! I'm sure, sir, I wish you joy!"

"Thank you, Mrs. Locke. I'll sit here on the mattress."

Richard had not forgotten how the eyes of the picture used to draw his, and he had often wondered since whether it could be the portrait of his mother.

In a few minutes Mrs. Locke reappeared, carrying the portrait, which had never been put in a frame, and knotting the cord, Richard hung it again on the old nail. It showed a well-formed face, but was very flat and wooden. The eyes, however, were comparatively well-painted; Richard imagined he could read both sorrow and disappointment in them, with a yearning after something she could not have.

He went out for a walk in the park with Wingfold, and there Richard told his friend as much as he knew of his story, describing as well as he understood them the changes that had passed upon him in the matter of his thoughts toward and relation to God, making no secret of what he owed to the spiritual influences of Barbara. Wingfold, after listening with profound attention, told him of his own awakening, saying that he had passed through an experience in many ways like his own, with the same root doubts. He added that, long before he was sure of anything, it had become possible for him to keep going, and that he was still—as strong as his belief now was—looking and hoping and waiting for a fuller dawn of what had made his being already blessed.

They discussed whether Wingfold should accept the baron's careless invitation, and concluded it better that he not stay to dinner. Then, as there was yet time, and it was partly on Wingfold's way, they set out for the smithy.

42 Richard and His Family

When the first delight of their meeting was past, Richard went in to see Adam. He had been all this time with Simon, to whom Richard had sent enough saved from his allowance to prevent him from being a burden. He looked much better, and was enchanted to see his brother again, and learn the good news of his recognition by his father.

"Is Alice still in the old place?" Richard asked. "I haven't heard of her for some time."

"Don't you know?" exclaimed Adam. "She's been at the parsonage for months and months! Mrs. Wingfold went and fetched her away, to work for her and be near me. She's happy now, and says if everybody was as good as her master and mistress, there would be no misery left in the world."

"I don't doubt it," answered Richard. "But I've just parted with Mr. Wingfold, and he didn't say a word about her!"

"When anything has to be done, Mr. Wingfold never forgets, but does it," said Adam; "but once he's done a thing, he forgets all about it, and never mentions it to anyone."

Richard then inquired eagerly about what Wingfold had done for his brother. First of all he had, by lending him books and talking to him, found out what was his bent and what he was capable of. For months he could hardly wake any interest in him, the poor fellow was so weak and weary. But at last he got him to observe a little. Then he began to set him certain tasks, and as he was an invalid, the first was what he called "the task of twelve o'clock"; for a quarter of an hour from every noon during a month, to write down what he saw going on in the world.

The first day he had nothing to show; he had seen nothing!

"What were the clouds doing?" Mr. Wingfold asked. "What were the horses in the fields doing? What were the birds you saw doing? What were the ducks and hens doing? Put down whatever you see any creature about."

The next evening, he went to him again, and asked him for his paper. Adam handed him a folded sheet.

"Now," said Mr. Wingfold, "I am going to lay it in one of my drawers, and you must write another for me tomorrow. We shall go on like that for a month, and then we shall see something."

At the end of the month, Mr. Wingfold took out all the papers. They read them together, and did indeed see something! The growth of Adam's observation was remarkable. The number of events and circumstances he was able to see by the end of the month, compared with what he had seen in the beginning, was wonderful, while the manner of his expression had changed from that of a child to that of a man.

Mr. Wingfold next set him "the task of six o'clock in the evening," when the things that presented themselves to his notice would be very different. After two weeks he changed again the hour of observation, and went on changing it. So at length the youth who had, twice every day, walked along Cheapside without seeing that one face differed from another, knew most of the birds and many of the insects, and could in general tell what they were about, while the domestic animals were his familiar friends. He delighted in the grass and the wild flowers, the sky and the clouds and the stars, and knew, in a real, vital way, about the world in which he lived. He entered into the life that was going on about him, and so in the house of God became one of the family. He had ten times his former consciousness; his life was ten times the size it was before. As was natural, his health had improved marvelously. For there is nothing like interest in life to quicken the body's vital forces.

Richard rejoiced with the change in Adam and walked back to Mortgrange with a heart light and thankful.

As the dinner hour drew near, Richard went to the drawing room, scrupulously dressed. Lady Ann gave him the coldest of polite recognitions; Theodora was full of gladness; Victoria was scornful and as impudent as she dared be in the presence of her father; Miss Malliver was utterly wooden and behaved as if she had never seen him before; Arthur was polite and superior. Things went pretty well, however. Percy, happily, was at Woolwich pretending to study engineering: of him Richard had learned too much at Oxford.

Theodora and Richard were at once drawn to each other. She was a plain, good-natured, good-tempered girl with red hair—which only her father and mother disliked—and a modest, freckled face, whose smile was genuine; she was proud of her new, handsome brother. Her mother considered her stupid, accepting the judgment of the varnished governess. Theodora was indeed one of those who continue to be children longer than most, but she was not therefore slow or dull. The aloe takes seven years to blossom, but when it does, its flower may be thirty feet long. Where there is love there is intellect: at what period it may show itself matters little. Richard felt he had in her another sister—one for whom he might do something. He talked freely at his father's table. If Lady Ann said next to nothing, she said nearly as much as usual and was perfectly civil. Arthur was sullen but not rude. Theodora's joy made her talk as she had never talked before. Vixen gave herself to her dinner, but the shadow of a grimace now and then reminded Richard of the old days in the library.

Having the heart of a poet, the brain of a scientist, and the hands of a workman—hands, that is, made for making—Richard talked so vitally that in most families all would have been interested; indeed, Arthur would have enjoyed listening, but he was otherwise occupied battling his pride. When they retired to the drawing room after dinner, and Richard had sung a ballad so as almost to make Lady Ann drop a scale or two from her fish-eyes, Arthur went out of the room stung with envy, and not ashamed of it. The thing most alien to the true idea of humanity is the notion that our well-being lies in surpassing our fellows. We have to rise above ourselves, not above our neighbors; to take all the good *of* them, not *from* them, and give them all our good in return. That which cannot be freely shared can never be possessed. Arthur went to his room with a gnawing at his heart. Not merely must he knock under to the foundling, but confess that the foundling could do most things better than he his superior in accomplishment as well as education.—*But let us see how he rides and shoots!* he thought.

Vixen had been saying to herself all throughout dinner, *What a mean fellow to come like a fox and steal poor Arthur's property!* But even she was cowed a little by his singing, and felt for the moment in the presence of a superior.

Sir Wilton was delighted. Here was a son to represent him, the son of the woman the county had refused to acknowledge! What was Lady Ann's plebian litter beside this high-bred, modest, self-possessed fellow? He was worthy of his father, by Jove!

He went early to bed, and Richard was not sorry. He, too, retired early, leaving the rest to talk him over.

How they did it, I do not care to put on record. Theodora said little, for her heart had come awake with a new and lovely sense of gladness and hope.

The next morning Richard came upon Arthur shooting at a target. He joined him, but found himself not up to Arthur's skill. When he began to talk about shooting pheasants, Arthur found in Richard a strong dislike to killing.

"Keep it quiet," he said with more than a trace of contempt. "You'll be laughed at if you don't. And my father won't like it."

"I pass no judgment on your sport," said Richard. "I merely say I don't choose to kill birds. What men may think of me for it is a matter of indifference to me."

They strolled into the stable. There stood Miss Brown, looking over the door of her box. She received Richard with glad recognition.

"How does Miss Brown come to be here?" he asked. "Where can her mistress be?"

"The mare's at home," answered Arthur. "I bought her."

"Oh!" said Richard, and went to the box, lifted her foot, and looked at the shoe. Alas, Miss Brown had worn out many shoes since Barbara drove a nail in her hoof! Had there been one of hers there, he would have known it. The mare sniffed about his head in a friendly fashion.

She smells the smithy! said Arthur to himself. "Your grandfather's work!" he remarked. "I should be sorry to see any other man shoe a horse of mine!"

"So should I!" answered Richard. "I wonder why Miss Wylder sold Miss Brown?" he added, after a pause.

"I am not so curious!" rejoined Arthur. "She sold her, and I bought her."

Neither could have known that the animal stood there as a sacrifice to Barbara's love to Richard.

Arthur had given up hope of winning Barbara, but the thought that the bookbinder fellow might now sweep her off her feet swelled his heart with a yet fiercer jealousy. Yet Arthur was not a bad fellow as fellows go; he was just a man who had not begun to stop being a devil.

At breakfast Lady Ann was almost attentive to her stepson. As it happened, they were left alone at the table, and suddenly she addressed him.

"Richard, I have one request to make of you," she said; "I hope you will grant it to me."

"I will if I can," he answered, "but I must not promise without knowing what it is."

"You do not feel bound to please me, I know! I have the misfortune not to be your mother!"

"I do feel bound to please you where I can, and shall be more than glad to do so."

"It is a small thing I am going to ask. I should not have thought of mentioning it but for the terms you hold with Mr. Wingfold."

"I hope to see him within an hour or so."

"I thought so. Do you happen to remember a small person who came a good deal about the house when you were at work here?"

"If your ladyship means Miss Wylder, I remember her perfectly."

"It is necessary to let you know, and then I shall leave the matter to your good sense. Mrs. Wylder—and, indeed the girl herself at various times—has behaved to me with such rudeness that you cannot in ordinary decency have acquaintance with them. I mention it in case Mr. Wingfold should want to take you to see them. They are parishioners of his."

"I am sorry I must disappoint you," said Richard.

Lady Ann rose with a gray glitter in her eyes.

"Am I to understand that you *intend* calling on the Wylders?" she said.

"I have imperative reasons for calling upon them this very morning," answered Richard, rising.

"I am sorry you should so immediately show your antagonism!" said Lady Ann.

"My obligations to Miss Wylder are such that I must see her at the first possible opportunity."

"Have you asked your father's permission?"

"I have not," answered Richard, and left the room hurriedly.

The next moment he was out of the house. Lady Ann might go to his father, and he would gladly avoid the necessity of disobeying him the first morning after his return. He did not know how small her influence was with her husband. He took the path across the fields, and ran until he was out of sight of Mortgrange.

43 Heart-to-Heart

When he came to the parsonage, which he had to pass on his way to Wylder Hall, Richard saw Mr. Wingfold through the open window of the drawing room, and turned to the door. The parson met him on the threshold.

"Welcome!" he said. "How did you get through your dinner?"

"Better than I expected," replied Richard. "But this morning my stepmother asked me to promise not to call on the Wylders. They have been rude to her, she said."

"Come inside. A friend of mine is there who will be glad to see you."

The drawing room of the parsonage was low and dark, with its two windows close together on the same side. At the farther end stood a lady, seemingly occupied with an engraving on the wall. She did not move when they entered. Wingfold led Richard up to her, then turned without a word and left the room. Before either knew it, they were each in the other's arms.

Barbara was sobbing. Richard thought he had dared too much and frightened her.

"I couldn't help it!" Barbara said, pleadingly.

"My life has been longing for you!" said Richard.

"I have wanted you every day!" said Barbara, and again began to sob, but recovered herself with an effort.

"This will never do," she cried, laughing through her tears. "I shall go crazy with having you! And I've not even seen you yet. Let me go, please. I want to look at you!"

Richard released her. She lifted a blushing, tearful face to his. But there was no pain in her tears, only joy. She gazed at him one long silent moment.

"How splendid you are!" she cried like a schoolgirl. "How good of you to grow like that! I wish I could see you on Miss Brown! What are you going to do, Richard?"

While she spoke Richard was gazing on the heavenly meadow of her face, and she for very necessity went on talking that she might not cry again.

"Are you going back to bookbinding?" she said.

"I don't know. Sir Wilton—my father—hasn't told me yet what he wants me to do. Wasn't it good of him to send me to Oxford?"

"You've been at Oxford all this time? I suppose he will make an officer of you now! Not that I care! I am content with whatever contents you!"

"I daresay he will hardly like me to live by my hands!" answered Richard, laughing. "He would count it a degradation for a gentleman!"

Barbara looked perplexed.

"You don't mean to say he's going to treat you just like one of the rest?" she exclaimed.

"I really do not know," answered Richard. "But I hardly think he would enjoy the thought of *Sir Richard Lestrange* over a bookbinder's shop in Hammersmith or Brentford!"

"*Sir* Richard! You do not mean—?"

Her face grew white; her eyes fell; her hand trembled on Richard's arm.

"What is the matter?" he asked, now his turn to be perplexed.

"I don't understand it!" she answered.

"Is it possible you do not know, Barbara?" he returned. "I thought Mr. Wingfold must have told you! Sir Wilton says I am his son that was lost. Indeed, there is no doubt of it!"

"Richard! I knew you were his son, but believed you were illegitimate. Lady Ann told me you were not—!"

"How then should I have dared put my arms around you, Barbara?"

"Richard, I care nothing for what the world thinks! I care only for what God thinks."

"Then, Barbara, you would have married me, believing me base-born?"

"Oh, Richard! Did you think that knowing your heritage made me—! No! no! It was *you*, not what you were! My father sold Miss Brown because I would not marry Arthur and be Lady Lestrange. I care no more for your birth than God himself does. The god of the world is the devil. He has many names, but he's all the same devil, as Mr. Wingfold says. I wonder why he never told me! I'm glad he didn't. If he had, I wouldn't be here now."

"I'm glad too, Barbara, but it wouldn't have made much difference. I only came here on my way to your house."

There came a long silence.

"How long have you known this about yourself, Richard?" said Barbara.

"More than four years."

"And you never told me?"

"My father wished it kept a secret for a time."

"Did Mr. Wingfold know?"

"Not until yesterday."

"Why didn't he tell me yesterday, then?"

"I think he wouldn't have told you if he had known all the time."

"Why?"

"For the same reason that made him leave us together so suddenly—that you might not be hampered by knowing it—that we might understand each other before you knew. I see it all now! It was just like him!"

"He *is* a friend," said Barbara.

A silent embrace followed, and then Barbara said: "You must come and see my mother."

"Hadn't you better tell her first?" suggested Richard.

"She knows—knows what you didn't know—what I've been thinking all the time," rejoined Barbara, with a rosy look of confidence in her eyes.

"She can never have been willing you should marry a tradesman—and one, besides, who—!"

"She knew I would—and that I should have money, otherwise she might not have been willing. I don't say she likes the idea, but she is determined I shall have the man I love—if he will have me," she added shyly.

"Did you tell her you—cared for me?"

He could not say *loved* yet; he felt like an earthly pebble beside a celestial sapphire!

"Of course I did, when Papa wanted me to have Arthur! Not till then; there was no reason. I could not tell what your thoughts were, but my own were enough for that."

Mrs. Wylder was taken with Richard the moment she saw him, and when she heard his story, she was overjoyed and would scarcely listen to a word about the uncertainty of his prospects. That her Bab should marry the man she loved, and that the alliance should be what the world counted respectable, was enough for her.

When Richard told his father what he had done, saying they had fallen in love with each other while yet ignorant of his parentage, a glow of more than satisfaction warmed Sir Wilton's consciousness. How lovely! Lady Ann was being fooled on all sides!

"Richard has been making good use of his morning!" he said at dinner. "He has already proposed to Miss Wylder and been accepted! Richard is a man of action—a practical fellow!"

Lady Ann did perhaps turn a shade paler, but she smiled. It was not such a blow as it might have been, for she, too, had given up hope of securing Barbara for Arthur. But it was not pleasant to her that the grandchild of the blacksmith should have Barbara's money.

44 The Quarrel

For a few weeks things went smoothly enough. The home-weather seemed to have grown settled. Lady Ann was not unfriendly. Richard bound her prayer book in violet velvet, and she had not seemed altogether ungrateful. Arthur showed no active hostility; indeed, he tried to behave as a brother ought to a brother he would rather not have found. They were even seen occasionally about the place together. Vixen had not once made a face to his face; I will not say she had made none to his back. Theodora and he were becoming friends. Miss Malliver, now an upper slave to Lady Ann, cringed to him.

Arthur readily sold him Miss Brown, and every day she carried him to Barbara. But he took the advice of Wingfold and did not remain long away from home any day, but close by to his father's call. He had many things for him to do, and rejoiced to find him both able and ready. He would even send him where a servant would have done as well; but Richard went with hearty goodwill. It gladdened him to be of service to the old man.

Then a rumor reached his father's ears, carried to Lady Ann by her elderly maid, that Richard had been seen in low company; and he was not long in suspecting the truth of the matter.

Not once since Richard's return had Sir Wilton given the Mansons a thought, never doubting that his son's residence at Oxford must have cured him of a merely accidental inclination to such low company. But almost every day that Richard went to Wylder Hall, he had a few minutes with Alice at the parsonage. Barbara treated Alice as a sister, and so did Helen Wingfold. Their kindness, with her new peace of heart, and plenty of food and fresh air, had made her strong and almost beautiful.

Richard usually rode over in the morning, but one day it was more convenient for him to go in the evening, and that same evening it happened that Adam Manson had gone to see his sister. On the way back from the Hall, Richard found him at the parsonage and proposed to see him home. Miss Brown was a good walker, and if Adam did not want to ride all the way, they would ride and walk alternately. Adam was delighted. They set out in the dusk on foot, and Alice went a short part of the way with them. Richard led Miss Brown and Alice clung joyously to his arm. The western sky was a smoky red; the stars were coming out; the wind was mild, and seemed to fill Alice's soul with life from the fountain of life, from God himself.

Alice had been learning from Barbara not to think things, but to feel realities, to see truths themselves. Often when Mrs. Wingfold could spare her, Barbara would take her out for a walk. When Alice saw her spread out her arms as if to embrace the wind that flowed to meet them, she began to wonder, and then began to feel what the wind was, how full of something strange and sweet. When she saw Barbara lost in silent joy, after wondering for a time about it, she concluded she must be thinking of God. Through Barbara she learned to feel that the world was alive. Of the three that walked together that night, she was the merriest as they went along the quiet road. And such was the foundation for the report that Richard was seen rollicking with a common-looking lad and a servant girl on the high road, in the immediate vicinity of Wylder Hall.

"He is his father's son!" reflected Lady Ann.

He's a chip off the old block! said Sir Wilton to himself. But he did not approve of the openness of the thing. Such things mustn't be seen!

But then an ugly thought came into his mind.

"It's that infernal Manson girl!" he muttered. "I'll lay my life on it! Dead and buried, the rascal hauls them out of their graves for men to see! It's the cursed socialism of his mother's relations! If it weren't for that, the fellow would be all a father could wish! I might have known! The Armour blood was sure to break out. What business does he have with what his father did before he was born? He shall do as I tell him or go about his business—go and herd with the Mansons and all the rest of them if he likes, and be hanged to them all!"

He sat smoldering in rage for a while, and then again his thoughts took shape in words, though not in speech.

How those fools, the Wylders, will squirm when I cut the rascal off without a shilling, and settle the property on the man the little lady refused! But Dick would never be such a fool! Hang it all, I shall never make a gentleman of him! He will revert to the original type! What's bred in the bone will never come out of the flesh!

Richard was at the moment walking with Mr. Wingfold in the rectory garden. They were speaking of what the Lord meant when he said a man must leave all for him.

As soon as he entered his father's room some time later, he saw that something was wrong.

"What is it, Father?" he said.

"Richard, sit down," said Sir Wilton. "I must have a word with you. What young man and woman were you walking with two nights ago, not far from Wylder Hall?"

"My brother and sister, sir—the Mansons."

"My God, I thought as much!" cried the baron, jumping to his feet. "Hold up your right hand," he went on—Sir Wilton was a magistrate—"and swear, so help you God, that you will never more in your life speak one word to either of those—persons, or leave my house at once."

"Father," said Richard, his voice trembling a little, "I cannot obey you. To deny my friends and relations, even at your command, would be to forsake my Master. It would be to break the bonds that bind men, God's children, together."

"Hold your cursed jargon! Bonds indeed! Is there no bond between you and your father?"

"Believe me, Father, I am very sorry, but I cannot help it. I dare not obey you. You have been very kind to me, and I thank you from my heart—"

"Shut up, you young hypocrite! You have tongue enough for

three! Come, I will give you one chance more! Drop those persons you call your brother and sister, or I drop you."

"You must drop me, then, Father!" said Richard with a sigh.

"Will you do as I tell you?"

"No, sir. I dare not."

"Then leave the house."

Richard rose.

"Good-bye, sir," he said.

"Get out of the house."

"May I not take my tools, sir?"

"What tools, curse you?"

"I got some tools to bind my lady's prayer book."

"She's taken him in! By Jove, she's done it, the fool! She's been keeping him up to it, to enrage me and get rid of him!" said the baron to himself.

"What do you want them for?" he asked, a little calmer.

"To work at my trade. If you turn me out, I must go back to that."

"Damn your soul! It never was and never will be anything but a tradesman's! Damn *my* soul, if I wouldn't rather make young Manson my heir than you! No, by Jove, you shall *not* have your cursed tools! Leave the house. You cannot claim a chair leg in it!"

Richard bowed, retrieved his hat, and walked from the house with about thirty shillings in his pocket.

His heart was like a lump of lead, but he was not dismayed. Outside the gate he paused in the middle of the road, thinking. Which way should he go, to his grandfather's or to Wylder Hall?

He set out, plodding across the fields, to Barbara. There was no Miss Brown for him now.

She was in the garden, sitting in a summerhouse, reading a story. She heard his step, turned, and came out and met him in the dim green air under a wide-spreading yew tree.

"What is the matter, Richard?" she said, looking in his face with anxiety.

"My father has turned me out."

"Turned you out?"

"Yes. I had to swear never to speak another word to Alice or

Adam, or go about my business. I went."

"Of course you did!" cried Barbara. After a little pause, she resumed. "Well, it's no worse for you than before, and ever so much better for me! What are you going to do, Richard?"

"I prefer to live by my hands."

"Will it take you long to get back into your old work?"

"I don't think it will," answered Richard, "and I believe I will be better at it now."

"It's horrid you have to go," said Barbara. "But I will think you up to God every day and dream about you every night. I will write to you, and you will write to me—and—and"—she was almost to the point of crying, but would not—"and the old smell of the leather and the glue will be so nice!"

She broke into a merry laugh.

They walked together to the smithy.

Fierce was the wrath of the blacksmith. "I might have known!" he cried. "But just let him come near the smithy! He shall know, if he does, what a blacksmith thinks of a baron! What are you going to do, my son?"

"Go back to my work."

"Not to that old wife's trade!" cried the blacksmith. "Look here, Richard!" he said, and bared his upper arm. "There's what the anvil does! You work with me and we'll show them a sight—a gentleman that can make his living with his own hands! The country shall see Sir Wilton Lestrange's own heir a blacksmith because he wouldn't be a snob and deny his own flesh and blood!"

"Grandfather," answered Richard, "I couldn't do your work so well as my own."

"Yes, you could. In six weeks I'll make you a better blacksmith than myself!"

"It would be best not to irritate my father with my presence so close. When I am out of sight, perhaps he may think of me again. There is more chance of his getting over it if I don't trouble him with sight or sound of me."

"Perhaps you're right!" Simon reluctantly assented. "Well, off with you to your woman's work, and God bless you!"

Richard took Barbara home, and the same night started for

London. His aunt was beside herself with surprise and delight at seeing him. When she heard his story, however, she plainly took part with his father, though she was too glad to see her boy again to say so. His uncle, too, was sincerely glad. Work had not been the same since Richard left.

He settled to his work as if he had never been away from it, and in two weeks could work faster and better than before. Soon he had as much in the way of mending as he was able to do, for almost all his old employers again sought him.

But how changed the world looked to him since that time in the far past! He had the loveliest of letters from Barbara. Mr. Wingfold wrote occasionally, and Richard always answered them both as soon as his work would allow.

As soon as his son was gone, Sir Wilton began to miss him. He wished first that the obstinacy of the rascal had not made it necessary to give him quite so sharp a lesson, and as the days and weeks passed he began to wish that he had not sent him away. He repented as much as was possible to him, and wished he had left the rascal to take his own way. He tried to understand how, always anxious to please him, the boy would yet not do as he said in such a trifle, especially when he had nothing to gain and everything to lose by his obstinacy. How could the fool make the Mansons a matter of *his* conscience? They were no business of his!

He pretended to himself that he had been born without a conscience. At the same time he knew very well that there were dusty compartments of his memory he preferred not to search in; he knew very well he had done things which were wrong. If he had ever done a thing because he ought to do it; if he had ever abstained from doing a thing because he ought not to do it, he would have known he had a conscience. But because he did not obey his conscience, he would rather believe himself without one.

For the first time in his life he was possessed with a good longing—namely, the desire for his son. Twenty times a day he would be on the point of sending for Richard, but twenty times a day his pride stopped him.

If the rascal would but make an apology, I would take him back!

he would say to himself over and over; *but he's such a chip off the old block—so infernally independent!*

A month after Richard's expulsion, the baron drove to the smithy and accused Simon of causing all the mischief. He must send the boy Manson away, he said: he would settle an annuity on the beggar. That done, Richard must make a suitable apology, and he would take him back.

Simon listened without a word.

"If you will not oblige me," Sir Wilton ended, "you shall not have another stroke of work from Mortgrange, and I will use my influence to drive you from the county."

He turned without an answer and would have walked from the shop, but the moment he turned, Simon took him by the shoulders and ran him out and right up to the carriage. In his rage the baron called out to the coachman to send his whip about the ruffian's ears. Simon burst into a loud laugh that, with the rest of the commotion, startled the horses. The baron had failed to shut the door of the carriage properly; now it opened and banged, swinging wildly as the horses reared and backed, and the baron, cursing and swearing, was tossed about inside, while Simon looked on, still laughing.

Before the next month was over, the baron was again in the smithy—in a better mood this time. He made no reference to his former ignominious dismissal, wanting only to know if Simon had heard from his grandson. The old man answered that he had: he was well, happy, and busy. Sir Wilton gave a grunt.

"Why didn't he stay and help you here?"

"I begged him to," answered Simon, "for he is almost as good at the anvil and shoeing as myself. But he said it would annoy his father to have him so near."

His boy's goodwill made the baron fidget and swear to hide his feelings. But his evil angel got the upper hand.

"The rascal knew," he cried, "that nothing would annoy me so much as have him go back to his filth like a washed pig!"

Perceiving that Simon looked dangerous, he turned with a hasty good morning and made for his carriage, casting an uneasy glance over his shoulder. But the blacksmith let him depart in peace.

45 The Baron's Funeral

One morning, about a year after Richard's return to his trade, the doctor at Barset was roused by a groom, his horse all speckled with foam, who, as soon as he had given his message, galloped to the post office and telegraphed for a well-known London physician. A little later, Richard received a telegram: "Father paralyzed. Will meet first train. Wingfold."

With sad heart he obeyed the summons and found Wingfold at the station.

"I have just come from the house," he said. "He is still insensible. They tell me he came to himself once, just a little, and murmured *Richard*, but has not spoken since."

"Let us go to him," said Richard.

"I fear they will try to prevent you from seeing him."

"They shall not find it easy."

They reached Mortgrange and stopped at the gate. Richard walked up to the door.

"How is my father?" he asked.

"Much the same, sir, I believe."

"Is it true that he wanted to see me?"

"I don't know, sir."

"Is he in his own room?"

"Yes, sir; but I beg your pardon, sir," said the man. "I have my lady's orders to admit no one!"

While he spoke Richard passed him and went straight to his father's room, which was on the ground floor. He opened the door softly and entered. His father lay on the bed, with the Barset doctor and the London surgeon standing over him. The latter looked around, saw him, and came to him.

"I gave orders that no one should be admitted," he said in a low, stern tone.

"I understand my father wished to see me," answered Richard.

"He cannot see you."

"He may come to himself any moment."

"He will never come to himself," returned the doctor.

"Then why keep me out?" said Richard.

The eyes of the dying man opened, and Richard received his last look. Sir Wilton gave one sigh, and death was past. Whether life was come, God knew, and those who watched on the other side knew.

Lady Ann came in.

"The good baron is gone!" said the physician.

She turned away. Her eyes glided over Richard as if she had never seen him before. He went up to the bed, and she walked from the room.

When Richard came out, he found Wingfold where he had left him, and got into the pony-carriage beside him. The parson drove off.

"His tale is told," said Richard, in a choking voice. "He did not speak and I cannot tell whether he knew me, but I had his last look, and that is something. I would have been a good son to him if he had let me—at least I would have tried to be."

"It is best," said Wingfold. "We cannot say anything *would be* best, but we must say everything *is* best."

"I think I understand you," said Richard. "But, oh, how I would have loved him if he would have let me!"

"And how you will love him!" said Wingfold, "and he will love you. They are getting him ready now. He had begun to love you before he went. But he was the slave of the nature he had enfeebled and corrupted. I hope for him—though God only knows how long it may take, even after the change is begun, to bring men like him back to their true selves. But surely, Richard," he said, "your right place is at Mortgrange—at least so long as what is left of your father is lying in the house."

"Yes, no doubt. And I did wonder whether I ought to assert myself and remain until my father's will was read, but I concluded it best to avoid anything unpleasant."

"Then until the funeral, you will stay with us!" said the parson.

"No, thank you," answered Richard. "I must be at my grandfather's. I will go there when I have seen Barbara."

On the day of the funeral no one disputed Richard's right to the place he took, and when it was over, he joined the company assembled to hear the late baron's will. It was dated ten years before, and gave the two estates of Mortgrange and Cinqmer, which had been Lady Ann's father's, to his son, Arthur Lestrange. There was in it no allusion to the possible existence of a son by his first wife.

Richard rose. The lawyer rose also.

"I am sorry, Sir Richard," he said, "that we can find no later will. There ought to have been some provision for the support of the title. Your title without money will do little for you."

"My father died suddenly," answered Richard, "and did not know of my existence until about five years ago."

"All I can say is, I am very sorry."

"Do not let it trouble you," returned Richard. "It matters little to me. I am independent."

"I am very glad to hear it. I had imagined it otherwise."

"A man with a good trade and a good education must be independent!"

"Ah, I understand! But your brother will, as a matter of course, respond to your needs. I shall talk to him about it. The estate is quite equal to it."

"The estate shall not be burdened with me," said Richard with a smile. "I am the only one of the family free to do as he pleases."

"But the title, Sir Richard!"

"The title must look after itself. If I thought it in the smallest degree dependent on money for its dignity, I would throw it away. If it means anything, it means more than money and can stand without it. If it be an honor, please God I shall keep it honorable."

As he left the room a servant met him with the message that Lady Ann wished to see him in the library.

Cold as ever, but not colder than always, she poked her long white hand at him.

"This is awkward for you, Richard," she said, "but more awkward still for Arthur. Mortgrange is at your service until you find some employment befitting your position. You must not forget the respect due the family. It is a great pity you offended your father."

Richard was silent.

"He has left it, therefore, in my hands to do as I deem fit. Sir Wilton did not die the rich man people imagined him, but I am ready to place a thousand pounds at your disposal."

"I should be sorry to make the little he has left you so much less," answered Richard.

"As you please," returned her ladyship.

"I should like to have a word with my sister Theodora," said Richard.

"I doubt if she will see you. Miss Malliver, will you go and inquire whether Miss Lestrange is able to see Mr. Tuke?"

Miss Malliver came from somewhere and left the room.

"There is just one thing," resumed her ladyship, "upon which, if only out of respect to the feelings of my late husband, I feel bound to insist. While in this neighborhood, you will be careful as to what company you show yourself in.

Richard was dumbstruck! Before he had half recovered himself, she had again resumed.

"If the title were receded to the property," she went on, as if talking to herself, "it might be a matter for more material consideration. Any *compensation* is only by courtesy. And suppose I referred my grave doubts of your story to the courts."

"My father has acknowledged me!"

"And repudiated you, sent you from the house, bequeathed you nothing! Everybody knows your father—my late husband, I mean—would risk anything for my annoyance. Had he really believed you his son, do you imagine he would have left you penniless?"

"The proofs that satisfied him remain."

"The testimony, that is, of those most involved in the case—whose very proof is a confession of a felony!"

"A confession, if you will, that my own aunt was the nurse that carried me away—of which there are proofs."

"Has anyone seen those proofs?"

"My father has seen them, Lady Ann."

"You mean Sir Wilton?"

"I do. He accepted them."

"Has he left any document to that effect?"

"Not that I know of."

"Who presented these proofs, as you call them?"

"I told Sir Wilton where they had been hidden, and together we found them."

"Where?"

"In the room that was the nursery."

"Which you occupied for months while working at your trade in the house, and for weeks again before Sir Wilton dismissed you!"

"Yes," answered Richard, who saw very well what she was driving at.

"And where you had opportunity to place what you chose at any time! Excuse me, I am only saying what a lawyer would say in court."

"You wish me to understand, I suppose, that you regard me as an imposter, and believe I put things, for support of my aunt's evidence, where my father and I found them?"

"I do not say so. I am merely trying to make you see how the court would regard the affair—how much appearances would be against you. At the same time, I confess I have all along had grave doubts of the story. You, of course, may have been deceived as well as your father—I mean the late baron, my husband. In any case, I will not admit you to be what you call yourself until you are declared such by the law of the land. I will, however, make a proposal to you. Pledge yourself to make no defense if, for form's sake, legal proceedings should be judged desirable, and in lieu of Mortgrange I will pay you five thousand pounds."

"To do as you ask me would be to endorse your charge against my father, that he lied in acknowledging me simply to give you annoyance! And I have the same objection with regard to my uncle and aunt, of whom you would make liars and conspirators!"

He turned toward the door.

"You will consider it?" said her ladyship in her stateliest yet softest tone.

"I will. I will continue to consider it the worst insult you could have offered my father, your late husband!"

"What am I to understand by that?"

"Whatever your ladyship chooses."

"Then you mean to dispute the title?"

"I decline to say what I mean or do not mean to do."

Lady Ann rose to ring the bell.

Miss Malliver met Richard in the doorway. Theodora was not with her.

"I am going to bid Theodora good-bye," he said.

"You shall do no such thing!" cried her ladyship.

Richard flew up the stairs and went straight to his sister's room.

The moment Theodora saw him, she sprang from the bed where she had been crying, and threw her arms around him. He told her he had come to say good-bye.

"But you're not going *really*—forever?" she said.

"My dear sister, what else can I do? Nobody here wants me!"

"Indeed, Richard, I do!"

"I know you do, and the time will come when you shall have me, but you would not have me live where I am not loved."

"Richard!" she cried, with a burst of indignation, "you *are* a gentleman!"

Richard laughed and Theodora dried her eyes. Miss Malliver was near enough behind Richard to be able to report most of the conversation, and the poor girl had a bad time of it as a result.

Richard went to see Barbara, and found her at the parsonage, where they both had a long talk with Wingfold.

Richard returned to London and to his work. Wingfold set himself to keep Barbara busy, giving her plenty to read and plenty of work. Among other things, he set her to teach his son, even in areas where she thought herself too ignorant. The parson held, not only that to teach is the best way to learn, but that the imperfect are the best teachers of the imperfect.

He made Richard promise to take no important step for a year without first letting him know. He was anxious he should have nothing to undo because of what the packet committed to his care might contain.

46 The Packet

At last the anniversary of the death of Sir Wilton arrived. Wingfold rose early, his mind anxious and his heart troubled that his mind should be anxious, and set out for London by the first train. There he sought the office of Sir Wilton's lawyer; when at last Mr. Bell appeared, Wingfold asked him to witness the opening of the packet. Mr. Bell broke the seal himself, read the baron's statement of the request he had made to Wingfold, and then opened the enclosed packet.

"A most irregular proceeding!" he exclaimed—as well he might: his late client had committed to the keeping of the clergyman of another parish the will, signed and properly witnessed, which Mr. Bell had last drawn up for him. As it was nowhere to be discovered, Bell had assumed that the baron had later destroyed it. But here it was, devising and bequeathing his whole property, real and personal, exclusive only of certain legacies of small account, to Richard Lestrange, formerly known as Richard Tuke, reputed son of John and Jane Tuke, born Armour, but in reality sole son of Wilton Arthur Lestrange, of Mortgrange and Cinqmer, Baron, and Robina Armour his wife, daughter of Simon Armour, Blacksmith, born in lawful wedlock in the house of Mortgrange, in the year 1863. The will was so worded, at the request of Sir Wilton, that even should the law declare Richard a fraud, the property must yet be his!

"This will be a terrible blow to that proud woman!" said Mr. Bell. "You must prepare her for the shock."

"Prepare Lady Ann!" exclaimed Wingfold. "Believe me, she is in no danger. An earthquake would not move her."

"I must see her lawyer at once!" said Mr. Bell, rising.

"Let me have the papers, please," said Wingfold. "Sir Wilton did not tell me to bring them to you. I must take them to Richard."

"Then you do not wish me to move in the matter?"

"I shall advise Richard to put the matter into your hands. But he must do it; I have not the power."

"You are very right. I shall be here until five o'clock."

"I hope to be back long before then!"

It took Wingfold an hour to find Richard. He heard the news without a word, but his eyes flashed, and Wingfold knew he thought of Barbara and his mother and the Mansons. Then his face clouded.

"It will bring trouble on the rest of my father's family," he said.

"Not all of them," returned Wingfold. "And you have it in your power to ease the trouble. But do not be hastily generous, and do what you may regret, finding it for no one's good."

"I will think well before I do anything," answered Richard. "But I must see my mother first."

He found her ironing a shirt for him, and told her the news. She received it quietly. Facing so many changes had caused both her and Richard to adopt a sober way of expecting anything; by this time there hardly seemed to be any surprises left.

They went to Mr. Bell, and Richard told him to do what he judged necessary. Mr. Bell at once communicated with Lady Ann's lawyer, and requested him to inform her that Sir Richard would call upon her the next day.

Mr. Wingfold accompanied him to Mortgrange. Lady Ann received them with perfect coolness.

"You are, I trust, aware of the cause of my visit, Lady Ann?" said Richard.

"I am."

"May I ask what you propose to do?"

"That, excuse me, is my affair. It lies with me to ask you what provision you intend making for Sir Wilton's family."

"Allow me, Lady Ann, to take the lesson you have given me, and answer, that is my affair."

She saw she had made a mistake.

"For my part," she returned, "I should not object to remaining in the house, were I but assured that my daughters should be in no danger of meeting improper persons."

"But, of course, I can give you no assurances that would meet with your satisfaction. It would be no pleasure for either of us, Lady Ann, to be so near one another. Our ways of thinking are too much opposed. I venture to suggest that you should occupy the old house of your father's."

"I will do as I see fit."

Lady Ann left the room, and the next week left the house for Cinqmer, which was not far off, the smaller of the two estates.

The week following Richard went to see Arthur there.

"Now, Arthur," he said, "let us be frank with each other. I am not your enemy. I am bound to do the best I can for you all.

"When you thought the land was yours, I had a trade to fall back on. Now that the land proves mine, you have no such means of making a livelihood. If you will be a brother, you will accept what I offer you. I will turn over to you for your lifetime, but without power to pass it on after you, this estate of Cinqmer, with the only burden imposed upon it that you pay five hundred a year to your sister Theodora till her marriage."

Arthur was glad of the gift, yet found it difficult to accept it graciously. Many men imagine that they shield their independence by not seeming pleased.

"I cannot see," said Arthur, "—of course it is very kind of you, and all that—but I should like to know why the land should not be mine to leave. I might have children, you know!"

"And I might have more children!" laughed Richard. "But that has nothing to do with it. The thing is this: the land itself I could give to you out and out, but the land has people. God did not give us the land for our own sakes only, but for theirs, too. The men and women upon it are my brothers and sisters, and I have to see to them. I know that you are liked by our people, and you have claims to be liked by them. And I have every feeling that you will prove a good and just landlord to them. I like you, Arthur, and consider you truly a brother, and therefore believe you will consider them as well as yourself or the land in the decisions you make. But suppose at your death it should go to your brother Percy? Should I not feel that I had betrayed my people?"

"He is my brother!"

"And mine. I know him. I was at Oxford with him. And not one foothold shall he ever have on land of mine. I cannot trust him as I do you. When he wants to work, let him come to me—not until then!"

"You will not say that to my mother?"

"I will say nothing to your mother. Do you accept my offer?"

"I will think it over."

"Do," said Richard, and turned to go.

"Will you not settle something on Victoria?" said Arthur.

"We shall see how she turns out by the time she is of age. I don't want to waste money!"

"What do you mean by wasting money?"

"Giving it where it will do no good."

"God gives to the bad as well as the good!"

"It is one thing to give to the bad, and quite another to give where it will do no good. God knows the endless result; all I see is the first link of the chain. I must act by the knowledge granted me. God may give money in punishment: should I dare do that?"

"Well, you're quite beyond me."

"Never mind, then. What you and I have to do is to be friends and brothers, and work together. You will find I mean well."

"I believe you do, Richard, but we don't somehow seem to be in the same world."

"If we are true, that will not keep us apart. If we both work for the good of the people, we must come together."

"To tell you the truth, if we did come together, I am afraid we should quarrel, and then I would seem ungrateful."

"What would you say to our managing the estates together for a year or two? Would not that be the best way to understand each other?"

"Perhaps. I must think about it."

"That is right. Only don't let us begin with suspicion. You did me more than one kindness not knowing I was your brother. And you sent Miss Brown back to Barbara after our father sent me back to London."

"She was your mare. I knew that is what you would have wanted done."

"Nevertheless, it was very considerate. I thank you."

Arthur turned away.

"My dear fellow," said Richard, "Barbara loved me when I was a bookbinder, and promised to marry me thinking me illegitimate. I had my sorry time of it then; your good time is, I trust, coming. I did nothing to bring about the change. God worked circumstances beyond the control of either of us. I thought about leaving everything to you, and simply keeping to my trade. But I saw that I had no right to do so, because duties attend the property which I could not neglect."

"I believe every word you say, Richard. You are nobler than I!"

47 Barbara's Dream

Mr. Wylder could not very well object to Sir Richard Lestrange on the ground that his daughter had loved him before she knew his position; within two months they were married. Lady Ann was invited but did not go to the wedding. Arthur, Theodora, and Victoria did. Percy was not at home.

Neither bride nor bridegroom saw any sense in setting out on a journey the moment they were free to be at home together, and they went straight from the church to Mortgrange.

In the evening they went out into the park as the moon was rising. The sunlight was not quite gone, and the moon's reflected light mingled with the light that had been given her.

"How different the moonlit shadow is," mused Richard, "from the sunny realm of the radiant Christ! Jesus rose again because he was true, and death had no hold on him. This world's day is but the moonlight of his world."

They wandered along, now talking, now silent, their two hearts lying together in a great peace.

The moon kept rising and brightening, slowly victorious over the pallid light of the dying sun; at last she lifted herself out of the vaporous horizon, ascended over the treetops, and went walking through the unobstructed sky, mistress of the air, queen of the heavens, lady of the eyes of men. Yet she was lady only because she beheld her sun. She saw the source of her light, and told what she saw of him.

"When the soul of man sees God, it shines!" said Richard.

They reached at length the spot where first they met in the moonlight. With one heart they stopped and turned, and looked in each other's moonlit eyes.

"Do you know that lovely passage in the book of Baruch?" asked Richard.

"What book is that?" returned Barbara. "It surely can't be in the Bible?"

"It is in the Apocrypha. I think I can repeat it; it was the moon that made me think of it. 'The stars shined in their watches, and rejoiced: when he calleth them, they say, "Here we be"; and so with cheerfulness they showed light unto him that made them. This is our God, and there shall none other be accounted of in comparison to him.' "

"That is beautiful!" cried Barbara, repeating, " 'And so with cheerfulness they showed light unto him that made them!' "

A silence followed. Then again Barbara spoke, clinging a little closer to her husband.

"I want to tell you something that came to me one night when we were in London," she said. "It was a miserable time—before I found you up in the orchestra seats there! London is a terrible city, full of misery. I was very sad, and saw nothing around me but a waste of dreariness. I kept asking God to give me patience. But the days were dismal, and the balls and dinners so frightful. I seemed to be in a world without air. The girls were so silly, the men so inane, and the conversation so mawkish and colorless! Their compliments sickened me.

"Then one morning, after what seemed like a long night's dreamless sleep, I awoke. But it was much too early to get up. So I lay thinking—or more truly, I hope, being thought into, as Mr. Wingfold says. Many of the most beautiful things I had read, scenes of our Lord's life on earth, and thoughts of the Father, came and went. I had no desire to sleep again, or any feeling of drowsiness; but in the midst of fully conscious thought, I found myself in some other place. I knew only that there was firm ground under my feet and a soft white radiance of light about me. Afterward I remembered branches of trees spreading high overhead, through which I saw the sky; but at the time I seemed not to take notice of what was around me. I was leaning against a form tall and grand, clothed from the shoulders to the ground in a white robe, full, and soft, and fine. The robe lay in thickly gathered folds, touched to whiteness in the radiant light, and the arms encircled without at first touching me.

"With sweet contentment my eyes went in and out of those radiant lines, feeling, though they were parts of his dress, that they were yet of himself. For I knew the form to be that of the heavenly Father, but I felt no trembling fear, no sense of painful awe—only a deep, deep worshiping, an unutterable love and confidence. 'O Father!' I said, not aloud, but low into the folds of his garment. Scarcely had I breathed the words when 'My child!' came whispered back, and I knew his head was bent toward me, and I felt his arms close round my shoulders. The folds of his garment wrapped around me and, with a soft sweep, fell behind me to the ground. Delight held me still for a while, and then I looked up to see his face, but I could not see past his chest. His shoulders rose far above my upreaching hands, for my head did not come much above his waist.

"And now came the most wonderful part of my dream. As I thus rested against him, near his heart, I seemed to see into it. And I was filled with a loving wonder, and an utterly blessed feeling of home, to the very core. I was *at home*—with my Father! I looked, it seemed, into a fathomless space, and yet a warm light like a hearth-fire shone and played in ruddy glow, as upon cottage walls. I saw, gathered there, all human hearts. I saw them—yet I saw no forms; they *were* there—and yet they *would be* there. To my waking mind the words sound like nonsense; but in my dream the contradiction did not perplex me at all. With light beyond faith, with absolute certainty, I saw them. But this part of my dream, the most lovely of all, I can find no words to describe; nor can I even recall to my own mind the half of what I felt. I only know that something was given me then, some spiritual apprehension, to be again withdrawn, but to be given to us all, I believe, someday, out of his infinite love, and withdrawn no more. Every heart that had ever ached, or longed, or wandered, I knew was there, folded warm and soft, safe and glad. And I seemed in my dream to know that this was the crown of all my happiness—yes, even more than to be myself in my Father's arms. Awake, the thought of the multitude had always oppressed my mind; it did not then. From the comfort and joy it gave me to see them there, I seemed to be aware of how my own heart had ached for them.

"Then tears began to run from my eyes—but easily, with no pain of the world in them. They flowed, like a gentle stream, into the heart of God, whose depths were open to my gaze. The blessedness of those tears was beyond words. It was all true, then. That heart *was* our home!

"Then I felt that I was being gently put away. The folds of his robe which I held in my hands were being slowly drawn away and the gladness of my weeping changed to longing entreaty. 'O Father! Father!' I cried; but I saw only his grand and gracious form, blurred and indistinct through the veil of my blinding tears, slowly receding, slowly fading—and I awoke.

"My tears were flowing now with the old earth-pain in them, with keenest disappointment and longing. *To have been there and to have come back* was the misery. But it did not last long. The glad thought awoke that I *had* the dream—a precious reality never to be lost while memory lasted; a vision which nothing but its fulfillment could ever be equal. I rose glad and strong, to serve with newer love, with quicker hand, and readier foot, the hearts around me."

Richard smiled down at Barbara and tightened his arms around her. "And we shall serve them together, my love," he said tenderly. "For he has drawn me, also, into his heart—forever."